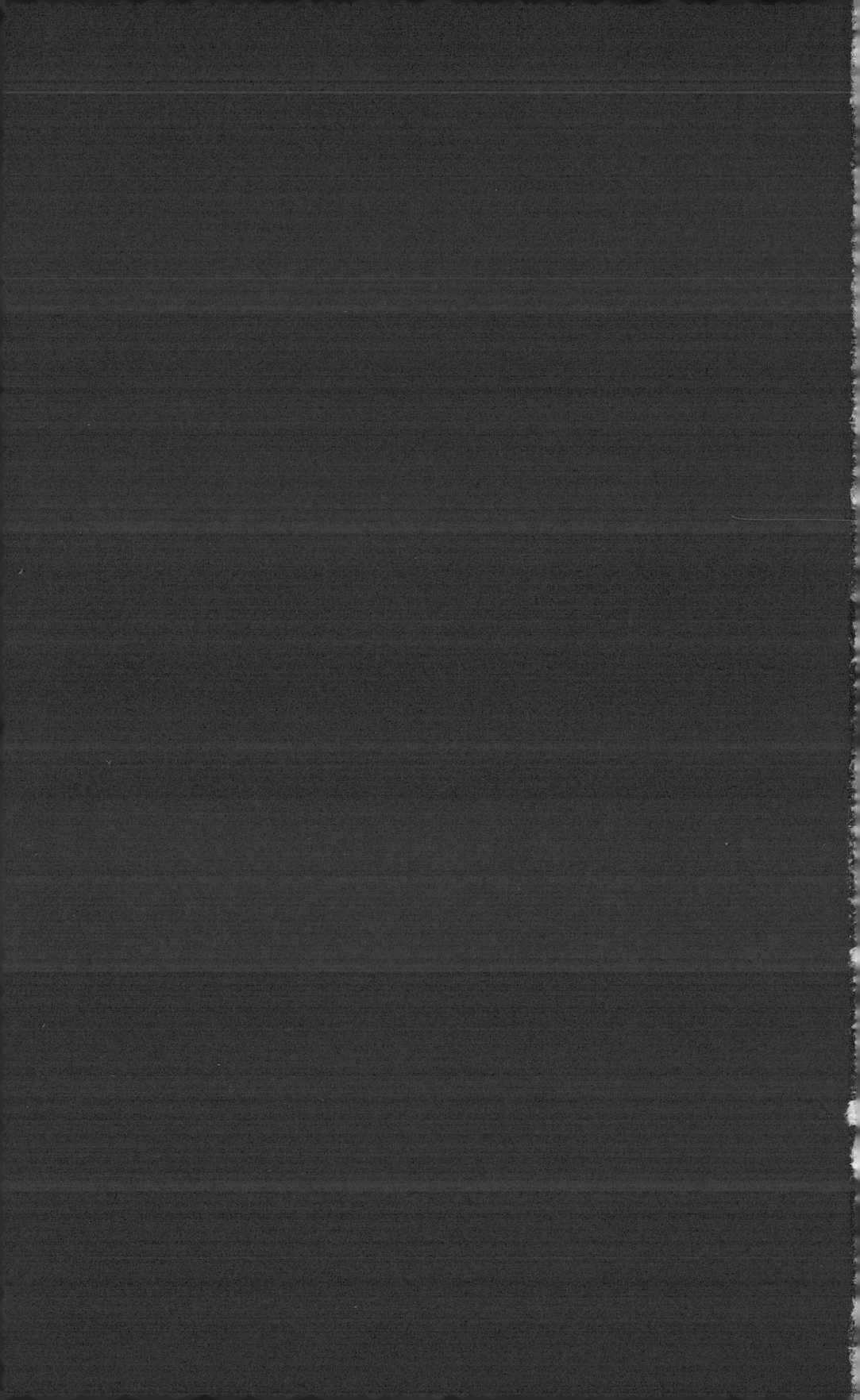

"*Seven Recipes for Revolution* is compelling, riotous, and utterly fresh! The delightful food-based magic is so unlike anything I've ever read in fantasy, and contrasts beautifully with a harsh, blood-soaked world of rigid social rules. Queer love, chef kings, giant monsters, and magical steaks—brilliant stuff!"—Sunyi Dean, *Sunday Times* bestselling author of *The Book Eaters*

"Tremendously unique; what fantasy needs at the moment."—Richard Swan, author of the Empire of the Wolf series

"Ryan Rose's debut is sure to whet your appetite with its cooking-based magic system, and please your palate with how its courses are served. If you enjoy good food, classic fantasy feeling, and charming nods to the culinary, this is for you."—R.R. Virdi, author of the Tales of Tremaine series

"*Seven Recipes for Revolution* is a pulpy, bloody blend of *Red Rising*, *Attack on Titan*, and *Iron Chef* with a splash of delectably detailed magic."—J.T. Greathouse, author of the Pact and Pattern series

"Vivid, vibrant and visceral, *Seven Recipes for Revolution* weaves a thrilling tale of twisting loyalties and revolutionary carnage through the gleefully unreliable narration of Paprick the Butcher. Rose's writing thrums with texture, taste and pointed humour, delivering a sensory feast with a jagged edge and a delicate seasoning of social conscience. And let's not forget the magical, delicious, monstrous kaiju!" —David Wragg, author of the Articles of Faith series

"If you loved *Babel* but wished it had more kaiju, this book is for you. Rose has created a fresh new world with a sensory explosion of scents and tastes, the flavors lingering long after I put the book down."—Amber A. Logan, author of *The Secret Garden of Yanagi Inn*

"Ryan Rose's *Seven Recipes for Revolution* stirs together a fascinating magic system, a fully realized world, giant kaiju, and a gritty, conflicted main character, combining them into a consuming story with the same care and attention as a delicious chocolate soufflé."—Clay Harmon, author of the Rift Walker series

From Ryan Rose and Daphne Press

Seven Recipes for Revolution
Eight Tastes of Treachery
Nine Courses of Calamity

SEVEN RECIPES FOR REVOLUTION

RYAN ROSE

D Daphne Press

First published in the UK in 2025 by Daphne Press
www.daphnepress.com

Copyright © 2025 by Ryan Rose
Cover illustration by Kerby Rosanes
Cover design by Jane Tibbetts
Maps by Luan Bittencourt

A CIP catalogue record for this book is available from the British Library.

Hardback ISBN: 978-1-83784-064-9
eBook ISBN: 978-1-83784-065-6
Waterstones Hardback ISBN: 978-1-83784-109-7
Broken Binding Hardback ISBN: 978-1-83784-111-0

The authorised representative in the EEA is Authorised Rep Compliance Ltd
71 Baggot Street Lower, Dublin, D02 P593, Ireland.
Email: info@arccompliance.com

Printed and bound by CPI Group (UK) Ltd,
Croydon CR0 4YY

1

MIX
Paper | Supporting
responsible forestry
FSC
www.fsc.org
FSC® C013604

To all those who cook so others can enjoy

The Lands of
EMPHONIA

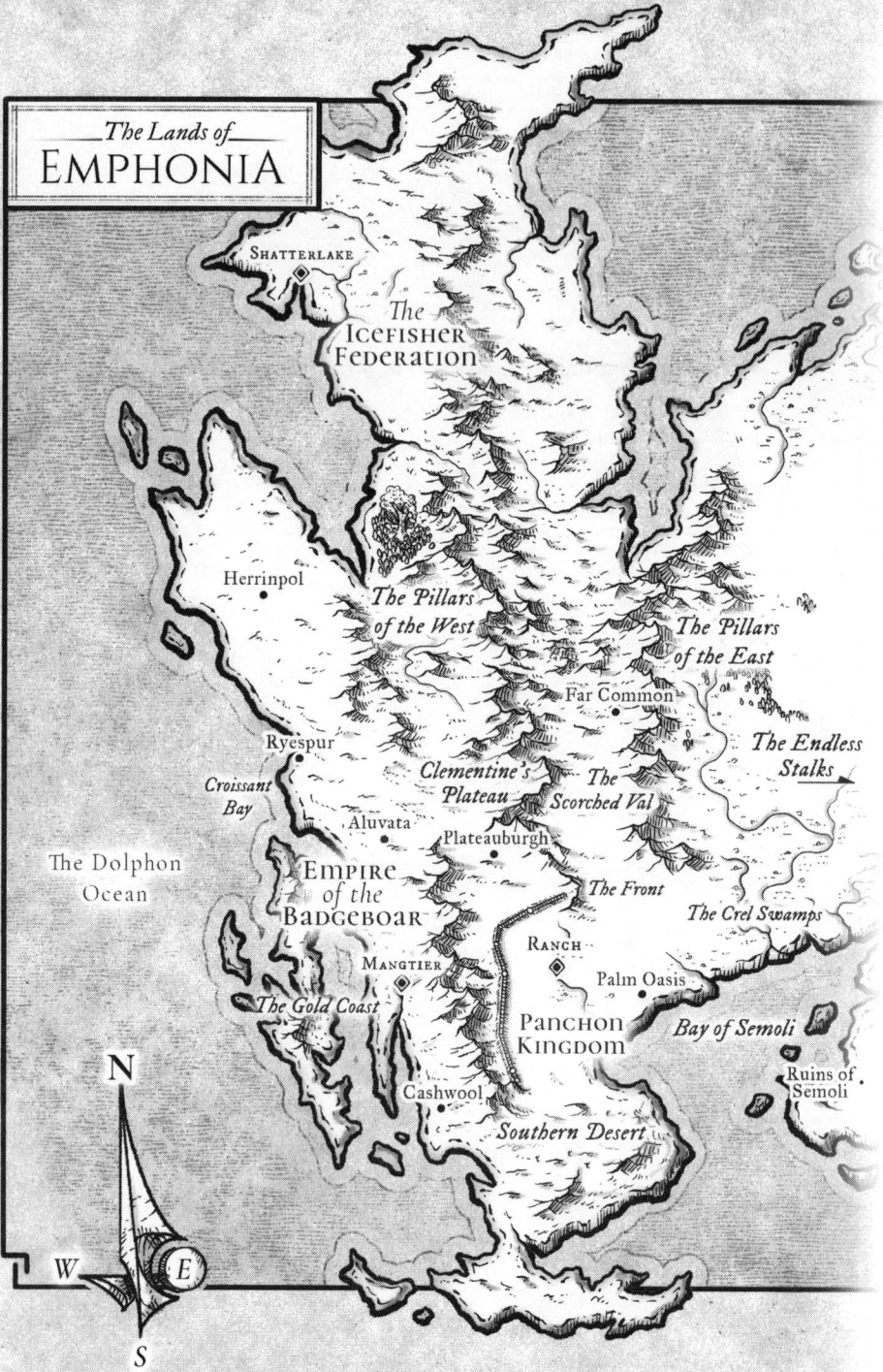

SHATTERLAKE

The
ICEFISHER
FEDERATION

Herrinpol

*The Pillars
of the West*

*The Pillars
of the East*

Far Common

*The Endless
Stalks*

Ryespur

*Croissant
Bay*

*Clementine's
Plateau*

*The
Scorched Val*

Aluvata

Plateauburgh

*The Dolphon
Ocean*

The Front

The Crel Swamps

EMPIRE
of the
BADGEBOAR

RANCH

Palm Oasis

MANGTIER

Bay of Semoli

The Gold Coast

PANCHON
KINGDOM

*Ruins of
Semoli*

Cashwool

Southern Desert

N

W   E

S

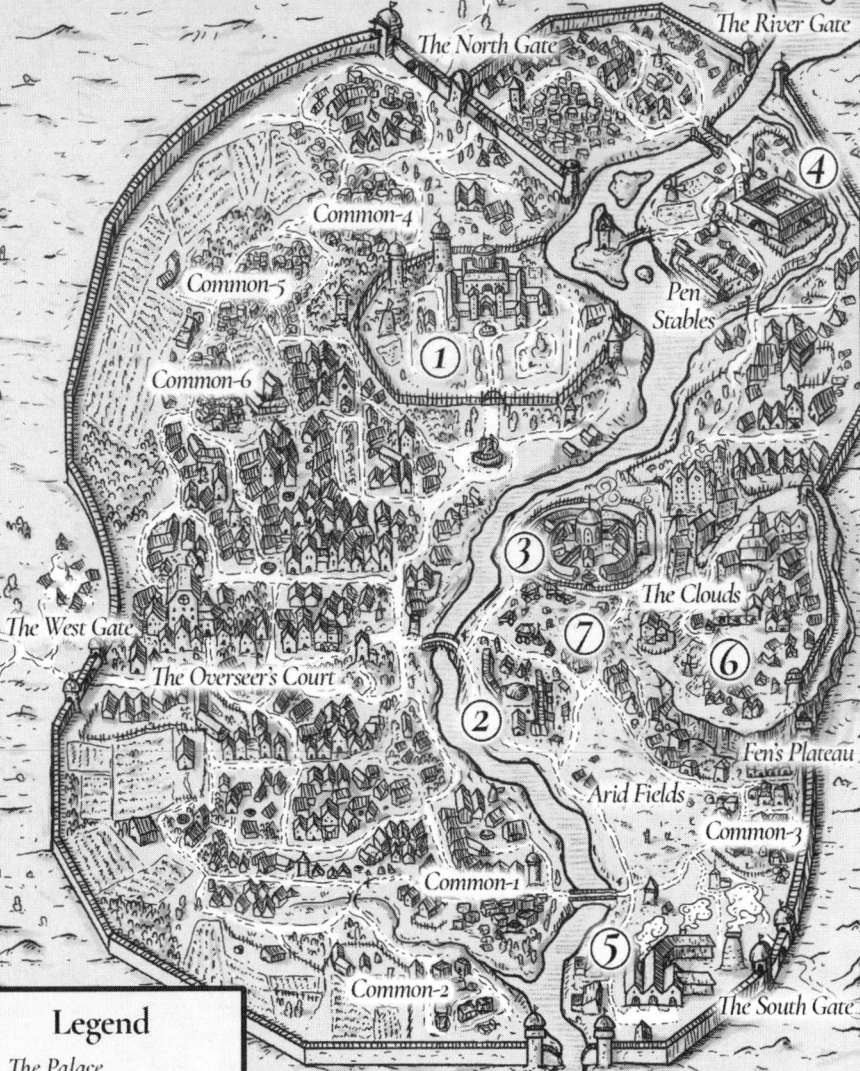

RANCH

The North Gate

The River Gate

Common-4

Common-5

Common-6

①

Pen Stables

④

③

The Clouds

⑦

⑥

The West Gate

The Overseer's Court

②

Fen's Plateau

Arid Fields

Common-3

Common-1

⑤

Common-2

The South Gate

Legend

1 The Palace
2 Black Spice
3 The Culinary Academy
4 The Barracks
5 The King's Factory
6 Cutler's Shop
7 Tall Grass

TABLE SETTING

BEFORE HE WAS Paprick the Butcher, he was Paprick, a butcher. Not in earnest yet, but an apprentice still. Little more than a common farmboy, indentured to the factory, slicing emphon flanks the size of a bison into strips and steaks. It is no wonder *he* became the Butcher. The King's Factory churned out but one product: flesh.

And Paprick got his pound of it.

For all the good it did.

"The charges are as follows," read the executioner from beside the young queen, his voice booming before a crowd so large. "Three counts treason, twenty score counts murder, one count blasphemy, seven counts espionage, one count regicide, and…" His sneer rose to the execution girder, where the Butcher hung by bound wrists, wriggling like a fish hooked above the street two dozen meters below. "Two counts cannibalism."

The Archivist of Law dutifully scribbled the charges into record, as the crowd jeered and roared in a clash of ideals. In the archivist's opinion, too many of the Butcher's dissenters had joined the royalists in the square for the queen's verdict to be assured. But such was the nature of audience, and the conqueror didn't yet the command the power to bar them.

"Butcher," Her Majesty addressed him when the crowd settled, "how do you plead?"

Several thousand eyes rose to the top floor of the four-story tenement where the emaciated Butcher dangled. The Butcher had always been lean, but his incarceration had withered him to a cord. His hair lay limp and uncut, not at all as he liked it. His exposed chest was painted with a violent mosaic of bruises and scars that matched the tattoos on his arms. Practically naked without his characteristic apron and cleaver. Yet his voice thundered.

"THAT IS NOT MY TITLE."

Shock chilled the archivist's nerves. The Butcher's words thrummed with Endurance, despite a fast imposed by his captors. To his herd, that magic was a feast of inspiration. Chants galloped through the crowd with the thunder of the bull emphon's hooves, rising and shaking the surrounding tenements as his supporters stamped their support.

"Chef King! Chef King! Chef King!"

"ENOUGH," the queen growled, her words carrying more Endurance than his.

The chants fell to silence, her words carrying a magical command sharp as teeth. Even the archivist's foot stayed its impatient tapping momentarily, halted beneath Her Majesty's authority. But one voice was not stilled by the command.

"I accept the charges," the Butcher said. "But not their grounds or chargers. I call for the Rite."

The archivist's pen paused, unaware that the Butcher was so well-versed in laws he'd risen to destroy. Several heads upon the dais swung between the queen and the Butcher. Dissent carried on the humid spring breeze as the emboldened supporters blasphemed their sovereign, jeering in support of their idol.

"Give it to him, you cannibal hypocrite!" called a common who snuck amongst the Rare nobility in the front row. Her removal was swift and exacting.

"And upon whose authority do you lay such idiocy?" barked the executioner, surmounting the growing support of the crowd. "You've no proof of Rarity anymore!"

This was one answer the Butcher could not give, and all knew it. The crowd's fire weakened with each passing moment, and the smiles upon the dais strengthened returned.

"Then—" the executioner began.

"Mine," the archivist interrupted feebly, forcing the words from a reluctant throat.

A thousand stares carried the weight of a bull emphon's gore. They struck the archivist in the gut and left anxious breath trickling away. Under all that scrutiny, the archivist yearned to slide beneath the table and disappear. To protect the wealth and security that subservience had afforded them this last decade. But the Butcher's truth was a delicacy like none before.

"I would hear it from the Butcher's mouth." The archivist's voice reached only the first rows of the crowd, the Tribunal, the executioner, and the queen herself, but the volume of its betrayal echoed to the children standing upon boxes of decayed meat in the very back. Cheers, both instantaneous and calamitous.

The crowd had expected this outcome. An incredible act of faith, given that until only seconds prior, the archivist had yet to reach that decision, and neither the Butcher nor his ilk could've known it could be reached. Not for certain. Not from the very person that condemned the Butcher's family to death.

And yet.

As the chants peaked, few heard the archivist's subsequent excuse: "He knows where it is." But the queen did, and her temper grew red as the spice for which Paprick the Butcher was named. Her Enduring glare could've set the dais ablaze with its fury. "**So be it.**"

A wave of power thrust the archivist into a teetering chair. An elderly Rare nobleman in the front—pressed already between the common at his back and the barricade against his ribs—gasped and collapsed over the fencing as the same power hit him.

A dozen times, the archivist dined as the queen's guest, and a dozen times over, the archivist would have sworn the woman could not have glut the portions necessary to wield so much Endurance. For the queen to have feasted in the present famine was a statement beyond words.

But the archivist managed to rise, and the crowd's roar frenzied as if its fickle nation had actually won the war. There was no recourse for the queen now, and her anger simmered to disappointment. "You always put God before country, and today it is your undoing. When he proves guilty, you die beside him."

"Lower him," the archivist instructed, feigning indifference to the threat.

The executioner's beady brown eyes found the resplendent, Enduring yellow of the queen's own. Without slaking her gaze from the archivist, she nodded. A pulley spun to life, and the Butcher lowered with the slow grace of Olearth's angels. Whatever fear might have wormed into common hearts boiled away. The crowd grew riotous in its exultation, smashing forward to crack the ribs of a dozen more Rare against the barricades.

Chaos.

Running, screaming. The common fought their way to the queen's dais to set it alight, and as the archivist was ushered to safety, the historian-turned-lawkeeper pondered whether future historians would see that moment as the start of a second civil war or merely the end of an intermission.

Hours later, in a dusty prison cell painted crimson by the fires burning outside the palace, the archivist taps a foot, guilty with responsibility and apprehensive of the Rite that will decide two lives. With perfect posture, the archivist suggests confidence and lifts a pen to begin.

For his part, the Butcher slumps nonchalantly behind the bars between them. Flagrant as ever in his casual approach to death. The archivist hates it. Or perhaps, still hates him. He who reeks of memory. Sweat and chicory. Smoke.

"I knew you'd bite," the Butcher says. "Curiosity was always your dish."

"I care little what you think of me, Butcher." A lie and both know it. But ever his mothers' son, the Butcher graces the archivist with an opening rather than objecting to the statement.

"That is not my title," he declares.

"You relished the mantle once, but you claim Chef King, now. What's changed? I remember when you hated that you might be royalty."

The Butcher's Enduring eyes flicker in the writing lamp's wan light as he leans forward. "There are two types of royals: those born into the curse and those who seize it. I'm neither." Shadows crawl over the contours of the Butcher's scarred face as his cell's darkness swallows him back. Only the yellow illumination of his eyes remains. "And both."

The archivist regards the shadow of a man some believe closer to a god. There could be some truth to his declaration, and by the Rite, it would be either validated or disproven by the end. But there is something more critical in the Butcher's story. The secret to Endurance itself. The secret of God's location. And there is very little the archivist would not risk to record *that* truth. Not the reopening of wounds. Not the deaths of people they both loved. Not even an impending execution should the Butcher fail to prove his innocence.

But maneuvering the Butcher into revealing it will be no easy feat. Admitting that would seal his guilt.

Ah, it will be a worthy duel between two former friends, the archivist expects. But not one quickly won. As a boom thunders the cell walls—a reminder that their conflict is but one of many—the archivist opens the Rite book to a blank page.

"From the beginning, then," the archivist instructs. "The factory. Meg."

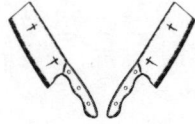

Course 1: The First Flavor

A meager cut, the First Flavor is best served as an appetizer or alongside a salad of herbaceous greens in a vinaigrette for acidity. Pair with a light red wine to start your evening.

Ingredients (serves 1–2):

50–100g bull emphon round steak
1 sprig of bull grass
1 clove garlic
Salt to taste
2 tsp coarsely ground black pepper
4 tbsp oil or butter

Steps:

1. Preheat oven to 135°C. Let steak sit at room temperature for 30 minutes.
2. Finely dice bull grass. Mince garlic.
3. Fork steak and rub salt and pepper into the meat.
4. Heat oil or butter over high heat in a cast iron pan for 30 seconds.
5. Sprinkle bull grass and garlic into the pan and sauté until aromatic, approximately 30 seconds.
6. Press round into pan for 15 seconds, flip, press for an additional 15 seconds, and transfer steak to the oven for 10 minutes.
7. Remove and let rest for 10 minutes before serving.

Expected Endurance Effect(s):

Endurance, 6–8 hours

1

THE KING'S FACTORY

THE GARGANTUAN MONSTROSITIES the Rare call bull emphon and the common call carnephon produce seven main cuts of meat living, and eight dead.

As an apprentice butcher, I was stuck with the shank. A terrible, tough cut in front of the brisket. Dry. Sinewy. Barely edible outside a stew. But the master butchers didn't post me there because it cut like tree bark and I was good with an ax. The glory of carving the shank was mine because our bull was a forty-ton carnivore, twenty meters from scaled claw to feathered shoulder, and slicing off its forearm didn't please its sword-length fangs much. Better the wiry sixteen-year-old common with a fresh indenture gets eaten than someone who knew the fine cut of sirloin.

The day Meg quit, I climbed the ladder anchored into the carnephon's bones, drudging my cleaversaw, a slicing tool as long as my leg that weighed twice as much, behind me. Not an elegant cooking knife but an unholy marriage of sword and ax, only faintly reminiscent of a butcher's cleaver due to its rectangular blade. Its length kept the sheathed blade far from the saw's handle in my hand, but my long torso meant the block knocked into my calf with each rung of the ladder. After a season on the job, the bruises ached endlessly as I bore my weight upward, but better them than the whip on my back—large target that it was—or worse, penalties on my indenture for laziness.

My work platform sat above the forward loop of the suspension harness, which held the bull off the ground with leather tanned from one of its long-dead ancestors. By the time I reached it, my labored breath fogged through the mouth slit of my head-to-toe butcher suit, the temperature frigid as imported ice slowly melted along the factory's walls. I sucked air through my nose, inhaling the stench of iron and offal without notice. Months had numbed it, but those first few weeks had been a constant battle against rising bile.

The well-liked apprentices were carving into the brisket off to my left, a stone's throw below me, splattering the ground with gore. Bessa—yes, I named her—trembled with pain as they bit into her with their saws. It was early yet, so her roars were faint, stored deep in the pit of her lungs, but my place at the shank exposed me especially to her hurt, so close to her terrified heartbeat.

"Sorry, girl," I whispered, laying my free hand against her scales as I caught my breath.

If I leaped up, I could run my fingers over the pink and green feathers that fluttered and twitched where they remained on the scales of her shoulder, but the pluckers had removed the feathers from her hide so that butchers could find the grain of her scales easily. Plucked, she looked more bovine than reptilian, though the reality was neither. While she might have the same general shape as the cows of Olearth, her milk secreted out of sacs above her sharp canines rather than udders. My grandmama said cows didn't have man-sized long claws on their forelegs, only hooves like Bessa had on her hind legs.

A hand tapped my foot, and I made room for my mentor to join me on the scaffold. In her butcher suit, Meg was a featureless rubber doll. Shorter than me by two heads but broad in shoulder and hip, she carried a strength that barely registered the weight of her flatsaw—similar to my cleaversaw, but thinner and angled more like a paring knife. Perfect for getting beneath the inedible scales and slicing them cleanly from the muscle. By all accounts, she was the best butcher in the Panchon Kingdom for her age, but that only made the overseers hate her more, which is why she was stuck with me.

"What are you waiting for?" she asked.

I scowled, knowing she couldn't see my expression. Cutting into Bessa wasn't something I did lightly. Blasphemous, I know, but I didn't want the emphon to think I was hurting her in spite. I always shared a moment with her, to thank her for the meat she was providing first. "I know you like the first cut," I joked.

"Just get in position before we get a deduction."

I didn't have time to move before Meg hefted the flatsaw and placed it perpendicular to the scale's grain. With a grunt, she began serrating between the scale and the muscle. Blood splattered across my mouth slit, filling my mouth.

"Starving rookie," Meg cursed as I cleared the blood from my mouth.

The last few weeks, my mentor had been less and less the friend I'd grown up idolizing. Angrier each day as she approached her eighteenth birthday and all that brought. But to intentionally splatter me wasn't like her.

"What's wrong?" I encouraged her as I got into position, gripping the scale she was cutting so that I could pull it away from Bessa as Meg cut deeper. When she'd gotten halfway down the scale, I'd support its weight so that it didn't peel off and damage the meat beneath.

"What's wrong?" Sarcasm edged her voice as her blade cut deeper and faster. Protocol dictated that she slice slowly rather than saw coarsely into the scale, removing it gently. Then I'd replace her with the cleaversaw to get deep into the tissue from the outside, cleaving to the bone so that we could both edge around it to remove the lean, working muscle cleanly, preserving as much flavoring from the tendons as we could.

Cleanly, as if it didn't involve draining a living thing of liters of blood.

But Meg was mad, and she didn't stick to protocol.

Meg shouldered through the hard clot of Bessa's epidermis scales and sank into the dermis flesh beneath it. Fresh arterial blood sprinkled the air, raining down on us, the platform, and a dozen more butchers cutting the length and breadth of Bessa's enormous body. The liters spraying from her at any given moment were little more than the bites of parasites. What would have killed any of us in moments barely registered. But enough blood loss would collapse even a twenty-meter-tall demigod, if the loss wasn't properly regulated by the cocktail of alchemics being pumped into her spine, stomach, and kidneys by the masters.

Meg's cut tipped the delicate balance, and Bessa's whole body quaked, straining the platforms anchored into her bones. Wood cracked below us. I grasped at the railing, but slipped on slick blood underfoot, wrenching my knee. Meg's hand snatched out and caught me by the forearm before I fell.

Suddenly, Bessa stilled, alchemics readjusted for the mishap. One of the overseers shined a spotlight on the geyser from the platform twenty meters above, drawn to blood like a vulture.

"Artery damage!" called the overseer. "Deduction levied to butcher Meg and apprentice Paprick."

"Confirmed, three percent!" replied another.

Black sludge splashed over the wound. An instant later, a gout of flames set the sludge aflame, cauterizing the wound and proving that the Enduring Defense Branch, the king's secret police, had a carver among the overseers to channel Endurance.

"Look what you've done now!" Meg shouted over Bessa's pained roar.

"Me? I didn't do a starving thing."

"You never do! Do you know what that three percent cost me?"

I did. But I wasn't in the mood to apologize, not for something

I hadn't done. "I'm not the one holding the saw." I punctuated the words by wrestling control of the cut away from her, forcing her blade to the proper angle by heaving my weight into the scale and tilting it up.

The flatsaw sank the final meter toward my ankle. Meg yanked it away in a huff so that I could drop the severed scale away into the offal and waste below. With the scale removed, about a third of Bessa's forearm shank glistened sanguine under the factory's dull red chandeliers. Individual muscle fibers thick as my arm interweaved as capillaries beat.

The first time I saw it, Bessa's exposed muscle mesmerized me. The enormous pressure of her heart moving all that blood. How it rushed then stopped and rushed then stopped. Then a master had cut a small artery no bigger than my hand and sprayed all of us with blood. I vomited into my suit. That had been near the sirloin though, where the muscle was tender and marbled with lack of work. The forearm shank, even strung up in the enormous contraption of leather the factory suspended her in, was tight working muscle.

We had five more scales to remove before we could remove the shank. The total portion would feed the army for a day or two if butchered properly. Which I would be sure to do. We'd already had a deduction. If we wanted any chance of making a dent in the debt we earned at birth, the shank would have to come away clean and whole.

"Cleaversaw's covered in blood," I complained, noticing gore stuck in the grooves of its handle. I was no knifehead, obsessed with having the cleanest saw and using it for precisely the right cut, but I knew better than to hold a giant slicing instrument when it was wet with blood. By the time I had it clean, Meg had produced a small pocketknife and cut three slices of shank from the greater mass. None was longer or wider than my hand, but each was worth a few hundred gold knuckles on the black market. More if you knew how to get it to the rebels.

"I said I wasn't down for this!" I whispered, hurrying to block any overseers—or worse, the EDB carver—that might see her. "How'd you even get that in here?"

Meg ignored me as she shoved a fourth slice into her apron pocket.

"They'll notice!" My hand snapped to her wrist, but she leveled the knife at my gut, low and out of sight.

"Meg," I said cautiously. "Walk me through this. Those aren't going to make a dent in your indenture."

"That's not what they're for."

"Then why? They won't just fine you for taking them. You'll dangle from a girder."

She didn't answer my question, instead folding the blade away and shoving the knife into a slit she'd cut into the thick rubber gloves we wore.

"Do you want to be a Chef or not, Pap?"

Another spotlight swooped over us. "Work stoppage! Point oh-two percent deduction."

"Confirmed, point oh two, Meg and Paprick!"

I growled and hurried back to my cleaversaw, hefting it inexpertly into a position and chopping randomly to get the light away. To get to the bone cleanly, I needed to reach the very top of the scales we'd removed and go in with a perfect 90-degree angle. The blood sluiced over us with enough volume and weight that I staggered, losing my grip. The cleaversaw fell across Bessa's exposed muscles, cutting through them like goat cheese.

And she roared.

The carnephon was then and is still the pride of our people. Its thick haunches carry a large bovine frame and an equally strong, squat neck. Four toes on each dexterous front foot, claws strong as endurium and sharp enough to cut through thick steel. Hind hooves like lead blocks. A stomp from one won't just kill a person but powder their bones and pressurize their blood to pop through the skin like a burst bladder. Claw, hoof, neither is as starving terrifying as its head.

Two goring horns long enough to stake five men each, and four fangs sharper than a flatsaw.

Bessa's head swung on us faster than the deduction lights could swoop. Her roar filled the air with the scent of her venom, a tangy seductive citrus, and the cadaverous stench of her throat. The volume of air leaving her lungs stripped the blood from my suit like a dust storm. Large yellow eyes fixed on us. The pain in them... I see them sharper than the faces of the people I'd kill. Those black, serpentine slits surrounded by yellow.

I froze.

Meg leaped forward to the platform's edge, hefting her flatsaw in one hand and my cleaversaw in the other. The strength, famines and locusts, I was a fool not to recognize it then—how anyone could lift both.

Bessa flinched back against the too-familiar knowledge of their bite. It was enough.

Enduring flame surged the length of her body as a carver cowed Bessa down. She roared against it, hated it in the way I hated the whip, but a moment later, her head lulled, no doubt filled with a pacifying cocktail. Yellow eyes layered gray.

"Eight percent deduction," an overseer decreed. "Additional three percent for resources expended."

"Eleven percent, confirmed!"

"Eleven percent," I muttered. On top of the 3.2 already incurred. The interest on that alone would be another two years of indenture for me. For Meg, it was a life sentence. Our saws *thunked* against the platform as they slipped from her hands.

It was cause for another percent for laziness, but even the overseers must have found a deeper disgust in the recesses of their Rare hearts because they didn't penalize us for it immediately. They gave us a moment to let 14.2 sink in, break us.

I hefted my saw and took my place back at Bessa's side. Meg joined, after a time.

Silence stretched between us until my numbness boiled to anger. Anger that we should even be in a situation where a mistake could cost someone a life of indenture. An indenture only earned because the king started a civil war he couldn't afford with the rebels holed up north in Far Common. My grandparents' generation had only had to be poor and hated for being common. My moms' got to be even less than that. And for what? The king was losing.

Blood poured around me, growing cold with each passing moment in the frigid factory. But I was hot.

"Keep hold of that," Meg whispered. "That feeling."

I did. For hours, until the rage gave way to exhaustion, hunger, and numbness.

"I'm quitting today," she said when we finished our ten-hour shift.

My arms shook with the cadence I used to pace my cut, a rhythm carved into memory by repetition and overexposure, but I still rounded on her. "You'll be exiled."

"I have to." She removed her hood. Her coffee-brown skin glistened with sweat and her black bob stuck to her cheeks. She should have been exhausted, but the faintest hint of yellow whispered Endurance in her normally brown eyes. "Been training my stomach for the South."

No one was close enough to see her eyes, but I tensed, uneasy. "What about your pa? What about…" I couldn't say 'me.'

"He'll be fine," she assured. "I've been passing him a slice a week for months." She reached for my shoulder. "I won't live under their thumbs, Pap. And you shouldn't either." She glanced around, lowered her voice, and slyly removed two of the strips she'd cut. As I stiffened, she slid them into the gap between my glove and my sleeve. Blood slid down my wrist and into my fingers. "You have the taste, Pap. I know it. Your moms know it. You just need a chance. Here it is. Stop sitting on your hands and practice with these before you turn eighteen."

"My moms put you up to this," I realized. "Stealing these."

"It was my decision."

"Don't do this. There're other options! You could report a thief or become a master."

She tore her hand from my shoulder and moved past me to the ladder. "I'm no snitch, and I'd rather die young and free out there than old and broken in here. Maybe I'll find the rebels. They have towns out in the desert somewhere."

Stories beneath her, two farmers struggled to pull a 90-kilo slab of shank onto the conveyor belt as the night shift sharpened their cleavers to cut it into portions. Cranks groaned as belters pulled the conveyor forward meter by meter. As Meg descended, the enormous factory reverberated with the organized beat of chopping flesh, and a lighter sound joined the factory's many drums as butcher paper unwound from waxy spools. The slap of meat. The crinkle of paper. The rattle of conveyor. They began to sing.

If the wrapped chunks made it to the front lines before spoiling, they'd be boiled in a massive stew to give carvers Endurance to use against the rebels. We'd removed that shank, Meg and me. And what had we earned for it? An exile and two years of debt.

Right before she left my sight, she covered her face and hid the yellow of her eyes. It would be a long time before I saw them again.

They wouldn't look nearly the same.

"The oven had been preheating my whole life," the Butcher says, changing his tone from storyteller to commentator. "But the day Meg quit, the timer dinged. A bit cliché, but I never did get the chance to write my cookbook, so you'll have to suffer a pun or two."

The archivist detects a hint of satire in that but says nothing, leaving the Butcher a moment to quench the thirst of his telling from the small cup he's been given. It's the only thing in his cell besides a thin blanket.

In truth, the archivist is far more concerned with the sounds from outside. Explosions echo as the battle for Ranch continues. The common so crushed by the Butcher's capture rallied with such force that even the palace is under threat, and the archivist worries it will be breached before the Rite reveals the truth.

"Brutal, huh?" the Butcher tries again, but the archivist is unwilling to engage the bait. The day Meg Common-3 quit is well-known. One of his propaganda pieces, sparking common hearts to fan the flames of war. No matter that the percentages were inflated, no matter that the overseer records reveal these successive infractions were spread out over several days rather than a single shift as he regales. Eyewitnesses dispute details, et cetera. But his story has velocity. Besides, what happened to Meg Common-3 later roused more common to the cause than the infamous final shift. Likely he will recount that fate, the Rite granting what should be enough time. What must be enough. The archivist suspects the secret of God came shortly thereafter.

Still, the archivist scribbles a footnote regarding the inaccuracies, not to turn any who read these pages against the Butcher or to earn trust. Because, to a fault, the archivist is more than a keeper of books and secrets, but a seeker of truth.

With his throat slaked, the Butcher regards the archivist's passivity. "You always were an unfeeling mask. Is that why you betrayed us?"

The archivist says nothing.

"Fine. You don't care for commentary. We'll keep chatter minimal."

The archivist taps the book twice, eager to continue.

"That night," he says, "I tasted magic."

2

A TASTE OF
ENDURANCE

"IT ISN'T MAGIC if you know how it works," my mother Sesa teased over my shoulder.

My moms and I squeezed into our kitchen, barely a distinguishable room in the tenement apartment. Only enough counter space for a butcher's block and a ceramic planter pot my mom Asabi had rescued from Meg's balcony the summer prior. We'd filled the planter with three wooden spoons, the good spatula, the *bad* spatula, a slotted spoon, and a pair of tongs that I had to scrape free of rust before each use. The icebox was more like a waterbox, and we didn't even have a thermometer. Still, we were lucky to have an oven at all—interior apartments didn't.

Of the ten thousand apartments in Common-3, the giant multi-block tenement we lived in, only a tenth were exteriors, and my moms had saved and scraped for forty years to earn ours. Despite their indentures. So yeah, it was small, but we loved it there, and we *used* it.

The oven was built into the exterior wall, smoke escaping directly from the back. It was large enough for a deep pot and several logs to build the fire on, but the metal between the stovetop and the oven was so thin it bowed under that same pot. With war ravaging the north, wood was hard to come by and we'd spent much of the summer only using the oven for bread, which was profitable at market.

Standing beside the stove, I pointed our breadknife threateningly at Mother. (I always called Sesa 'Mother' and Asabi 'Mom'.) "But we don't *know* how it works, not really."

Mom nodded sagely in my defense and passed me a sourdough loaf. By all rights, she should've packed it for sale. There wasn't a common in Ranch that didn't know Mom's bread on smell. But when I'd gotten home from my shift and shared the news, she'd elected to reserve it.

Mother tutted. "We know enough to keep that bread handy. So at least tonight, it ain't magic."

"It's a *real* recipe?" I asked, lowering my voice despite our privacy. "A greater one?"

"Passed down by family," Mother assured. "Before they murdered her, your grandmama would test me without warning. She'd say, 'Sweetmeats, remind me of Stew.'"

A tear shadowed the pot Mother prepared. I squeezed her hand and focused my trembling arms, still sore from work, to cut gently into the bread, treating it with the respect it deserved. Some Olearth cultures once forbade cutting into bread at all, deeming it unholy and irreverent—or so Grandmama said—and I wasn't about to cut a jagged toast for a meal that might very well be my last.

It was a crime for a common to eat a greater recipe.

"So how do we make it work, the mag—Endurance?"

My moms busied themselves with the stew, talking me through it as they went.

"Oil and Holy Trinity first," Mother instructed, spooning carrot, onion, and green pepper into the pot—all diced by her steady hands.

"Then the garlic," Mom added when the trinity softened. "And it's time for thyme."

My moms giggled as I rolled my eyes.

"Salt now?" I was so eager for salt back then. It made everything better, every little trickle of food we managed on our three meager indentures. I didn't know how flattening it could be to flavor, how singular.

"Not before the broth," Mother informed. "It'll upset the boiling."

"Right," I recalled. "One magic stew and I've forgotten how to cook."

Mother smacked a spoon against her palm jokingly. "Best not! In this house, we don't just cook…"

"We live," Mom and I finished simultaneously. Because we did. We lived through food and all that it had to offer. In those days, it was all we had. Fun. Community. Calm. All of it came from food.

As the aromatics filled the space, I prepped my famous vegetable broth, homemade with the skins and leftovers of our vegetables from the previous week; seasoned it with pepper, chili powder, cumin, and oregano; and stirred it red with tomato paste. Mother mused that a broth made from carnephon bone would provide more magic, but she was guessing. We didn't know how Endurance worked. We remembered the greater recipe's flavor but not its power.

Truthfully, we didn't care all that much. We could afford bison meat only once a fortnight, and this wasn't half-spoiled Rare scraps but actual *emphon*. Meat stripped from gargantuan creatures that roamed the planet killing humans like ants. The taste was supposed to be unequaled. Magic or not, we salivated for a taste. And knowing what Meg had given up to give it to me… I had to honor that, angry as I was with her.

Remembering Mother's lessons, I brought the broth to a simmer, delicately sliced the shank strips against the grain, and lay them in a pan with oil and lime juice to get them tender. Onion and butter aromas floated within a citrusy hickory smoke, perfumed with beets. Astoundingly unlike the ingredients in the pan. It was my first time smelling emphon, and I twitched to consume it raw.

"Windows, swe'me," Mother instructed Mom.

Mother was the taller of the two women, with beet-red hair and freckles that stretched from the left side of her face to her fingertips.

A blotchy white scar, evidence of an overseer punishment gone wrong, bleached the right side of her face, but the smile she wore— stern yet so full of love—always distracted from it. Whenever she used her pet name for Mom, she sang it. I can describe a thousand tastes, but I can't distinguish an alto from a—whatever one of the others is called. Her sound was like windchimes.

Mom scampered to the windows and threw them open. Emphon drew noses, and we didn't need anyone inside Common-3 knowing we had it. Better it head outside.

As Mom crossed the small kitchen back to us, her crooked smile set lines into her eyes. My eyes, brown as mesquite wood. Her salt and pepper hair pulled back, revealing the dark smile of a scar along her lower neck. The pot's steam collected a visible ray of sunlight, one of the day's last, and the light struck her back through the window, giving her too-thin frame a glow.

Her starved thinness soured my throat. Too often she went on beans and barely a fork of rice so that Mother and I could eat more, always saying she wasn't hungry. A lie.

Mother clicked her tongue suggestively. "Oh, swe'me, this light does you justice."

Mom dipped her chin and waggled her hips. Mother strode around Mom, hugging her from behind and planting a kiss behind her ear. The two women shared a look that my age caught onto years before. It was a small apartment.

"Please don't spoil this meal for me."

Both women chortled, but I was secretly glad for them. For the rest of my life, long or short as it will be, I'll remember the two of them like that, that evening. Before it went wrong.

The Butcher's eyes bore into the archivist's for one moment. Then two, before he continues.

∽

As they kissed, I lifted the slices into the now boiling pot, reduced the char and oil in the pan with some water, poured that into the pot, added chopped potatoes, and lowered the heat to a simmer.

Sixty minutes passed like molasses over an ice cube. The smell. Famines, that smell. I've made a thousand meals with emphon since that night, but that first whiff filled me with something divine. Power danced on the steam at the edge of my grasp. I've heard it described as finding water in the South, and I don't doubt it. I ached for it.

The front door of the apartment banged open. "What's going on in here?" called a distorted voice.

My heart stopped, only to grow annoyed as my Uncle Macen entered the room with his hand cupped over his mouth to deepen his voice. On his hip, he carried my infant cousin, Musta, who smiled and giggled at the raspberries Uncle blew into that hand.

Mom took Musta and welcomed them with the customary common greeting, offering him a small cracker. "Treat, Macen?"

It was customary to take a greeting and either eat it or save it in a pouch all common wore on their belts, but Macen said, "Not yet, Sis," which meant he was staying for dinner. It wasn't unusual—Auntie worked the night shift at the cayenne bottling factory and he needed the help after his long shifts outside the walls—but I wished he'd chosen a different night.

"You can't barge in like that."

He handed me a toffee as greeting before noticing the look on my face hadn't budged. "What's wrong, Paps?"

After closing the door, I whispered, "We're making emphon."

His eyes flicked to Musta and then to the pot, his brow growing serious, no doubt weighing the risk of having his daughter at the scene of a crime. He didn't leave, though, and I couldn't blame him. Wasn't every day you ate emphon.

Speaking of, when we took the lid off the pot, steam coiled up at us like a pillow drawing us in after a long day. It hit us at once, and each of us sighed. It took all my strength not to drop my hand in the simmering liquid and scoop it into my mouth.

"Almost there," Mom said. She removed the final collection of ingredients from the pantry: salt, cayenne, and red pepper flakes.

"It's spicy?" I asked.

My moms exchanged a laugh. "All the best things are."

"But with sourdough?"

I was skeptical until I dipped my bread in that stew, which came after I slurped my spoon for the first few tastes. Those first slurps were good, which likely sounds anticlimactic. Be assured that at this point in my young life, this was up there with the vanilla ice cream that my moms spent three years saving silver knuckles to buy me for my sixteenth birthday. But it wasn't magical. Not in the way that the scent of the toasting bread and the simmering stew had been. Those mingling smells teased me with a grandeur of flavor that would fill me with Endurance and break the limit of the sky.

"It's good," I said… to say something.

My moms laughed and met my gaze. A yellow halo circled Mom's walnut eyes—my eyes. Mother's and Uncle's olive eyes, too. I shifted in my seat, arching my spine to fix my gaze upon my reflection in the window. No yellow. No change. I thought I was broken, that somehow, I was the only person in Ranch that couldn't use Endurance.

"Dip your bread," Mom encouraged.

It wasn't going to taste good. Sour and spice didn't mix. They activate different sides of the tongue and fight each other. They were supposed to complement subtler tastes. Or so I believed. I hadn't studied what tastes worked together or what tastebuds even were then. Couldn't define piquant and astringent in percentages.

The sensation that struck me when I bit into the bread was neither spice nor sourness. It was the sixth flavor: emphonic. The heat was present, the tartness of the bread too. But they were both accents to the bold, forward grip of emphonic. We call it the sixth flavor, but it's more of a feeling. The relaxing tickle of fresh a breeze on the first day of spring. The pleasure of the chase finally manifesting in the first kiss. The appreciation for the pink flash that concludes a sunset.

As the bread settled in my stomach, heat radiated through my limbs. My exhausted arms tensed as fibers reknit. All senses sharpened, and my mind relaxed, plucking stray distractions from my brain and carefully setting them aside so that I was focused. That strength, that clarity of mind, that was Endurance.

Since then, I've learned every greater recipe hits different. The First Flavor stops there, providing only Endurance. Emphon Milk also heals wounds and resets bones. The greater that bears my name would—well, we're getting there. But what of Shank Stew? What else would it do?

Eager to know, I scarfed the rest of my stew and mopped my bowl with the bread. I ate until I was fit to pop, and then I ate more. I didn't want to eat too little to get the full benefits. My moms laughed, enjoying their Endurance in slow serenity, forty years of knots unwinding from their shoulders. They were calm and thankful. I was ravenous with jealous rage. Anger that this was forbidden. That common would never know fullness, let alone *this*.

A few minutes after my last bite, the additional effect washed over me. An impulse. A *feeling*. As I tried to comprehend, the overseer and their black sludge crept front of mind, how the flames lashed Bessa's body close enough that the heat breached even my rubber butcher's suit. Almost without meaning to, I flexed my hand and a gout of flame roared into life on my palm. Everyone in the room, me included, shrieked, and I flapped my hand, trying to put it out.

It took me a moment to realize I had to consciously suppress the flow of energy moving through my body from stomach to hand, but when I did, the flame snuffed.

Mother chuckled. "I think we can find some better uses for this than burning the whole Common down, swe'me."

Clearly understanding her wife, Mom strode back into the kitchen, lighter and stronger than ever on her thin frame, and curious, I followed.

The tongs lay where I left them in the drying rack. Already, little bits of red speckled the tarnishing metal. She took the utensil in hand as I leaned forward, really examining it. Smelling the iron tang of the rust. Tasting the evaporating water on the air. With a much subtler flick of her hand, embers jumped from her fingertips to the tongs, instantly boiling away the liquid and scouring the rust from its holding place.

No wonder this power was kept from us. Sure, we could raze palaces with a single communal meal, but creativity could take us beyond destruction. With a million common using their diversity to problem solve, we could do anything with a single greater recipe.

As I took the tongs from Mom to examine them closer, I resolved to make real a dream I'd mostly given up. For a common, there were only four ways to escape indenture: pay it off (impossible), become an officer in the military (impossible without some truly prodigious ability *and* a Rare to fight for your advancement), get adopted by a "philanthropic" Rare as a kid (gross), or become a Chef (only slightly shy of impossible, maybe). A childhood of hunger had taught me to cherish food. Mom's bread and Mother's musings about flavor had inspired me to cook as reverently as some worship. I knew even the simplest staples could change a person's life with love, care, and a little spice. And I had spent years learning new techniques because I loved every second.

With Shank Stew stoking my emotions, I knew that happiness in this life lay only in a Chef's apron. I had eighteen months until my indenture locked. If I didn't become a Chef, I'd never have Endurance without the fear of being caught. I'd never *feel* like I could burn the Rare the way they burned Bessa. But if I was a Chef, I'd have a lifetime of power.

It's funny. Any Rare can choose to attend the Culinary Academy. "Daddy, I want to be a Chef," was all it took. But common had only one path into those hallowed kitchens: invent a greater recipe. Something that can only be done with emphon meat.

SEVEN RECIPES FOR REVOLUTION

Quite the feat when it was illegal for us to touch it, right?
I didn't care. I chose it. I *chose* that as my future.
Anything it took. Any cost.
I had no idea how steep it'd be.

3

A NEW PARTNER

ENDURANCE CAN'T ADDICT. But once you've had it, you can't help but feel powerless without it. Craving hooked its claws in me immediately.

Even though there were dozens of common ready to drop everything for a job in the factory—including some of my friends in Common-3, who I'd commiserated with about Meg the next day—the overseers didn't replace her right away. Alone on my scaffold with Bessa, I stole more slices during each of my next three shifts.

I was betting my life, my moms' lives, and maybe my little cousin's life on whether the overseers caught me. It was reckless, driven by craving and fury, but it was my only chance to achieve something Rare could simply ask for. Each time I thought about leaving the cuts untouched, fury at the unfairness moved my hand.

If my wrath was quenched by anything, it was how much I missed Meg. We'd grown up together. My next-door neighbor, the leader of my little group of friends, and eventually my mentor when I started. She was there for years before my indenture began, teaching me knife skills alongside Turmer and Peppa, who never got chosen for the factory despite their skills. Working alone was a numbing, lonely tax

36

on top of the deductions I took for working slowly, doing both parts of a two-person job.

The second night I brought emphon home, my moms cautioned me—ironic, given that they'd encouraged Meg to steal when she'd started thinking about quitting—but they savored their taste of power as hungrily as I did. When I told them why I did it, they encouraged me to follow that dream because they understood what I needed, and I think they feared I'd disappear forever like Meg had if they told me to stop. We used the Shank Stew's flames to scour metal and boil pots for our neighbors, earning a few silver knuckles here and there.

After a week, we had earned enough to buy wood and experiment, but my first attempt went nowhere. I tried to make a different type of stew—that's all shank's good for, seriously. But I came up short, even if the meal tasted good. I got no Endurance at all.

When I arrived at my shift the next morning, I was *normal* and dreading the taxing work of a shift alone without extra strength. An overseer stopped me as I came through the door from the changing room. "You're off foreshank, cockroach. Head to the left rearshank."

The rearshank was a tougher cut; the hind legs do more work than the forelegs and the scales are thicker. But if the foreshank was bad because it got the horns, the rearshank was hell because it got the tail. No mask could filter literal tons of shit, and no suit could protect against a tail that could slap through a wall.

Suffice to say I wasn't excited.

Enter, Cori Common-5.

Wearing the butcher's suit, everyone was they and them at first. Covered head-to-toe in black, there was no way to guess a stranger's gender. On shift, we recognized people by voice, the greeting snacks we tossed between scaffolds, or by height and build if you really knew someone well, which most didn't, working in isolated pairs. Cori was average height and svelte. When I hefted myself onto the platform, exhausted already from trudging both the flatsaw and the cleaversaw without Endurance, I had nothing to go on.

"Who're you?" I labored.

"Cori. Your new mentee," they explained, a slight drawl at the end of *Cori* and *mentee*. As a greeting, they tossed me an entire habanero.

I might've startled at the drawl and its ramification, but I damn near stumbled at *mentee*. I couldn't even process the habanero. Only on the job for six months, *I* was still a mentee. I was supposed to teach someone? Teach them what? How to rack up penalties on your indenture?

Customarily, I should've tossed them one of my spiced almonds, but I was agape.

"You always just sit around with your mouth hanging open like that?" Cori asked.

I recuperated and fished out my almond. "Pronouns?" I asked.

Cori hesitated for a moment. "She and her." Again, I caught a drawl, which meant she was from the northern region of the country, part of which the rebel army controlled.

"He and him," I replied before she could ask. "You from the north?"

"That going to be a problem?" Her accent grew stronger as if in accusation.

I'd heard country common were a proud folk, despite how rough they had it compared to us city common. They had no walls to protect them from wild emphon like we did in Ranch. A third of them got indentured into the military, where they ended up fighting their own cousins in the civil war up north, and worse, most of them were practicing emphonists, which was technically treason. But they continued working the fields to keep us fed. Despite all that weighing on their shoulders, they held their heads high.

After a week of Endurance clearing my mind, all that and more rampant thoughts pulled my Endurance-less attention in too many directions: If Cori was an emphonist, being sent to the factory was damn near sacrilege, and she couldn't even admit it or she'd be killed for heresy. I wouldn't be able to share private moments with Bessa as she deserved now that I had a partner again, and a flavor on the edge of my tongue was starting to call out to me when I cooked emphon. Not right for shank, but there out in the distance. So yeah, it was probably going to be a problem, but I couldn't say as much without seeming like an asshole or looking suspicious.

No," I said. "Just haven't met an indenture from outside the city. You ever handle either of these saws?"

"It's my first day."

"Right, duh." I rolled my neck to relax my shoulders. "Sorry. I'm Paprick. Did they explain how this works? Did you see your indenture?"

"Not really, but yeah, I saw. More knuckles than I could count."

"Yeah, well don't overcommit. You aren't erasing it today. Just watch me. Do you get squeamish with blood?" I laughed darkly. "It's a long drop if you do."

"No." The conviction in her voice gave me confidence, and a hint of fear, too.

"This is Bessa." I was breaking protocol already, but if I was going to mentor, I was going to mentor my way. That meant respecting our bull, which she might appreciate if she were secretly an emphonist. "She's a kicker, but she means well. Don't you, girl?" I placed my hand against the green feather before me. The pluckers hadn't come for whatever reason. Probably someone had gotten injured in one of a thousand different ways.

"We need to clear these feathers. Come say hi."

Cori didn't miss a beat. She hurried to my side, folded her hand beneath the feather's vane, and reached deep toward the quill, grabbing the rachis right where it met the scale.

"You done this before?"

"Once or twice."

It turned out Cori had done quite a few things once or twice. She plucked the feathers expertly. When I showed her how the flatsaw was used, she said, "I've descaled before, just not with one of these."

39

"Is that how you got indentured here?" I aimed to make polite conversation, build up the familiarity that Meg and I used to get through the day without dying of exhaustion. But Cori's arms folded into a protective shell like this was an interrogation. "Sort of."

I tried cracking that egg for something to do mostly. "Who taught you to descale? Have you cleaved? Cooked?"

"Is this part of the training?"

"Point taken."

We worked the rest of the day without further questions. Between plucking, dodging Bessa's tail, and lessons on the safe use of the saws, we removed only one scale. If our accounts hadn't been flagged as first-day mentorship, we'd have been heavily deducted. But even still, we'd done a lot. I barely touched a saw my first day. Cori had been able to finish off the scale as the shift bell dismissed us.

"You'll probably be sore tonight," I said. "Rolling out the muscles in your upper arms and legs will help."

"You offering to help?"

I missed a step and stumbled as thoughts of what that might entail emulsified. Even though I hadn't seen Cori's face and she'd rebuked my questions about her past, I liked her. What can I say? Hard work and competence are hot as habaneros.

The archivist groans.

"I'm sorry," the Butcher lies. "Does the mass murderer have something to say about how I exercise my Rite?"

"No," the archivist grumbles.

"Right, where was I? Ah, right. Flirting."

"I'm kiddin'," Cori chuckled after a beat. "How old are you anyway?"

"Seventeen," I lied, rounding up for obvious reasons. "You?"

"A bit older." She teased the words out as if to say, "Too old for you."

I didn't embarrass myself by pushing. She couldn't be eighteen, not with a freshly signed indenture. Definitely not too old for me. "Good. Wouldn't want you to get all hot for teacher."

Cori scooped up the flatsaw, chuckling in a way that might have been at my expense more than at my joke, and climbed down the ladder, leaving me beside Bessa's exposed rearshank. It was the first time I'd been genuinely cheerful in the factory since Meg quit and sudden grief darkened me with guilt.

Meg never said goodbye, never even went home. Wasn't allowed to.

The moment Meg quit, she was sent through the South Gate into exile. Probably couldn't have died of hunger that quickly. But thirst, emphon, sun-stroke—any of those could've claimed her. I was so sure that I would never see her again, never know her fate.

The next several shifts together went about the same, save I found that I was starting to hope Cori was interested in being more than friends. I know I was. She had a wit and a charm that gathered me in and made me feel warm despite the cold factory air.

It was about three weeks later, one of the last shifts we'd be at the shank, that it all went wrong. Rebels had been attacking carvers, city guards, and Rare citizens in the city, putting overseers in a whipping mood and common on edge, me included. Cori had descended the ladder, and all the overseer spotlights illuminated the chuck where the masters were finishing up for the day. As Rare, they couldn't be penalized, so I figured the lights had to be there to help see some trickiness or because someone was watching closely.

Nervous though I was, I was no longer one to waste an opportunity. I removed my pocketknife and cut. Two slices for Shank Stew and a third to experiment with. It had been weeks since I'd failed the first time, and I knew I'd have to do it eventually if I wanted to become a Chef. Why not start then?

As I went to cut a fourth, a metallic sound snapped my focus back to the ladder. The figure was devoid of features in a butcher suit, but I recognized Cori's lips through the mouth slit immediately. I'd been, well, noticing them a lot until then.

Panicking, I thrust the slice into my sleeve and tucked the knife away.

"When you didn't come down," she stammered. "I—"

"You had a long day," I interrupted seriously. "Your mind is tired. Your eyes are playing tricks on you, you understand?"

Cori nodded and hurried down the ladder. A moment after, I realized I had just admitted to the crime; a confession was a death sentence. If Cori sold me out, she'd be rewarded enough gold knuckles to end her indenture. Without that debt, she had a chance at actual freedom.

I dashed after her, sliding onto the ladder while hefting the cleaversaw. Its length batted me with each rung, leaving fresh bruises, but I barely felt them. Too focused on getting down to deny or threaten or something.

Cori didn't waste a beat at the bottom of the ladder, hurrying across the bloody floor to the changing room. I gave chase as surreptitiously as I could—walking with the urgency of someone who wanted to get home after a long day—but she was already inside when I arrived, her flatsaw in its cubby alongside everyone else's.

Two score common milled in various stages of undress. I knew some by height and stature, a few by name, but Cori only by her lips and her voice. A baker's dozen were average, slender, and the right age to be her. I was about to ask around for her, but one of my friends from Common-3 walked up with a greeting snack to invite me out dancing later. By the time we got things settled, the only women left in the changing room were too old to be Cori.

I bit my lip and hoped she'd keep her mouth shut.

She didn't.

4

BLACK SPICE

IF CORI REPORTED me and I was still carrying slices the overseers could use as evidence, I only had myself to blame. I could've cooked them, sure, but that meant walking around with Enduring eyes and going home to risk my moms as accomplices. I needed to offload them and quick—to people I could trust.

There were two common markets in Ranch: one everyone knew in Tall Grass, and the one most didn't.

Tall Grass Market was a sprawling mosaic of competitive flavors and dazzling speed, serving seemingly anything before you could get your gold knuckles out of your purse to pay. There wasn't a cuisine you couldn't find, from local empanadas to semoli pastas from across the bay, or a product you couldn't buy—except emphon. Only Chefs in the Rare districts could prepare or sell emphon. Still, the place was beautiful. The moment the opening bell rang, hundreds of vendors rushed through its gates. Wagons would collide as merchants shoved them—and the bison that pulled them—into each other, trying to edge the competition out of coveted corners. At least once a year, a wagon flipped, someone died, and the market closed until the merchants learned how to "behave." But in a city where god is in the food and capitalism is as powerful as god, there's no stopping Tall Grass for long. Not without the king stepping in. And he didn't do shit.

The other market was better.

That evening, I ascended a rickety staircase. Several common kept me silent company, none of us uttering so much as a grunt for fear of being kicked out. At the top, a guard examined the person ahead of me for weapons, and a second guard tapped a rolling pin against his palm threateningly. Mom had vouched for me years before, and I had the tattoo to prove it. Showing it earned me entrance, but not without the standard threat. "Whatever you buy, you got from Tall Grass."

"Or you die, to feed the mass," I responded.

As melodramatic as it was, it was important to all who had the tattoo. To us, that market's secrecy was as sacred as greater recipes are to Chefs. As far as we knew, that market was the one place the Rare didn't know about, that the king couldn't touch. The king could usurp his God by halting trade in Tall Grass, but even he couldn't bring his wrath down upon Black Spice.

Black Spice Market thrived inside a derelict tenement building, the whole fourth floor gutted save its doorframes. Around those, produce crates and spice barrels rose halfway to the ceiling to create low walls for each stall. Dusk's light slithered through the narrow gaps in the blocked-up windows, adding with a thousand candles to color the stalls turmeric, and from each stall came smells. Paprika, cayenne, chili powder. Cilantro, oregano, basil.

Breathing was tasting and sight was salivation. Despite its name, Black Spice was the most colorful place in Ranch, thanks to its wares and to the personalities who sold them.

In stark contrast to the chaos of Tall Grass, Black Spice was order incarnate. The first rule was given when you entered. Never tell anyone where you got your supplies. The rest were easier: No bartering. No stealing. No tasting without permission.

Rushed as I was to get rid of the evidence, I walked the hall as slowly as I would hallowed ground. For all the learning I did in my mothers' kitchen, I became a cook here. When I was six, Halapen taught me the capsaicin scale. At eight, Old Man Banan explained the difference between kebab and satay. At ten, Cinna tested me on kitchen measurements in exchange for sweets.

That night, I needed Crooked Rish, a man that took what he was—a crag of a man, all elbows, knees, and sharp angles—and made it a moniker first and a profession second. As a child, he'd fallen from Common-4's third floor and struck his back against a cart. By sheer luck, he'd survived, but his injury left him forever bent sideways and forward, requiring a wheelchair to move. To the bigoted Rare, he was unsightly, never worth attention. That made him lethal.

"Pappy, baby!" he shouted as I approached, handing me a candied lemon wedge. "What brings you to the most crooked stall in Black Spice?"

He always spoke like that, ridiculously and dramatically. I loved him for it.

And his stall *was* crooked. Literally. The wooden door was intentionally slanted so he could pull a tarp closed at a moment's notice. When I gave him "the look," he raised a hand to do exactly that, leaving us in a private pocket of a secret market.

When I produced my shank strips, he didn't show surprise or reproach me for doing something illegal. He simply wheeled forward and gave one a tentative lick. "You're a butcher in earnest, now, eh? I can give you three hundred gold knuckles, but no more. This is a lot to relocate even for Crooked Rish. Especially with these attacks."

It was more wealth than I'd ever had—almost a year of indenture—but I was sullen to part with the meat. I wanted to cook, to find that flavor dancing ahead of my grasp. "I'll take it."

With the transaction complete, he pulled a string behind the wood counter and the flap opened the stall to everyone.

"How are your moms?" he asked, flowing right back into conversation as if nothing had happened.

"Nervous about the increased rebel activity," I said, "but good."

He double-tapped his chair arm. "Give Sesa my best."

For the hundredth time, I played into our little ritual. "But not Asabi?"

"Never." He winked.

It was like that with everyone. Black Spice was my community, my place of self-care and confidence, my people. Starving good people who cared about your mother's sister's brother's uncle way out in Plateaubrugh's pepper fields.

As I turned to leave, Rish caught my sleeve and pulled me back in closer. "And Pappy. Something is stewing, eh? Keep your nose up."

I thought he meant the rebel attacks until I followed his gaze to the one stall rarely filled. Not because there wasn't a handful of merchants that wouldn't have filled it, but because it belonged to a traveling merchant named Ruda. She was away from Ranch more often than not, but the respect her stall had earned laid her claim to the space in iron. Nations could rise and fall, and Ruda would be allowed that spot. Just as no one could take Rish's or Banan's. A dozen people loaded boxes and crates into its space.

"She's back?"

"Looks that way," Rish replied. "After two years."

I had only just received permission to enter Black Spice alone then, and I couldn't afford to think about her stall, let alone shop there. She trafficked in spices from countries we were forbidden to know existed. Her cart had crossed the deserts of the south, entered *and* exited the jungle mountains riddled with the deadly badgeboar emphon to the west, and gone farther north through rebel territory than anyone else who lived.

"How long until she's open?"

"Some things even Crooked Rish does not know," he answered, a hint of bitterness in his tone. "They arrived but an hour ago with her seal and order, but no sign yet. It smells wrong."

"I'll be back in a day or so," I decided. "If Ruda pops up, don't let me miss her, yeah?"

Rish tilted his head sideways. "Eager to buy?"

I lowered my voice. "There's this... flavor I can feel. It's... I don't know how to explain. It's when I smell the emph—meat," I self-corrected, "I can feel it daring me to make it."

"And you think Ruda can help with this?"

"I don't know," I said truthfully. "This taste, this thing I'm feeling, it's different than things I've had. Sweet in its spiciness, but nutty and citrussy hints to it?" I shrugged. "I sound raving."

He turned me about, looking at me seriously. "There are stories, Pappy, of those who invented greaters, back when it was allowed. A feeling on their tongue like you describe. I know of no spice like that, and I know most. Like cumin but not, eh?" He eyed me closely. "Yes, if someone is to have it, it is Ruda. I will ask if you cannot."

"Thank you, Rish. You're a good friend."

His smile faltered for a moment. Touched or displeased, I couldn't tell. But it returned quickly. "I owe Sesa my life for rescuing me from that accursed wagon. Least I can do."

That night we returned to our regular staples: root vegetables, spiced to all hell so we could feel something, rice, and beans. I barely stomached it, thinking about Cori.

"Why not go to Common-5?" the archivist asks. "You knew Cori lived there from her surname."

"Maybe I was too scared to remember. What're you after? Famines, you were there for most of this story."

"I want the truth."

He snorts. "No, I think it's the same as before. You want the Source, and you've heard I touched it. Tell me, old friend, do you think I touched it *before* you left? Is that why you're here?"

"You're delaying," the archivist counters. "You think you can distract from the verdict of your guilt by pushing me? I'll call a Defense Branch officer in here and have you whipped, Butcher."

"Oh, my very own EDB carver? Is that a promise? Don't tease me, scribbler."

"Enough with your games!"

He leans back. "You always were so dull. Fine."

5

CONFRONTING CORI

THE FIRST SIGN of disaster came when I entered the factory. I intended to make up for missing Cori the night before, but I was barely there when an overseer with a ruddy complexion blocked my path.

"Paprick Common-3," she said, disgust lingering in her Rare accent. "You have been reassigned from the rearshank to the left ribs."

"Why?" I asked incredulously.

"You dare question me, cockroach?" Her hand flexed to the whip at her belt.

I mumbled an apology and hurried away. I'd never even seen a fine cut up close, let alone performed one, so in my mind, Cori must've told. The Rare needed to inspect the rearshank before I could cut it to prove my guilt, and so they'd moved me.

As I pulled on my butcher's suit, I scanned for Cori. She was northern, so I immediately eliminated all the blonds and the one redhead. Of those remaining, my leading candidate had brown skin and burns on her left arm that spoke of fire. The king said rebels burned northern crops all the time, so why not?

I was about to flag that person down when she paired up with an older man I knew from my tenement. Not Cori then.

"Famines and locusts," I cursed. By then, I was the last common without a hood up, and I risked penalties to my indenture for tardiness. Assuming I even had an indenture. For all I knew, I was about to approach the rib ladder and find a carver ready to kill me.

I considered making a run for the South Gate and exile. But I couldn't leave my moms and my community. My hands shook, and I could barely carry my cleaversaw as I stepped out into the factory's biting chill.

Bessa hung limp in her leather cradle, weak after weeks under the knife. Others had already started cutting, so blood waterfalled from her belly to the ground.

Unlike the shanks, the ribs had no bones beneath them to anchor into, making ladders impractical. One gentle sway of the cradle and Bessa could tip a ladder over while someone was climbing. The masters didn't care if we died, but the inconvenience of training new butchers outweighed the joy of watching us fall. Scaffolding was the solution.

Up and across. Up and across. I went back and forth, zigzagging my way to Bessa's upper ribs. Blood dripped through the cracks of the lower levels, falling from where three pairs of experienced butchers worked on the short plate—the soft meat that clings to the bottom of the rib cage. The raining gore prevented me from seeing up to the final platform and slicked each rung of the ladders, slowing my progress. The fact that a carver hadn't met me at the bottom calmed my breathing somewhat, but I was still shaking with anxiety. I resolved to never steal again.

I passed the short plate without ceremony, and the sanguine sluice died down. A flatsaw whistled through flesh above me. Cold wisps of frost steamed my visor as I hustled up to the platform.

As I crested it, Cori maneuvered her flatsaw to the top of a long, thick side-scale. Unlike the scales on the shanks, these had evolved to protect against being gored, bitten, and slashed. Each was as thick as my chest, twice as large in each direction, and easily fifty kilos each.

As soon as she caught sight of me, Cori began to cut. I hurried into position, throwing all my body weight against the scale so it wouldn't move as she brought the flatsaw through the tendons that connected it to the muscle.

"Hey," I grunted awkwardly. We were a bit past wasting time to share greeting snacks by then. Deductions and all that.

"Howdy," she drawled back.

"About yesterday…" I started.

"I was tired."

I relaxed, my breath practically collapsing my lungs in its haste to exit my body.

"Wow," Cori commented. "You were sure I sold you out, huh?"

"Why didn't you?" I couldn't wrap my mind around it. She'd known me a few weeks. What reason did she have to keep a decade of indenture?

"I still might," she admitted.

Blackmail? I tried to feel her out as we worked to remove the scales for our cut. We needed to do the entire top of the rib, using three different levels of the scaffold. It would take us at least two shifts to remove the scales and another three or four to cut the meat from the bone. If Bessa died in the process—and after weeks of cuts, she could— we'd leave the bone in to preserve flavor. I hoped she wouldn't, but maybe I should've? I guess I just hated how powerless she was to her own suffering. If I wanted her to die to ease her suffering, I was only a step away from wanting that for all common.

The city only had three bulls left: one male and two females. The other female, who I called Heffa, had survived her yearly flaying and was a few months from laying eggs for the male, Angus. Technically, that made Bessa expendable; she was past her egg-laying years. But she wasn't scheduled to die this round. The war effort couldn't afford to lose her. Not that I really cared about that side of it. I had faith she could withstand at least two more flayings. The civil war with the rebels pushed the masters to get everything they could out of her, but she was a strong old cow.

The end-of-shift bell rang right as we dropped a scale into the offal.

"Where does all that go?" Cori asked, her first words since subtly threatening me that morning.

"I don't know," I realized. "It's inedible, so they probably bring it to the farms to rot and become fertilizer."

"Bones, too?"

I hadn't given that much thought. Heffa had been my first, and she still lived. "I guess they probably would go to the farms, too?"

Cori grunted, clearly unconvinced. "Pretty sure that would poison the crops."

She pushed back from the edge of the platform and examined the exposed meat of the rib. Closer to Bessa's heart, the heartbeat slapped ripples of blood through the flesh.

"Amazing, right?" I laid a hand against the muscle.

Cori matched me, recoiling a smidge at the first beat. "Ain't necessarily the word I'd use, but she's something fierce, alright." She hid a chuckle that bordered on a snort as a second beat pushed her back half a step. It was an inviting sound, and as I heard it, the anxiety of being blackmailed slipped away.

"So do we take our cut now, or do we wait for something else?"

The anxiety came right back, and I instinctively checked the air above us for spotlights. Again, they were clustered around the chuck, and it occurred to me that we hadn't had any surveillance during our shift, despite a few delays. Where were the overseers?

"You could be killed for this. You know that right?"

"Show me a common who ain't living in fear of being killed and I'll introduce you to the missing princeps."

Well, she wasn't wrong. It'd been centuries since the old royals were deposed by the Rare, coincidentally about the same time common started dying for Rare enjoyment. The rebels claimed to have a legitimate heir—the princeps—but that was a myth to keep the stove burning, and nothing more.

"You're sure?" I said.

She stepped closer. "I didn't come to Ranch for its *legendary* safety."

The sarcasm emboldened me to slice away a forearm-long chunk of rib and cut it into a half-dozen cubes to split between us. So much more delicate than the slices that I'd taken off the shank. Marble glistened in the fibers, so seductively juicy I nearly took a bite right there to explore the flavor and begin getting a taste for it. But I restrained myself, shoving the meat away.

Cori did not.

She removed her hood, upsetting a tumble of black curls that parted to the right and cascaded a smidge past a sharp jaw. *Those lips* smirked below a slightly crooked nose, made more pronounced by a marbling scar that bridged it and the bull-ring septum-piercing that hung from it. Brown eyes lingered on me as she gave the meat a tentative lick. The mirth in those eyes grew, and I reached to remove my visor to try it too.

I didn't get the chance.

The metal overseer's platform above screeched and listed sideways, crashing into the pulley that connected both ends of Bessa's cradle. As they collided, spotlight lamps along the platform exploded in cascading eruptions, sending fireballs into the pulley's ropes and freeing the cradle.

An instant later, Bessa and the platforms anchored to her slammed into the ground, sending shockwaves. Blood splashed across the factory before a triumphant roar blasted through her lungs and Bessa rose triumphant among the bodies of dead butchers and shattered platforms.

Our unanchored scaffolding groaned. Boards cracked.

Before we could move, Bessa leaped from the rubble, bucking, and kicked the wall behind her. As the wall crumbled under the force, buckets of black sludge fell against her and one of the lamps set it ablaze. Feathers burst into flame, and she teetered into our scaffolding, screaming.

Cori and I reached for the railing, hands scrabbling, but we skewed sideways. I caught myself on the rail, but the blood-slicked metal loosened my grip. My moms, Meg, my other friends all flashed across my eyes before I lost my hold and fell.

Air burst from my lungs as my ribs cracked against something hard and metallic.

Seconds or minutes later, I reached out in all directions, groaning. Splintered scaffolding pinned me like a cushion, but a hand caught my forearm and pulled me out of the debris.

"Kick, damn it," Cori instructed as I squirmed through, gawking at the chaos.

Bessa had bulldozed the Factory's brick wall, cracking a spiderweb of brick thirty meters across. With a roar, she reared onto bloody haunches and kicked with her forelegs, bursting through. Human screams pierced Bessa's low roar of triumph as people outside scattered.

This wasn't supposed to be possible. Where were the carvers to stop her? Where was the king and his recipe to control the minds of emphon?

With a flick of her tail, Bessa jumped through the hole to take her revenge on Ranch.

"That's gonna be bad," Cori said.

"We have to do something," I said. "Stop her until the king can take control."

Cori looked at me like I was raving, but I didn't care. My moms, my friends, everyone I cared for lived in this city. I could hate my job and the king and his indenture, but I couldn't stand by as it was destroyed by a tortured carnephon.

I didn't know how I'd help, but I ran after Bessa anyway.

"Paprick, stop!" Cori shouted.

I can't help but wonder what the world would look like if I had listened.

6

THE RUNNING
OF THE BULL

AS CORI SHOUTED at me, Bessa leveled four grain silos. She charged through each like a godly hammer striking anvil. Screams rang across the crowded avenue, bison-drivers risking charges of treason as they frantically abandoned the long multi-axle carts that left the factory each day with Bessa's spoils and waste. Common and Rare alike ran in every direction.

Smelling the stolen flesh, Bessa lowered her neck, charged back toward me, and crushed a four-axle wagon into splinters with her forepaws, reducing her severed flesh to pulp. I barely dove off the road in time, and Cori was nowhere to be seen. I hoped she was okay. A score of people weren't, groaning or dead in Bessa's wake.

Horns raking to her left, Bessa pierced through the back of another wagon and lifted it over her head. The vehicle and its bison flung across the cobblestone street and into a fifth silo, which crumpled on impact. Grain spilled into the street, and despite Bessa's threatening presence, dozens of common flocked to scoop rice into their bags and pockets, desperate for that next meal.

Bessa roared, her yellow eyes glaring over fleeing humans. There was disgust there. Rage. She stamped and snorted, let out a bellow and ran.

The King's Factory, now crumbling as everyone hurried out, was in the south of Ranch, just inside the forty-meter-tall wall that circled the city and kept out all twelve breeds of emphon. If we were lucky, Bessa would head for the wall. She couldn't get over it or through it, and when the military scrambled to take her down or subdue her, she'd be penned in by its height.

She wasn't that stupid. She ran west toward the river.

I struggled to keep up, sprinting through her wake of screaming children and silent corpses. Cracked water towers slicked the street alongside her dripping blood. A crowd called for me to stop and help pull a man from an overturned cart, but I didn't. I couldn't. I had to follow. I felt responsible.

Where was the Rare military? The carvers? The king? Within a minute, the king should've used his magic to assert control over her or the EDB should have swarmed her. But in eight minutes, she'd already gone over two kilometers. Rumors always spread of the war effort thinning the guard, but the war had raged for years. Nothing seemed any different. Why today?

Bessa's path took her to the river that bordered Common-1 and Common-2. Each was like my own, an enormous block of connected four-story tenement buildings. Ten thousand apartments each, and uncountable common within, including my Uncle Macen in Common-1. I hoped without reason that Bessa would turn north at the river rather than cross it. Make for the palace or the Rare districts.

She stopped at the river, allowing me to catch up as she lapped water like she hadn't drank in days. Then, finally, six carvers wearing bull-scale mail armor and helms dropped out of the sky wielding their customary war spears—two prongs at the end like a carving fork. It was my first time seeing the military in action, and it slowed my sprint to a jog.

The second the boots hit her back, Bessa bucked and spun. Three carvers tumbled into the river, but the others held on. One stabbed straight into Bessa, ignoring the scales by using one of the holes Cori and I had cut at the rib. Blue lightning—from some greater recipe—arced down the polearm and into her. She screamed and twitched uncontrollably, tripping at the riverbank and slamming into the water.

The carver tried to wrench the spear away, but it was stuck below the waterline. Lightning webbed away across the waves. The carvers yelled and jumped away, but the one holding the pole was too slow. The Endurance shocked back into them, running tremors through their body until their scream was swallowed by the water.

The three carvers that had been bucked regained their feet on the riverbank and jumped incredible distances in a single bound, floating like feathers on their descent. In unison, they landed on Bessa's back as she picked herself up. Water sloshed from her remaining feathers, their oil slicking it away as she stood fully.

Three more lightning prods speared into her.

Foreboding knotted my stomach.

Bessa continued to twitch. Two of the three remaining carvers returned to her back and unspooled a long, braided robe from a bag. With inhuman strength, one of them began to lasso the rope in a large, sweeping circle overhead, larger and larger until it was ten or eleven meters across, a loop sizeable enough to wrangle even Bessa. All the while, the other carvers used lightning to stun her still.

Then five figures ran past me and hurled themselves onto Bessa's back as the carvers had. They weren't wearing tactical armor or the livery of the king but common clothes. My mouth hung open as the one at the head, a tall, black man with multicolored cornrows, dropkicked the carver with the lasso. Endurance must've flowed through him because the target of the kick rocketed into the water. The lasso fell limp around Bessa and slid into the waves as the rebels—even then, I knew it had to be the rebels attacking the carvers—brandished hammers, spears, and even one sword. Squaring up atop Bessa's back, the carvers removed their spears and engaged.

Bessa took the distraction's opening. Scrambling in the waves, she righted herself and sniffed the air. Something caught her nose and she hurried to the opposite shore. Toward Common-1. Eight tenement buildings, each five stories tall, shaped into a square around a stone courtyard. Half dilapidated, wood replacing some windows, but all full of life.

Terrified, I ran to the bridge at my right and sprinted with the madness of a boy sure he could stop a hurricane if he tried hard enough.

Bessa lowered her head and bulldozed Common-1.

I felt the splintering columns like spurs in my own bones. Windows shattered. Screams silenced as half the building collapsed in an instant. Fire leaped from the wake.

Bessa turned round and kicked her hooves, spinning into a bucking tornado of carnage. Horns smashed into the building as if it had been stabbing her and cutting her, not the carvers, not me.

By the time I reached the end of the bridge, Common-1 was a smoldering ruin. Bessa continued her assault, sending bodies into the air like sand beneath a digging dog. She filled her mouth with common blood and bellowed proudly.

My face went numb. Maybe most weren't home yet. The day shifts only got out ten or fifteen minutes ago. Maybe, maybe Uncle Macen was with Mother in Common-3...

I pretended they were fine, these common who believed that while the king didn't care for them, he'd at least value their labor enough to protect their lives. I pretended even as I stared at a mass grave.

For five minutes, I stood motionless in my butcher's suit. The sky grew sanguine with evening and fire. People I loved were dead. Last conversations had without knowing. Had I left a sour taste in any of them? Did my uncle kiss my cousin this morning?

I would never know.

Four of the five rebels leaped over me. One landed only a handful of paces away. Clad in a black suit like mine. Gone before I could identify them, jumping again to land on Bessa's back. The carvers lay behind me, unconscious or dead.

I wiped ash from my face as two rebels attempted to get ahold of Bessa's horns, one on each side. As she bucked, they yanked her horns back with their enhanced strength, slowing her chaos. She strained and fell immobile, unable to move her neck. For a moment, a twinge of hope. They'd done what the carvers couldn't. They'd stopped her.

But then she bucked them all and charged off back across the bridge toward the center of the city.

Rage replaced the numb spreading across my chest. Every moment of compassion that I'd nursed for Bessa bubbled into self-loathing. I should've made her suffer. I should've bled her like a starving pig and used her blood to drown her hatchlings. I wanted her to feel *pain* for the dead in Common-1.

I started to run after her. Stopped.

No. She didn't engineer these deaths. She was escaping her prison. Lazy carvers hadn't shown up. The rebels didn't stop her. The *king* let this happen.

Unnoticed by dozens of soot-covered common milling about, I hustled after the bull. If no one would stop her, I would. Then I'd find the carvers who couldn't do their starving jobs and I'd avenge Common-1. I was convinced to my marrow that I was the hand of its justice.

Not the king. Not the Rare.

But a common that knew the pain of their boots and the hurt of their inaction.

7

THE FIRST BATTLE
OF TALL GRASS

"I DON'T REMEMBER much of what lay between me and where I ended up," the Butcher admits. "Wreckage, obviously. Your histories know which streets were destroyed, but near two thousand common died that day. I remember them."

"Oh, starve. 'I remember them.' This Rite isn't for you to expand your mythos, Butcher. It's to record the truth before God and determine your guilt. You expect me to believe that you 'followed' the emphon to Common-1 and then from there to Tall Grass on foot without Endurance, *while* wearing a heavy butcher's suit? That's nearly ten kilometers in an hour, not to mention the standing around you did."

"'Before God,'" the Butcher mocks. "You don't even believe in your queen's god."

"You're deflecting."

"Why would I lie about this, before I even get to the charges?"

The archivist snorts. "You're an idol built on propaganda. You and I both know you kept hold of that meat you'd stolen. You might pretend you followed her to Tall Grass, but I've never been able to prove you went to Common-1 at all. Witnesses remember you going to Tall Grass. Only there. It makes one wonder if you'd always planned to."

"Don't dare throw stones about lying. Not at me. Not after what you did."

Never one to rise to bait, the archivist calms and nods at the book. "According to my histories, the rebels herded her toward the palace in an attempt to destroy it, and her path strayed through Tall Grass and into a full squadron of carvers. Do you agree?"

As is his way, the Butcher only shrugs and continues his tale; tall or short, the archivist would be sure to find out eventually.

When I arrived in Tall Grass, dozens clashed atop burning wagons among smoke. Destruction pocked the battle zone as Bessa trampled through the market. I didn't stay, running to Black Spice instead. Crooked Rish was carefully descending the stairs as I raced, Cinna and Old Man Banan carrying his chair as Rish took each step slowly. "Pappy? What brings you here, now?" Even then, he tried to hand me a candied lemon.

"I came for you," I said. "You're okay?"

"Yes, but it's not safe."

"Is there anyone else up there?"

"Ruda," Old Man Banan answered at the same time that Rish said, "No."

Banan eyed Rish, but I hurried past them.

Black Spice was empty of customers. Clearly, every merchant had hastily abandoned their wares, not bothering to secure them from looters—no common would—but one was still rooted to her stall. Like me, Ruda had brown hair, skin, and eyes that allowed her to blend in easily in Ranch and the rest of the Panchon Kingdom— even though she hailed from one of our neighbors, Semoli. I envied the colorful tattoos of emphon on her arms: two bulls, a badgeboar, a drakephon, and others I only vaguely recognized from religious texts. But more, I was jealous of her mysterious history as a trader, which took her all across the world.

"You have familiar eyes," she regarded as I slowed my approach. She didn't move from her chair at the center of her stall, didn't drop her boots from the crate they rested on.

"We've never met," I said, thrown slightly, but I managed to recall my manners and produced a spiced almond from my greeting pouch for her. "I saw you last time, but from afar. I'm Paprick, but we need to go before Be—the bull knocks the building down."

She waggled a finger and pointed at my eyes, ignoring the almond. "No, no. Not that." Her words were slow as molasses, grinding against the urgency of my task. "Death," she decided. "It has its hold on them."

I frowned, annoyed. "I just watched a thousand people die, so yeah, I'd starving say so."

As if on cue, the building shook, unsettling a century's dust from the room. It spilled around us like the ash that had fallen over Common-1.

"Yes," she agreed, too slowly, too... pleased. "And that brings you to me, Dead Eyes?"

"I came to help, to—" My voice trailed off as a whiff of something seductively familiar, yet totally unknown, stopped me. As I scanned her wares, my nostrils found a scent sweet in its spiciness but with nutty, citrussy hints. The exact taste I was chasing when I spoke with Rish. Beside barrels and barrels of spices was a pouch the size of my hand, left open to reveal an earthy auburn powder.

Ruda clicked her tongue knowingly as she followed my gaze to it. "A curious nose you have, Dead Eyes."

"What is that?"

Slowly, she rose from her chair and came to stand across from me. She smelled like road dust and honey, and she moved with all the carefulness of a coiled snake.

"Your language has no name for it," she answered as she pinched a bit within her fingers and held it up for me to smell in earnest. "Most languages do not. What would you call the roots of a tree so tall that it would dwarf your tenements? With leaves that touch the moon when it blooms at night under her glow?"

62

My rage fled. Though I'd worked all day. Sprinted kilometers. Watched my home destroyed. Felt my people's death. I was full of energy to try that flavor. I reached for the pouch.

Ruda slapped my hand away. "No, no."

"How much is it?" I pulled out my pouch of gold knuckles.

"Not for sale."

"Then why have it out?" I spat, irritated. "Why stay, if not to sell?"

Even as practiced as she was at the mysterious merchant act, she flinched against my outburst. Then she caught herself and her eyes turned spiteful. All as I reached for the pouch.

"*Paprick!*" Old Man Banan locked his grip on my wrist and wrenched me to face him. "That is not how we do business here."

Crooked Rish frowned behind. Had they come back to check on me? I felt betrayed and chided, as if the entire world had been set against me. I pulled my hand free of Banan like a child caught stealing from a cookie jar.

"What has gotten into you?" he demanded. "No son of Sesa's should behave so."

I hadn't meant to knock him so hard, but his comment stoked something in me. "No common should watch a Common fall either. But here we are, Old Man."

Banan's mouth opened in shock. I'd never spoken to him that way. Famines, I can think of only one person who ever spoke to Banan like that, and he was family. But I didn't care. I turned back to Ruda. "I want that—"

Masonry imploded with a vicious *crack*. Everything behind Ruda ripped away as Bessa crashed through the side of the building. Four stalls worth of goods fell over a new edge as the whole floor lurched downward like a bridge cut at one side. Ruda, Rish, and Banan spilled to the ground alongside the contents of a dozen spice barrels, but I stayed upright, used to balancing on the swaying scaffolds.

The last rays of evening light poured in through the wreckage with a breeze that swept spices across my face. Outside, the battle continued.

Rebels wielded enormous weapons with their Endurance, while others blasted lightning, threw fire, or moved at speeds that couldn't be tracked. The carvers fought back with their own powers. A woman threw an entire wagon at the rebels. Another simply extended his hand and called the wind to sweep one into a campfire. Bessa ran rampant among it all, unchecked.

Without thought, I swiped the pouch from Ruda's fallen stall and poured something more than a pinch and less than a teaspoon into my palm. She sprang to her feet but too slowly. Through all the running and riding, climbing and chaos, I'd only lost one of the three cubes of Bessa's ribs I'd taken. I rubbed the earthy-red spice without a name into the two that remained.

Ruda snatched the spice pouch and my pouch of knuckles with one hand as she slapped me with the other. I stumbled back.

"Your stall!" Rish shouted as he rose into his chair.

She turned as one of the candles that had fallen set a barrel aflame. Forgetting me, she swatted at it with a banner. Banan and Rish fell in beside her, leaving me holding the rib chunks.

A dozen small fires caught the remains of the market as more candles spilled. Smoke filled Black Spice with the smell of applewood and ash. Charred flavors like cast iron's unique residue—a flavor that can't be matched by any other. My mouth salivated, still clinging to the unknown flavor of the unnamed spice.

The smell of applewood roused a memory: Uncle Macen grilling mushroom tacos over an applewood flame. A caress of powders: chili, onion, garlic. Color from paprika. Enhancement from salt and pepper. The kick of a lime. And then cumin, too, to enrich the earthiness. I could taste those tacos in the air. The meat sang in my fingers, pulsing with Bessa's powerful heartbeat, wanting it.

I stumbled into a barrel of paprika. As I snatched pinches from this barrel and that, I formed a dry rub in my hand. Last, I went for cumin, remembering Macen's lesser recipe, but as I smelled it alongside the unnamed powder, I couldn't stomach the idea of the two mixing.

I moved on to salt and my rub immediately smelled of my uncle's deep, earthen voice, my infant cousin's smile. I reached for the final barrel: tortillas. But a pillar cracked and the floor fell away beneath my feet.

I tested the taste of a rib chunk tentatively. Thank gods I hadn't used the cumin. Mushroom tacos relied on the earthiness of the fungi for balance, but emphon didn't have that base. It needed something heavier. The new spice, the one that was earthy like cumin but deeper and unique in its way. The flavor rang across my tongue, nearly complete. My lungs shimmered with anticipation. There was something more I needed.

A kiss of lime.

Rish tried to usher me out. Flames raged around us, and even the concrete began to stain with soot. "Your lungs cannot take much more, Pappy," he pleaded, but his words passed through my brain like flour through a sieve. He, Banan, and Ruda waited a moment longer before Banan coughed so hard he nearly lost his balance.

Ruda rattled a curse. "I will not stay to die with him."

"Be safe, Pappy," Rish said as he turned away. I barely heard him.

The flavors swam through my mind like cheap ale, dulling everything, whispering a promise of power. Hazy, I found a bruised lime, half-squeezed, and crushed its remaining juice over the meat. Some of the spices washed off with it, but the sense of precipice remained. It was like when the bread and stew mixed scents in the air. I was *close*.

I only needed to cook it.

Open flame danced all around me, but I needed a way to control the exposure and mine. I'd pulled the top half of my butcher's suit down to run over there, hanging them about like overalls, but now I pulled them back up over my sweating arms.

Banan's stall, Spear and Spearmint, stood mostly intact near the entrance, though a ring of fire surrounded it. Protected by my suit, I dashed through the flames, unaffected but for the smoke stinging my lungs. Skewers smoldered across the ground, all short. Holding one meant gloves in flames.

I should've stopped that madness. But every few moments, Bessa roared. It'd been, what—an hour? more?—since she'd escaped. How was she still being allowed to run free? Someone had to corral her. Why not me? It seemed impossible, but I had emphon meat, and that meant Endurance and power. Maybe it would be enough to somehow wrestle her to the ground and keep her from hurting herself or anyone else.

I slid both cubes of spiced emphon rib onto a skewer and found a barrel that burned in a bright column. Its scent was a lodestone.

My eager hand extended the skewered emphon into the fire. I nearly fainted at the sizzling crackle of charring meat. A breeze whirled around me, shifting the smoke away to leave only the smell. My knees weakened. My tongue drowned in saliva. And my hand *burned*.

Melting leather shrank into my palm after the first minute. Blisters cracked my fingers, shaking my hands well beyond safety. The skewer's smell should've been overburdened by ashen gloves and charred flesh, but it was as fresh as lime in the air, intoxicating as the finest wine.

I didn't cook it long. Three minutes, maybe four. I can't remember rotating it either.

I was half-mad with pain. Pulled my hand away to see shaking flesh and blackened skin. And yet I didn't fear. I knew the bite would sustain me.

I expected an explosion of flavor and got instead a delicate opera in a language I didn't speak. Each tastebud became a stage for a ballet of citrus and acid. Capsaicin didn't bite and water; it tingled my lips with a bee's buzz. Buttery, sweet saltiness lined the base of my tongue as the meat's juices sprang free under my teeth. An aftertaste as I swallowed: the smoke of a ruined city, saying its last goodbye.

Endurance slammed through my lungs and popped blood vessels in my eyes. The pain in my hands turned to a vibration that evolved into the strength of a regrown muscle. Fear, grief, and anxiety drained from my brain, leaving one thought: eat.

It was a thousand times more intense than the stew. I felt immutable, immortal, invincible. And I hadn't even eaten the second piece.

I ripped it from the skewer viciously. The moment I swallowed, my legs carried me through the flames to the edge of the ripped-apart building.

The battle in Tall Grass raged on. Rebels and carvers. Bessa rampaging. Fires everywhere.

A pang like my deepest hunger punched me in the gut and brought me to my hands and knees. Pain like nothing I'd known ignited my bones. My clear mind fixated on the fire raging in my body, my bones, and I couldn't imagine a worse death. Rumors said ingesting bad emphon could kill you. But I was so sure I hadn't. The flavor had been divine.

The building shifted beneath me, and I slid over the side.

Falling.

I closed my eyes, cursing myself for dying for... nothing.

I fell half as far as I should have.

I landed in a crouch, aware of tremendous weight pressing down on my legs but fortified with a strength I'd never felt before. My head swam as I opened my eyes to a perspective that made no sense.

I'd landed in a wide crater. My hand was braced between my legs, atop the crushed-flat ruin of a wagon. I lifted it in my hand, marveling as I stood on instinct. The vehicle was a toy in my hand.

My shoulder came level with the top of the tenement as I straightened.

I was twenty meters tall.

ENTREMET I

[decorative knife illustration]

SKEPTICISM

"DO YOU TAKE me for a fool?" the archivist interrupts.

"You've seen me in that state," he says, tilting his head to the side.

"My skepticism isn't of your growth. I object to the sequence of events, to the conveniences and emotions that pushed you toward your so-called discovery. Am I to ignore that you didn't once think about your mothers in all this chaos? Asabi would've been three blocks from the Factory when Bessa escaped. You didn't think about her? Didn't rush to Common-3 to see them safe?"

A flash of anger channels more Endurance into the Butcher's eyes, making them glow in the darkness of his cell. "Starve, locust. Maybe I don't want to talk about my moms. I don't have to explain my grief."

"Fine, but your story ignores any exploration of the ruin, and there remain no records of a Macen Common-1 dying that day or any other since. Inconsistency after inconsistency!"

"You asked for the story. *You* staked your own life on its truth."

"And I object to these lies as such!" The archivist has to shout over an explosion that rattles the barred windows. "I won't be drawn to the girder to feed into your legend. I want *truth*. How did the Source teach you the greater recipe?"

His yellow eyes lift with a smile. "Is that how you think it works?"

"You would have me believe that emotion and flavors pushed you at the right moments toward discovering a greater, and ignore the whispers? Was the Source talking to you somehow?"

Slowly, he pulls himself from the wall and closes the distance to the bars that separate him from his biographer. "Go on, you've clearly got a theory."

"And I quote, 'The flavors swam through my mind like cheap ale, dulling everything, whispering a promise of power.'" The archivist taps the pages hard.

"Nothing about the Source." His grin widens. "It was instinct."

"Who gave you the greater? Rish? Ruda?"

The Butcher's eyes cut with disgust. "She wishes."

"Then your mother? Macen made the mushroom tacos. Was this passed down from their family, too?"

"Is it so hard to believe that I invented it? I would've thought it to be the one thing I'm actually credited for with you and your people."

"You overstep, Butcher."

"And you overwrite. I told you this was *my* story, not your book of pious bullshit. If you want your answers, you might try listening. You always were good at that."

Glowering at his accusation, the archivist lifts the pen. "You may recall that I was present for some of what came next. History won't be the only tool I have to dismantle your lies. Experience has its benefits." And its curses, too.

He smiles. "I was twenty meters tall."

8

THE H⊕RNS

IT ATTRACTED SOME attention, understandably. But slower than you would think.

Fires jumped from wagon to wagon, racing across the plaza. A dozen more isolated skirmishes flitted through the haze in flashes of lightning and fireballs, smoke rising from everywhere and filling the world with an acrid stench. Bessa bucked a dozen carvers and rebels who fought each other while they attempted to wrestle control of her stampede, and trapped common screamed as they were trampled underfoot.

Only those nearest to me stopped fighting right away, so I had a few moments to examine my hands. They'd been healed by the change that had come over me, the fire's touch erased.

Swirling winds pushed away the smoke, revealing that my clothes hadn't grown with me. I was shy back then, so despite a sick satisfaction that I was certainly the biggest man in the world, I reached down and tied camp banners into a loincloth.

The task allowed me to reckon with the perspective of my new height and the strength my body held. But what to do with it?

I'd wanted it. I'd wanted a way to confront Bessa. Famines, I got

70

it. But I was terrified. Whoever said bigger is better didn't know what it meant to stare down a carnephon from across a burning field.

Bessa stopped and faced me. Big as I was, I barely came level with her chin and weighed a quarter what she did. But I was a new threat in a day of anger and pain. Inhaling sharply, she stamped her right foreleg into the dirt and dug for traction before she charged.

A charging carnephon covers a kilometer in about ten seconds. I had half that distance.

Meg taught me carnephon have one real weakness: a bone between the skull and the ear that works like a sort of stabilizer, keeping equilibrium. If you can break that bone, the bull loses its ability to hear and balance.

My first instinct was to plant my feet and dive at the last moment, letting her charge straight into the tenement to crack her skull against it so that the impact would break the bone. But that would've destroyed what was left of Black Spice, and from what I'd seen, slamming her head into buildings wasn't having much of an effect on her.

At the last second, I lunged right, hoping she wouldn't be able to maneuver and I'd get more time to think. She pivoted, reflexes sharp as the blades I'd used on her, lowered her head, and flung me into the air.

I crashed through Black Spice's roof. Four floors crumbled inward with me in an explosion of dust that left me gasping. Bruised bones needled my lungs, but after catching my breath, I pushed smoldering debris off my chest and wobbled to my feet in Black Spice's ruin.

Before I could see straight, I took another full charge from my side. Her horn missed my head by centimeters, striking air on either side of it, but her steel-plate of a skull cracked the side of my head. Vision black, I crumpled over like a stringless puppet, and she trampled through me. Pain exploded in my right thigh. Fresh dizziness choked my throat, and I vomited blood and chunks of meat onto the rubble.

Instantly, I felt weaker. I swear I shrank a meter or two.

I was losing and needed help. Fights continued between the two factions all over the field and the sight fueled me to my feet. Not a damned person had tried to use my distraction to intervene and gain control of Bessa. Was I the only one who wanted to stop this?

My cry of frustration shattered glass and cleared the smoke around me. As my lungs had grown they'd become powerful, and it shocked even me into stillness. The entire field stopped to look at me, including the one creature whose attention I wanted a break from. Bessa roared, mistaking my cry for a challenge.

I stumbled back as she charged, pressing my shoulders against the adjacent building's wall, and foolishly pinned myself with nowhere to go. She dove, horns poised to gore me in the chest, but I rotated on instinct, throwing my hands up feebly to cover my face. By sheer luck, I struck her chin as I did, and her horns angled into the masonry on either side of my head. Her steel-plate of a forehead struck me upside the head, again, and I reeled, biting my tongue. Blood pooled in my ear and my mouth, and I spat it away as the world tilted around me.

She bellowed her own frustration into my bloody ear as she failed to free her horns from the brick. It was like hearing a god's scream muffled by water. The wrongness of it...

My palms rushed into her armpits, and I pushed with all my massive strength. The wall cracked around her horns as she wrenched upward. I strained my legs, lifting her fully onto her hindlegs in the most absurd chest press the world has seen. Her neck thrashed and her forelegs slapped at me with her meter-long claws. One raked my exposed shoulder, drawing across my flesh like knives.

Which, you know what? Fair.

Screaming, I bit into the closest thing I could reach: the shank. My teeth smacked through thin fibers and straight down onto bone. Even as quickly as she regenerated flesh, she hadn't been able to heal the damage I'd done with my cleaversaw.

Her roar turned into a screech. Her thrashing became flailing.

Before I could do anything else, she pulled back on her haunches, smacked me in the face with her claw, and backed away.

Panting and sore, I pushed off the wall and strode out into Tall Grass, raising my fists and bending my knees. The next time she came for me, I'd feint to the left, bounce right, and punch her in the eye.

I lost the will for it almost immediately.

As she recovered from my bite, she limped around the field, keeping her distance. Each step came with a hitch that cut through my rage. Even with the death and destruction behind her, it was obvious that she was nothing more than a scared animal. She wanted freedom. I registered as a threat that stood in the way of that. It sickened me.

"WILL NONE OF YOU SUBDUE HER?" I shouted. My voice was a thunderstorm, loud and deep with the bellow of six-meter lungs. "RESPECT THIS CITY! STAND TALL! HELP US!"

If there were any fighters in the field that hadn't seen me yet, they did then. Unspoken truce ceased the conflicts, and someone even called back, "Who the hell are you?"

I didn't get a chance to answer.

Bessa must've mistaken my bellow for another challenge because she charged again. I didn't have the wall at my back anymore, but I wouldn't underestimate her dexterity either. As she closed and lowered her head to strike, I ducked and shuffled slightly left. She predicted I'd go right, flipping her horns in that direction to fling me again, but she missed me completely, sailing past, her hind legs bucking up to support her fling.

With my feet planted, I wrapped my arms around her passing back legs. Every enormous muscle in my body strained against her momentum, but I braced my legs and yanked her back. She keened as we tumbled backward. Her spine and head slammed into the street in a suplex. Buildings shook and the cobblestone cracked under our combined weight.

Hurriedly, I scrambled up her back while she lay stunned and locked my arm around her throat to knock her out. She thrashed and clawed at my arm. Rolled me onto my back, pressing tons into my chest. In a sick reversal, I couldn't inflate my chest. Even as I choked her, I suffocated. Bones in my chest broke—it would be a while until I invented the Enhancement that turned my bones to endurium like hers—and several punctured inward. Blood coughed over my teeth as I drowned.

My vision spotted around the edges and my very mind seemed to buzz like a cicada, distracting me, but I maintained my grip on her throat. She deserved that much. The city deserved that much.

I don't know who it was, carver or rebel. Someone in all black slammed a war spear into her neck. I rasped, trying to breathe out the word *no*, but it came out like a death rattle. They drove it in further and raked it to the side. Blood trickled out of Bessa's carotid artery as I kept pressure against the throat.

"Let go!" a different voice screamed into my ear.

I flinched and released my hold on her throat. The trickle exploded into a geyser. Bessa, dying now, thrashed and rolled off my lungs. But I still couldn't breathe.

"This guy's toast," someone remarked.

"Shame," another answered. "I'd love whatever greater accomplished this."

"They're coming!" a final voice warned.

I tried to shift to find the sources, but Bessa lay dead or dying across my hips, and my ribs blinded me with pain.

"Cut as much off as you can and get the hell out of here."

"What about him?" a voice at my ear drawled.

"Leave him!"

Unable to move, I stared into the smokey sky, gasping like a fish, sure I was going to die for the second time in a handful of minutes. At least I'd stopped the rampage.

Footsteps pattered away. Someone leaped over me.

I felt cold despite the heat.

"Status," a muffled voice called.

"Unclear, sir. But the bull is dead."
"What about him?"
I felt footsteps on my chest like the pattering of mice.
"Dying?"
"If he dies, you die with him."
I blacked out sometime after.

9

RARE CARE

I WOKE STRAPPED to a bed, which meant that someone had either built the largest mattress in Ranch or I had shrunk to my normal size. Groggy, I spent several minutes thinking it was the former.

Eventually, I sat up as best I could, given my restraints. Despite bandages wrapping my chest, throat, and right ear, I felt no pain. A figure leaned over me and examined my eyes, stretching them wide open.

"I'm Doctor Veroan," she informed as she extended a hand, which I stared at blankly. Without missing a beat, she marked her clipboard and tapped her pen twice.

I was in some kind of hospital room—or so I guessed. I'd never seen the inside of a hospital. My "doctor" on the third floor of Common-3 boiled flowers and herbs into tonics. Hospitals were for Rare. But the fact remained that Veroan's was a relatively small room with a bed for me, a desk for the doctor, and a closet.

My throat proved dry as the south and my tongue as useful as the time I'd gulped scalding tea when I was four. Only a whisper made it out as I tried to speak.

"I wouldn't recommend speaking until after." She handed me a cup with a white, opaque liquid within it. "Drink this."

Even though I was still restrained by a Rare, I would've done anything for a drop of liquid. It was thicker than expected, more like heavy cream than skimmed bison milk. Not nearly as sweet as milk either, almost bitter like dark chocolate. A citrus quality too. When I swallowed, I immediately felt a kick of Endurance, and my throat vibrated with energy.

"What—?" I couldn't finish the question, but Doctor Veroan must've understood.

"Emphon milk. Drink it all."

I did so without questioning it. When the magic set in, I realized how stupid that was. Rare executed common for eating emphon— and drinking their milk. Unless I was a sorcerer of Olearth, I'd consumed emphon to grow big, which was illegal enough for me to fall from a girder. Famines and locusts, I was consuming more. Right in front of her.

But famines, it felt good. Cool waves pulsed down my arteries with each heartbeat. My throat was more than quenched; it tickled as lacerations and bruises healed. My broken ribs twitched and refit into place, cool numbness rebuilding them.

As I drank, she undid the restraints at my wrists.

"More?" I asked as I finished what she'd provided.

She gawked like I was raving and stopped releasing my bond for a second, as if worried I still needed them. Then she laughed. "Aren't you the clever one?" She laughed again, released my bond, and moved over to a desk at the side of the room. "Joking about gorging with a doctor! I like you, hero."

I didn't know what gorging was, but I realized she thought I was Rare. No common could be heroes.

"Do you recall what happened?" she asked.

I kept my statement simple and adopted a Rare accent. "Scorching sun, I wrestled a bull emphon in Tall Grass, didn't I?"

"An understatement. And when you brought it to ground?"

It. I had to keep my face straight despite that. Bessa was an animal, not an object.

"I couldn't breathe."

She chuckled again. "You broke three ribs and punctured a lung. You also cracked your breastbone. If not for the Endurance and whatever it was that made you so bloody large, you would've died. If Lt. Vyson hadn't cut the bull off you before you shrunk, you *would have* died. Scorching sun, had this happened any farther from the palace, you would have died. Do you see where I'm going with this, lad?"

"Lucky to be alive, aren't I?"

"Lucky?" She frowned. "Rare are never lucky. You're blessed by the Consumer."

I grasped desperately for knowledge of the Rare religion and their god, the Consumer. I remembered something about being made in Their image with strong jaws and deep stomachs. That much better to eat emphon with, or something.

I flexed my jaw like I saw the overseers do at the factory. If I messed this up, my moms' lives might be on the line. "Yes, ma'am. Blessed with a deep stomach. Sorry, my mind's a little jumbled."

"What's your name?"

I feigned a cough and reached for my glass as if asking for more milk, but for all my charisma, I've never been a good liar. For my lies to work, they usually have to be rehearsed. She called out immediately, and three carvers entered the room with spears readied.

I lifted my hands. "I—"

"Stand down."

A fourth figure entered the room with efficient, thundering bootfalls. Short blond hair over blue eyes. Pale skin and thin lips. His lapel was decorated with the king's livery and a motley of colored strips. The guards immediately stood at attention and saluted him.

"Paprick Common-3, isn't it?" He eyed me without hostility, but I felt undressed. I *was* undressed, but this was different. Like I had no secrets under his astute gaze. No future either. Did they know about my moms? Were they okay?

Behind him, the doctor's face implied she'd accidentally eaten a spider.

"Yes," I admitted, hoping the truth would spare my moms.

"I swear by the Consumer," the doctor said, "I didn't know, Lieutenant! I wouldn't have given him—"

"Be silent, Doctor. You've done enough." He turned back to me. "Rise and be dressed. You're to speak with the Tribunal."

"The what?"

"I won't repeat myself, *common*."

One of the guards tossed me a pile of clothes nicer than any I'd ever owned. Both the shirt and the pants were white as sour cream and made of linen. I hesitated for a moment, wondering if I could escape, but three-on-one didn't look good. I dressed quickly and stood barefoot on the cold tile floor.

The guard shoved me toward the door, but I'd be starved if I missed a chance to take a potshot at the bigoted doctor. "Lucky I got that milk," I called. I swear she hissed at me.

The hallway was much larger than the narrow corridors of Common-3, and adorned with white ceramic tile. The king's emblem— a three-eyed carnephon, the third eye completely red in the center of its forehead, and a hand hovering above it, guiding it—sat at the center of each square.

The guard pushed me again as I examined the hall, and I stumbled into step behind the leading soldier. I nearly swung around to punch the guard in the jaw, but common sense warned me that I wasn't dead yet and should behave. Unless they hadn't known who I was until a minute ago and my death was coming.

I decided if I was going to die, I wanted to jab at a few Rare on the way. I clenched my fist and hoped for another opportunity.

79

Before I got it, I entered a large, sparkling chamber lit by an enormous glass wall. Dawn shone through pink, as the sun yawned over Fen's Plateau to the east, its shadow stretching back toward the river. The manicured cacti garden roused to life between the palace and the river, flowers popping open in the sun.

"Execute him, and let us be absolved of this," a deep, Rare accent decreed as I arrived.

10

THE TRIBUNAL

ANOTHER RARE YAWNED. "A bit early for execution, isn't it?"

"Blessed for its efficiency, then," a high, lilting voice suggested, trailing off as my escort was noticed. "Even the Consumer must break fast."

The soldier clicked his heels and saluted. "Esteemed Tribunal."

The "esteemed" Tribunal I had the pleasure of addressing was uniformly unhappy to see me. Though it was set for five, four Rare sat behind a gray stone table shaped in close likeness to a carnephon's horns. It curved from the unoccupied center seat toward me on a shiny stone platform, elevated off the ground so that I had to raise my gaze to meet their disapproving nods.

I only recognized the white woman at the right hand of the empty throne, the one who'd expressed how efficient my death would be. High Consumer Orega Marzona, head of the Consumer religion. Her hair was mostly white with fading hints of red and brown, tangled into a massive headdress of metal wrought to stick two carnephon fangs into the air like curved swords. It must have weighed ten kilos, but it did nothing to bend her neck—probably because her eyes blazed the buttery yellow of Endurance.

Beside her was a bearded black man whose eyes—brown, not yellow—focused on a stack of papers before him. He mouthed different numbers to himself as he scribbled, as if doing calculations, and for the entirety of what came next, he never looked up.

Across from him was a clean-shaven man with skin like the southern sand dunes, coarse and beige. He wore a uniform somehow more starched than my escort's, but heavier with medals and lapels. I figured him as the source of the deep voice because his anger was hotter than a grill, and because beside him was a bespectacled, bookish-looking person with brown eyes ringed with bags, who I doubted had the voice for it.

Clearly the youngest at the table, the academic sported a boxy torso, a loose, shoulder-padded suit jacket, and a series of earrings on their left ear and nose, which were all connected with different chains. Beneath the web of linkage, disguised but still somewhat visible, a scrawl of brown scars against their tawny skin.

I didn't notice the fifth member until she called the group to attention. She had a voice like bitter greens, in your face with authority and eager to get it all done with for both of your sakes. Sat at her own small table below the main table to the side, it was as if someone was unwilling to leave her on the floor but refused to equalize her with those at the big kids' table. Her chef's jacket, stained at the cuffs, rustled beneath a face weathered by a million years of scowling. Her eyes were yellow bordering on brown, but something about them spoke of naturalness rather than Endurance, and she had a knife of a nose, a tool that would slice down on you with her glares and cut through your defenses.

Two people at the higher table had spoken casually of my death, but it was the woman at the low table that frightened me.

"Well," she said, "what do you have to say for yourself, kid?"

The blood drained from my face. "I'm sorry?" I rasped. Truth be told, I don't know if I was asking her to repeat or trying to repent. Besides the terror her demeanor inspired, I was realizing exactly how dead I was.

The bearded man chuckled as he flipped another page. "Ah, an apology. See? We can go."

"Don't be flippant, Hoppus," chided the Chef like a whipcrack, but the bearded man only chuckled again and returned to his papers. She refocused on me. "Do you know where you are?" Her tone was gentler, in the way that cheese graters can be slightly gentler at different coarseness.

"The palace, ma'am."

She scowled. Famines, was she made for scowling, the old bat. "Chef," she corrected. "You will address me as Chef or Chef Ilantra."

I nodded sternly, but I was in awe. A Chef! Capital-C! That meant she'd graduated the Culinary Academy and cooked emphon. Ilantra was a Rare name, so she hadn't needed to invent a greater recipe like a common to get in, but she no doubt knew greaters. How many? What powers? I wanted to know.

Needed to know.

Unlike the other members, I granted her a small amount of respect.

"You have no idea with whom you speak, do you?" the military man said, voice deep as the Melting Mines.

"I recognize the High Consumer."

"Did I ask you to speak, cockroach?" he lanced back.

I opened my mouth to say he had, but was cut off.

"Hoppus Florento," said the bearded man, introducing himself. "Treasurer of His Royal Majesty." His eyes flicked to the bookish person. "He and him, if it please you."

"Dean Dyl Corzon," the academic said, smiling politely. "They and them, please."

"We're doing this for a common?" the military man complained. At the dean's glare, he muttered, "Commander Thymen Wensoan, First—"

"From whom did you steal your greater recipe?" the High Consumer interrupted.

"I didn't."

"Lie!" Commander Wensoan announced, slamming his fist against the table. "This is absurd! He's not even afforded the Rite. Humoring him will only—"

"I didn't!" I insisted, my voice cracking a little.

The High Consumer charged over the weakness like a carnephon to blood. "Paprick Common-3, you are an imbecilic common and you will fall thrice! Once for lying to your betters. Twice for stealing from a Rare. And thrice for using a greater. That is my d—"

"Enough!" Chef Ilantra ordered, silencing the High Consumer. "The king may be absent, but you've no authority to decree, you old goat. Only the king can do so. *We* come to a decree by vote in his absence."

The way she said *we* struck me as defensive. Without the position of her table, I would've ignored it, but there was exclusion there. Whatever the power dynamic, the Chef was fighting for her place as much as for my life.

"A waste of time," the High Consumer responded. "To vote, immediately. All in favor."

The High Consumer and the Commander raised forks that I hadn't seen from my angle. After a pause, both glared at the Treasurer, who did not lift a hand from his papers.

Chef, for all that she had just won that bout, did not smile. Her scorn for them deepened her scowl, which she turned on me. "Paprick Common-3, you stand accused of theft, heresy, and now perjury. What do you have to say for yourself, kid?"

I knew what was being asked of me now, and Endurance whipped my thoughts into the only story I thought would save my life. "I didn't steal the greater. I invented it. Using it myself was a foolish crime, but as you said, I'm an imbecile. I had no reason to believe that I'd actually invent a new greater. I just wanted to help save the city."

The chamber stilled, the only sound Hoppus's scrawling.

"A new greater recipe hasn't been invented in a generation." Dean

Corzon addressed the others. "And it was better suited for brothels than the military. We would be fools ourselves if we kill this child before we learn it."

"The law is clear," the Commander declared. "A common who uses Endurance without Rare authorization must fall for heresy. Even Rare fall for heresy. Only a royal can commit such a thing and go without. Drop him and let us be done with this!"

"Commander, be calm." The High Consumer stared at me now, the full weight of her Enduring gaze like a slap.

"You are a butcher." It wasn't a question.

"A butcher's apprentice," I corrected, feeling bold.

An eager glint caught her eyes. "Commander, I believe we have placed our scrutiny in the wrong direction. Carrion feeder, where did you get the meat for your greater?"

Famines, she had me there. I couldn't admit to stealing from the King's Factory without falling for that. But almost before my mind caught up to the solution, I was speaking. "As the carnephon escaped, the bent beams of the building snagged some exposed flesh at the ribs. Several pieces tore off and fell nearby. I rushed to find a Rare I could give them to, but the city was in chaos. I never found one." In retrospect, it was a pretty decent lie.

Everyone but Hoppus looked down at me keenly. I don't think any of them bought it, but for all the greater recipes in the world, none gave the ability to know when someone is lying. The Tribunal needed evidence, but that would take time.

Chef spoke again, her bitter voice full of opportunity. "Bold, claiming to have invented a greater recipe. Describe exactly how you made it. Be specific about the ingredients and the process. I'll know whether you're telling the truth."

I sensed eagerness from all of them, even Hoppus, who stopped writing for a moment.

Greaters were sacred. Beyond their holiness to the Consumer religion, they were the secret currency of the Rare, the infrastructure of the military, and an entire field of study at the Academy. That concerned the high table, each with fingers in one pot or another, stirring for power. The Chef spent every day converting the meat I butchered in the King's Factory into the strength of his army, the intelligence of his Academy, and the pleasure of his Rare.

"I've always wanted to be a Chef," I declared after half a heartbeat. "It wasn't just because I'd be elevated either. I love to cook."

"She asked you a question, cockroach," the Commander insulted.

"Respectfully, Thymen," Dyl said carefully, "I believe he is answering, in his way."

"If I give you this recipe, I'll never cook again." I affected as much sadness into my voice as I could, which wasn't hard. It did hurt to even imagine. "You would never trust a common with the knowledge of a greater. You'd cut off my hands, cut out my tongue. Anything to stop me from communicating it."

"And we would be within the law to do so," the Commander reminded.

I had to barrel forward as Bessa had. I was a caged animal before them and only my strength would see me out of the room alive. I knew it like I knew my mothers' love. "But even then, someone could ask me yes or no questions, and I could nod my way to the greater's rediscovery. So your only solution to keeping this secret is to kill me."

Chef Ilantra rolled her eyes. "But if you were elevated to Rare, there would be no reason for you to die nor reason for you to keep it a secret. That's where you're going with this?"

I nodded.

Dyl nodded back to me. It was a quiet thing, a thin thing, like the line between a simmer and a boil. "Clever common," they mused.

"Do not speak such blasphemies in my presence," the High Consumer snapped.

But it was the Commander who saw my weakness. "You would have us believe you found some meat and then managed to cook it into a greater recipe the same day with no training? Lies. Give me an hour with him, I'll get the recipe."

"If he's that strong a liar, you'd never know for certain you got it," Hoppus remarked.

"I won't stand for it," the Commander boomed. "There is a procedure for elevating common to the Culinary Academy."

"One that hasn't been used in three generations," the Dean countered. "For good reason!"

"For no reason," Chef declared. "Because there's been no reason to employ it." She regarded me carefully, and for all the Endurance keeping me focused in that moment, my vision doubled with the memory of Bessa staring me down from across the burning field of Tall Grass. They had the same eyes, Chef and Bessa. "Are you so eager to leave behind your common people and join us? You will be hated by both sides. What of your parents?"

"I would rather be hated and able to cook than dead. My moms know that."

"Moms?" said the Commander. "Is your father one of those common degenerates with multiple wives?"

Without speaking aloud, I leveled every curse I knew at the bigot. Polyamory was celebrated alongside monogamy and partnerlessness. To remain calm, I reminded myself that this was good. If they were asking this question, my moms weren't here. For now, at least, they were okay.

"I have no father," I answered.

"Leave us," Chef ordered.

The soldier that escorted me in hooked me by the elbow and turned me around. I'd all but forgotten he was there. We moved quickly into the hallway. "Wait here."

Two other guards held spears to my throat. After a moment, the soldier pulled up beside me, facing the opposite direction and speaking so softly it could have been my imagination. "I'll pry that greater from your bleeding throat, cockroach."

"Try," I said.

Before he could, the doors swung back open.

"Return!" boomed Chef.

The soldier pushed me forward and took a step to follow, but the voice of the Commander called out, "Remain outside, Lieutenant Vyson."

So he'd been the one to save my life. "Regret saving me?" I asked.

The soldier narrowed his eyes at me but said nothing and retreated, leaving me half a mind to dash for the enormous window and throw myself out. The uncertainty of how long the drop would be and the desperate hope that I might actually be made a Chef stayed my feet.

It was the Dean who spoke, which surprised me. "At what temperature does bull emphon become medium-rare?"

I honestly looked to Chef thinking the question was for her. She scowled back at me and lifted an eyebrow, daring me to answer.

Confused as I was, I answered. "Fifty-eight degrees, Dean."

"Define salad," they continued.

Define *salad*? Famines. "A collection of two or more vegetables, often served with a dressing, sometimes served with fruits, meats, or even nuts. Am I—"

"If I gave you one cup diced onion, one cup diced green bell pepper, one cup diced carrot, four cloves of garlic, and six cups of broth, what would you be making?"

"Is the broth seasoned?" I wasn't sure if I *could* ask questions, but by then I knew I was being tested, and I wouldn't fail without being thorough.

Chef answered through gritted teeth. "Yes."

"A stew, or I guess, a sauce in one case."

"Which case?" Chef demanded.

"If the broth was mostly tomato-based."

She snorted. I couldn't tell if that was an insult or if I'd impressed her. I risked a look at the High Consumer and the Commander. Both simmered.

"How many grams of endurium are present in one liter of emphon milk?" Dyl continued.

Endurium? That was the stuff in emphon meat that gave people magic. They could measure that?

"I don't know," I admitted.

"In ten kilograms of a female bull emphon's femur?"

"I—I don't know."

As the High Consumer and the Commander smiled, I felt my life slipping away from me. I could see my moms in the crowd below my girder, weeping as I dangled. Looking away before I fell.

"And in one kilogram of sirloin?"

I swallowed. "I don't know."

"See!" Commander Wensoan celebrated. "Nothing but a common fool."

"One last question," Dyl continued.

I'd just missed three questions, after answering three correctly— probably. My life rested on answering the next correctly.

"What is food?"

"What is food?" I repeated dumbly. It was so open-ended, but also so obvious. Food was anything you could eat without getting sick. Grass was food. Paper was food, technically. It didn't mean they tasted good or provided any sustenance, but they were food.

That wasn't the answer they were looking for. How could it be?

"Food is..." I trailed off to buy myself time. My attention fell on Chef Ilantra. The Dean had been asking all the questions, but when I'd asked a clarifying question, they'd turned to her for the answer. Was she the one asking the questions, really? If this was a test for me to become a Chef, then surely she'd be involved. What did she want to hear?

I racked my brain for what I knew about her: basically nothing. Ilantra was a Rare's name, named for cilantro. A Chef, so she probably knew taste. But she sat below everyone else. Was she unimportant? Doubtful. Chefs made the Rare powerful. Without them, the other four seats didn't matter.

But the same could be said for common in a way…

She wanted the greater that got me large, but not because she thought it could give her power. Because… It clicked. It was the same reason I'd wanted to make one.

"It's community," I suggested. "We set schedules and holidays around meals, gather around tables, form bonds over tastes. Without it, we'd be no different than animals. But it's also… identity? I mean, what I consider good food and what you consider good food defines us. Even when we disagree on good, people unite around some meals because they're important or sacred or traditional or whatever. It's community identity, too. Rare eat things common don't. It defines us."

My answer wouldn't win awards for cleverness or oration. It was a rambling jumble. But it was my truth, and if I was going to die on the fate of one question, I'd speak it.

"You swear on your life you don't know your father?" Dean Dyl probed.

Truthfully, I never let myself think about it. A small part of me occasionally whispered that Mother might have transitioned. But I looked so much like Mom and nothing like Mother. So I didn't let myself think about it. I chose to be what they wanted me to be. Their child and their child only. I never asked. "I swear."

"On the charges of theft, heresy, and perjury, we will now vote," Chef said. "High Con—"

"Guilty!"

"Agreed," echoed the commander. "The cockroach is clearly guilty."

"Noted," Chef said. "Dean?"

"Not guilty."

My heartbeat sped up. There was a chance.

"Hoppus?"

Without deviating from his calculations, the treasurer yawned. The moment seemed to stretch with each centimeter of his gaping mouth. When he finished, he nodded to himself. "Not guilty."

"What?" the High Consumer shrieked, but before she could do anything, Chef said impassively, "With a vote of three to two, the Tribunal finds Paprick Common-3 not guilty, on the grounds of enrollment at the Culinary Academy, retroactive of his discovery of the yet unnamed greater recipe for emphon-like size and growth."

I couldn't believe it. Despite missing three of the questions, I wasn't going to die.

I was going to be a Chef.

Or a Chef's apprentice? I wasn't sure. I'd heard of the Culinary Academy, but that was for people who didn't know how to cook yet. I had already made a greater.

"Shouldn't I be a Chef?"

Chef Ilantra barked out a laugh so hard she choked. "God, no, kid."

But before I could think anything else, Dyl said, "Congratulations, Rare," and my brain reeled.

Rare?

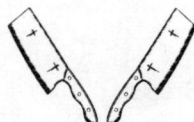

Course 2: Sleepless Salad

A sharp salad best enjoyed at midday beneath the sun. For a fuller flavor, serve in a tortilla bowl and pair with iced limeade (with or without tequila).

Ingredients (serves 1)**:**

Marinade:

- ◊ 1 lime, juice and zest
- ◊ 1 jalapeño, minced
- ◊ 2 cloves garlic, minced
- ◊ ¼ cup cilantro, ground into a paste with a squirt of lime in a stone pestle
- ◊ pinch paprika
- ◊ pinch black pepper
- ◊ 2 tbsp oil

100–115g bull emphon flank steak
Dressing:

- ◊ 1 cup cilantro
- ◊ ½ lime, juice (reserve the other half for grilling)
- ◊ 2 tsp white vinegar
- ◊ 1 guavacado
- ◊ pinch black pepper
- ◊ pinch salt
- ◊ 2 tbsp water

Oakwood for grilling
Salad:

- ◊ ½ cup lamb's quarters
- ◊ 1 cup mixed greens
- ◊ Handful of cherry tomatoes, sliced in half
- ◊ ¼ cup hominy
- ◊ ¼ cup black beans
- ◊ Salt to taste

Steps:

1. In a large mixing bowl, combine marinade ingredients.
2. Fully submerge steak for one hour.
3. While steak is marinating, process dressing ingredients into a creamy liquid.
4. Preheat grill to hot with oakwood. Test by placing half a lime against grill. Lime should char immediately.
5. Add lamb's quarters to a large salad bowl with half of the dressing. Using your hands, massage the dressing for one minute or until the greens become softer. Let sit to absorb the dressing.
6. Gently place flank steak onto grill. Immediately squirt remaining lime juice onto flames beneath the grill. Immediately flip steak, reduce heat to low, and cover for 3 minutes.
7. Uncover and flip again. Cover for 3 minutes.
8. Remove steak from heat and let rest for 5 minutes.
9. While steak is resting, add remaining salad ingredients to bowl and toss gently.
10. Slice rested steak into thin strips no more than 7 centimeters long and 4 centimeters wide.
11. Add to salad with remaining and dressing and toss. Serve.

Expected Endurance Effect(s):

Endurance, 20–24 hours
Heightened Senses, 36–48 hours
No apparent need to sleep or drawbacks from going
  without sleep, 36–48 hours

11

NAMES AND
KNIVES

AFTER THE DECISION, Chef Ilantra escorted me to an incredulous administrator. After nearly an hour spent arguing to convince him that this was happening, he opened a book covered in so much dust you couldn't read the cover. With the guidance of the book, he maneuvered me through several bureaucratic processes necessary to become a Rare. As I filed paperwork, Chef instructed me to report to the Culinary Academy at the end of the summer—in two days—to begin classes. She gave me a course schedule that was only half culinary. Military Matters, History and Logic, Alchemic Gastronomy, Knifecraft, and Theory of Flavor.

"Alchemic what?" I complained. "History and Logic? What do I need this stuff for?"

"I'm sorry, were you expecting us to hand you a cookbook with 300 years of secret greaters? To name you Chef today and give you a restaurant with no formal training? Tell me, do you even know what tartare is?"

"Like tartar sauce?"

"No, not like tartar sauce, stage."

"Stage? Is that a Rare insult?"

"It's the term for an apprentice chef."

Chagrined, I returned to my schedule. My courses required materials I could never have afforded on indenture wages, but Chef informed me that they would be covered by an Elevation Stipend. I nearly fainted at the number of knuckles. Barely enough to draw a breath from even the lowest Rare, but more wealth than my moms had accrued in their lifetime. The bulk would go to course materials, but I immediately considered where I could skip meals or avoid costs. I'd gone without before and if I did so again, I could buy any spices and ingredients I wanted, even an oven. Assuming I wasn't killed before I could, I might even afford to move my moms out of Common-3 and into one of the nice Tall Grass tenements for merchant common. At the least I could give them something to save. Pay back that ice cream they'd bought me for my birthday.

Before I could leave, the bureaucrat demanded I choose a surname that wasn't taken already, because Common-3 wasn't going to suffice in Rare society. I had to do it then, and put on the spot, I blurted the first thing that came to mind.

"Bessa."

"Bessa?" he repeated incredulously. "That isn't some common innuendo, is it?"

"No."

"It's dreadfully boring. If I had gotten to choose mine—"

"Bessa," I interrupted resolutely.

He rolled his eyes but scribbled it in a book. Carefully, he prepared a small piece of thick vellum parchment, writing my new name, a seven-digit number, and a description of my features. He then signed it and heated an elaborate wax stamp, which he pressed into the back. "This card identifies you as Rare. Without it, you can't access Rare Districts, receive healthcare at hospital, or gain access to your classes. Don't lose it."

I took it carefully, hating that I had it.

"The Treasurer will disburse the money to cover your indenture and provide any remaining balance in knuckles down the hall," he said, concluding.

"You're taking it out of my indenture? I won't be able to afford anything."

Chef Ilantra sighed. "Then get a job."

I frowned down at my course schedule. I would be in class six hours. It was at least an hour across town from Common-3 to the Culinary Academy, and all my classes were smack in the middle of the day. The King's Factory only hired ten-hour indentures. I was going to have to do something else if I wanted to pay for meals.

Chef Ilantra escorted me to the Treasury office and then toward the palace exit.

"Can I work for you?" I asked.

"You have some stones on you. I appreciate that." She considered it a moment before saying, "I run the student-staffed restaurant in the Academy. Lucky for you, someone graduated."

Lucky?

"If you run late, you will spend the remainder of the shift chopping onions. If you still have fingers, you'll come back the next day on time. If not, you're gone. Do you understand?"

"Got it, sure. But you won't be so concerned after you taste my food."

Chef snapped her attention back to me. "Remember that my vote was the difference between life and death, stage. You think you're special because you discovered a greater? You're fresh meat under the sun, spoiling with every breath. The moment Wensoan has it from you, he'll cast you back without tongue, hands, or eyes as a warning." Her eyes grew distant, staring away from me through a window. More softly, she added, "Unless you learn to refine your bloody talent. Refinement takes perfect service. Perfect service runs on time, so you will, too. Understood?"

As angry as I was, I bit off a retort. I'd been Rare all of an hour, and I was already acting like it. The truth was, I was losing my grip on who I was. Sixteen years I'd hated the Rare for who they were and how they behaved while coveting what they had. Now that I was here, I couldn't ignore it. I'd be able to buy my moms a home they deserved one day. I'd get to explore a whole new world of flavor with access to legal emphon and the knuckles to buy it. But at what cost? Had I just given up the possibility of being a good person? Was goodness more important than comfort and wealth?

Ilantra took my silence as compliance or some rational control over my emotions and nodded. "Good, because here's the bloody truth: I don't care about you, and I don't think your recipe is nearly as useful as the others seem to think it could be. I saved you in there because you weren't a complete idiot and because Hoppus has voted in line with Consumer and Commander on every meaningful vote during the last three years. Until today. Today, he aligned himself with Dyl. Over you. I don't know what he's up to, or why he dares risk animosity for a brat who thinks himself clever, but the best way for me to understand is to have you near."

I wadded my fist in the pockets of my new linen trousers. "I'm a tool."

Chef's laugh wasn't light like a bell or deep like an echoing well. It was the groan of a grave, rattled and dying in its disuse and disgust. She strode out into the sun and raised her nose over the palace cacti gardens. "We're all tools, stage. The only meaningful choice in life is to determine what tool we become. I chose to be a chef's tool, a knife. If I teach you anything, let it be this: be a knife. The rest are worthless."

I nodded. I could be a knife. A sharp one.

12

DINNER GUESTS

AS I LEFT the Rare-only Palace District, I drew more stares than the two carvers who trailed me home "for my safety," which was saying something. I assumed the scrutiny was for my clothes.

Then someone yelled, "That's him! That's Paprick!"

Suddenly, everyone pointed at me, whispering "new greater," and "big as a bull." It'd only been half a day since what was being called the Battle of Tall Grass, but I'd learn that carvers across the city had rounded up common, beating them in search of information about *me* overnight.

Bolder common swarmed me, quickly transferring the dirt and soot clinging to them like a marinade to my fresh linen clothes as they offered me greeting snacks I couldn't carry by myself. They thanked me for my martyrdom, for giving up the great secret of my greater to save the city. Others leaned in to whisper, "Stand tall," in my ear conspiratorially.

By the time I got to Common-3, I'd been proposed to by three women and two men, a woman had asked me to bless her child, and untold common had begged me to share greater recipes I didn't know.

"Please, I know there's one that can cure my boy's blindness."

"Brother, if I could only read my overseer's mind, I'm sure he'd stop beating me."

"Is it true you can fly? Please, it's been nine years since I could walk. I just want to see over the walls…"

And then, on the front wall of Common-3, a mural of an enormous human silhouette, standing among the wrecked but identifiable buildings of Tall Grass. The myriad body shapes of common lined the edges, hand-in-hand, backs straight, posture defiant. Beneath, written in red paint, were the words *Stand Tall*.

"We'll be back in the morning," one of my guards informed me at my door.

"What?"

"Until you move, you aren't safe. You'll be escorted. We'll be back tomorrow to escort you to Fen's Plateau to buy your school supplies."

I sighed. "Fine, whatever."

They both wore hoods remarkably similar to the one I'd worn at the Factory, and androgynous scale mail. I doubted I'd recognize them.

"And one more thing," the same one said, stopping me with a punch to the gut. "Wensoan's watching, cockroach."

I gritted my teeth against the pain. Looked like I wasn't getting away from the military so easily.

"Eight-hundred hours."

I opened the door and swooned into the embracing aroma of bread, butter, and something surprising: honey. I realized suddenly that I hadn't eaten all day. Between the Tribunal, registration, and the walk back, I'd been moving on Endurance from the milk, but the sour caress of dough cradled me in a loving hug. I was more than ready for a quick meal and a long sleep.

As the door shut behind me, Mom hurried from the kitchen and scrambled me into a hug. She smelled of sweat, panic, and flour. Mother hurried over from behind the curtain that enclosed my "room," and enveloped us, taking us in with her long, strong arms, smelling like cayenne.

"Pappy," Mom said, "we were so worried. When they took you inside the palace…"

"I'm okay."

"More than okay," said a third voice, somewhat familiar.

Over my mom's shoulder, a figure rose from a seat at our kitchen table. He was tall and thin, but sturdy like a stalk of celery, with cornrows dyed a motley of different colors and scented with honey. His clothes were remarkably clean but distinguishably common: a homespun cotton shirt the color of dust and a pair of ripped trousers.

Beside him, a second, more familiar face rose with him. I pushed away from my moms, staring at Cori with an open mouth. They wore—

"They?" the archivist interrupts.

The Butcher's brows furrow in confusion for a moment. "Oh, right, Cori wasn't using 'they' yet then. Force of habit."

She wore similar clothes to the man, but her shirt was sleeveless, to reveal arms like braided rope and sun-browned skin that was flawlessly uniform. It was the first time I'd seen her outside of the butcher's uniform, only the second since time I'd even seen her face. My original impression of average height and svelte build proved slightly incomplete. Her build was that of an athlete or a soldier, and her sleeveless shirt made sure everyone knew it. I felt scrawny and lanky in comparison.

"What are you doing here?"

"I am afraid Cori's with me," the man said.

I gauged my moms' demeanors. Mom smiled a fraction, but it didn't reach her eyes, and Mother's shoulder blades protruded from her thin dress as if coiled for a fight.

"And who are you?"

He strode to me and offered a honeycomb. "Where are my manners? I am Vanil Common-1. He and him."

"Common-1. I'm so sorry." I handed him back a spiced almond.

He acknowledged the loss of his home and neighbors as he stepped back. "All homes can be replaced, except the one in here, eh?" He pointed at his heart. "I am sorry about your uncle. Our doors were always open to one another."

My knees weakened as the confirmation of my suspicions set in. My head fell to Mother's forehead, and she rubbed my back. "Vanil and Cori will be joining us for the mourning dinner," Mother informed through gritted teeth.

That wasn't how common typically grieved.

"It is a necessary imposition," Vanil explained at my confusion, and I finally placed his voice. I'd heard it in Tall Grass, lung collapsed and Bessa on top of me. A figure in an all-black suit leaped over me with Enduring strength. A butcher's suit. Cori.

They were rebels.

As I looked at her in the new light, Cori politely tossed me a habanero, which I caught on instinct. "This is too much."

"Can't handle a little heat?"

"*You're* a rebel! You lied to me."

"I'm sorry. It wasn't personal."

At a loss for words, I tossed her an almond and shuffled to the kitchen. Preparing the mourning dinner—tomato and red bell pepper soup with sourdough—calmed me, and gave me some space from Vanil and Cori.

As I chopped the bell pepper, a pair of arms wrapped me from behind, pulling me into a hug. "You okay?" Mother asked, her words muffled into my shoulder so our "guests" couldn't overhear.

"No," I admitted. "It's—"

"I know, swe'me." She pulled me tighter. Her arms were so strong. "We'll keep them busy. Relax and take your time cooking. It always helps. Your mom will come check on you, too."

"Thank you."

"Always, swe'me. We love you always."

When the meal and I were both ready, we pushed the table and chairs against the wall so we could all sit together on the floor. I couldn't wait to get the warm soup in my belly and for this all to be over. I had suspicions as to why Vanil and Cori had come.

Mom served Vanil first, as he was the elder of the two guests.

"Thank you, Asabi," he said quietly. "For your hospitality and your labor during this period of grief. The dead are honored by your care."

"That's rich of you to say," I said sharply. "Considering you probably orchestrated the stampede."

"Paprick," Mom reprimanded, but Vanil waved her off.

"I heard you were a sharp one."

"Not from me," Cori said with a smile.

"Why are you here?" I repeated.

"Let us dip our bread for the dead, first," Vanil instructed. "Then to business."

Each of our bowls was barely half-full, a meager meal for meager people, but common persisted in hunger, and so we looked at our bounty like it was that. Hungrily.

One by one, we tore chunks from the loaf and dipped for the dead. "Uncle Macen," I whispered.

"Macen," Mom agreed, stifling a sob.

"Little Musta," Mother offered for my cousin.

I didn't recognize the names Vanil and Cori gave, but they were delivered with the same severity as ours. They'd lost people, too. Even if the stampede was their fault.

"May they be fuller in death than they were in life," Vanil said, raising his bread.

We raised our dripping bread, and each filled our mouth to bursting so that the dead could have one last full bite in their name. Then, as promised, Vanil got to business.

"Your elevation offers us a unique opportunity," he said as Cori sat. "By tomorrow morning, the entire city will know of it, and in three days' time, there won't be a soul in the country who hasn't heard about Paprick Bessa."

I was galled by the statement and spoke timidly. "How do you know that surname?"

"Our information network works quickly." His smile turned smug. "I know what classes you will be taking, the exact value of the stipend hidden in your boot, and of your job with Chef Ilantra Andala. Does that surprise you?"

Truthfully, it scared me. He spoke casually, but anyone who has knowledge has power, and he knew where I would be and when. It felt like a threat.

"We also know that they plan to claim your 'father' was a Rare, which was recently discovered. We're already fighting that propaganda here. You're common, and we won't let any common forget that."

I hadn't yet tried my soup, but I tossed my spoon aside. No wonder the Tribunal asked about my father. But also, where did Vanil get off acting like a savior fighting propaganda after causing all this? "What makes you think I would want to help you?"

"Pappy," Mom warned. "Be respectful."

"Respectful? This guy and his 'network' got a thousand common killed yesterday."

"And every day, the king kills a thousand more," Cori retorted.

Vanil hushed her with a look. "His anger is justified. We made mistakes yesterday."

"Mistakes implies a plan," Mother said coldly. "I saw chaos and desperation."

"Without me," I added, "you would've lost so much more, and you know it. Now you entreat our hospitality to threaten me?"

Vanil slurped loudly from his spoon. "Is that what you think?"

"I've already been interrogated and threatened by five Rare and none of them got the greater out of me."

"I don't want your greater recipe," he said matter-of-factly.

"My only son will not be the poster-child of your rebellion." Mother gripped my hand firmly as she spoke. "He is going to be a Chef."

"A Chef that feeds murderers sows the seeds of his own reaping," Vanil retorted.

"Is that a threat?" Mom asked. For all her grief, she was as fierce as Mother when she wanted to be.

"No. If Paprick wishes to become a Rare Chef, then he is welcome. None of you will ever see me again, and I don't mean to imply that is because you will be dead. We don't operate that way."

"Then what do you want?" I asked sharply.

"It's been a generation since Rare have seen a new greater recipe. I'm curious how they will respond to its temptations. Already, they have surprised me by leaving Paprick with his head." He bowed his head a fraction to me. "I understand that has much to do with how you held yourself before them and the quickness of your wit. Those two skills will get you far within the Rare and their silly school."

"You want a spy," I decided. "But they'll never trust me. Even if they call me Rare by some unknown father."

He lifted a finger. "Rare hoard information, secrets, and most of all greaters with the greed of the drakephon. They will not trust you at first, but eventually their arrogance and their cravings for knowledge will make them desperate for your favor. Those that don't know the truth will pity you. They will convince themselves you are Rare so that they never have to consider a reality where a common surpassed them. Time will make you a story of their success."

"You will be the lost boy they elevated to proper Rareness," Cori said sourly. "They'll love themselves for it."

I hesitated, and Vanil picked up on it.

"You don't believe me? Consider this. They are so sure elevating you has made you theirs, they let you return, even with a greater in your mind. They fear nothing and no one, which only makes them easier prey."

There was truth in that, but I was still angry at them for what they'd caused. "Once I become a Chef, my moms will never work another day in their lives, never be hungry. I will be Rare and reap all the benefits. Why risk that for people who leveled a Common?"

Vanil nodded at my words and scratched the stubble at his chin. "I cannot in good conscience tell a man to throw away that which will fill his belly. I will not in good faith tell you that your risk will garner reward. But I will say that anyone with common sense can see that this nation is at an inflection point. Yesterday, common fought carvers in the street without being slaughtered. How do you think we did that? What essential resource would that have required?"

"Emphon," I answered.

"Emphon." He grinned wide and sly. "The king thinks he has a monopoly on it, but I have worked for a generation to bring it to my people. I have discovered things that your Rare teachers will never learn. The stories say that Aion and her children discovered the greaters by necessity and ingenuity. I ask you, who among our nation has those two traits?"

I took his meaning.

"Yesterday you risked everything to save this city," he continued. "You discovered a greater recipe after, what, a month from your first taste? What could you discover with a year? With an entire bull at your disposal?"

"The Rare offer the same thing with more security," Mother countered.

"Under their supervision and their thumb. Would you really grow to become that which you grew up hating? Would you shun all but your moms? I would let you work to your heart's content."

"Why trust me?" I reproached. "You don't know me."

"I do not," he admitted. "But Cori does, and she spoke well of you. I trust her more than most. And even if I didn't, I have spoken with others that know you. Do you know what word I have heard over and over to describe you?"

"It better be 'Mommas' boy,'" Mom joked in what felt like a desperate attempt at lightening the mood.

"Righteous," Vanil corrected, his eyes trained sharply on mine.

I'd barely touched my soup since the first bite.

"I would take one righteous person with wit and instinct over an army of dullards." He looked to Cori approvingly. "But I am lucky to have far more than one."

I met Cori's eyes and felt a silent pleading, a hope I would agree. "I refuse to believe the butcher boy who named his bull won't stand tall against the real animals," she said.

Stand tall.

"A storm is coming to Ranch, Paprick," Vanil added. "Yesterday's strike was but the first within the walls after more than a decade fought in the north. More will come. But you could rally thousands more to those battles. Your support could turn this from insurrection to revolution."

With a nod and another offer of thanks to Mom for her hospitality, Vanil stood.

"What would you need from me?"

"For now, go to school. Stay in Rare districts while we play up your exploits here and Rare focus elsewhere. If you feel you have something useful to share, find Crooked Rish and he will find me."

"Of course he's involved," Mother said.

After they left, my moms took me in another suffocating hug and I slumped into the security of their arms. I couldn't help but remember the Stand Tall mural. Did no one understand that these women were the reason I could stand at all? I just wanted to collapse into the floor, but they held me up. They were my pillars. A sob choked my throat. "I thought the Rare might kill you."

They only squeezed tighter, holding me until hunger got the best of me and I squeezed free to drain my cold soup.

"We're proud of you," Mother said as I ate. "No matter what you choose. You set a dream for yourself, and you achieved it."

"And now you're both at risk."

Mom lifted my chin to meet her gaze. "Your first thought was for us, for what we could have because of your work. That makes it all worth it."

I couldn't bring myself to admit that wasn't true. They'd come second to my excitement about the classes I'd be taking. I hadn't thought I could feel any worse, but my stomach turned. How could they come second? If I could've justified the waste, I would've stopped eating.

Instead, I forced down another spoonful.

"Any life worth its salt risks death," Mother said, seeing my face. "You did the right thing."

"Leave the cold soup," Mom said, pulling me toward the icebox.

"But—"

"It's fine," she insisted. "I'll make sure it doesn't go to waste later. For now, you did something no common has done in three generations. I think that deserves ice cream."

"You didn't," I said, smiling despite my roiling gut.

"We did," Mother said.

And for a few minutes, I forgot the world, entirely focused on the soft sweetness only food and a mother's love can provide.

ENTREMET II

CLARIFICATION AND CONCESSION

"POINTS OF CLARITY," seeks the archivist, raising a pen to the air and looking the Butcher in the eyes—no longer Enduring, finally. "Did Vanil speak about your father that night? Beyond what you said, obviously."

"I have no father." The Butcher's voice could've shattered ice. "Only mothers."

"Right… What happened to Bessa's remains?" the archivist asks quickly, hoping to catch the Butcher off-guard.

He barely twitches at the mention. "The rebels cut what they could from her. Then she was harvested by the Rare, all eight cuts taken overnight. Why?"

"And the bones?"

A grin lightens the darkness of his cell. "Where all emphon bones went."

"Need I remind you of the importance of the truth?" the archivist complains.

"Why do you care? What exactly do you think the Source is?"

They share a look, the Butcher's smug and the archivist's all but aflame, before a separate emotion rises unbidden through the biographer's memory.

"Don't worry," he assures softly. "We'll get there by the end."

Need weakens the archivist's voice to a whisper. "You would tell me?"

"We both know your queen won't excuse my crimes. I just admitted to joining the rebels, and if only for that, I'll die tomorrow. But I'm here for a reason, and that book will have answers for someone that needs them."

The archivist's eyes narrow as the Butcher chews idly on his too-long hair. "Did you let yourself get captured?"

"We can't just skip to the end! This next part is where the fun begins, where all the secrets start to come out. That's what *you're* here for, isn't it? The secrets."

"While we're on the subject, I want you to admit to one." The archivist waits as the Butcher's gaze shifts back to confusion. "Your uncle didn't die. He was one of the five rebels who fought on Bessa, alongside Cori and Vanil."

He shakes his head. "Macen died in Common-1."

"Why is that lie so important to your mythos, Butcher? I've never understood it."

The Butcher looks down as he sucks his matted hair and rubs his eyes. When he looks up, a change comes over him and he regains his strong conviction. When he speaks again, his voice and eyes thrum with Endurance, commanding enough that the archivist would have left the desk and unlocked the door had he ordered it. "LISTEN CLOSELY."

The pen rises. The archivist can only oblige.

13

CUTLER

AS THREATENED, MY guards arrived in the morning to escort me. They claimed it was for my protection, but as we reached the gate to Fen's Plateau, a Rare district, they had to confirm with the patrol at the gate and the patrol's supervisor that I was actually supposed to be let through, despite the fact that I could show a Rare ID.

On another day, I would've enjoyed the disgust spreading like warm butter across the faces of the patrols as I passed, but I'd slept poorly. With all that had happened, I couldn't still my thoughts. Excitement at the possibility of learning to be a Chef, fear that they'd discover I'd been stealing emphon, memories of the Tribunal's judgment playing over and over. One thing I couldn't shake was Chef Ilantra's suspicion that Hoppus Florento was up to something, too. I'd forgotten him while speaking with Vanil and Cori, and as I took a punch from my escorts on behalf of Commander Wensoan, Florento's lack of obvious motive felt like a bigger threat.

And what about when they'd asked about my moms? Were they in danger? Were they going to try to force Mom to admit to having me with some starving Rare?

Thoughts of intrigue left my mind as we crested the height of Fen's Plateau, via a heavily guarded staircase. Forbidden to common— supposedly because it was unsafe to be above the walls and at risk of attack—the district was the highest point of the city, and I knew only its striking silhouette as seen from Common-3, clearest when the sun rose behind it. I never imagined I'd one day be up there looking down at Ranch stretching below, but now that I was, I knew the real reason they kept us out.

With walls blocking the way, I never realized how small the Rare districts in the city were compared to the common ones. Common-5 and 6, the newest tenement complexes, might've been bigger than the entirety of the Overseer's Court, the only Rare district in the western half of the city. How many more of us were there? How tentative was their grasp on power, really? Up on the plateau, the questions begged asking.

As if aware of my thinking, my guards shoved me away from the western edge and into the shopping district. Unlike most of the city, built tall to take advantage of all the space within the wall's protection, the Plateau's buildings peaked at two stories. I won't bore you with my shopping or the disgust plain on the Rare faces that served me. Though my stipend was meager by Rare standards, I bought new clothes and all of my materials, which had seemed impossible until I found an adobe shop that looked older than the wooden shops surrounding it. Most Rare gave it a wide berth.

I'd decided early that I would buy my culinary supplies last because they were the ones I understood best. If the supplies I didn't understand—like the aerator for Alchemic Gastronomy—cleaned out my knuckles, I could at least cobble together the supplies I needed for Theory of Flavor and Knifecraft with secondhand common equipment.

A sign inside the entrance claimed the shop was established in 28 P.L., 23 years prior to the formal founding of Ranch under the first original royal family more than 300 years earlier. It had to be the oldest building in the city. Older even than the palace.

"Well, come in!" squawked an old man from across the entrance with about as little welcome in his tone as any other Rare shopkeeper I'd encountered.

I nearly tripped on the threshold. On my life, I would have sworn him to be the identical twin of Old Man Banan of Black Spice. They had the same thinning white hair, gentle brown eyes, and resilient leathery skin. The only thing that marked them as different was that I had never once seen Banan stand up completely straight, and this man was rodlike.

"Are you just going to block real customers from entering or are you here to buy?" he asked. "Well?"

I entered.

The man had commanded my attention, but the shop stole it as I entered. A wonderland of riches. Cast irons of different diameters and heights. Chopping blocks with built-in drainage paths. Spice jars. Spice racks. Spice cups. Knives—more than I knew the names or shapes of. I couldn't control myself.

He threw a walnut at me. "Greetings." It slammed right into my cheek. No one in Rare districts greeted people properly, and I hadn't been remotely ready for it. After picking it up, I tossed him an almond and pointed to an angled, oblong cup made of some green material. "What's that?"

"A guavacado cutter," the man snapped. "Are you daft?"

"What's a guavacado?" I asked. It sounded expensive.

"What?" the man barked, aghast. "Were you raised by wolphon?"

As he hustled around his little counter with quick, shuffling feet, I decided not to tell him that I didn't know what wolphon were either. One of the Twelve emphon the emphonists worshipped, maybe? Practicing emphonism was treason. Would it get me in trouble to ask?

"What is your name, boy?" He inspected me like butchers examined emphon before cutting.

"Paprick Bessa."

"Bessa," he teased out. "Unfamiliar! You have not been in my shop."

"No," I said, though it wasn't a question.

"That wasn't a question!" he snapped. Without missing a breath, he changed tone and demeanor. "I'm Jives Cutler. This is my family's shop."

"It's incredible," I said earnestly.

"Take that back."

"No?" I wasn't sure why I even cared, but I wasn't going to cow to some rude Rare.

"Then you really are daft," he decided. "Now, what do you need? Your smell will scare away customers."

For all the beautiful cutlery and products in that store, there was a layer of dust on everything more than a meter from the counter. He hadn't had a real customer in weeks. But I handed him a list of course requirements that I was actually looking forward to purchasing, unlike the books I needed for History and Logic.

"Scale, measuring cup set, knives, yes, yes, I can do this. Make yourself useful, will you? Grab that for me." He pointed to a large iron pot at the top of a tall shelf.

I did as I was told, struggling slightly under the surprise of twenty-five kilos.

"You're stronger than you look, wiry and thin as you are," he remarked with such a snap that I couldn't tell if it was a compliment or an insult. "What're you going for? Military?"

"Culinary," I corrected.

"Waste of time if you ask me."

"You own a kitchen supply store."

He winked at me. "Didn't say it was a waste of *my* time."

I laughed, and immediately scowled at doing so. I shouldn't be laughing with Rare. But he was loud and eccentric in a way that felt common. The first person who had bothered to have a conversation with me that morning.

He commented on everything, informing me why this item I was buying sucked or why that one really should've been one my teachers asked for, as I continued to fetch items for him—even ones he could easily reach. In another store with another owner, I would've told him to do his own job, but Cutler's was akin to a messy, disorganized Black Spice. I felt at home there, craving to know its shelves as intimately as I knew my favorite flavors. So many tools, some so specific I couldn't even imagine a world where they were necessary, which filled me with an even stronger desire to use them. Accessories I instantly craved more than what I already needed, the most unnecessary being a leather apron that screamed *grill master*.

But the price of my supplies made my face fall. I would only have enough knuckles left for a week's worth of food, and I couldn't risk that for an expensive apron.

"So you're daft and poor," Jives speculated at my frown. "Shite luck."

My disappointment boiled over. "Are you always so rude?"

"Would you have me bow and dance? I'm a Cutler."

"You're an old bat," I whispered under my breath as I counted out knuckles.

"Bats have sharp hearing!" He flicked my ear.

"Ow!"

"And sharp teeth."

I bit back another retort that would only earn some other clever insult as I loaded my goods into the iron pot to carry them. I was halfway to the door when he called after me. "Come back next weekend at dawn."

"Dawn? Why would I do that?"

"For work," he said.

I cast a narrowed glance back over my shoulder. Cutler sat behind his desk with his tongue pushed into his lower lip and his bulbous eyebrows scrunched in a ridiculous mockery of a glare. It was so startlingly odd that I choked out a laugh and fumbled the heavy pot in my arms. "You're serious?"

"Never," he replied. "But you have a respect for this place most don't deign to notice, and my kid is at the Front. Without them, the shop's a mess, and no one wants to shop in a sty. Besides, a Cutler has never been too proud to recognize when they need help. I won't be the first."

I nodded, understanding. And I could admit that I needed the knuckles. Chef Ilantra hadn't told me how much I'd make with her, but I wasn't holding out much hope that she would keep me around long, let alone pay me well. "I'm not sure I'll have the time, but I can try. Why so early?"

"Someone's got to stock before customers arrive. Famines, you're daft. Now go, before I change my mind. And make sure you bathe before you set foot in here again!"

I considered saying something snarky, but I nodded and simply said, "Thank you, sir."

His eyes brightened with something approaching satisfaction, but he quickly overcame it and waved me off. "Or don't. I don't care!"

14

THE CLOUDS

MY GUARDS STOPPED me outside. "We sent your other things to your flat," one informed me.

"My what?"

"Your *apartment*," they said, using a common accent with disgust.

I started to walk south toward the stairs back to the common districts, but the same guard who'd spoken turned me north by my elbow. "You aren't going back to Common-3. You'll live at the Academy."

"And if I decline?"

"Non-negotiable. Not if you want your parents to wake up tomorrow."

They led me north from Fen's Plateau to the Clouds, the largest Rare district in the city. Everything there was tall and sharp, from the lampposts to the palm trees. Commons degraded by the day, paint flaking and windows boarded, but the *flats* of the Clouds sparkled, pristine and boring: blue building, white door; white building, red door; red building, blue door; on and on. So uncomfortably sterile. No grime between the cobbles to keep you from tripping. No one cooking on stoops. No guitars or drums or singing. Wrong.

117

"Did someone at least tell my moms?" I asked. "They're expecting me."

"If they know what's good for them, they'll get over it."

It wasn't at all how I pictured moving out. It'd only been a day, but I was already excited to bring what I learned at the Academy back to them. The three of us cooking together, using Rare techniques, Rare ingredients. All gone in an instant.

I barely registered the next several blocks. Then a gate welcomed us into a bustling courtyard centered around a fountain. Four marble figures stood within the pool of water, a man in a chef's jacket sharpening a knife, a robed woman carrying a stack of books, an androgynous figure in scale mail crouched with a war spear, and a larger crowned and suited figure looming behind the other three. Chef. Scholar. Soldier. King.

Behind the courtyard rose the iconic twenty-story tower visible from any point in Ranch, sparkling white under the desert sun, windows swirling around it and dozens of chimneys jutting from strange angles to accommodate its many kitchens' exhausts. Several smaller buildings surrounded it, bridges and covered stairways linking them to various floors of the tower. Looking at it made me dizzy.

My guards led me to one such six-story with DORMITORIES written over the entrance, and one dropped a key into my hand. "Your flat is on the sixth floor."

"Am I supposed to pay for it or is it covered?"

"I don't care."

I sighed and lugged my stuff up to my floor, my calves reminding me that they used to work in the King's Factory, and my still-healing ribs ensuring I recalled how recently that was. By the time I reached my apartment, I was sweaty and light-headed. The building held heat better than my moms' oven.

The rest of my purchases blocked a rickety wooden door, and I quickly learned that I had one of those shoddy locks—the type that never slides in or out easily. I played with it so long I began to think it wasn't my apartment, but eventually the door swung in to reveal a small studio with an oven, an icebox, a counter beside the oven, and a thin mattress on the floor.

It was more space than I'd ever had, and I walked the perimeter of it proudly. I'd earned it by inventing a greater. *I'd* done that. Me. A factory boy from Common-3. It was the first time since waking up in the palace hospital that I really got to appreciate that. No more butchering powerless creatures. No more calculations to see if I could afford a churro. I was about to be surrounded by food, living in it, cooking. I was on the literal doorstep of my dream: chefdom. In a month, I'd gone from never eating emphon to discovering something about it that no one had.

But there was also the reason *why* no one had, the one that I hadn't really let myself think about: Ruda's spice. I'd played the part of the strong, willful common, refusing to tell anyone, but what could I have told them? That a mysterious merchant had a spice with no name, and I'd used that to make a greater with measurements I could barely remember?

I was alive because the Rare thought I could replicate that recipe. Ilantra had said how much the Tribunal wanted it.

I was valuable to the rebels because they thought I could discover more, serve as a distraction, and *because they also thought I could replicate that recipe.*

I couldn't do that.

All of that and more rattled around my mind as I finally looked down at the mattress on the floor of my apartment—the apartment that I didn't know the cost of.

A small piece of folded paper rested at the center of the pillow. White on white, impossible to notice from any meaningful distance. Handwriting I didn't recognize.

REVEAL THE GREATER AND YOU DIE. KEEP YOUR MOUTH SHUT AND THE ROOM IS FREE.

The note shook in my grip. It solved rent, but it was the difference between medium-high and high heat on my anxiety. I felt the flames licking up my stomach and throat. There was no way out of the frying pan.

Too many threats surrounded me and my moms, and I hadn't done anything yet.

Famines, I hadn't even properly grieved yet. Thousands had died two days ago. People I knew and loved. I'd *watched* it happen. When I closed my eyes then, panicking, I saw Common-1 collapsing, and it stayed when my eyes opened.

I didn't even know what I wanted. I wanted to cook because I loved cooking. I loved using my hands and my creativity to turn something raw and bitter into something beautiful and sweet. I loved bringing that to the table with my moms or my friends and laughing as we told stories.

Now that I lived here, how often could I actually do that? I'd agreed to two jobs!

I roared as I slammed a fist into the thin mattress. My knuckles cracked against the floor, sending a wave of pain up my arm. I wasn't even good at punching!

With the rebels, I would fight for equality. That was important. But I'd be a soldier. Potentially expendable. Did I want to die for equality? I wasn't sure I wanted to die for anything.

But it would be a better world…

Nursing my throbbing fist, I fished a handful of spiced almonds out of my greeting pouch and threw them down my gullet. Mother's spice blend danced across my tongue, nutty beside heat and hickory, numbing the distraction of my knuckles.

The Rare's Culinary Academy would better prepare me to fight. Give me the freedoms I always wanted—that those same common deserved.

Assuming the Rare let me live through graduation.

I crumpled the paper and looked at my new oven. I needed to relax, and that meant cooking, not just eating.

So that's what I did. And as I boiled rice, I recognized a need for a plan, or the beginnings of one. Something I could hold onto as I tried to escape the pan and live in the fire.

I didn't know a starving thing yet. Not really. So that became the plan. Go to class. Go to Chef's. Help out Cutler for some extra knuckles.

Above all: learn.

And I did. I learned that knowledge is a double-edged sword.

15

KNIFECRAFT

I DEPARTED THE next morning already screwed. Nightmares of Common-1's collapse plagued me into the early morning, and I had accidentally slept in, leaving no time for breakfast.

Scrambling, I packed my books, which included such doorstops as *The Encyclopedia Organica* and *The Unabridged History of the Panchon Kings*, into my new pot alongside a notebook, pen, and a leather-wrapped bundle of knives. Though they fit nicely, I was left cradling a new cleaversaw in the crook of my elbow while I hefted the pot awkwardly. We were required to bring a weapon we "had experience with" for Military Matters, and cleaversaws had surprisingly made the list. The weapon banged against my body with each step across the bridge into the Academy, a sick symmetry with my days at the Factory.

My bridge led to a lobby with a small cafeteria. They had several things I'd never heard of, like a black sludgy liquid called coffee and strangely-shaped sticky breads called cidered croissants. Both smelled inviting—the former like warm, nutty earth, and the latter like a sickly-sweet apple—but I didn't want to risk an upset stomach or my dwindling knucklebag on the unknown. I ordered a plain bagel, buttered, and a tea that tasted nothing like the tangy, flowery green blend Mother made.

It was *good* though. With sweet citrus oil in it to balance the earthy black-red leaves. The server called it Earl Grey, and I was ready to swear fealty to him. Mom's bagels were leagues better though.

Twisting maze-like hallways brought me to the central staircase, an enormous spiral that spoked off to each floor until it reached the 16th floor, where a gate halted progress; the top floors required special credentials I couldn't provide. The Practical Wing, where actual cooking was done, was contained within floors five through fourteen and housed twelve kitchens, two freezers—mind you, I'd never even heard of a freezer at that point—a dining hall, a wine library, which was very different from the book libraries, and an anatomically accurate scale model of a carnephon spread between floors. It felt endless, like everything that I could ever need could be found in those walls. Older students shared tales of secret rooms, lost basements, and even the skeletons of dead classmates hidden in the walls.

But that day? Simply chaos. Hundreds of people marched the spiral. No one would look at me, let alone direct me, and I worried I was the only student who wasn't Enduring. Everyone passed with golden eyes. (Yes, people were spending tons of knuckles on greater recipes to gain advantage in class.) Knifecraft was only about three minutes from starting, and my head was walloping around like dough on a hook when a voice sharp as cheddar but equally inviting called out, "Mate, hold up!"

Its owner was a stocky black guy about my age with a patchy beard and jolly, full cheeks. He dressed in a vibrant yellow linen suit that I immediately feared would match his eyes, but his irises were ruddy brown beneath circular spectacles. On his shoulder, he carried a packed black messenger bag, and on his back, a giant wok that looked more like a shield than a cooking utensil. Best of all, he lumbered under a pot full to the brim with the same supplies as me. We had to be in the same courses.

"You looking for Knifecraft too?" he asked. His accent was Rare, but his eyes were surprisingly desperate.

Confirming that he was in fact talking to me. "Yeah, with Chef Ilantra?"

"Thank the Consumer, I won't be alone." He shrugged his pot as if about to one-hand it but thought better of it. "I'd toss you a mint, but... I'm Laven, anyway. He and him. Knifecraft's this way, ain't it?"

"Paprick," I said, falling in beside him and giving my pronouns. "Did you say 'mint'?"

"Is that presumptuous? Sorry, mate, I read about you in the news sheets, and thought I should greet you the common way. It true you discovered a greater?" Unlike most Rare, his accent was almost common, his Ts more like soft Ds.

I gawked. The Rare sheets weren't claiming I'd stolen it *and* this Rare was actually planning to respect common traditions. "That's right."

"Lish!" he exclaimed in response to my expression. "That's my dream."

"Yeah, lish," I nodded, testing out the word.

"It's like delicious," he whispered under his breath. "Slang for, like, wonderful."

"I guessed as much."

He stopped walking, even though class would be starting any moment. "Sorry, I didn't mean to imply you couldn't. It's just everyone's already heard about you." He lowered his voice. "Some are bound to stir your pot, and I thought you should know the word for sure. That's my bad. I won't insult you like that again." He shook his head. "And think, me and all these other gits got into the Academy because our parents wrote a letter to Dean, but you had to invent a whole scalding greater yourself. Of course you can figure out lish. You're probably a bloody genius."

I didn't know what to do. A Rare had apologized to me. For having good intentions. And he was rambling. Was he nervous around me?

SEVEN RECIPES FOR REVOLUTION

"So, yeah, sorry mate. No more insulting you until we're friends. If we end up as friends, that is. Which we don't have to. Like, we just met each other, and—oh thank the Consumer, this is our classroom."

The archivist can't help but laugh. "That's how he won you over?"
The Butcher ignores the comment and continues.

I followed him into a small auditorium. At the bottom of the semi-circle, Chef Ilantra scowled over a chopping block and a set of knives. Behind her, a slate read: *KNIFECRAFT. NO CUTTING.*

"Huh. Didn't know she'd be here," Laven whispered beside me.

I followed his gaze as he waved to a young woman in the back row. She was maybe a year older than us, but one look at her serious, observant demeanor made me feel even younger. She struck me as the kind of person that looked at adults with jealousy and other teenagers with suffering indifference. Like she'd wanted to be an adult since she could breathe. Metal pins held her wavy hair, dyed the green and pink of emphon feathers, into a messy bun. The asymmetric layers framed a sharp, angular mouth sporting lipstick that matched her hair: top lip green, bottom pink. In contrast, her clothes were perfectly neat: a white linen blouse and a high-waisted pleated skirt—its matte so black the folds seemed to run into each other—that fell to the ankle.

"This is Yenne. She and her," Laven introduced. "Yenne, this is Paprick, he and him."

"From cayenne?" I questioned, disbelieving her common name here of all places.

She sneered at Laven. "Is he always this direct?" Her accent, dry and easy as a desert wind, all but confirmed it. She was common, or had been.

Laven shrugged. "Maybe. I just met him outside."

I apologized quickly and handed her an almond. "I didn't expect there to be another—"

"Another what?"

"Common," I said.

"I'm not," she said, matter-of-factly. Then she laughed. It was a mischievous sound, like a crackling fire still deciding whether it wanted to cook or burn. But cruel, too. Cruel in the way that she knew she was smarter than me and that she could wield that against me.

"A jest," she said, as she extended her hand. If Laven spoke like a Rare with some common tendences, she spoke like a common mimicking Rare airs. "Apologies, I don't often carry greetings anymore. I'm adopted Rare, you see. Two years hence, and have had little need."

Before I could ask more, Ilantra berated the class. "Listen up, maggot brains. Anyone who walks in after this owes me a two-page report on the difference between a boning knife and a filleting knife. I won't stop class to assign it. Do yourself a favor and let them know. If someone comes in late and subsequently says they weren't informed of the assignment, you all receive a failing grade for today."

"Well, that isn't fair," a man in the row in front of us grumbled.

"Life isn't fair," she snapped. "A kitchen is a team where everyone has a role. Most of you are in this class because you want to be in kitchens for the rest of your life. A few of you from the Theoretical Wing are here because you thought this would be a fun elective. You're both idiots. But while you remain, you're on the team. If you have a problem with that, save your fellows the trouble and leave now."

In the front row, a person with eyes as yellow as a lemon departed. Quick as that.

"Good. For the next six weeks, you will learn the importance of knifecraft." She pointed to her knife block. "There are thirteen knives in this block. You will learn what each is for, how to hold it, and how to move your hand or arm to use it properly."

I sighed and slunk into my chair. I knew knives. I was a butcher.

"Bessa," Ilantra cracked. "You don't think you need this class?"

I sat up straighter, but knew better than to answer.

"Come down here."

"That's not necessary, Chef. I know—"

"Did I ask you what was necessary?"

Chagrined, I hurried down to join her, and she motioned at her block. "Which would you use to separate emphon shank from the bone?"

"None," I said seriously.

A few students snickered. "Stupid cockroach," someone whispered. "Heard he stole a greater to elevate."

"I heard he's someone's bastard."

"And why not?" Chef asked, ignoring the students.

"The boning knife here is barely as long as my forearm. I'd use a flatsaw or I'd be at it for a month."

"Good. The first lesson for the rest of you is that these tools are for civilized preparation. Two days ago, Bessa here was a butcher in the King's Factory. His tools would bend your back without the help of Endurance. But they served him well, and even he isn't dense enough to use one in a kitchen."

Was she actually giving me credit?

"Return to your seat, stage."

As I did, I realized that she'd done much worse than give me credit.

"Common rat," someone muttered.

"Indentured scum."

"You butchered emphon?" Laven asked with a tone that approached awe.

"It's not pretty work," I said, trying to understand why a Rare would care.

Ilantra cut off whatever Laven meant to say next. "You have just learned that a member of your team has knowledge that you lack. You may have already told yourself that his knowledge is useless. It isn't. I can tell you already that Paprick Bessa is the most advanced student in this class. If you have a problem with that, you can follow the young lady out."

Six more left. Each one turned their noses up at me as they did, and I boiled in my seat. But not at them. Them I was used to. But Ilantra? She hadn't merely mocked me for not paying attention, she'd made sure to make half the starving school hated me.

"Good," she said, surveying the rest of the room. "Now, place your knives before you. We're going to cover the uses of each. Bessa, since you're so smart, you can tell us their names."

I did my best, but there were five I'd never even seen before, let alone knew the name of, and three of them looked almost exactly the same.

"Paring," she said, holding up one I could identify. "Part of the chef suite." She lifted another. "Utility, same suite. And peeling, vegetable suite."

I frantically made note of the tiny differences in their widths and curves. Beside me, Laven had full sketches with annotations in his notebook. I'd never seen someone write so quickly and neatly.

"Mate, that was brutal," Laven whispered as she continued with the salmon knife, which was apparently for a fish Rare enjoyed, even as he took notes.

"She's got a reputation for being severe," Yenne added. "But she hates you. What did you do to her?"

"I asked her for a job."

"A job?" Laven gasped. "In the Academy House? First-years never work there."

I blinked, surprised. "She gave me one."

"You aren't serious?" he said. "I would give a kidney for a job at her restaurant. It has four Missiloan stars."

"What stars?"

"They're a Rare company that ranks restaurants," Ilantra snapped from directly beside me.

When had she climbed the stairs?

"The three of you can deliver me a one-page report on them and the importance of *paying attention* tomorrow."

We each groaned and she offered one of her rare smiles. "Your names?" she asked of the other two.

"Yenne Corzon, Chef." She looked dutifully abased.

"Ah, Dyl's orphan. Shouldn't you be in the Theoretical Wing?"

"I chose an elective, Chef."

"And you're still here. Interesting. You?"

"Laven, Chef."

Her eyes snapped from Laven to me and back to him again. "Florento's kid?"

"Yes, Chef."

Her lip curled. "Interesting coincidence, the two of you here together."

I looked back at Laven, seeing now the resemblance to Hoppus Florento, the Treasurer. How had I managed to end up with the children of the two Rare who voted for me? Part of me wondered if someone named Wensoan was about to pop out of the shadows and stab me in the back.

"It appears I can't trust you in the back, stage. Move to the front row."

I couldn't help but wonder if Chef was trying to break their hold on me as I followed Chef to the front of the classroom.

"You better memorize those knives, butcher," Yenne warned as I descended the stairs to the front. "She might try to kill you with them."

I wasn't sure if she was joking.

16

LAVEN FLORENTO

LAVEN WAS IN Theory of Flavor as well, but we headed to different classrooms before and arrived at TOF at different times. I was both glad and disappointed not to be sitting with him.

Glad because I didn't know how to interpret his parentage. Was it pure coincidence that the first and only true Rare (Yenne not counting) who'd been kind to me was the son of the person who'd mysteriously voted in my favor? Or was it just that his dad was a decent person and he'd been raised to be the same?

Disappointed because I'd come from Military Matters, where every student called me bastard or cockroach and the teacher, none other than Lt. Vyson, the soldier who had escorted me to the Tribunal and saved my life, was no kinder. He started by demonstrating sixteen ways to take down an opponent on me. And by that, I mean he disarmed me and threw me to the ground repeatedly. I could barely sit in my TOF chair comfortably from the bruises on my ass.

The other students mostly laughed as I was forbidden to fight back. When we got to spar later in the term, though, I'd get my revenge. One class assured me I could wield a cleaversaw far better than all but a couple could wield their chosen weapons. I wouldn't be anyone's target practice.

TOF was taught by Chef Sagen Clo, who quickly became my favorite teacher. Barely a meter and a half tall, stocky and jovial with gentle eyes, a bushy red beard, and a shaved head. His class analyzed why flavors tasted as they did, and he began by explaining the five base tastes: sweet, sour, salty, bitter, and umami. "It's when you combine the five at different measures that you begin to get different flavors, chefs. Sweet is sweet. Sour is sour. But what do you get with equal parts of both?"

When he realized the question wasn't rhetorical, Laven's hand shot up. "Tangy?"

"Tangy! Yes!" the Chef boomed emphatically. "Pull out your paring knives and grab an orange from that basket. Let's begin to break tangy down!"

The class went by in a blink. I left feeling as if I'd learned nothing new but understood everything in the kitchen better. His class always went that way, and if I hadn't had it to excite me before two miserable hours of History and Logic, I don't think I ever would have made it through that horrendous excuse for a class.

Let me be clear, there was no Logic to be done in that class, and the history was suspect at best. Our final was to develop an argumentative paper for why the current monarch, King Fennel Panchon III, was the best yet. The guy whose creation of indentures, destruction of carnephon mating grounds, and rampant Rare corruption started a civil war he was losing. It was a propaganda machine, and it made me question the whole Academy's credibility.

Which brings me to the last class of the day: Alchemic Gastronomy.

"I think we have the same culinary courses," Laven remarked as he joined me.

We rode stools at a table made of cold, waxy stone. At the center of each table, a metal canister leaked white smoke that I would've been afraid to inhale if any other students showed concern.

I might have been uncertain in TOF, but I was happy to have Laven beside me in AG. Each of the tables had two stools, and all of the other students made it clear they weren't going to be sharing a table with me.

"What did you have before this?" I asked. I figured that I couldn't do myself any worse by befriending Laven. At the very least, Yenne seemed to like him, and she was common once.

He groaned. "Dad's forced Economics as my elective. Thankfully, I have Maths before TOF to keep me sane."

"You got an elective?" I said, grumbling. "I'm stuck with History and Logic and Military Matters."

"History and Logic?" he said incredulously. "That *is* an elective."

A resonant voice instructed us to open our textbooks. Laven and I both yanked open *The Encyclopedia Organica* before turning to face the teacher. He had a sepia complexion, gray mustache, gray military cut, and wore a coat matching the one the doctor in the palace had worn, but beneath it was a chef's jacket.

"You," he said, pointing to the table beside us. "First paragraph, page forty-two."

"Yes, Chef Chikor, sir," the student said as she began. "'One of the eight fundamental techniques, flash-freezing involves exposing food items to L N Two—'"

"Liquid nitrogen," Chef Chikor interrupted, with clear annoyance.

"'—to liquid nitrogen for three to six seconds. The process freezes the outside layer of the food, protecting it from rot, without solidifying the inside or creating ice. The technique can also be used to vaporize ice in cold foods such as ice cream.'"

My ears perked at ice cream.

"Each of you has a canister of liquid nitrogen at your desk. To prepare yourself for using it, you can lift the cap of the canister and place your hand inside for a moment."

I reached to follow Chef's instructions, but Laven snapped his hand around my wrist. I was about to question my decision for friendship until three students cried out at once.

"Each of you will report to hospital immediately. Do not bother to return to this classroom. I do not suffer those that don't do the pre-reading."

Pre-reading? No one told me about pre-reading. I snapped around as the woman who had read from the book cradled her hand, which was a ghastly shade of blue and starting to blacken around the tip of her middle finger.

"The rest of you are either diligent or blessed that your partner reached in first. Now, let us begin."

I didn't know if I should be excited or terrified, but I knew that I was very, very glad to have made friends with Laven.

"I owe you one."

"You can give me three-quarters of the ice cream we make, fair?"

"I could live with that."

He wagged a finger. "That's what you think, but *I* think you've never had hard ice cream. You'll regret it."

And I did.

I came to regret much about Laven Florento. The ice cream was the least of them.

17

THE ACADEMY HOUSE

THERE WERE THREE classifications of restaurants in Ranch, or four if you asked a common. The lowest of the four were the commonsaries—small takeout joints run illegally within the Commons. Unlike Mom, who sold bread at market, the commonsary chefs sold meals straight from their kitchens, usually sandwiches wrapped in palm leaves or rice dishes spooned directly into a bowl that you brought to the apartment door. None dared use ground bison or rattlesnake sausage at all in fear of attracting the wrong attention, let alone emphon. They were purely vegetarian.

Officially, the three were food wagons, sit-downs, and houses. Occasionally, you could find lesser recipe emphon at a sit-down, but only houses could serve greater recipes. To cook in a house, you had to be a Culinary Academy-licensed Chef or a student of the Culinary Academy.

Chef Ilantra's Missoloan-starred Academy House was the jewel of the Culinary Academy. Built at the back of the tower's first floor, it opened into a small foyer where guests were directed to either the first dining floor—a large open space with thirty tables surrounding a concert stage—or the second, which was more intimate, with ten tables on a balcony that overlooked the first. Large windows provided a view of the river behind the tower, and a mesmerizing chandelier graced the diners with rotating light.

Of course, Chef didn't let me step foot on that dining floor for a week after I started, so when I rushed down after my first day, I saw only the kitchen—and it was even more spectacular than the dining room. As complex as a small city with traffic lanes and patterns of movement, its storage spaces containing proportions so precise that to waste an onion could throw off the whole ecosystem: the kitchen was efficiency.

"You're late, stage," Chef accused when I finally entered through the back door. "Grab an on—"

"I was here on time," I interrupted. "If anyone had believed that I was supposed to be here, or, I don't know, been told to expect me, I would've found you two minutes early."

"Two minutes early, *Chef*. And yet you were late," she said, pushing past me to inspect a pile of julienned bell peppers. "What does that tell you?"

I recalled the roundabout nature of her questioning at the Tribunal, and how she'd simultaneously used a simple question in Knifecraft to damn near defenestrate me in class. I wouldn't be answering any question she ever asked me again lightly.

A fact she picked up on. "Well, stage?"

I chose my words carefully. "A team is only as valuable as its least forward-thinking member, Chef. I should've anticipated that there would be obstacles and budgeted more time."

"Heard," she acknowledged. "Maybe there's hope for you, yet."

She led me to a woman with spiky brown hair and vivid flowers tattooed on her left arm, chest, and neck, all of which I could see because, unlike the other staff in the kitchen, who wore full-length chef's garments covering most of their skin, she wore a simple halter top. The lack of sleeves also exposed her right arm, which ended at the elbow.

"This is Wintagren," Ilantra introduced. "Top of the third-year class, and my sous."

I didn't know what sous meant, and it clearly showed on my face because Winta, as she preferred to be called, guided me. "I'm responsible for keeping the kitchen clean, orderly, and stocked so Chef can oversee the food staff. If the Tribunal or some other duty calls on Chef, I put on my big girl trousers and take over."

"See that Paprick learns his duty, Chef."

"Yes, Chef."

With that, Ilantra surveyed the kitchen like a hunting bird looking for prey and calmly approached a chef butchering a leg of bison to offer assistance.

"The kitchen is broken into areas," Winta explained, walking me through them. "Different menu items are prepared in different places to maximize efficiency. Each night is an educated guess in what will be in highest demand." She pointed to a second-year whose sole responsibility seemed to be chopping chard. "Salad here. Grills there. Right now, we're heavy in flank, so on that station, we prep chimichurri."

"Emphon flank?" I asked excitedly.

"For those with the knuckles for it. But we mostly serve bison."

We continued to the pastry station, the freezer—not an icebox but an actual walk-in freezer!—the stock rooms, and all three wine cellars downstairs, which were painstakingly kept at different temperatures for red, white, and bubbly by the house's sommelier, another third-year. As we finished the tour, I noticed that I hadn't seen any emphon anywhere. I didn't want to seem overly eager to find the "good stuff," but I was genuinely baffled as to how I missed it. Winta turned out to be one of the more insightful Rares I've met, and read me like a book.

"Chef will inform you of emphon procedures when she feels you're ready. *If* she feels you're ready. Don't take it as an insult. It's this way at all houses."

I thanked her for her honesty, and we moved to one of the supply closets.

"What am I cooking?" I asked.

She chuckled. "Eager, are you? Listen, this kitchen, above all else, is efficient. Every station needs its expert, and right now, each does except one."

I looked back at the empty grills. I *had* discovered a greater, after all. That meant was I easily more talented than everyone else. And if someone was cooking emphon there, it made sense.

"Before the dining room opens," Winta informed, "you'll be on stock inventory." She pulled a clipboard off the door and put it in my hands. "Double-check all ingredients for the night's menu are stocked in the quantities needed. If something is missing or bad, notify me and I'll send the runner to the wholesale for more."

I stared at the clipboard.

"As you've seen, we've got several stock rooms, and your classes only get out an hour before doors open, so you'll need to be efficient. Memorize the organization system if you can." She pointed across the kitchen to a large, double-basin sink. "When the dining room opens, you're on dishes. We use the finest, so you'll need to be careful but quick. We can't afford to be backed up on plating because you're afraid of breaking something."

"Stock and dishes," I repeated.

She placed her hand on my shoulder. "We all start somewhere. You're still part of the team. Chef rotates the menu monthly, and she always picks everyone's brains for new lesser recipes. If you want to move up, impress her and give her reason to find you capable."

"Pretty sure she already finds me *in*capable."

"Don't be so sure." She pointed to the second-year chopping chard. "Bayle is top of his class and started on dishes end of last term. *I* had to stage with two food wagons before I touched the grill. She respects you. But we're a team, and every team member earns their knives."

A bell rang as the maître d' reached into the pass—the counter where Chef passed plates to the waiters—and struck its cord.

"That's doors," Winta said, straightening up.

"Alright, people!" Ilantra called into the kitchen. "Fires hot!"

As one, the cook staff shouted back, "Knives sharp!"

"Plates clean," Ilantra finished, much less forcefully than the rest, but in a way that made my hairs stand on end. "Let's make someone's day."

18

SALAD SAVES LIVES

I WOULDN'T SAY I settled into my routine so much as collapsed into it.

Chef kept me until midnight on weekdays and later on weekends. Most of those nights, I was the last one out. All dishes had to be clean before we reopened. If the inventory was finished before my shift started, it meant I could spend the beginning observing the brigade or shadowing Winta, which made the late nights worth it.

On weekdays, I hurried to buy an Earl Grey tea to wake up as fast as possible before Knifecraft sapped the energy away immediately. Chef punished us every class with techniques that required uncanny dexterity. For all I hoped working for her would tame her tongue, Ilantra came to every class wide awake and spiteful that I was tired. Like it was some great sacrilege that I should be tired when she wasn't. Even though I had twice as much work as any other first-year, balancing the restaurant work with her ridiculous papers (how can anyone write 1500 words about the importance of elbow angle in the slicing of sourdough versus the cutting of barley bread?).

After Knifecraft, Lt. Vyson inflicted my daily beating—I won my first bout against a Rare in our second class and never once got to spar with a student again, partnered with Vyson ever after. But I made him work for it, practicing with my cleaversaw each morning until I started landing bruises back.

Sagen's class, though! I began to comprehend the world through flavor. I almost never had time or knuckles enough to cook for myself—Ilantra always prepped Family Dinner for the staff, so I never went hungry or uninspired by her genius with spices—but when I did cook, I practiced the theories Sagen taught alongside the techniques Ilantra drilled with something approaching reverence. By the third week, I hoped to leave the Academy House to work for him, but though Sagen loved me—and I'm pretty starving confident Laven and I were his favorites—he didn't hire help. It was just him and his husband, serving three tables a night at an exclusive pop-up. He even washed his own dishes, which only increased my respect for him.

I suffered more of History and Logic, snoozing through lecture after lecture of propaganda with no ability to ask questions or contradict our glorious professor. As it was essentially Rare for the Rare, I was consistently bottom of the class in marks and quickly in danger of being expelled if I failed.

That's when I learned how Yenne got into the Culinary Academy. After complaining about H&L one day, Yenne shared how she'd snuck into a Rare library and anonymously written a historical analysis of the heretical common religion (more on that later). The paper was so prodigious that it inspired Dean Dyl to track down the author. When they learned the author was a brothel orphan from Common-4, the Dean personally adopted Yenne and enrolled her at the Culinary Academy on academic merit. Adoptions happened from time to time, but I'd never heard of anyone getting into the Academy that way.

Yenne knew the H&L syllabus like I knew carnephon anatomy and offered to tutor me. I slept even less, but my grades improved, and I learned more about her, like how she had a mysterious partner outside the Clouds—something I kept in mind because I still needed to figure out a way to see my moms, who I ached to check on. I'd sent them letters, but nothing came back. I told myself it was because Lt. Vyson and the military controlled the post, but if I let myself think about it too often, I fell down a hole where the only reality I could comprehend was their deaths, and I couldn't afford to dig myself more holes. Not with how much I was trying to balance.

Anyway, the last class each day was Chef Chikor's.

He didn't hate me, not like Vyson or Ilantra. Hate would mean he felt *anything*, which I was convinced he couldn't. He was a compass pointed toward information with no deviation. I couldn't ask questions in H&L because they weren't allowed. No one asked questions in Alchemic Gastronomy because doing so was as likely to get you an answer as putting your hand in a burner was to get you a piece of cake. It was the hardest class, riddled with inexplicable alchemic phenomena, and without Laven, who excelled in it, I barely would've passed.

I'm what you would call street-smart. But damn if I wasn't hard-working.

On the weekends, my exhausted body dragged itself to Cutler's shop. For all his huff and puff, he was a font of culinary knowledge and a renowned home-cook. Half the customers came to ask when his next dinner party would be or if he could walk them through this lesser recipe or that one.

My workday ranged from utter silence to panicked chaos. When he had a thought, we did stuff. When he didn't, I tended the shop and he found ways to make fun of me.

And he did. Often and flavorfully. But as cutting as his words were, he became a true friend. He paid me far too much and took an interest in my problems when I voiced them.

Which is how it was that Cutler taught me the greater recipe that kept me alive.

"You look like you fell between the coals, were plucked out by a gryphon, and dropped in bison shit," he said as I walked in after a particularly late night at the Academy House. Starving Rare birthday party.

It'd only been three hours since I'd left there, and I'd stayed up rather than sleep and accidentally miss my shift. If I was going to free my moms from the Commons, I needed every knuckle I could get from Cutler. "Good to see you, too."

"Nothing?" he grumbled with disappointment.

Cutler was as much a connoisseur of comebacks as of cutlery, and I prided myself on getting a jibe in. "I'm exhausted, Cut."

"As I so eloquently said." He threw a walnut at my face. I only realized after it bounced off and hit the floor. Sighing melodramatically, he waddled beside me and opened a box of kitschy kitchen tools he stocked specifically so that he could dissuade people from buying them and instead buy the more expensive thing they *really* needed. Half the time, they fell into his trap, but occasionally they bought the stuff, broke it a week later, and returned to buy the good or cheap ones they'd grown addicted to. Win-win for Cutler either way.

"When was the last time you slept more than a handful of hours?" he asked seriously.

"What's today?"

"Stop what you're doing."

He could've told me to impale myself with the carving knife and I'd have done it, tired as I was.

We entered the back room where he did demonstrations during weeknights. I'd yet to join one, but he swore they sold wares "like the devil." The stock said otherwise.

Humming to himself, he pulled out a host of greens, beans, oils, seasonings, vinegar, and limes. He directed me to start chopping the greens, which I recognized as lambs quarter, a wild green that common often collected outside the city. "I'll be right back."

He came back ten minutes later with a fruit I'd only heard of, and a parcel of something wrapped in butcher's paper. "Go out back and start the grill. Oakwood only!"

Realizing we were actually going to be cooking together sent me into the giddy stage of exhaustion where everything was exciting and nothing seemed half as bad as it should, not even the little tremors running through my vision from sleep deprivation, or the way things smelled backward. I returned to him cutting a guavacado, green-skinned at the bottom, shading up toward its pear-like top, where it was paler, like an underripe lime. The inside was an unappetizing blend of pink and green, almost brown, that looked fleshy and smelled extraordinary.

The scent of lime pulled my attention to a bowl where purplish meat marinated. "*Carnephon?*"

"Of course, you half-daft halfwit. Now come help me here."

Cutler walked me through the preparation of Sleepless Salad, belittling me and chiding me through the whole process.

"Why are you teaching me this?" I asked as we finished.

Cutler gave me three truly serious looks in the time that I worked with him. This was the first, and it was as if I was staring into the wisdom of a god or a library older than Ranch. "Equity."

He didn't eat any of the salad, which almost dissuaded me. As if I could've been. The smell was like... In TOF, we often discussed "the Perfect." Everything had a "Perfect." There was a Perfect apple. A Perfect chip. Theoretically, there was even a Perfect bitter, something so purely and unequivocally bitter that nothing could be as bitter or as inarguable the essence of bitterness. The salad smelled like the Perfect lime: a bright, vibrant tartness that creeps up the back of your souring tongue with a kiss of sweetness to keep you sane. My fork skewered through greens and emphon with as much resistance as it would a cloud, and as I pulled the bite into my mouth, the delicate texture washed over my tongue like a deluge of rain. Its taste was more like lightning, trembling my fingers as the emphonic taste leaned into spice and tang. It was incredible. And I felt *awake*.

"How's that now?" he asked as my eyes vibrated with Endurance.

"You're a cockeyed genius, if genius was measured by the amount of smoke they've blown up their own ass!"

He waffled his hand. "The salad takes some time to kick in. Keep eating."

RYAN ROSE

We both laughed well into the night.

"I have to close the shop tomorrow," he said, as my shift came to a close. "Business to attend to on the other side of the city, and as much as you're a sycophantic sack of sod, I can't leave you to run the place on your own."

I started to protest, but he cut me off.

"I don't judge, Paprick. You least of anyone. But the rebel attacks are getting worse, and more frequent, too. The king's people strike back at the common worse each time. Too much death. Too much misinformation. People are scared, and half the Rare that come in here complain about you."

"Why?" I asked defensively. "I'm a good worker, and I'm polite to the assholes."

"I agree. But they hear rumors that you're a rebel spy. 'Stand tall!' They tell me their housekeepers talk about you like you're here to liberate them all."

"What? That's... I'm not." But I couldn't deny that the rumors existed. Each time I took a beating in Military Matters, someone brought it up. How I was some kind of rebel hero, despite the fact I'd done almost nothing. I hadn't even been to the Commons since classes had started. "I don't know where those rumors come from," I lied.

"I know this city, and I'm not ready to leave a common in here alone. Not because you can't be trusted, but because I can't trust myself not to second guess it or find some stupid reason to let prejudice color my reaction to anything unexpected that might come up."

"That's unfair," I protested.

"Undeniably. But what if some haughty Rare walked in here and beat you or burned the place down because of the rumors? I'll think about that the whole damned time I'm away, and I can't have that. Not tomorrow." He pushed his tongue into his lip. "Sorry, boy."

I swallowed back a retort that might've gotten me fired completely. It was the first time he'd given any indication that he even knew I

144

was common, let alone mentioned it. And for all that he insulted me every ten seconds, he never meant it.

"You'll get full wages for tomorrow," he added.

"That's not necessary."

"You think I don't know that?" he snapped.

"I think you don't know that change requires risk."

The frown that was so often playful on his face grew authentic. "Go home."

Home. As I left, his words hit the mark. Between exhaustion and schedule, there'd been no time for me to leave the Clouds and see my moms or Black Spice, but Cutler assured me I wouldn't need to sleep until the next night.

I could sneak back to Common-3 in the middle of the night. Without needing to be back at his shop in the morning, I could spend the whole night with my moms. Finally show them what I was learning, tell them about my plans to move them into the Clouds, maybe even host a midnight meal for them and my friends in Common-3 like I did for my fifteenth birthday. And then go to Black Spice to see Crooked Rish the next morning before I was needed at the Academy House for stock inventory.

Whether he realized it or not, Cutler was right. I was connected to the rebels, and tomorrow I would see them.

19

HOME

DRESSED IN MY nicer, Rare clothes, I shrunk into myself, self-conscious that I was much less likely to be recognized as Paprick the common here than when I'd returned from the palace. It'd been weeks since I'd been in a common district, and with all the rebel attacks, I worried I'd be mugged or attacked for being Rare.

I was utterly unprepared for the changes to the Commons.

As I walked through the streets, I saw carvers painting over murals *of me*. "Stand Tall" written beneath them.

As I stuck to the alleys, I heard whispered conversations through broken windows. "Tomorrow, we stand tall! Screw the overseers by slowing the conveyor, start some fights, anything. Who's with me?"

As I entered Common-3, I smelled Shank Stew on the air. Someone was cooking it. And not doing a particularly good job of hiding it either. I quickened my step, afraid the scent was coming from beneath my moms' door.

And then I was standing in front of it. No smell crept from beneath, but no candlelight did either. That hole—the fear of why I received no letters—started opening beneath me again. My arms shook as I lifted my hand to knock. What would I do if no one answered?

I don't even remember knocking. No idea how long it took for a light to appear beneath the crack. But I can remember the sweat dripping off my chin and plummeting toward the floor like that endless abyss of worry.

"Pappy!" Mom shouted in surprise when she opened it, shoving several zaatar crackers into my hand in greeting. "Come in, come in."

I smothered her in a hug, burying my nose in her hair to inhale the scent of sourdough and home.

Mother poked her head out of their bedroom and dashed out to join our hug. "Swe'me, finally!"

"You're too thin," Mom chided as I pulled away from Mother. "Are you eating?"

"Yes," I insisted as she immediately began cooking. "I'm just working a lot."

"Too much to see your mothers," Mother commented.

"They haven't been letting me out of the Clouds! I had to sneak out to come here."

She played the disbeliever for a moment longer before she drew me into another hug. "I'm just glad to see you, swe'me. Tell us everything."

I explained my jobs for Cutler and Ilantra and how that kept me fed. Then school, my growing friendship with Laven, how Yenne was tutoring me.

"A common?" Mom asked earnestly.

"Another woman?" Mother asked with much less subtlety. "And here I thought he had eyes for that Cori. I liked her."

I cleared my throat. "We're not doing this."

Mom lowered her voice. "Have you, you know, *seen* Cori recently?"

"I haven't been able to get out of the Clouds." I dropped to a whisper. "What's going on? Those murals, and I smelled *stew.*"

"We're trying to stay out of it, swe'me," Mother said. "But we did share the Shank Stew greater. People were suspicious at first, that we weren't helping. They talk about you all the time. Paint those murals.

Vanil and his lot have been organizing disruptions at factories and educating common about the rights they used to have when the Herdon royals ruled here."

"Rights? What rights?" I said in disbelief.

Mom chuckled from the kitchen. "Some school they sent you to. People used to be able to worship the Twelve openly, not just the Consumer. Common could have their own newssheet to say whatever it wanted. Stuff like that."

"And your mother and I could be legally married, not just 'cohabitating.'"

They filled me in on more of the rebels' actions as we ate a salad of berries and melons with a side of tea. A decent midnight snack, but so much less than I was growing used to at Family Dinner. The quality of the berries was a shock too. Had our food always been so close to going bad? Both my moms appeared satisfied by the meal, and when I suggested cooking something for them and my friends, they waffled politely about whether it was kind to wake people up or rude to show off by making an extra meal on a whim. It showed just how quickly I'd left behind the efficient metabolism of poverty. I had to cover my stomach with a blanket to stifle a growl, still hungry. And I'd eaten a greater recipe today. I doubted my mothers even understood the level of fullness I enjoyed daily. What would they think of the Family Dinners I treated more like lessons than sustenance?

I spent the night in my old room, and even though I didn't need to sleep, the nightmares returned. Common-1 falling. Common dying. I found myself staring out our oily, opaque window, imagining common trying to climb the stairs to assail the Rare in Fen's Plateau. There was no chance. Dawn cracked, and parents ushered their five-year-old kids toward the river to catch frogs for stew before school in hopes of giving them meat. I remembered learning to swim so I could dive down to hide if a Rare happened to be down by the river. As much as I was starting to like Laven, I doubted he'd ever hidden in the silt while trying to feed his family.

When Mother was ready for work the next morning, I walked her toward her factory, which was on the way to Black Spice. The streets were crowded, common heading to day shifts, and it was impossible to go unseen in my Rare clothes. Within a block, common swarmed me to hand me greetings.

"I'm sorry you have to deal with this," I apologized to Mother as our progress ground to a halt.

"It's like this every day, swe'me," she admitted. "Most, especially mothers, congratulate us for seeing our child into a better situation, but some blame us for 'giving you' to the Rare. Want us to get you back so you can fight."

I wanted to be comforted by how highly the common regarded me, but the truth was I hadn't done anything meaningful since stopping Bessa. Yeah, Vanil ordered me to keep the Rare distracted, but I spent more thought on improving my cleaversaw technique than on whether Common-1 would be rebuilt for those its collapse left unhoused.

Common seemed to notice they were waylaying Mother's progress and quickly started clearing a path for us. She thanked them and told them it was unnecessary, starting forward with a smile I recognized as proud.

Proud.

I hadn't done anything. I just stood there, the common starting to look at me with concern, until Mother turned around to see what was holding me.

"I'm sorry," I said, hurrying back to her. "I have to go. I need to talk to Rish and do more."

"Swe'me," she started, but I pulled her into a hug.

"I'm going to be back more. I promise. I love you."

The warmth of her smile could've melted ice cream. "I love you too. Go on. I can get to work by myself."

I might've slunk my way into the Commons the night before, but in the light of day, I damn near ran to Black Spice.

I needed to prove to myself that I hadn't forgotten my roots.

20

NEW BLACK SPICE

BLACK SPICE WASN'T repaired but moved. The original remained a husk of rubble, split open like a cicada's back. My blood stained the wood that hadn't been scavenged, and my treatment of Rish, Banan, and Ruda was a memory inked in that blood. Guilt sickened my stomach as I passed it.

A few blocks away, a spice pouch emblem marked an alley door. I would've missed it without Mom's careful direction; it was the kind of door people passed without a thought, or if they did think about it, assumed it was a back entrance to the building it was housed in. A door no one opened by accident.

Behind it, a cellar staircase delved the building's dank bowels. If not for the candles, I would've been sure I was in the wrong place, but I followed them through the dark for so long I surely left the original building. The journey's length allowed me to formulate an apology to Banan for my behavior.

"What do you want, Paprick?" the guard asked, raising her rolling pin as if to strike me. "You broke the rules last time you were here. You know what that means."

"You know who I am?"

"Do you know who I am?" she mocked. "I've let you in here twice a month since you could barely toddle."

Feebly, I offered her a spiced almond and said, "Crooked Rish is expecting me. I have… time-sensitive information for him. Please?"

She sighed and motioned me to come through the doorway. "If I get shit for this, your mom owes me a loaf of her sourdough, you hear? Vanil doesn't like me bending the rules."

I nodded and passed through, my mind racing. Vanil? Did Vanil set the rules of Black Spice? The whole place took on a new perspective, and not because it looked completely different.

I surveyed the new layout of the market, aware of the glares and silence that greeted me. My lips formed a thin line. If this place was controlled by the rebels, you'd think they'd be happy to see me, but then again, I'd insulted the sanctity of the last location and probably gutted a hefty sum of knuckles in lost wares from the merchants.

Each stall, fewer now, sprawled across a half dozen meters, asymmetric and disorderly, rather than packed between neat walls. Almost more like Cutler's than the original Black Spice. It struck me as unnatural—this had always been a place of order—but as I looked closer, I saw how unfinished it all was. Where stall edges were jagged, it was because broken crates were held up by barrels; what I mistook as clutter proved to be tools and equipment for rebuilding. But the absence wasn't misjudged. At least five stalls I used to love were missing. Two of those traders had been from old Common-1, and I hoped their absence was due to dealing with personal things, and not the obvious alternative.

Ruda wasn't present, but Old Man Banan was. His supply was thinner than it had been, and despite the space he had to spread out, the stall was neatly packed, a perfect replica of the original. A smile fell off his face as I approached, but he handed me a dried banana slice anyway.

"You should not be here," he said dismissively.

"I wanted to apologi—"

"If you had wanted to apologize, you would have done so weeks ago. What you want is to be forgiven."

I didn't have a defense against that.

"Go. I'm expecting someone and you will not find service here from me again."

It stung, and I itched to squeeze Banan's wrinkled face so that he would listen when I said I was sorry. But I was lucky to enter Black Spice at all. Vanil and his rebels may have organized this place, but Banan's word was law. He could've barred me from far more than his own stall, so I slunk away with my head down and found Crooked Rish examining a stone with three crystals, teal and jagged, growing out of its side. Unlike anything I had ever seen.

"Pappy, baby!" he exclaimed as I approached, and fished into his chair for a candied lemon wedge. "I was wondering if knocking your head against that bull had made you forget about dear old Rish. Come in, come in."

I pointed to the crystal growth. "What is that?"

"Oh, this?" he drawled, raising it before my eyes. "But a gift from a friend far to the south. Did you know, down there, small emphon— no bigger than you or me—feed only on these gems?"

"Emphon eat rocks?"

"Caprishells, they're called." He caught candlelight in the prism of the crystals, splaying a blue-green wash of color over my face. "This is called endurmite."

"Like endurium?" I reached out to touch it, but he pulled it away.

The Butcher stops speaking suddenly to drink from the meager cup his jailors provided, and the archivist's eyes flick from the Rite book to the sleeves of his threadbare prisoner's shirt, imagining the teal ocean waves tattooed beneath them. "Do they cover the Black Spice tattoo?"

"No," he answers, showing the spice pouch at his wrist. "Why?"

152

The archivist chooses the next words carefully. "There are rumors that scars manifest on those who touch the Source, that sometimes the best way of hiding those scars is with tattoos."

"And?"

The archivist ponders why the Butcher isn't as angry as he'd been. Is talking of the good ole days easing the pain of betrayal and loss? Or is it a trap to goad the archivist?

"Have you?"

"*If* I had, if, they wouldn't be a part of this story, the charges. It would be information I'd have to share." His eyes flick to the cell door. "Or perhaps trade."

Trap.

"Then let us not waste time," the archivist says. "To the past."

"What brings you to me today, Pappy?" Rish asked in a more serious tone.

"I owe you an apology."

He waved a hand. "You were under the madness. It is forgiven."

"Not by Banan," I grumbled.

"Banan is called Old Man for a reason. His memory is as long as the wrinkles in his face. But I cannot help but wonder if there is more to your visit. You could say Crooked Rish hopes there is more."

Lowering my voice, I leaned forward. "I want to speak with Vanil. About how I could help. I've learned something."

Rish began to stow his stall's trinkets. "We must move quickly. There is already much afoot today, eh?"

Before I knew it, he was rolling through Black Spice, away from where I'd entered. I'd never seen him move his chair so quickly, and, admittedly, I didn't think him capable of it.

"I am full of surprises," he said, somehow reading my thoughts.

21

MAPLE AND ROSE

RISH STOPPED BEFORE a pile of crates in the back of Black Spice and rapped his fist against one. What appeared to be the side of a crate swung open, revealing a hole in the wall behind it. I ducked in, following Rish, and was immediately flanked by two guards with rolling pins similar to my friend at the entrance.

The four of us traveled to a door that opened into a large indoor garden with grass underfoot and two huge fountains straight ahead. One was a carnephon spraying water through its fangs as it bucked its hind legs, and the other was the badgeboar emphon. It was positioned as if digging down into the fountain's marble column, its thin, clawed hands scraping into the top of the column as its thick haunches pushed it deeper. Spined tusks appeared to scrape against the stone, assisting in the digging process, as its beady eyes looked out over a flat nose that sprayed water in a star pattern toward us.

Rish hurried me into a garden housed below a domed glass ceiling. Light poured in, bathing enormous trees thick with star-shaped leaves and rows of multicolored flowers. I reckoned the garden extended at least a hundred meters to my right and left, and maybe even another hundred ahead. The size of a large tenement floor.

I couldn't reconcile how I'd returned to ground level or where this could be in Ranch. Neither seemed possible, but I was too stunned by its beauty to dwell. I'd seen the palace cacti garden, and two Rare garden spaces had grass, but they were mostly barren of trees. Even the Cloud's rows of palm trees paled in comparison to the greenery here.

"What is this place?" I asked.

"The Greenhouse." Vanil arrived from an adjacent path, its winding turns barely visible within the trees, and handed me some honeycomb. He'd changed his hair since I'd last seen him, the multicolored cornrows undone and left natural and undyed. His clothes were different, too. When he'd visited, he'd dressed in common clothes, but now he dressed in Rare linens, and he even carried a weapon on his back—which only Rare adults could do—a long quarterstaff, knobbed at one end in the shape of a serving spoon. Maybe he pretended it was a walking stick. "Do you like this place?"

Crooked Rish bowed his head slightly and departed back the way we came. "Much to do, excuse me."

"It's beautiful," I answered. "I've never seen anything like it."

He motioned for me to follow as he walked farther in. "Tell me, Paprick. What have you learned about Ilantra's Academy House?"

It seemed a strange, sudden question. I shrugged. "I could tell you all the inventory they keep and how the dishes are done."

Vanil brought my attention to a nearby tree. "This tree produces a sticky blood called sap that can be boiled and refined into the most exquisite syrup. Would you like to try it?"

I stammered, confused. "Y-yes. I never turn down an opportunity for a new taste."

He pulled a spiked funnel from inside his jacket and jabbed it hard into the tree, startling me. A moment later, a light amber liquid trickled out. He motioned for me to taste a drop. It was waterier than I expected of something that could become a syrup.

"Forty parts sap for one part syrup," he shared. "And often, one cannot even get that much from a single tree. You have to bleed a whole grove to tap its wealth. But one drop is enough to hint at what can be found. It's why I have you looking for Rare secrets. One drop could be enough for me to start tapping Rare trees."

"That's why I'm here. I learned a new greater."

"That's very good, Paprick. Very good. Truth be told, I've stretched your heroics in Tall Grass as far as I could. 'Stand tall,' and all that. Common were starting to lose faith. This new recipe will go a long way to keeping the faith. But what can you tell me about the Academy?"

As we did a lap around the park, I shared what I'd been up to for the last month, sparing no details so that I didn't inadvertently leave something important out. He stopped me only once, and asked, "And what do you think of Yenne?"

"She's very smart," I said cautiously. "Kind of distant though. Why?"

"No reason," he mused, smiling. "Only that I would not think Cori so pleased to hear you're spending so much time with her."

"Why would Cori care?" I asked, failing to hide eagerness in my voice. "Is she around?"

"What do you think is the purpose of this place?" he asked, clearly ignoring my question.

We'd been walking for a while now, and though I'd counted a few more of the maple trees, it was a far cry from the forty he would need to make sap. "It's not a sap farm," I said confidently. "Or an orchard, or anything resembling orderly. It has to be some kind of Rare garden. Just a place to mill about and enjoy nature."

"Rare, you say." He stopped to pluck a red, thorny flower from a bush. "Would it surprise you to know that only two Rare before you have ever set foot on this grass?"

"This is a common place? Why haven't I ever heard of it?"

"When the Herdon royalty were banished from Ranch, they left it to my organization's stewardship. We've maintained it for them."

"Oh, right, the *Herdons*," I said, as if acknowledging an inside joke. I'd heard this myth. But fine, if he didn't want to tell me how the rebels got ahold of this place, he didn't have to.

He handed me the flower. "A rose."

I turned it naively in my hand, nicking my thumb on a thorn. "Ah!" I cursed, and handed it back. "It's sharp."

"Beauty can be deceiving, Paprick, and this place is nothing if not beautiful."

"Okay, but how is it dangerous? It doesn't seem like a strategic position to plan a revolution from."

"You spent the last twenty minutes telling me about the Culinary Academy, its beautiful tower, its many rooms. About the dining room at the Academy House. About this Cutler's shop, which you find more incredible than this garden. That's the danger of beauty, Paprick. If common walked this garden, it would blind them to all the subjugation and oppression they face."

"No," I said. "You underestimate them. It could inspire them. Give them hope."

"Hope? From beauty? No, hope comes from *action*. Like what you did at Tall Grass. Like what we've done in the factories. In fact, my agents lie in wait to ambush the military and rob the king of a newly captured carnephon at this very moment. If they succeed, we'll deal a significant blow to the Rare and supply my troops. That will give hope."

I took a moment to consider that. He was right, but it didn't feel *right* to me.

"Still," he continued, "hope won't do anything to stem the king's true power."

"True power?"

"You have heard all your life that the king can control emphon. How?"

"It has to be a greater recipe. He's no god."

Vanil pointed at me emphatically. "Yes! Yes, exactly. You want to help? Figure it out."

"How am I supposed to do that?"

"The same way you discovered your greater in Tall Grass."

"I don't know how I did that," I admitted. "It was an instinct. One I haven't felt since."

"Youth," he complained as he rolled his eyes. "Have you had sex?"

I tensed, and then forced a laugh. "Yeah, tons of times. Yesterday, even. Why?"

"Indeed."

I was a great liar, as you can see.

"Some of us find our way to sex on instinct the first time, and then it takes a few more before we understand it, eh? I imagine your discovery is much the same. You need merely to return to it. Make your greater recipe again. Feel it in your body and capture that feeling like you would capture the heart of a paramour." He gave me a knowing look.

"I can't."

He stopped walking. "And why is that?"

"I used a spice that I can't get. From Ruda."

He tilted his chin. "I see. And what was this spice?"

I described it quickly, noting that it had no name and came from a tall tree.

"Tricky... Ruda won't be back for some months. You will have to make do in the meantime. You say that you have learned a new greater? What does it do? What does it require?"

When I finished explaining, he spun the rose in his fingers. "We have time before you must be back in the Clouds for your shift at the Academy House. I have carnephon flank here, and I can send for the remainder of your ingredients. Make it. Consume it again."

"But..." I struggled to think of a reason why I shouldn't. "Isn't that a waste?"

"If it helps you to find this feeling? No. Besides, you came here to give information, and now that I have you, I will not waste you. I will have others shadow and learn this greater, and while you have its effects, you will be of greater use. A first step toward your potential."

"And what is that?"

"As good as Ruda is, there's nothing she can procure that Rare cannot. Your spice exists somewhere in that Academy, I'm sure of it. Maybe even in the Academy House. After your shift, while you are still awake, look for it."

"You want me to sneak around her restaurant? If I get caught, she'll fire me. Or worse."

"Then start elsewhere, Paprick. Ranch wasn't built in a day, and the Academy is a big tower."

"I'll do it," I decided.

"Good man. Now, let us cook together. I am curious to try this salad. And I have a timely gift for you it seems." From his pocket, he produced a small white case, shaped almost like a rounded hourglass but thinner. I popped it open to reveal two nearly transparent concave disks with brown circles within them. As I tried to make sense of them, he pressed a finger to his eye, making me squirm with discomfort, and then I gasped as his finger pulled a disk away from the ball. "Contacts, they're called. They hide Enduring eyes. A useful trick, eh? Come, let us see what tricks you have now."

As I followed after him, I examined the contacts. "What would I need these for? I can eat greater recipes whenever I want at school."

He smiled over his shoulder at me. "Who said I always want you at school?"

I showed him how to make the salad, and my mind raced with what I'd learned. By the time I got back to the Academy, I'd be out of Endurance. Vanil's task would have to be done late, so I took any serving with me. It was a good thing. I didn't think I would be able to sleep with everything rattling around my head.

What I would discover that night would ensure that I didn't sleep soundly for weeks.

22

A DEADLY
BISQUE

MOST NIGHTS, WINTA greeted me with the day's menu so I could double-check the pantry. But that night, Winta hurried me to the center of the kitchen where the entire cooking staff crowded around Ilantra, who had her hair up. She wore it up for every demonstration there and in Knifecraft, so I assumed she was going to teach us a technique or lesser recipe.

"We have an unexpected guest this evening," she announced. "He's bought out the entire venue for his guests and made specific requests for the menu."

"Someone can do that?" I whispered to Winta. Beyond the knuckles it would require to buy out a house for a night, I couldn't think of a single living person whose demands would make Ilantra change her menu. Even the members of the Tribunal hadn't bullied her successfully, and that'd merely been about my life or death. Her menu was more important to her by leagues.

"It's infrequent," Winta admitted in a whisper.

"The king," Ilantra informed, when it was obvious the brigade wouldn't get to work without knowing.

I wondered whether we had any rat poison I could knock over

160

his plate, but as everyone else whispered excitedly, I realized Vanil probably wouldn't appreciate the chaos of an assassination—nor would I live through it long enough to protect my moms from the fallout. Better to smile and pretend I was eager too.

When everyone else got themselves under control, Ilantra handed Winta a parchment.

"This is our menu," Winta announced. "Lobster bisque main, following an emphon tartare and a watercress-radicchio salad. Salted caramel chocolate fudge mousse for dessert. Scalding sun, Paprick, I'm not sure we have some of this."

"Remember," Ilantra said as everyone started to break to stations, "the king graduated top of his class and even worked in this kitchen. I taught him, and he's starving brilliant with flavors. Especially his emphon tartare. Be excellent!"

Everyone scrambled to stations, but I stood rooted, my self-confidence reeling. I thought I was a prodigious Chef in the making, proving myself worthy of a place at Ilantra's stations. I was sure I could perfect our regular dishes—flank with chimichurri, asada salads, steak burgers, gourmet tacos, even fish dishes that I'd only recently tasted. But Winta had spoken another language. Bisque? Radicchio? Mousse? I didn't know what any of those were, let alone what we needed from the pantry.

Winta yanked me toward the nearest pantry. "I grant that cooking for the king is a lot, but we need to move."

"I don't know what to get," I admitted.

Her expression fell, understanding dawning. What common would know meals like that? From her apron, she produced a pen and quickly annotated the menu items, indicating the ingredients and quantities from each. I can't know if she realized she was giving me a greater recipe by doing so, but I doubt it; she was too empathetic to mire her thoughts with secrets and power.

Like every item on our standard menu, I memorized those ingredients and started playing with their combinations to predict the flavor in my mind as I rushed off to find everything. The service was for twenty people, and now that Winta had given me recipes, I worried. Twenty lobster bisques on short notice could undo our timing on its own. But the rest could destroy us.

Our runners, mostly second-years who hated me, scrambled to the wholesale. Winta tapped me to help chop, finally getting to cook a little, while we waited for them to get back. Every station was a flurry, from patisserie to garden.

And Chef was a force among it all. Sprinkling lessons through each station like seasoning. Maintaining everything. When the bell clanged for doors open, she didn't just begin the same rote mantra we repeated every night, she stopped the kitchen.

"We'll have a special Family Dinner tonight. It's called the First Flavor, because it was the first greater recipe to be discovered. But to me, it's also the first meal that made me want to cook. Tonight, we share it."

Excited murmurs sizzled through the staff. "You honor us, Chef," Winta bowed.

"Earn it."

Three servers came to our stations and produced a small plate of garnished carnephon steak. Despite how full I felt from the greater I'd made for the rebels, my mouth salivated at the smell of lemongrass and the perfect diamond pattern of the grill marks. Purple, medium rare tendons glistened between the char, sweating in their butter baste. Famines, I wanted to try it, but my stomach bucked instinctively at the thought.

Even if it was only a salad, it was a dinner portion, and emphon leaves you satiated in a way that nothing else does. It's nearly impossible to eat anything within a few hours of eating an emphon dinner, let alone more emphon. And I had my contacts in. Shortly, everyone's eyes would be Enduring, but unless I managed to somehow swallow this food *and* get my contacts out unnoticed before all those dishes rushed back to my sink, I would be in suspicious circumstance.

"Sir?" my server asked hesitantly when I didn't take the meal.

Chef noticed from across the kitchen. "You're Rare now. You need no permission."

I nodded, attempting to make my face eager as I accepted the plate, cut a piece of steak, and forced it down. I don't even remember the taste—a shame because the First Flavor is so special. But I remember the feeling as it hit my stomach like a lead weight. I think I actually gasped.

"Good, eh?" my server remarked.

I forced a nod and kept eating until it was gone.

"You gorged?" the archivist interrupts. "That wasn't another one of Vanil's fictions?"

"I didn't know the consequences. Obviously, I didn't die as I could've, but I should've at least lost consciousness from endurium poisoning. What happened to me next was far worse."

"I won't swoon to your propaganda, Butcher."

"I'm not ly—" He cuts himself off. "Look, like I said, it was a night I won't forget for *many* reasons."

"It's impossible. You must be lying."

"Oh, for the love—"

"No!" the archivist interrupts. "That is far—"

"LISTEN!" he commands.

Face strained and twitching, the archivist's lips snap shut.

As we finished eating, Chef roared our mantra. "Fires hot!"

"Knives sharp!" I called back, feeling like I was about to puke, and slipping the contacts from my eyes while everyone was distracted.

"Plates clean!" Ilantra demanded. "Let's make His Highness's day."

Dishes quickly surrounded me, but none were so disgusting as the mains, which have no equal in the kitchen. Lobster bisque requires boiling the shells of the horrendous bug-fish that gives it its name. What's left after is a crunchy, flaky, pink-orange mess that you can smell halfway across the country.

Each noxious inhale thickened the inside of my throat. I struggled to wheeze and swallow, and though I was offered a taste, I couldn't imagine sucking that pale spongy meat down my tightening throat. I was appalled that anyone would make it, let alone eat it, but my dizzying mind reminded me that because the king liked it, it must be decent. I thought maybe I would taste it later, after the pain in my overfull stomach subsided.

I remember coughing violently as the final pot was brought over. Elbows deep in another, scraping and retching against the smell that filled the kitchen, and the final pot was nearly full of unused bisque. Extra in case His Highness wanted more.

I was sweating and cramping hard in the gut with every movement.

My soapy hands moved sluggishly to push the pot where I stacked the dirty dishes, but I knocked it like a drunkard, waterfalling creamy orange soup over the floor. The drain would get most of it, but my brain—which I didn't realize at the time lacked the sharpness of Endurance—thought it a huge disaster. Spilling soup in Chef's kitchen. And on the day the king was in attendance!

I scrambled for the mop, berating myself almost as loudly as Chef cursed me from across the kitchen. I needed a break, a moment to myself. I whipped off my cleaning gloves and braced myself over the hissing sink, head hanging.

My head was a fog thicker than the rising steam.

A server wheeled another tray of bisque dishes to my area. If this stuff was so good, why was everyone sending it back half-finished? As Chef kept telling me to get my act together, I started to doubt her. Maybe she wasn't the genius I thought she was. Grabbing one of the clean spoons, I scooped some of the lobster.

Again, my stomach buckled at the thought of more food, but I figured I could taste it and spit it back out.

My doubt dissolved like the delicate flesh over my tongue. The king was right to order this. Ilantra was a genius. It was buttery with hints of the mirepoix that started the pot, slightly acidic and sweet with the white wine that deglazed it, and so creamy. All punched on top of a meat, soft and smooth. I marveled at how unlike the smell it was.

Now, if you know about food, you know that almost everything has a smell that mingles with its taste. Most of what we think is taste is actually smell in the back of our throat. Greater recipes are the only things that have a dichotomy. Well, emphon and one other thing. People who are allergic to foods tend to smell them differently. Those foods don't smell inviting. It's the body's means of protecting itself.

My moment of bliss was shattered by a pulse of breathlessness. Everything in my lungs seemed to explode through my neck. Irons clamped my throat shut as breath escaped. My eyes bulged. Vision blackened.

"Chef!" someone screamed, dull and far away. "Root!"

Someone forced a liquid into my mouth, my throat reopened, and I sprayed the sink with a stench that has no place in the kitchen. I fell to the ground, gripping my neck. Lights danced pink and blue and starry as the night closed in on them.

Someone stabbed hot fire into my leg. The fire in my lungs froze and burned cold like the inside of the freezer. I gasped and coughed. My heart was a thunderclap in my ears, frantic and manic and mad. Mad that I had put it into a slumber when it could *race*.

23

SEEKING SPICE

I WOKE SOMETIME later on a small cot in the produce pantry. Ilantra leaned over me, her yellow eyes no longer pale but fire-bright with Endurance and annoyance. "What were you thinking?"

My throat was raw and stung sharply when I tried to speak. With a sigh, she handed me a tablespoon of emphon milk. Healing and Endurance welled through me with a single swallow. Like summer to fall, my throat transitioned from dry and hot to wet and warm. It wasn't a miracle cure. It would be days before I could swallow something as terrifying as a tortilla chip, but it was enough.

"I don't know what happened," I said. "Was that food poisoning?"

She laughed cruelly. "You really didn't know."

"Know what?"

She explained allergies and anaphylaxis to me.

"I'd heard peanut butter could do that to common, but I didn't know meat could."

"Shellfish," she explained. "And it appears your allergy is severe. You will not be allowed in my kitchen when we prepare it."

"But I—" I sat up in the cot.

"There's no negotiating this, stage. If there's a cicada bloom this year, you won't be here for that feast either. Do you understand? You could die."

I tried to protest further, but I was so, so tired that I could barely form words. Whatever the reaction had done, it'd scoured the Sleepless Salad and all Endurance from my system.

Ilantra pushed me back down, gently. It was an unnerving thing from her, tenderness. "Rest. I've sent for your friend to help you get back to the dorms. You can skip Knifecraft in the morning if you're still groggy, but don't make a habit of it." She rose. "I have a mousse to prepare. Try not to die in the meantime."

To ensure we're not here still here when the Empheron arrives to kill us all, I haven't covered every little thing in my daily life. Suffice it to say in the last few weeks, I'd grown closer to Laven. Between classes and the occasional pub lunch or late-night "study" beer, we'd become friends. As real as the ones I had in Common-3. In a way that I couldn't have imagined with a Rare. I didn't trust him with anything approaching rebel secrets, but I shared things, like how I missed Mother's fermented hot sauce, and I even gave him Mom's lesser sourdough recipe. Mostly because he was always sharing something with me, unprompted. How he carried the wok on his back because, as a kid, other Rare kids would throw rocks at his back while he was bent over a notebook, or how he wanted to be remembered for inventing a new use for eggs—because apparently scrambled, deviled, whipped, fried, and the million others weren't enough.

He rushed into the room like a kid in a candy store. "They're making mousse for the king with an actual alchemic..." He cut himself off, cringing as he looked at me. "Mate, you look proper scorched. What happened?"

"Dared sample the king's soup," I joked, though my voice was a rasp.

He hooked me by the elbow and pulled me up. "Lesser men have fallen for that, probably. Let's get you back to bed."

My body ached like I'd run the length of Ranch's walls. My breath was short by the time we got to the central staircase. "I can't do six flights," I gasped, my eyes traveling up the spiral.

For a moment, it seemed like he might try to carry me, even with the heavy wok on his back, but stout and strong as even he was, I think Laven knew six flights was out of his league. "I could take you back to mine, but I've only got one bed. Probably best to leave that for later in our friendship, ain't it?"

He lowered his voice. "If anyone asks, we got lost." Quickly, he led me—or more accurately, carried me—down a corridor I'd never entered. I'd actually hoped to investigate it after my shift, because Winta occasionally sent a runner down it when we needed something that wasn't in the pantry. But I wouldn't have gotten far. At the end of the hallway, we passed under a sign labeled RESTRICTED – SUBSTACK to arrive before a padlocked door.

Laven cast a glance over his shoulder before retrieving a key from his pocket, which opened the lock and revealed a staircase that descended into the basement.

"You trying to make the climb worse?" I complained.

He raised a finger to his lips and helped me down into a musty maze of shelves, some neatly lined with academic tomes, others packed with cans and jars. "The libraries on the upper floors can't hold everything," he explained when we confirmed no one was waiting at the foot of the stairs. "Same for the classrooms and pantries in the Practical Wing. They exchange things using a dumbwaiter lift"—he saw my confused expression—"oh, uh, elevator, I think you'd call it. But it's technically teachers and staff only."

A jolt of alarm raced through my drained body. This could be my ticket to finding the spice. Laven scrutinized my sudden reaction with a raised eyebrow.

"Oh, right, elevator," I said as if it were the cause. "The overseers had those in the King's Factory so they didn't have to climb like us. How'd you get a key?"

"Nicked it off my dad." He pointed. "This way."

Slowly, we flitted through shelves, passing doors I assumed branched off into other storage rooms. As we came around another turn, the dumbwaiter waiting for us at the end of the stack, a muffled feminine voice shouted, "Please, no!"

Hair rose along my arms and neck. "Did you hear that?"

"Hear what?" Laven kept pulling me toward the dumbwaiter, but whimpering drew me to a nearby door.

"Someone's in here."

As Laven pressed his ear to the door alongside me, a wet slapping sound cut off another scream. His eyes widened and he pulled away. "We should get someone."

"What if we're too late?" I said. "They're being hurt."

Laven cursed and looked around before nodding to himself. From his messenger bag, he removed a small glass bowl covered by a piece of butcher paper secured with a rubber band. He opened it and handed me the bowl. "I nicked this off the pass in the Academy House when I came through to get you. I was planning to eat it myself, but—" Bits of Ilantra's carnephon tartare, raw and cold, called to me from within the bowl, the creamy smell wafting up. "You try to stop whatever's happening. I'll get help."

"You're going to leave me?" I protested. "I'm exhausted."

"We only have enough for one, and"—he looked away—"I'm afraid I'll freeze up."

"Okay," I said, not sure I was any more confident.

He took off as I plucked the tartare into my mouth. An explosion of flavor hit me, a Perfect balance of spicy and cream, more like a salsa crema than a meat dish. My eyes brightened, reflecting off the dusty jars around me, and strength raced down my arms. Instinctively, I flexed my hand and felt the skin over my knuckles rip to reveal dull metallic plates where my bones should be. Not painful but exhilarating. I felt heavier and sturdier, like every bone in me had become steel.

I took a deep breath and grabbed a glass jar from a nearby shelf to throw, or something. No plan, only the idiocy that calls itself bravery. I eased open the door, and cold air rushed out of the room like it was desperate to escape.

Flickering candlelight revealed a meat locker, and at its center, a pale, blond man in Rare heavy traveling clothes, the type people wore when crossing the desert during winter, his gray sleeves coated in blood. Splatter painted his face, drenching his Enduring eyes and mustache red as the row after row of bison cuts hanging from butcher's hooks.

They weren't the only things hanging. Two men and a woman, clearly common, in homespun clothes, swung behind the Rare man, all of their hands fully impaled by hooks to hold them up. I nearly dropped the jar as the sweat in my hands went cold. The common bled from gaping cuts. At least one was surely dead, the crown of his head removed, and his brain resting in a bowl of his own skull on the floor beside the Rare. Beside it, discarded and bloody, was a mask etched with the star-nosed likeness of the badgeboar emphon.

I'd seen blood. I'd seen offal. The Factory was a horrifying, gruesome place.

This was not like that.

Vomit rocketed up my throat, but I remembered how I'd vomited some of my greater on Tall Grass, how I'd just puked in the kitchen, how they'd each robbed me of Endurance to some degree. Clenching, I held it back, my cheeks fit to pop. When I swallowed it back, I realized the Rare hadn't seen me.

I launched the glass jar at his head, missed, and charged forward, raising my iron fists. The Rare flinched before raising his own. In one, he held a thin carving knife, and as I closed the distance, he jabbed with it, attempting to slice at my arm. Ducking sideways, I swung for his face. As my iron fist connected with his cheek, I felt the buckling of his teeth in their sockets, one shooting loose through the pucker of his bloody lips.

Before I could throw another, he backpedaled, and we circled one another. The heightened focus of Endurance emphasized his every movement, the way he favored his right side, and the advantages of my environment. Blood puddles littered the floor. The air was stingingly cold. I thanked Lt. Vyson for my regular beatings because they'd sharpened me like a blade. I only needed that moment to calculate my attack.

I feinted at his left side, aiming a punch at his knee. He rotated into a jab, stabbing at my eye with his knife, but I was already turning, taking the slice hot and gushing across my cheek. Too little. My steel fist crunched into the meat of his right thigh. The shockwave rippled and bones crunched. He slammed into the tile floor, cracking his head against it. The sound reverberated in my teeth and made me gag, but I tumbled to the floor after him, raising my fist.

He tried to spin away, but my knees pinned his hips as I landed. As my mind screamed "don't do this, don't kill him, don't don't don't," my knuckles sunk right through his forehead—my Enduring strength and steel fist a tenderizing hammer. He didn't even rattle. The room's copper stench soiled a moment later as his bowels relaxed in death, and I fell off, shaking. I'd killed a man. Committed murder. (That's one of however many scores, but it hurt like all but one other.) I felt changed. So instantly different. No longer Paprick, but other.

Whatever was left in my stomach spewed across the floor. My bones and hands returned to normal and Endurance left me. Exhausted, I rolled onto my back and heaved breaths.

The woman screamed as a figure in a horned carnephon mask pushed through the hanging meat and charged me. I scrambled to my feet, but the slippery blood that had felled my first attacker caught me too. The smaller assailant shouldered me in the chest and tackled me to the ground. The ceramic horns of the mask pressed into my flesh. Without warning, I was haunted by memories of my fight with Bessa.

Before I could clear my focus, I struck the tile, and pain raged up my tailbone and through my spine. Two fists like cast iron pans fell from the sky. Once. Twice. Vaguely, I realized they were like mine. This person had eaten the tartare.

After the third, the world swam. There may have been more.

Eventually, the Rare's blade scraped against the tile as the new masked attacker lifted it. The sound wriggled through my bones and made me twitch. It was enough to bring my senses back as he sliced the throat of the screaming woman, silencing her forever.

Numbly, I fumbled to stand. Done with her, the bull-masked Rare stalked forward toward me.

Then their body spasmed as a gasp rattled from their throat. Blood stained their shirt red from within and they tipped forward, falling flat to the ground. Protruding from their back was a long knife— and not the kind you find in a kitchen, but a serrated dagger meant for violence. Standing where the masked person had just a moment before, her mouth hanging open and her hand still outstretched, was Yenne Corzon.

I passed out.

The Butcher waves a hand, ending the command's hold on the archivist's face, and reaches for water.

"Anaphylaxis," the archivist says immediately. "You overcame gorge by vomiting and flooding your blood with white blood cells."

The Butcher chuckles, a warm sound, genuine. "You would know better than I." The words feel out of place in their current circumstance. He should not be so comfortable, so genial.

"The truth disappoints the rumors, then."

"Please. Your Rare cite rumors about what I've done as evidence for my crimes as readily as you invalidate them. And that's supposing you didn't invent the ones you cite. Someone once told me the people who write the stories of our lives change them."

"As if you don't revel in the everchanging narrative. We both know there was no storybook heroism to your butchery. One kill in self-defense does not beget innocence for wholesale slaughter at the Palace."

"ENOUGH!"

The archivist's spine snaps to attention at the command, but it isn't from the Butcher. Its source sweeps into the room in her finest silks—marred by soot.

"The law abides this farce, but I will not waste hours listening to the two of you prattle while deluded sycophants attempt to kill me and the Empheron's bloody gryphon conduct flyby reconnaissance." Her Majesty's words drip with power and duty. In such a small room, the smell of foreign meat hints at the greater recipe that gives power to her commands. Her eyes darken as they confront the archivist. "You disappoint me."

"And you disappoint millions," the Butcher retorts on the archivist's unwilling behalf. "Or can't you hear how they fight for their true king?"

"ENOUGH," the Queen commands again as she sweeps out of the room. "RESUME AND BE DONE WITH THIS BEFORE YOUR OWN PEOPLE BURN YOU ALIVE HERE. OR I'LL KILL THE OLD MAN."

That, it seems, affects the Butcher. His eyes linger on the door with true want. "So he is here," he whispers to himself, so faintly the archivist barely catches the words.

The door slams shut behind the queen, leaving the pair to their privacy, but the tension radiates throughout. All the world knows well what happens in the wake of the masks—or presumes to. The archivist will hear the truth, finally, and so then will have answers.

"Where was I?" the Butcher asks, his voice almost wistful.

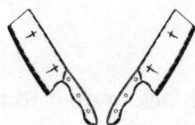

Course 3: Emphon Tartare

Best served in small quantities as an appetizer, Emphon Tartare is the meal of choice for those who want the benefits of Endurance without the emphon being the centerpiece of the meal. Unlike many others, this greater recipe's effects apply immediately after the first bite and last longer if the meal is enjoyed slowly. Pair with white wine—or silver tequila, if you're feeling dangerous.

Ingredients (serves 1)**:**

100g bull emphon chateaubriand or filet mignon
For the pickled jalapeño:

- ◊ 1 tbsp vinegar
- ◊ 1 tbsp water
- ◊ ½ tsp white sugar
- ◊ Pinch salt
- ◊ ½ clove garlic, minced
- ◊ 2 tbsp jalapeños, finely diced

1 guavacado
¼ cup capers
1 cup frying oil
For the chipotle aioli:

- ◊ ½ cup mayonnaise
- ◊ 2 tsp lime juice
- ◊ 1 tbsp chives, chopped
- ◊ 1½ tbsp smoke-dried chipotle peppers, minced
- ◊ Salt to taste

2 tbsp tomato, finely diced
1 tbsp shallot, finely diced
1 egg
1 slice sourdough bread
Radish slices for garnish

Black pepper to taste
Cilantro, chopped

Steps:

1. Prepare the pickled jalapeño:
   - Combine vinegar, water, salt, sugar, and garlic in a small pot over medium heat.
   - Stir at a boil until salt and sugar dissolve and remove from heat.
   - Stir in peppers and let stand for 15 minutes.
2. Cut emphon into 2cm cubes and pack in ice for 10 minutes.
3. Mash guavacado into a chunky paste.
4. Deep fry capers on high heat in oil. Remove with a slotted spoon and drain oil.
5. Prepare the chipotle aioli by whisking all ingredients.
6. Remove emphon and hand chop to desired texture.
7. Combine emphon, pickled jalapeño, tomato, shallot, capers, and 2 tablespoons of aioli in a ramekin.
8. Poach egg and toast sourdough.
9. To plate, smear avocado paste atop sourdough slice. Invert ramekin and give a firm thrust to release tartare from ramekin onto slice. Top tartare with poached egg.
10. Garnish with black pepper, radish, and chopped cilantro. Serve.

Expected Endurance Effect(s):

Endurance, 1–4 hours
Strengthened Bones, 1–4 hours
Burst-knuckles made of metal, 1–4 hours

24

FINDING
QUESTIONS

I AWOKE A minute or two later, Yenne and Laven cradling my back. As I groaned, Yenne removed a small teal pill from some mysterious fold in her skirt. "Swallow this."

A licorice taste gave way to warmth that radiated through my fingertips. Like a whisper of emphon milk, condensed somehow, healing and passing quickly without the cool wave of relief the milk brought about.

"What was that?" I asked.

"Dehydrated emphon milk," she answered as if it were obvious. "For emergencies."

Groggily, I surveyed the wreckage in the meat locker. The bound woman's eyes were open but vacant, blood trickling down from her hands and throat. She looked so much like my old mentor, Meg, I impulsively moved toward her, but Yenne said, "We need to leave."

"What? We—no," I argued. "We can't. Shouldn't, these masked Rare—we don't know what they're doing, why. Yenne, they—they killed them. They…" I motioned to the splattered brain as a gag tied off my words.

Her eyes trailed to the debrained man, but I saw no change in her stoic expression. My mind started working again. "What are you doing here?"

"Laven encountered me at the central stair. It seems Chef Ilantra entreated both of us to return you home, but he arrived first. I'd only just come down when he rushed up. Now, think clearly, Paprick. The substacks are restricted, and whatever this is, we don't want to be associated with it when Rare authorities investigate it."

"We can't leave them," I repeated, staring at the dead common. I think I convinced myself that if I looked at them and not the Rare, I could somehow forget what I'd done.

"I'll take care of it," Laven said, his voice thin and his face waxy. "I'll say I was sneaking around with my dad's key and found it like this already."

"You'll be punished," Yenne said placidly.

"Nothing new. Besides, I won't leave them either. Take Paprick in the dumbwaiter. You two can't be here. People already think you're dodgy because you used to be common. They'll accuse you somehow. Worst case, I pull the 'do you know who my father is' card."

Yenne pulled me to my feet. "Be careful. Others might be involved in this and may return to evaluate its progress."

As Laven headed back toward the central stair, Yenne hurried me to the dumbwaiter and slammed the gate shut. I didn't begrudge her. I could barely see straight.

"Famines," she cursed. "What were you thinking, fighting them?"

"Me?" I gasped as my memory started to fully return. "You... you killed someone."

Her lip trembled, but she nodded confidently, as the floor began to rise. "A necessity."

"Necessity? Yenne, I'm shaking so hard the blood in my clothes won't dry. You're not...?" I didn't know how to finish the question. When, I closed my eyes, I could already see the screaming face of the man I killed. "Do you need a minute?"

"Why, because I am but a frail woman? I asked what you were

thinking." Her tone left no room for me to contradict the first question. But for all her straight posture and seriousness, her eyeliner was smudged from tears or wear or shock or something, and it weakened her everything. I kept my gaze trained on her.

"Are you okay?" I asked softly.

"No," she admitted.

I wanted to reassure her, hug her maybe, but that wasn't what Yenne wanted from me. She steeled herself. "I will adapt. This isn't the first time I've seen death. So I ask again, what were you thinking? Were you searching for the spice as Vanil instructed and happened upon that scene? If so, why would you risk searching alongside Laven *Florento*?"

Several thoughts flicked through my head simultaneously. The first was dread. I'd been caught as a rebel spy. But then I focused on the words. Vanil. Spice. Instructed. Yenne knew about my mission. Unless she was an even better spymaster than Crooked Rish, the rebels told her. If the rebels told her...

It made sense. Vanil came to me the day I elevated. Why not her? Because she was in the Academic Branch instead of Culinary? Because she was adopted by Dean Dyl, a Tribunal member? That made her even more appealing.

"He was taking me back because I couldn't climb the stairs. I got sick in the kitchen. That's why Ilantra called for you."

We reached the sixth floor, which was utterly devoid of light, but Yenne seemed to know where she was going. I followed her, still seeing the Rare's face each time I blinked. "Who were those people? Why were they cutting commons' brains out?"

She turned down an adjacent hall, its length as black as the alchemic pitch carvers poured on Bessa to seal her wounds. Another turn brought us to a dying candle illuminating a small door, locked. Sighing, Yenne pulled the metal pins from her hair and materialized an L-shaped wrench from her skirt to pick it. As the door swung into a well-lit hallway, she answered me. "No one with permission to be there."

"How do you know?"

"Because I keep track of many aspects of this building on Vanil's behalf, and you are merely one."

"Do you always have to speak so pretentiously?" I complained. Not the nicest thing, obviously, but I was in a bad mood with the whole killing-someone thing.

She answered my question with silence, but when we got to my room, she finally said, "We'll need to report this to Vanil, together. Meet me tomorrow morning. I'll tell Dyl that you're ill and have them excuse you from classes."

"Ilantra excused me from Knifecraft already."

"Good, that'll lend support to the excuse." Without a glimpse back, she left me with the weight of what we'd done.

I lay awake on my bed for hours, unable to get the scene out of my head. The dead common, strung up like starving animals. The Rare I killed. In my desperation, I tried to convince myself that I was a soldier on the side of good, killing for the greater good, but I never wanted to be a soldier. I wanted to be a cook. People like Lt. Vyson delighted in fighting—I saw it every day in Military Matters, how their grins curved higher and higher with each drop of blood spilled. It made me sick. People should only smile like that while eating and laughing with the people they loved.

I tried to expunge the horror with good. I forced memories of my moms, Mother hugging Mom from behind, smiling in the sunlight. The three of us grilling with Uncle Macen, Musta, and Auntie at Mother's birthday. The taste of my greater, which I'd started calling Emphon Rub. The way I'd made half the Tribunal hate me. To my surprise, Cori came to mind, funny and challenging at the Factory, quietly comforting at my uncle's mourning feast. I wondered what she was doing. Probably out under the stars somewhere, with those arms…

"Is this necessary?" the archivist interjects, annoyed. "Don't you have an important conversation coming up?

"A good story needs romance," he replies. "And yeah, I do think it's necessary for you to understand how shaken I was. I didn't just kill that man and become 'The Butcher' like your queen pretends. I grieved for him. Even though I didn't know him. Even though he attacked me."

"Spare me."

In the same Greenhouse grove where I'd met Vanil the previous morning, I waited, exhaustion heavy on my eyes. I hadn't slept. But dawn glittered through the glass dome above, and crickets sang within the garden.

"Back so soon," Vanil commented as he stepped into sight and tossed me a honeycomb. "And so early, too. Good thing I needed no sleep." His eyes shone with Endurance, but they sunk as he took in Yenne's expression. "What happened?"

"He nearly died last night," Yenne informed Vanil. "I found him in a restricted locker with two corpses and a masked person a step away from killing him."

At Vanil's request, I began to recount everything since I'd left. "The king bought out the restaurant, so to make sure we were on top of our game, Chef fed us the First Flavor, but—"

"You ate the First Flavor with the salad in you?" Vanil asked.

"It was a little hard to get down, but—"

"A little hard?" Vanil awed. "Paprick, you should have died."

"What? Why?"

"It's called gorging," Yenne informed. "Too much endurium is poisonous. Your pancreas explodes."

I didn't know what a pancreas was then—carnephon don't have them, and they accounted for the majority of my anatomical knowledge—so I just nodded. "Right."

"You should have died within the hour," Vanil added. "This is very good. Your legend will grow when the world hears of this."

"Well, I mean——"

"No," Vanil said. "Don't tell me anything else. I don't want it to affect the way I spin it."

So I told the rest about Laven and the locker.

"I don't like the sound of this at all," Vanil said finally, "but I don't know any groups that wear masks shaped like emphon. We will need to learn more. Paprick, return to your duties as if nothing's happened. If anyone asks, you left with the Florento boy. His lie about poking around down there after being seen collecting you may become problematic, but I trust you to figure something out. Maybe you got separated when Yenne came down to answer her summons? Think about it on your way back. Yenne, you will need to enroll in another Culinary elective next quarter."

"But I need——"

"We can't risk you being too far from Paprick."

It felt unnatural seeing her ordered around. Ilantra did it in her classroom, but that was different. Yenne was a student, deferent as expected. And maybe that was why. She didn't strike me as the type of person to involve herself in rebellion. Too distracting from her studies. "Yes, sir," she grumbled.

"Go rest. I'll handle Paprick from here."

She left with a frown.

"I don't want to be *handled*. Someone's killing common. I want to help. I can look into the masks."

"An unnecessary risk," Vanil said, waving the concern away. He put a hand on my shoulder. "Paprick, you're so valuable. It hasn't been long enough for you to have heard, but people are already sharing that greater salad recipe and using it to our benefit. Last night, we disrupted a Rare supply line to the front with the extra manpower. Common are standing taller. Leave this mask business to me. Stick to what you've been doing. Keep looking for the spice."

"Let's say I find it. What then? I don't even know what your group is really up to. You say you want to empower the common, but how?

Who rules if we depose the king?" I crushed the honeycomb he gave me in my fist. "What am I even doing here? I'm a cook, not a soldier."

It was a long moment before Vanil responded. "Do you know how the Panchon monarchy came to rule this country?"

Despite the non sequitur, History and Logic's propaganda rolled off my tongue. "They settled the War of Eleven Recipes by taming the carnephon and establishing Ranch."

"'Taming.'" He laughed. "No, they ended that war by weaponizing a greater that no one could stand against. It's called Chili Control," Vanil said, staring up into the stars, "and it was discovered by a woman who lived on Fen's Plateau. Almon Panchon, a neighbor and apprentice in her kitchen, killed her and stole it. With it, he reached into the minds of carnephon, controlling them to destroy the Eleven Families, and established his kingdom.

"You ask who we are. We are the Herd, and we aim to reclaim that weapon of injustice and turn it back on the family who stole it. We have agents in every facet of the country, from the fields where its spices are grown, to the factory where its meat is carved, to the Academy where its knowledge is kept. We know that, somewhere, the king's secret waits to be discovered. Only time keeps it from us."

"It sounds like a great mission," I acknowledged. "But I killed a man tonight. I see his face each time I blink. If I work with the Herd, he won't be the only one, will he?

Vanil took me into a hug, surprising me. "I'm sorry, Paprick. I know this is more than you expected, but the common need a symbol to rally around. I thought to use the story of the long-lost princeps returned, but for every common that believes, there are five who don't." He paused and gave me a significant look. "And then you stood tall, out of nowhere, on your own merits. You showed them they needn't fear the king's most powerful weapon: his carnephon. You gave me an even better story."

"So you have the missing princeps here somewhere? Why is he any better than the king we have?"

"I had hoped to have this conversation farther down the road," he said.

"What do you mean?"

A flat line balanced Vanil's features. "What do you know of your father?"

Venom spat from my mouth. "Seriously, you too?"

"This is a world of family lines," he pressed on. "Fathers and sons, mothers and daughters. Kings and princeps. All passing down their greater recipes, their legacies, their trauma. You really never wanted to know?"

"I don't care who he is. Mom never saw a need to tell me, and that's enough for me to know that *I don't care.*"

"But the world will," Vanil insisted. "We can make you anyone we choose. With a whisper in the right ear, you could be the missing princeps himself. Gods know the people want to believe. *You* could ensure the new king is different."

"You would name *me* king? You don't even know me."

"Some opportunities, some conveniences, they can't be wasted, Paprick. The Herd has many people who could advise you. And it wouldn't be forever. We planned to name the princeps Steward, to rule as we transition to a democracy."

"I don't even know what that is, democracy. I—I just love to cook. I can't be king or steward. I'm barely capable of being a symbol."

Vanil clutched my shoulders. "It's a lot, I know. It's not going to be today, or tomorrow, or next week. It'll take months to organically grow the revolution, if not years. In the meantime, you get to go to school, to cook. You won't need to be in the Commons while we make you out to be our savior. You just have to smile and nod when the king falls, and we present you."

"And if I don't?"

Vanil shook his head sadly. "You invented a greater recipe and became a symbol. Like it or not, there's no going back from that."

"Is that a threat?"

"Need it be?" he asked. "I thought you wanted to help."

"I do. But how can I keep looking for the spice, ignoring the masked Rare killing common, and become steward one day with any dignity? Even if I'm meant to be a symbol, I can't become someone who ignores things like that. Not for the Herd, not for anyone."

"Is *that* a threat?" he asked, turning the question back on me.

"Can't you just agree to help protect common from these masked Rare?"

"Of course I want to do that. But you're in no place to be making threats. Think about it. What's the 'or else?' Are you going to leave the Herd? Tell the king about us? Hurt all these common?"

"No," I admitted.

He put a hand on my shoulder. "You're a good kid. But you're still a *kid*. You can't do everything. Let me do my job. Trust *me* to worry about the masks. Can you do that?"

25

TRUST

HOURS LATER, AS I headed to The Steer's Snort, a pub on floor eleven of the Academy, I couldn't stop thinking about the conversation with Vanil. Asshole. If the Herd was going to exploit my moms and me, make up lies about us, the least they could is protect the people they claim to represent. But unless I found a way to empower myself further, I had no leverage. They already used my image and my words for their own ends. If I tried to steer common away from the Herd, they'd just claim I was trying to lower my profile around the Rare or something. My own words didn't belong to me. But if I found the spice, maybe I could hang it over their heads and force them to investigate the masks.

Laven waited at the bar, salsa and tortilla chips in front of him, two beers dripping condensation flanking the basket.

I'd paid an entire gold knuckle to send him a message via one of the trained carrier birds Rare often used, a hungry, brown-and-white feathered thing called a roadrunner which fed on lizards and bugs. I still hadn't gotten used to them, running faster than a man as I tried to walk peacefully through Rare districts. The first time I saw one flying up the Academy's central stair, I almost screamed. Who thought it was a good idea to let birds inside a tower?

Laven greeted my cut face and bruised eye like it was raw kale forced down his throat. "Scalding sun," he cursed. "I didn't realize how bad it was, mate."

I forced a smile and handed him an almond. "Good to see you too."

"Sorry." He reached into his bag, produced his notebook and a mint. "I took notes for you in Knifecraft."

"Thanks, I wasn't feeling up to going after everything," I lied. "Couldn't sleep much either. At least I got out of Military Matters."

Our server came, and I ordered spiced potato tacos for the third week in a row. They weren't as spicy or rich as Uncle Macen's, but they added something to them that provided a weirdly inviting bitterness, and you could add guavacado slices for an extra knuckle. Laven always treated me—he absolutely refused to let me pay—and he reiterated that money really was no object for him.

"You must really like them," Laven noted.

I shrugged. "You ever feel like you need to understand a taste? There's something bitter in them that I still can't place. It's bothering me."

"Before Sagen's class, no way. But now? Yeah, I get it."

When the server was out of earshot, I lowered my voice. "What happened after we split up last night?"

"Ran straight up the tower to Dyl's office. They were skeptical but followed me back down. By the time we got there, though, the freezer was completely empty."

So those common wouldn't be mourned. No final bite. Sneering into my mug, I said, "And what did Dyl do?"

"Took my bloody key, for one. But I think they took it seriously when I showed them into a restricted area. Too horrible to be a joke, ain't it? So they flagged down some other faculty and sent me off. I think the area's under observation now, but who knows if they'll actually investigate. My dad's raving, too. Dyl already told him about the key—as if that's the important bit—and he threatened to pull me out of here."

"Rares," I complained without thinking. Immediately, I realized what that sounded like. Halfway to treason. But Laven was my friend, and in my sleep-addled mind, anyone who was my friend was a common who hated Rares.

"A right bunch of gits," he agreed.

I proceeded cautiously as we ate, making small talk about our classes. If he said something like that about a common, I would've lost my mind. How could he be okay with what I'd said? Let alone agree?

I kept thinking about how Yenne had been working for the Herd this whole time and never told me. I couldn't shake suspicion, and I blurted, "Did your dad tell you to befriend me?"

Laven choked on his burger. "What?"

"You were nice to me the first day when everyone else called me a bastard and whatever. Your dad voted in my favor even though he only ever votes with the military and the High Consumer. Did he put you up to it?"

"That's a shite thing to ask, mate. But no. He told me about you after the Tribunal, but I already knew from the sheets. Everyone did. Well, except for the you not actually being a bastard bit. The sheets kept repeating that part. Dad told me the truth."

"Why, then? What do you get out of befriending me other than Rare hating you?"

"Already have that." Laven's face grew sullen—something damn near unnatural on him.

"Because your dad audits people?" I asked.

"More or less. Why do you care suddenly? Does this have to do with last night?"

I sighed and downed the dregs of my beer. "Kind of? Like, who were those people? They could've been anyone, yeah, but they were definitely *Rare*."

"As am I," he acknowledged. "Yeah, I get you, mate. People hate me because of my dad. Like you said. So much I'd been dreading coming here this year even though I love to cook. Right next to the

Military Academy? Full of gits my dad taxes the hell out of for the king's war. I think I told you people used to throw stuff at me?

"Truth is, mate, I knew you'd be ostracized, too. Took a risk that maybe the enemy of my enemy could be my friend, an' all that. All it cost me was some mints." His smile faltered. "But you'd rather stick with Yenne. Safer bet than some random Rare, ain't it?"

Did I rather?

No. Yenne kept things from me. Laven answered any question I asked. He shared *everything*.

"Can I trust you with something?" I said, tentatively. "About my greater?"

His eyes widened. "Lish, yeah, course."

"I want to make it again, but I'm missing an ingredient."

"What is it?"

"It doesn't have a name in this language." I described its taste and the tree it came from.

"Never heard of it." But he pulled a book out of his bag and flipped to the index in the back. "Don't tell anyone about this. I'm not technically supposed to have it."

"What *is* it?" I asked, leaning across the table. "And, seriously, anything else in that bag you aren't supposed to have?"

"It's a record of all the library books with restricted access," he answered. "I've been using it to try to find Chef Chikor's lessons ahead of time. So that I, uh, can be better than you in that class."

"I don't think you need to cheat for that." I chuckled.

"Nothing stands out," he said, a moment later, snapping it shut. "Where'd you get it?"

"A Semoli trader. She comes through the Commons from time to time."

"Semoli? Maybe from their peninsula then. Though I haven't heard of trees like that there. Don't remember seeing any either. I'll do some research."

"You've been there?"

"Yeah, once. Tons of Rare holiday there."

I'd heard of this thing, holiday. Supposedly, Rare could stop working for up to a month and even leave Ranch. I thought it was a common myth.

"There might be some here somewhere." I gestured to the tower. "I mean, if a common could get it, surely they have it here."

Laven left his burger in front of his face. "You want me to get my key back."

I hid my chagrin behind the final bite of my taco. The bitterness was coming into focus, its touch beginning to make sense. I hadn't realized it initially—the spiced and fried potatoes' texture subsumed them—but tiny chunks of nopales cactus strengthened the crunch. It'd been years since I'd had nopales, a favorite of Uncle Macen's.

When I swallowed, I decided to be honest. "If I don't find a way to recreate my recipe, *if I don't get that spice*, I can't protect common from those masked Rare. I don't know about you, but I couldn't sleep last night. I need to help."

Laven put his unfinished burger down. "I know what you mean. I'll do it. Can't risk grabbing the key again so soon, but I'll do research in the meantime and get it eventually. You have my word."

"Thank you. Seriously."

He clinked his beer against mine. "Cheers, mate."

26

TECHNIQUE

I BARELY MADE it to my shift at the Academy House on time, fatigue and dread slowing my pace. I'd screwed up our line. Might've even delayed service the night before. *To the king.* Chef was going to kill me, *should* kill me.

That guilt surprised me. Before working there, I wouldn't have ever cared about messing up a Rare's day. If anything, I'd hoped to. But even though Ilantra was a cold Rare, the type common sometimes called raw, I cared about the prestige of her kitchen.

My kitchen.

It'd become as much a home as Cutler's shop. Neither stood even with my moms' apartment in Common-3, obviously, but even though I was only doing dishes and counting inventory, I was essential to the team. It was important, and I'd failed it.

Chef's hair was up for a demonstration when I arrived, which drove a deeper spike into my gut. A tower of dishes wobbled next to my station as the other chefs passed it on their way to Ilantra's station. They'd get to learn with her while I cleaned up before tonight's service, and I'd fall even more behind. Never getting the respect I'd need to earn a cooking position. But Winta's arm caught me on my way to the dishes.

191

"I'm proud of you," Chef announced. "One of us revealed a weakness last night, and the first response from all of you was to fill in. Our service stayed on time, and the king expressed his satisfaction with both the tartare and the mousse. So much so, he wishes to do a demonstration for you all in a couple weeks."

"We get to meet the king?" the third-year pastry chef asked, but all I could think was, not the bisque?

"If he has the time. But that's not all. I've canceled tonight's service and prepared a special demonstration for you tonight. We did well, and the king appreciated the meal, but I saw desperation last night. Twinges of chaos. All of you have room for improvement."

I sulked. Whatever this was, I was going to miss it.

"What defines our cuisine?" Chef asked.

Perplexed looks answered her silently until the second-year garden chef, Bayle, ventured, "The ingredients and flavors we use?"

Chef shrugged, noncommittal.

"How it tastes compared to other cuisines?" suggested the second-year fry cook.

"And climate," said the pastry chef. "It determines what we have available."

"Technique, Chef," answered Winta.

"Technique," Chef agreed. "Everything we serve thrives on technique. How we cut, how we flavor, how we grill. When. How long. At what temperature. Anyone can make a burger. It's how we do it that defines us."

Chef produced ingredients, the most obvious being a dozen tomatoes. I started to slink toward my station, but Chef called out. "You, too, stage."

"What about the dishes, Chef?" I asked.

"You'll get to them after. Even if you're here all night."

Everyone laughed, but I couldn't keep a grin off my face. I wouldn't be falling behind.

"What do you see?" Chef asked, eyes on me but motioning toward the ingredients.

Including the tomatoes, I considered what to make with green bell pepper, carrots, olive oil, garlic, some herbs I couldn't identify at distance, and onions. "Are there chilis roasting somewhere, Chef? It looks almost like a salsa."

"Who's visited Semoli?" Chef asked. "Paprick hasn't."

A couple hands rose, and embarrassment colored my cheeks. I should've known she'd use any opportunity to humiliate me.

"Bayle, what do *you* see?"

"A semoli pasta sauce, Chef?"

Chef slapped the cutting board in front of her. "Paprick sees salsa because the way he sees these ingredients, the techniques he would use *here*, typically produce salsa. I asked you about Semoli, so your mind switched to a different technique. Had I asked about the Empire of the Badgeboar, what then?"

Winta said, "I would've asked if we were making a curry, Chef."

"Exactly. This evening, I'm going to teach you the traditional Semoli techniques used to produce a marina sauce. Then we'll make a badge curry. As we make them, think about what each teaches us about red salsa."

"I don't understand, Chef," said Bayle. "We know how to make salsa. How do these teach us anything?"

"Last night, I asked you all to prepare a lobster bisque. What does it have in common with these dishes?"

Everyone nodded, even me. It was making sense now.

"By my standards, you added lobster to a scalding salsa. Unacceptable. The king expressed satisfaction with the tartare and the mousse. That means he hated the bisque. And I can't blame him. Now, wash up and take a station. Stage, make sure each has these ingredients exactly."

"Yes, Chef!" we all called.

"Fires hot!"

"Knives sharp!"

193

"Plates clean," Ilantra finished. "Let's bloody learn."

I scrambled to set the stations, ignoring the dishes created with each demonstration. One of my biggest shames, though, is that I didn't really *get* her lesson that night. I learned how to make the dishes, sure, but Chef wanted us to see how making each influenced the others. Other than that Semoli squeezed their tomatoes into pots rather than dice them, I didn't see Chef's point.

It was even more humbling than the tower of dishes.

She'd told us there was a point, and that meant there starving was. At least I wasn't the only one who missed it. As he brought his dishes to me after, Bayle admitted the same.

"Bloody evil, she is, always asking questions rather than telling us the answers. At least Chikor and Sagen spell it out for us thick ones. I haven't the foggiest what we were supposed to learn from this, you?"

Contemplating the question, I caught up on inventory and dishes—two nights' worth now. My sink stank like rot and ruin, and I gagged on approach. Not because it was really that bad, but you have to understand, I hate the idea of left-out dishes. At home, I do a dish the moment I finish my meal if I can, if not while cooking. The idea that little bugs and who knows what else could crawl around on there and lay eggs or multiply…

When the Butcher, the Bone Lord, the man who supposedly slew a drakephon singlehandedly, shudders with disgust over dirty dishes, the archivist falls into a fit of uncontrollable laughter.

"Starve," the Butcher complains, but the curse lacks conviction to the archivist's ear. It certainly wasn't a command.

Alone and free for the first time since seeing the common butchered the night before, I channeled my anger and grief into ripping grime from those dishes like they were the heads of masked Rare. I scraped the gristle from pans like I would scrape a knife across their throats. I was so engulfed in my work I didn't hear anyone enter the kitchen.

"Howdy, killer."

Fear and shock shot through me so quickly, I didn't even think. I took the cast iron pan I was salting and swung it around like a hammer. Cori deftly managed to dodge out of the way, never in any real danger, but the glower she sent my way was sharper than any knife in this kitchen.

"Simmer down," she said, throwing up her hands, and dropping the habanero she'd brought.

My heartbeat thundered in my chest. "Don't do that!" I rasped. "Locusts, I almost killed you."

"As if you could." Cori shrugged, but there was definitely more distance between us now than there had been when I swung. She reached into a pouch and produced another pepper. "Peace offering?"

I cast about to make sure we were alone. But the kitchen was long cold. "What are you doing here?" The last time I'd seen Cori, she'd been courting me into the Herd alongside Vanil, and while I'd joked and flirted and felt something for her at the Factory, things were different. She was part of the Herd, and I didn't know if the Factory had been an act.

I hoped it wasn't.

"I heard about last night and wanted to come check on you." She leaned against the island opposite my sinks and plucked an apple from a basket. As Cori chomped down, I noticed a wince and a bruise against the corner of her jaw, mostly concealed with makeup that also covered the scar across her nose.

The concern for me, my feelings from before, the clear pain she was in—I don't know which got the better of me. Maybe they all did. But I deflated. I could reckon with the Herd stuff later.

"What happened?" I asked, instinctively reaching up to touch the bruise.

Cori eyed my approaching hand like it was the most curious object in the world, one eyebrow rising high into her tumble of curls. I cleared my throat and pulled my hand back, drawing a chuckle.

As every boy should, I glared my way through a blush and repeated myself. "What are you doing here, really?" It didn't have half the scorn the first one carried, and I tossed her an almond.

"Besides enjoying your wonderful nuts?" she joked, and again I blushed. She went serious. "You killed someone. I needed to check on you."

"Really?"

"Really."

"Aren't you worried someone will see you? This is a Rare district."

She motioned to her clothes, which I admit I hadn't paid much notice to, her bruise drawing so much of my attention. She wore an ankle-length white jacket over a partially buttoned man's shirt—also white—that rolled over the three-quarter-length sleeves of her jacket and a pair of high-waisted white shorts fastened over a large black belt buckle, which was complemented and also somehow thrown off by black military-style boots. From the belt hung her Factory flatknife, scabbarded like a sword. Rare could get away with wearing weapons, but it shocked me she'd chosen a flattknife. Any Rare looked too close, and there'd be questions.

The attire wasn't exactly fashionable for a woman, not like Yenne's exquisite dresses. But I liked it. It was unique, fresh. Like she was. And it was definitely Rare quality. Paired with Cori's shove-off expression, it was unlikely any Rare would look close enough to ask those questions.

My gaze lingered too long to go unnoticed, and when it returned to Cori's face, a knowing eyebrow waggle met my gaze. "Paprick," she teased, drawling my name with such slowness I ached. "I know it's been a minute since I've graced you with my presence, but it's impolite to stare. What would people think?"

I babbled an apology that only earned me more chuckles and promptly returned to my dishes. "I appreciate you checking on me, but it was unnecessary," I said, smiling. "It was self-defense. I have nothing to feel guilty about."

"Are you sure?" Cori rotated to press her back against the sink, moving right beside me. Close enough that if I kept washing, it would splash against her jacket.

I stopped. "Should I feel guilty? He killed common."

"That's not my place to say. Killin'… hurts. Feeling upset, guilty, anything, that's valid."

I shook my head. "I can't get his face out of my mind. But I don't understand why. I want them to pay, all of them. Their victims deserve justice. So why should I be haunted by it? I did the right thing."

Silently, she pulled me into a hug, just like Vanil had. But it was different. More genuine. Real. Her firm, calloused hands stroked my spine as my breath stuttered out, and all at once, I felt validated. When she let me go, I almost imagined I could sleep.

"Doin' the right thing don't mean it feels right. I take it you haven't seen your moms since?"

"Haven't had time."

"Make sure you find it. You don't have to carry things alone."

I nodded, but I couldn't imagine telling my moms I'd killed someone. Did Cori have that kind of relationship with hers? Did she have parents here? I was about to ask, but I found her smirking again. I was starting to really appreciate that look, and the play in her eyes said she knew it. Cheeks warming, I returned to my dishes. For all my bravery in standing before the Tribunal and killing a man, I couldn't deal with the eager emotions Cori stirred.

Not that I was inexperienced. I'd kissed enough common to lose count, boys, girls, and otherwise. But my moms had raised me to be respectful and patient. Famines, I did not want to be patient right then. I wanted to flick the soap from my fingers, close the two steps to Cori, lift her onto the kitchen island, and—

⁓

The archivist groans.

"And give her something to smirk about," the Butcher completes, smiling.

But that wasn't me. I was the first one in TOF to raise my hand with an answer, the first one to run into a fight, the first one to do almost anything if I could. I liked being first. But when it came to romance, I always moved second. It's the uncertainty. When I know the answer, I plunge forward. When I know someone needs to be protected, I interpose myself. But I second-guessed myself with Cori continuously. What if she was just naturally flirty? What if I was misreading?

"It's been a while. Whatcha been up to?" I asked to clear my mind.

"I was on hunting duty for a minute. Went up to the Scorched Val to capture some wild carnephon for the Herd with a team. Got three in as many weeks."

"That's north of the Front," I said. "Y'all can get through that?"

She smirked. "Easily. The hard part is getting on the back of a bucking bull twenty meters off the ground. You ever ride a bison? Not easy. Even harder to jump off one."

I finally gave up on doing the dishes and faced Cori. "You're taking the piss."

"Well, well, only been a couple months and you've already mastered Rare lingo? You're not plowing new fields, are you, Bessa?"

I startled. I had been spending a lot of time with Laven. "Okay, first off, don't call me that. It's weird when you do it. But no, definitely not changing sides. You really hunted carnephon from the back of a bison?"

"I wanted to take you, but Vanil wouldn't risk it. Barely approved me. But I'm back now, and you get a two-week break coming up between this term and next, right? To celebrate the Flyover?"

"Yeah, but I'll be working," I groused. "Doubt I'll even get the festival off."

"Did I miss something, or didn't you get elevated out of your indenture?"

"I need groceries, supplies for next term, and I've been wanting to change the layout of Cutler's shop. Wait, speaking of, are you still indentured to the Factory?"

"No. Legally speaking, I never existed." Cori tossed the apple core into the compost next to my station. "What if there was something more fun planned for your break?"

"Like what?"

"A party in the Commons that ain't likely to be forgotten."

"You want me to go with you? What happened to 'too old for you?'"

"With? Why, Paprick," she said as she got closer. Much closer. "Are you implying I'm asking you on a date?" Her fingers walked up the center of my chest. Stopped at my clavicle. "Former coworkers. Rebel spies." Lips leaning closer. "What would people think?"

I gasped, hot, and she pulled away, laughing without shame. "Maybe I am. You're not interested?"

"I am," I said quickly—too quickly to get away without Cori giggling. "But I can't that night. I need the knuckles, and there's no way Chef would let me miss the festival shift. Chefs don't get holidays. Another time?"

She shrugged. "I'll talk to Vanil about your finances. If he can give me the knuckles for this outfit just to come check on you, he can help you out. Besides, I think it's important you spend time with our people if you're going to lead them one day. And it won't be all play. You'll have a job to do."

I wasn't sure how I'd get out of the festival shift, and I didn't want to leave Cutler without help. Until I remembered that he hadn't trusted me to watch the shop. But there were still the masked people, and Laven was looking into the spice for me. And I'd also hoped to see my moms during the break. Famines, there was too much going on with my life.

199

"If you did come…" she said after a beat.

"Yeah?"

"We'd be out pretty late. Too late for you to come back, even. You'd probably need a place to sleep, and well… I'm told you inherited common sense."

That damn near sealed it. I wouldn't miss it for anything. "What would my job be?"

"Simmer down, killer. That's a surprise."

I should've hated that nickname. I didn't want to be a killer, but the way she said it, the look in her eyes. I sighed and returned to my dishes, far too many thoughts in my mind. Cori's smirk high among them.

ENTREMET III

CONFLICTS AND INTERESTS

"WE ARE HERE for a particular reason, Butcher. Need I remind you?"

"As I understand the letter of the law," he counters, "they who call upon the Rite are afforded the opportunity to explain away the infractions for which they are being charged. I *just* explained one of the murders, and I think we can both agree that the first was self-defense."

"You and I both know you'll never be cleared. If anything, this Rite is your last chance to define your legacy. Yet you spit on it to remember when you got your cherries jubileed."

"'Cherries jubileed'," he remarks. "I like that. Mind if I use it?"

"We have serious work to do."

"Serious?" he complains. "You search for a mythical god and call it serious?"

"That isn't for you to decide," the archivist argues. "And you call the kettle black. I don't know why you're here, but it isn't to prove your innocence and it isn't to chronicle your courtship."

"How would you know? You Rare never believed I invented Emphon Rub or any of the others, not really. You think someone told

201

me, and if not someone, the Source. To think your Rare berate the emphonists for worshiping the emphon."

"Don't compare me to faunatics," the archivist retorts, too sharp and easy for the slur to be infantile in its use.

"Seriously?" He shakes his head. "You call me Butcher and throw that word around?"

The archivist glowers. "I staked my life on there being more to this story than what we've all heard. I don't record this for my health or even my archives. I do it because the Source is the only thing that is going to save this country from the Empheron. So, yes, I grow frustrated."

Slowly, the Butcher rises to his feet and approaches the bars. The archivist joins him, taking pen and book. It is the closest they've stood in nearly ten years.

"What do you know of the Empheron?" the Butcher asks.

The archivist fights a smile. So that's his game. "What do you know of the Source?"

A moment later, the archivist sits back behind the desk, head swimming as if coming from a dream. "What did you just do?"

The Butcher, now slumped at the back of his cell, runs a hand through his limp hair. "Your eyes lost focus. Are you feeling well?"

"I don't know what you're up to, but this gambit may be my last. I won't stand for more flippancy."

The Butcher sneers. "So many of the people in this story died because they knew me. And not *because* of me. Because of you and your masks! You accuse me of flippancy?"

"No more bullshit. No more waxing poetic about Cori because 'all good stories need romance.'"

"Most good stories *do* need romance," he insists. "Because the heart makes us do things that the brain cannot, and it's in *those* actions that the most important discoveries are made."

"If this comes to nothing, I will burn those pages," vows the archivist. "I don't know why you care they be written, but I can think of no other reason that you'd invoke the Rite than to demand it. It'll be the last thing I do, and I'll do it proudly."

"Fine, you want the meat and potatoes?" The Butcher returns to his seat on the cold, stone floor of his prison. "Then perhaps we should cover some ground quickly."

27

QUICKLY

TWO WEEKS SEPARATED me from the Flyover Festival, but among them lay finals designed to cull our class by half. If I failed even one, I risked being cast back down into the common—assuming I wasn't killed to protect my secrets.

I had to pare a fruit platter into flowers for Knifecraft, disarm Vyson blindfolded in Military Matters, correctly identify the tastebud breakdown of obscure flavors like piquant and name a baker's dozen of sources for TOF, *and* demonstrate a brain-breaking spherification technique in Alchemic Gastronomy. None as frustrating as the propaganda paper I had to write for History and Logic. Without Laven, Yenne, or Sleepless Salad, I wouldn't have survived.

Meanwhile, Laven discovered a few interesting things about Ruda's spice, the most important being a paper so thoroughly redacted that only the description of the spice's flavor revealed the paper's relevance. Thankfully, the byline hadn't been redacted, so we knew Dean Dyl authored it, which was a lead he could pursue.

What else? Oh, yeah, turned out the king planned to do his demo Flyover afternoon, so we had to cancel service that evening, which got me out of work.

Before the Butcher can continue, blades clash in the hall, and a Rare guard, bleeding, crashes into the jail to bar the door behind him. Several hands burst through, stopping the gap, and the guard can only resist as the door is slowly forced open to reveal common with rolling pins for clubs. One strikes down at the guard's arm, snapping her bone with a *crack*.

The archivist leaps forward, driving a knife into the attacker's side through the door.

The Butcher whistles, impressed.

Several more thrusts stab through the gap, rapid and rabid as the archivist returns to training long abandoned. The common pull back, giving the guard enough room to close it fully.

Shouts echo down the hall followed by footsteps as the archivist returns to the desk.

After a minute, another out-of-breath guard enters the room. "We've pushed them out."

"Good," the archivist says, before turning to the Butcher. "Disappointed?"

He shrugs. "The only disappointment appears to be your guards. If I were you, I'd start thinking about what might happen if real soldiers show up."

The archivist stiffens. "Alert the commander. There may be more happening here."

"Of course," the guard says before saluting.

With a frown, the archivist motions for the Butcher to continue. The Source, the archivist remembers. It's all that matters.

"You were saying, Butcher?"

With finals finished, we celebrated. Students flocked to the pubs within the central tower, and beer rained from the taps. Most Rare left the pub the moment I entered, but I liked it better that way. Laven,

Yenne, and I celebrated with a pub crawl that displaced half the tower, and by the time we were done, we were so drunk Yenne admitted she was in love with her mysterious partner, whoever they were.

For Laven and me, it was the first step toward achieving our dreams to become Chefs. Not only had we taken the step, we'd leapt to the finish line in style, crushing our exams because of how we complemented each other—his knowledge of gastro, mine of knifecaft, our combined love for TOF. As we drank, we confessed as much to each other, promising to stick by each other's side in every kitchen we could. I think that promise was largely responsible for the zeal with which Laven pursued the spice over break. I barely saw him—not that I was around much either—and when he missed our regular pub lunch, I realized I had no real way of contacting him. I didn't see him again until after the Festival.

But we'll get back to that.

In the meantime, I worked myself ragged, spending a week completely reorganizing Cutler's for my own sanity, and slaving away in the Academy House, which overflowed with Rare from across the country who came for the festival.

Though we had a date scheduled for the Festival, Cori was no stranger. Practically a bodyguard, really, escorting me from Cutler's to the Academy and back, and helping me find time to visit my moms. I got to make Sleepless Salad for the pair of them, and we spent the whole night sharing all that'd transpired during my term, sipping tea and licking the last dewdrops of ice cream from our spoons. It was nice, just casually walking around with Cori, relaxing into each other's company. Without it, I think I would've been so nervous about the date, I would've ruined it.

Plus, seeing Cori carry her flatsaw as a sword inspired me to carry my cleaversaw while in Rare districts. Rare didn't like it, and I often had to show my ID to EDBs sent to disarm me, but I wasn't going to let that dissuade me from protecting myself.

I hadn't forgotten those masked people.

And as it would turn out, they hadn't forgotten me either.

28

KING
CONSOMMÉ

ON THE AFTERNOON of Flyover, Cori, Yenne, and I came down the central stair of the Academy. Though they'd both been in the Herd since Cori got to Ranch, they hadn't spent much time together until Yenne started watching me for Vanil and Cori got back. The first time we hung out as a group, it took them ten minutes to realize they shared a mutual passion for making fun of me, and they'd become fast friends. So much so that Cori had just spent the last two hours doing Yenne's hair for a date with her mysterious partner that night.

"This damn humidity better not mess it up," Cori was saying as she finished the final check of Yenne's new style.

My eyes flicked to the adjacent hall, which led to the substacks, but it was as still and dusty as usual. I checked before and after every shift, a dark, hungry part of me hoping I'd see a mask in the darkness, but that wouldn't be the afternoon.

Instead, Yenne and Cori headed back to the Commons, and I proceeded around the corner to the Academy House's staff entrance, nearly slamming into Vyson, who guarded the door alongside another carver.

"You." He scowled, the bruise on his cheek especially green so close to his Enduring yellow eyes.

"Howdy, teach," I said with as much common accent as I could muster. "How's that bruise? I'd've thought it'd heal by now. Must've *really* hurt."

It was too much, even for me, and Vyson lost it, slamming a baton into my gut with the full force of his Endurance. The wind shot from my lungs, and all my training—his training—evaporated from my mind. My muscles crumpled.

Before I could regain my feet, he wrenched my cleaversaw from my back. "How dare you attempt to bring a weapon before the king, you scalding cockroach. I should kill you right bloody here. Do us all the favor."

"Lieutenant," cautioned the other carver, though not out of remorse for me. "The king specifically mentioned his desire to speak with the carrion tonight."

Vyson dragged me up and slammed me into the wall. "Well, we better make sure he stands tall then."

I shoved myself free of his grasp and pointed to the cleaversaw. "I'll have that back when I leave."

"You'll never see this blasphemous excuse for a weapon again, cockroach. Not unless it's back at the Factory where you belong. Now get inside. His Majesty's waiting."

I shouldered through him and into the kitchen, where most of the staff already waited. Several more carvers stood at attention around the perimeter, disrupting the hyper-efficient space. At the central station, where Chef normally stood alone to do demonstrations, she practically disappeared into the shadow of King Fennel III.

His muscular frame made Vyson look like a common. Shoulders and arms pushed against his tightly fitted chef's jacket, the buttons threatened by his barrel chest. On his back, he carried a double-headed, polished chrome hammer. Like a meat tenderizer, one head threatened exsanguinating pain by way of pyramid-shaped studs, while the other did things the old-fashioned way with a flat bone-breaking mallet. I doubted I could even swing it without Endurance.

Far more threatening were his eyes. Enduring, of course, but maliciously dark like his hair and twice as flat. Bagged and exhausted in a way I'd rarely, if ever, seen on a Rare. The weight of an entire kingdom seemed to hang in their shadows, which surprised me. I hold no empathy for him, not even today, knowing what I know, but famines and locusts, did I ever recognize the toll of nightmare and pain in those eyes.

When I entered, he turned their full attention on me, and I stopped in place, chilled as if I'd walked into his Factory without my butcher's suit.

"It's customary for one to bow before his king, but total shock and awe? I knew I'd like you, butcher." His voice scoured like lemon and vinegar. Overpowering, closer to a cleaning solution than a hint of acidity balancing a dish. The way he called me butcher back then, I *knew* it was an insult, like he was refusing to give me a name or accept I was anything more than the factory boy.

Belatedly, I bowed. Even I'm not that raving.

He motioned casually for me to join the staff. "You and I will speak after, but first, I will demonstrate the only acceptable way to prepare the most technically difficult dish on the planet: bull emphon consommé, or as my servants say—and I admit I'm partial to the alliteration— carnephon consommé."

I naturally rejected the king's declaration that it was going to be that difficult. I didn't know what a consommé was, but it couldn't be that bad. Plus, in no circumstance is there ever *only one* acceptable way to prepare anything. The starving arrogance to even say so.

Famines and locusts was it hard. I *hated* that it very well might have been the most difficult dish I'd ever prepared. But what annoyed me more—and got me thinking—was that carnephon consommé didn't have an Endurance effect. Here was something so technical, so difficult, that when we produced ours, even Chef's was slightly imperfect. Winta, the best of us students, was barely in the same color palette, and mine? Awful. All that, and it didn't even add Endurance.

Chef mentioned offhand that it was used in some greaters as the main source of endurium, but I couldn't even imagine what kind of Chef would risk a greater recipe on a consommé they were as likely to ruin as to produce.

It made me realize that *meat* wasn't everything. You couldn't just add it and get powerful. Sure, I'd learned that months before when I tried to invent a greater with stolen carnephon shank, but, to use a Semoli expression, I'd been throwing spaghetti at the wall and hoping it stuck. Now, I was learning that even technical perfection wasn't a guarantee.

It made me wonder *how* one took emphon and turned it into a greater recipe.

But I wouldn't get long to wonder because the king made good on his threat. When everyone had presented their results and he'd critiqued them, his words sharp and cruel, he dismissed everyone but Chef and me for a private conversation.

"I must admit, butcher, I'd been looking forward to meeting you. The way the High Consumer describes you, I imagined a three-meter devil frothing at the mouth with blood. You're barely more than a child. Tall, but not that tall."

I didn't respond. How would I? Besides, every time he spoke my teeth clenched. That voice. Those eyes. My gods.

"Speak when spoken to, common!" the king demanded.

"Yes, Your Majesty," I said, rebelliously obedient.

He laughed. "I love how you lot turn those words into a curse. Truly. Does it irk you, common, to have climbed so far and still lack any authority? Ilantra tells me you're little more than a pathetic busboy. You who invented the first greater recipe in a generation."

"I'm quite pleased with my position here, Your Majesty. Chef is unparalleled."

He sneered. "*Chef* is unparalleled in her lack of creativity, I'll give you that. Tell me, Chef, has anyone failed to produce an original greater as often as you?"

"I can't say, Your Majesty."

"Yet you so often lecture, so tediously question." He turned back to me, rolling his eyes. "Speaking of questions, common, I have many for you. Vyson!"

Lt. Vyson strutted gleefully into the room.

"Hold him."

Before I could react, Vyson pinned my arms behind my back, executing his hold with Enduring speed.

"Let's start with a simple one," the king said as he sharpened a carving knife. "Have you touched the Source?"

"The wha—"

A pain like a paring knife into my brain stole the words before they were out of my mouth. His question, even sharper, even more acidic, burned inside my head, speaking from within like fire. *Have you touched the Source, cockroach?*

"I don't know what that is!" I shouted, my head searing.

The king tilted his head, considering. Behind him, Chef looked away.

"From whom did you steal your greater recipe?"

Again, he asked the question in my mind, his words burning like the sludge they poured on Bessa, a flame meant to prolong suffering.

"No one!" I stammered to make it stop. I had to make it stop. It was unlike any pain I'd survived before, worse.

"How, then?"

My mind felt scraped by his knife as he tried to carve out my memories. I saw flashes of that night in Tall Grass. My memories of Uncle Macen's tacos. The flavors whirling around me. Somehow, some instinct told me I had to close off the thought of Ruda's spice, to hide it. I thought of my moms. Just as I did every night before staving off the nightmares.

He smiled lasciviously. "Mums, eh? I enjoy multiple women. Maybe I'll bring them to me."

"I'll kill you," I promised.

"You dare threaten your king?" He slapped me so hard the sound rang off the copper pots hanging above the island beside us. Pain stung up the side of my face, but it was nothing against the pain searing through my skull from within.

How did you make it? His words were coldly calm, but the force of his need screamed into my brain.

"I don't know," I whispered. "Please, I don't know."

His next words didn't come into my head that time, and famines, how I thanked him for the reprieve even as I cursed him. He stepped close, and I smelled the familiar buttery death of lobster bisque on his breath. "Have you found the recipe for control?"

Vanil had called it Chili Control. Did he know I was looking for it?

"No," I admitted.

"No," he agreed, patting me on the cheek. "Vyson, release him. I wouldn't want him to miss the festivities. Roaches get one day off a year. Be a shame if his mums missed him for it."

I fell out of Vyson's arms like a bag of flour, but he gave me a kick for good measure.

"Kneel before your king, cockroach."

I tried not to groan, desperate not grant them the satisfaction as the king removed parchment and quickly scribbled something. I'd talked myself out of killing him when he came to Chef's House for his starving lobster, but I promised myself I'd do it. Maybe not today, but someday. He thought he could silence us, call us roaches? I'd cut out his tongue and leave his body so grotesque not even roaches would touch it.

He passed the parchment to Vyson, and then said, "It was an absolute disappointment, butcher. Enjoy your silly festival."

When they left, Chef scrambled away quickly, returning before I even regained my feet.

"Milk," she said, handing me a cup.

"You just watched him," I said, condemning her even as I accepted the offering.

She stared away from me so long I expected no answer, but eventually, she turned back and said, "I'm not a knife, kid. The best I can do is sharpen the steel around me."

I regarded her, noting for the first time how old she really was. Not ancient like Cutler, but older than Mother. Just as tired.

"What's the Source?" I asked.

"Some nonsense he raves about from time to time. Says his ancestor, Almon, touched it."

"Almon, the first king of Panchon?"

"Yes, stage, the one who invented Chili Control and a dozen other greater recipes. Who founded this very academy."

Inventing Chili Control was a lie, but I didn't tell her that. "Why did he ask if I touched it?"

She took the glass from me. "Go enjoy the festival. I'll do the dishes."

With Vyson's threat and the king willing to assault me in front of other Rare, I wouldn't risk traveling to Cutler's unarmed. As Ilantra started the dishes, I slid a butcher's cleaver free of the knifeblock at the carving station and tucked it between my waistband and back. The steel was cold, and if I shifted too much, sharp against my ass cheek, but the comfort was unparalleled.

"He asked you if you touched it, truly?" the archivist asks.

"Does that surprise you?"

The archivist ignores the question. "And did you answer truthfully? Had you touched it?"

A sigh escapes the Butcher like a dying breath. "Do you enjoy asking the same question repeatedly? I swear, you're no better than he was. Should I treat you the way I treated him?"

"Be my guest. Get on your knees and beg for more meaningless lives."

213

The Butcher's eyes flash from within his cage. "They weren't meaningless."

"So you insist. But let's hurry this up. I'm sure you're eager to overindulge about your perfect Cori and your insufferable teen insta-love."

"Oh, I can't hardly wait, but first we have to go talk to Cutler. Or would you rather I not share what I would learn about the Source that night?"

"What?" The archivist nearly drops the pen. "What would Cutler know of the Source?"

"Listen closely," the Butcher mocks.

29

WHAT CUTLER KNOWS

ON THE NIGHT of the autumn equinox, the largest of the twelve emphon flies directly over Ranch, crossing from the northwest to the southeast, like clockwork. Its passage signifies the start of hurricane season, when a storm could whip off Panchon's east coast without warning and decimate Commons and fields alike. I always found it odd that we celebrated its arrival, but I realize now that common celebrated the season. Hurricanes *could* come, but rain almost always came in its wake, and that meant coolness, water, and reprieve for common working the arid fields that grew our survival.

The combination of Rare telescopes and the plateau's altitude made it the best place to observe the Flyover. The district's narrow streets thronged with Rare, many of which had traveled hundreds of kilometers to celebrate, drink, and spend money earned on our backs. Even with my cleaversaw and height, I had trouble pushing through to Cutler's, and by the time I made it, I was worried I'd miss my first—and maybe only—chance at ever actually seeing the Flyover.

Cutler threw a walnut at me as I ducked into the store. Ready, I caught it and tossed back an almond. It'd been a few days since I'd been in, but the new layout already felt familiar. I'd been angry with

Cutler after he shared his lack of trust that day, weeks before, but time had numbed the sting. I'd come around to accepting he was right, and decided to get back at him by messing with the layout. I doubt he realized what I was doing at first, but by the time I was finished, he couldn't find a godsdamned thing in that store without me.

"Where's my telescope?" he barked the moment I arrived.

"Row three, column four, shelf five," I said, as if it were obvious. "Don't tell me you couldn't find it."

"I'll find you," he threatened, scurrying into row three.

"One," I counted. "Two…"

"Damn it, papwit, I can't reach that!"

Beaming, I followed him into the aisle and retrieved it. "How foolish of me to put it out of your reach."

"So clever," Cutler mocked. "Wait until Soryl gets back from the Front next week. You'll regret pushing me around then. They'll slap the arrogance right out of you."

Besides the name and pronouns, the only thing Cutler'd mentioned about his kid was that they were a conscientious objector to the war, serving only as a medic. As I understood it, Rare couldn't be required to serve, but something Soryl had done had gotten them sent anyway. I'd yet to find out what.

Cutler hurried upstairs. Twilight grasped much of the city, the mountains to the west casting shadows that touched all but the palace roof and the whole of Fen's Plateau. That late sunlight contributed to the plateau's viewing advantage, and despite the lingering effects and ringing head from my encounter with the king, I was giddy with excitement.

You can't see the Flyover from the Commons. Even if you managed to get to a roof, which would be packed with celebrations, the darkness and the distance made it impossible. Sure, a handful every year claimed to see it, but each one had a different, ridiculous description for the god among emphon. Up here with Cutler's telescope though? I'd finally see it. Cutler's adobe was one of only a few two-story buildings in the district, and the only with a flat roof. The crowded streets around it radiated with jealous murmurs as we climbed up, telescope in hand.

Other than that, it was surprisingly hushed. Rare parents assuring the children on their shoulders that they'd see. Unnaturally quiet for a holiday. On Flyover, the Commons resounded with guitars and drums. Half were kids with pots and spoons, sure, but the tenements danced. Maybe because we weren't focused on trying to see. Maybe because we needed it in a way Rare didn't. Probably both.

"What's it look like?" I asked.

"You really haven't seen it?" Cutler grumbled. "Ridiculous. Absolutely ridiculous they don't let you on top of the tenements they make you build."

Ever since Cutler restricted me from running the shop that day, he'd opened up about the inequalities between Rare and common. I think, at first, he worried he'd drive me away by saying the wrong thing or by pointing out my status. But now that we'd gotten past that dispute, he spoke more freely about his opinion of the divide.

For one, he hated the idea of Rare and common. "When this shop was founded," he said the day we finished reorganizing the shop, "everyone was a rancher. That was it. All that mattered. Wasn't until that upstart Panchon came around and decided some people were better than others that you ever heard the word 'rare' outside of a restaurant." And I think that meant something to him. He was always yammering on about the plateau's history and its supposed importance.

"Are you going to tell me what I'm looking for?" I prodded, pointing at the telescope.

"Of course not. Why the hells would I? I brought a damn telescope for a reason, almond-brain. Look around. You'll know."

It hadn't occurred to me that I'd be the one using it.

"Oh, don't look at me like that. I've seen it two hundred times already."

"How much longer?" I asked.

217

He scrunched his gaze toward the sky, tilted his head as if listening, and said, "Two minutes."

We used the time effectively, him not-so-politely instructing me on how to use the telescope. When finally I got the hang of it, he told me to use my naked eye first so I didn't end up missing it by staring at the wrong cloud, and then he pointed northwest.

At first, it was nothing but a silhouette against the darkening sky. Vaguely lizard-shaped, in that it had a pair of limbs toward the front half of its thin, serpentine body. But unlike a lizard, its wings extended wider than it was long, and its tail was at least four times the length of its head and torso. When I spotted it through the telescope, I gasped. Twisting antlers like those on a stag sprouted from a flat, snakelike face. I don't know why I expected its head to resemble a carnephon's, figured they were related I guess, but other than the scales—black, purple, and teal—and feathered wings of the same color, it barely resembled Bessa.

As it approached, wings rippling, more detail came into focus: finlike ears, thin and papery trailing in the wind, three hooked fans protruding either side of its thin lips, a knuckled knob of teal scales at the end of its tail, threatening as the king's hammer, and some strange, moving dots that seemed to fly around it. When it passed directly overhead, those dots came into focus, and my body went cold with fear.

They were vultures. Vultures, which I knew to have wingspans of two or more meters, were *dots* against the enormity of this thing. If it landed, it would sit on the whole of Ranch like a roost.

"How big is it?" I stammered.

"Hmm, that one? I'd say something like two hundred meters from snout to tail. Maybe two hundred and fifty from wing to wing."

Incomprehensible, and yet I was seeing it.

"Still smaller than the older dolphon in the Bay of Semoli though. Those ladies can get up to three hundred meters long in the deeper parts."

One enormous emphon was enough. "What could they eat? Famines, what do they taste like?"

"That drakephon will eat four or five bulls or badgeboar on its trip, then sleep for a couple days. Maybe go pick a fight with a herd of emphalope when it wakes up."

"You know where it's going?" I asked.

He seemed to consider whether he wanted to answer for a long while. "Aye. It's headed back to the Source. Never did figure out why it leaves at the start of summer. It probably knows even it can't handle the heat and flies to the mountains to mate with the other one, but I never made it up that way."

I dropped the telescope. Could it really be a coincidence? The same day the king asked me about the Source, Cutler brings it up?

"Hey, that's fragile!" He scooped it up and threw another walnut at my head. "No respect these days."

"What's the Source?" I asked tentatively.

"Of your idiocy? Even I can't say," he deflected.

"Cutler," I said. "What is the Source?"

"Nothing you need worry about. Forget I mentioned it."

"The king attacked me today. He asked me if I'd touched it. Cutler, what is it? How can this be a coincidence?"

"He what?" Cutler froze, one foot on the stair back into the shop. "He said, 'touched?' You're sure."

"Yes."

Sighing, Cutler motioned back into the shop. "Come inside. Too many ears on the street."

The archivist shakes with anticipation.

"I could lie. Right now," he threatens. "Tell you *anything* about what he said."

"Please, Paprick," the archivist begs. "I'll prove your innocence. I'll repent for my part in what came next. Anything."

Another explosion echoes outside.

"I don't need you for either," the Butcher counters. "They're both in my hands."

"I could unlock the cage."

"I could make you do that."

"Then what do you want, Butcher? What do I have to give you?"

"Your queen and the asshole that preceded her claimed to know the greater for Foresight Fried Gryphon. Do you know it?"

"What do you need Foresight for?"

"This isn't a negotiation," the Butcher counters. "Do you?"

"Yes."

"Answer the next question truly, and I'll tell you what Cutler said."

"I swear on the Source."

The Butcher laughs. "Fitting. Have you or anyone else in this bullshit court used it to look into the Empheron? Can it be killed?"

The archivist sighs in relief. Thank the Source. "You're lucky I'm trusted, Butcher. Yes, the queen's intimately familiar with the Empheron. And yes, it can."

"But you've never looked yourself?"

"Me? No. Why?"

"Just curious."

"I'm sure."

"I won't tell you where it is or how I know, so don't even ask," Cutler began. "And you need to understand, knowing this puts you in danger, and not just with that shriveled cashew posing as king. His head's so far up his arse he can smell his breakfast. But if he thinks you touched it, smart people may come for it. People with resources far beyond those limited to carnephon greater."

I wondered if the masked people fit that description. "I understand."

"I don't think you do, Paprick. I really don't." I think it was the only time he used my name, and that made me all the more uncomfortable.

"So what is it?

From beneath the front counter, Cutler retrieved a rock with teal crystals jutting from it, practically identical to the one Crooked Rish showed me weeks before. "Do you know what this is?"

"Endurmite," I said.

He looked genuinely impressed. "You know too much already. Where'd you learn that? No, don't tell me! I don't want to know." He sighed. "Yes, crystallized endurium. More than you'd find in a carnephon flank. If you ate it, you'd die of gorge. Assuming you could digest it, which even a bottomless pit like you can't manage.

"Some think the Source is a god. Some think it's *the* God; you know the one the Consumers always yammer about? Others say it's a machine like the doodads used in alchemic astronomy or whatever it's called. Really, it's not all that different from this rock. About the size of this shop, but an egg-shaped flower of crystallized endurium. Somehow alive or aware or something. Not important!"

"Why would the king care if I touched a rock?"

"Hard to say," Cutler admitted, his face scrunched. "Depends on how stupid he is. Legends talk about connecting to the Source, touching the Source, calling the Source, you name it, papwit. But all the same legends say doing so grants you unparalleled power. Because this is Ranch, everyone assumes that means knowledge of greater recipes. What greater power is there?"

"Does it?" I said, a hint of longing in my voice.

And believe me, Cutler sensed it. "Do yourself a favor, boy. Forget about the Source. You saw what guards it. Anyone who tries to get near it gets incinerated by drakephon flame and eaten. You've already done what millions dream of, inventing a greater recipe." He flicked my forehead. "There's more power in that thick skull of yours than in half of Ranch. If the king wants the Source, he's afraid of you for what you've already got."

"It's late and I'm hungry. Go back down into the Commons and find that lady you won't shut up about. For whatever reason, she seems to actually enjoy your company." Cutler stood sharply. "Unlike me," he added, as if that wasn't obvious.

"Why have I never heard of the Source?" I asked anyway. "How could it come up twice in one day and never before?"

Cutler shrugged. "Its legend predates Ranch. I'm shocked the king even knows it, though I guess old Almon might've written something down, assuming he could read. Look, dungtongue, he must know the drakephon guards it, somehow. I'm guessing the Flyover reminded him of it. It isn't some sign you need to worry your ugly mug about. Find the girl, enjoy your youth, kiss your mums. You'll never get those opportunities back. Myths and legends have a way of staying around forever. Chase them later."

"It sounded like the advice of a wise old man," the Butcher adds, remorseful. "But all these years later? I think he knew."

Silence lingers too long, too heavy.

"I wish I could still ask."

30

THE FESTIVAL

BEFORE WE GET into exactly what happened that night, a few things I learned during my walks with Cori those few weeks before the festival:

First, she hadn't lied. She *had* come from the north, specifically from parents who led the Herd army at the Front as generals. Practically royalty, she had the clout to extort Vanil into buying my supplies and doing what she wanted, like organizing Bessa's release from inside the factory.

Which she'd done because she was an emphonist, like many common. Emphonists, also called faunatics by bigoted assholes, revere the Twelve, an idealized menagerie of the twelve different emphon. Not gods, exactly—at least not like the Consumers' God, who demands the slaughter of emphon, emphonists, and everything else—but powerful, intelligent creatures worthy of respect. To eat sparingly and considerately. To love and thank for their sustenance. Not to torture in stirrups with alchemics to keep them alive. Working in the factory had been hell for her, but refusing an indenture at the factory when she was assigned her indenture would've outed her as an emphonist. Apparently, the way I respected Bessa had earned me her trust and made it bearable.

For emphonists, the festival wasn't only a holiday, but a holy day, where a revered creature signals the changing of the seasons, unperturbed by humanity and its infinitesimal place on the planet. It meant a lot to Cori, and I was deeply committed to making it memorable.

As we bustled through a throng of singing people toward my surprise destination, she and I shared churros made in Common-3's commonsary and talked about what we cared about. How excited I was I'd be taking a course next semester all about greater recipes, how I still wanted that apron hanging in Cutler's shop, how Mom was going to give me some of her sourdough starter to bring to my apartment for my birthday.

Cori dazzled me with tales of the country outside Ranch's walls and the wild carnephon herds. She told me how she missed her parents, who'd somehow made time—at the Front—to teach her swordplay, medicine, music, sculpture, painting, tracking, history, and practically everything else I asked about. A walking encyclopedia of experiences and knowledge.

"Okay," I said, wiping some raspberry filling from her lips and failing to keep my thumb from lingering, "what about cooking? They teach you any greater recipes?"

"Well, *how-dy*, killer." She licked the path my thumb had just taken. "When did you get so bold?"

I rolled my eyes.

"Not really," she answered. "Serious cooking's taboo in my family. With all the focus on surviving and staying ready for threats, food was something we did quickly, and greaters belonged with the warchefs. Rice. Beans. You know how it is. Plus, Mama didn't have time, running the medical tent."

"So I'll do the cooking then," I suggested. "Leave you everything else."

"My own private chef, only an apron to clothe him? I could get behind that."

Gods, kiss me. If she just would, I could do it whenever I wanted to, needed to, like I did in that moment. I *hated* that I didn't have the confidence to do it first. Plus, despite the singing and dancing in the streets, everyone watched us. As we'd walked, common pointed at me, handed me food, whispered, "Stand Tall." I couldn't risk being denied and looking like a fool. Symbols don't get rejected.

"I'll commit right here if you tell me where we're going," I said. "Personal chef for life."

She took my hand, sending a tingle up my fingers. "Going? Who says I don't have you exactly where I want you?"

"Do you?" I asked, practically breathless.

"Well, I don't see a bedroll, so not quite."

She smirked and leaned forward, daring me to take her, before quickly easing right back to arm's length, strong arms going taut to pull me along. "Come on, killer, we're nearly there."

The throng seemed impenetrable before us. Music vibrated from everywhere, percussion and strings and clapping hands lifting feet and spirits alike. Men, women, and everyone between or beside laughed, kissed, sang. And among it all, smells. Sweets and spices thickened the air, steam clouds billowing from campfire pots, woks, and all manner of street vendors. Greeting foods changed hands faster than they could be eaten. Beer taps ran like rivers. Empty tequila bottles piled high. The common saved and fought all year to afford this festival, to keep the party going.

But as Cori pulled me forward, common parted for her. Us? Me? I didn't know, but dancing people opened like an embrace for her and then me, fires illuminating her in red and gold. I wanted that every night. Every minute.

"They deserve this every night," I said suddenly. "I'll make sure *this* is always theirs."

Cori stopped short and pulled me to her. Calloused hands snapped to my neck and pulled me in with need. Her lips pressed to mine, playful and quick, tasting like lime and wheat, smelling of sandalwood smoke and bull grass lemon. I drank her in, my tongue reaching into her lips like they held the last water in the desert.

Cori eased out of it with a satisfied snort, and I laughed, tried to pull her back in. "More of that later," she said. "Time to work."

We entered a nearby building, slightly smaller than the King's Factory. Hundreds of common filed inside to its large central doors, which had been broken inward.

"This is the cayenne sauce factory," I said. "Mother works here."

"Worked," Cori corrected. "We instigated a workers' revolt last week, shattered all the glass bottles. Now, normally that ain't much of a problem, but four days prior, we commandeered several wagons full of sand headed to the glassblowers."

"What about her indenture? She won't be able to afford food."

Cori continued to lead me forward. "The Herd's getting food to all the displaced workers. Your moms especially. Fact is, we had to get her out of here. The overseers targeted her every chance they could, and we can't risk your moms. Not with how much you mean to these people."

"Vanil said he'd take care of them when I demanded it, but shut down a factory? What about everyone else? They're out of jobs."

"All these people? Half of 'em worked here, I reckon. They wanted it."

Common continued to hand me greetings as Cori led me to a stage. "There're going to be some speeches. For motivation. You only need to keep your posture straight and nod along, alright?" She didn't stop to confirm, just pulled me up the steps to face the speakers.

I recognized a few Black Spice vendors, a couple from Common-3. "Who are all these people?"

"The Herd," she said proudly. "Growing larger every day."

The speeches were moving, and my job did itself. The speakers promised freedom, liberation, and justice. Occasionally, they pointed to me, talked about what I did. How I'd stood tall, of course, but also how I shared Sleepless Salad, how I survived gorging, how just today

I'd taken a beating from the king himself without giving up any information on the revolution. I hadn't told anyone about that yet, and my genuine surprise only rallied the crowd more.

Cori went last, which surprised me, but my greatest surprise was that she didn't speak. Instead, she pulled a chair to the lip of the stage and accepted a guitar from someone. I have no ear for voices, let alone strings, but I was dazzled by her skilled fingers, moving and plucking both sides of the instrument in unison. I'd seen Meg's father strum with a pick and sing soft melodies, but Cori played that instrument like it was the Rare piano in the Academy House. I wanted to kiss those calloused fingers.

Then she sang, her drawl deeper than I'd ever heard it, and I nearly melted.

> *I don't believe in wasted chances,*
> *don't care for spoiled meat.*
> *Ain't forgot my ancestors,*
> *nor the things that they dreamed.*
>
> *I stand tall 'cause I'm asked to,*
> *I believe 'cause I should.*
> *Wouldn't stop if I had to,*
> *kill 'em all if I could.*
>
> *We ain't meant to go hungry,*
> *Ain't supposed to fear whips,*
> *All we want is to eat right,*
> *drink beer, eat some chips.*
>
> *Their God says to kill us*
> *Their king tries his best.*
> *Can't even do that right*
> *A kid stood tall to the test.*

We don't believe in wasted chances,
don't care for spoiled brats.
Ain't forgot our ancestors,
Won't be treated like rats.

We'll stand tall 'cause we have to
Believe in freedom like a prayer!
Wouldn't starve if we had to
Fuck 'em! Eat the Rare!

I don't know what shocked me more, the lyrics or that every common in that room sang along with her.

"Eat the Rare! Eat the Rare!" As the last notes of the guitar died in the corners, the chant grew louder and louder. Cori turned and gave a bow before walking back.

"Eat the Rare?" I asked over the noise.

"A little lesson learned from their religion. Their Consumer says to eat emphon because it's unholy? We'll eat something unholy first."

Then, without preamble, she pulled me into another kiss as the crowd roared behind us. I melted into it, fueled by the calamitous atmosphere. As we broke apart, someone handed us tequila bottles, and we toasted the crowd.

It became a blur, dancing, singing, drinking, jumping, shouting, chanting.

I don't know when the rioting started. Right after her song? Before? Hours later? I only remember sobering in the street, watching as a bottle of tequila, a cloth pushed into its neck and set aflame, hurtled over my head toward the King's Factory.

The explosion. Flames licking. People shouting. More bottles. Carvers all around us, cracking batons into heads and stomachs. Smoke choking at my lungs.

"Stand Tall!"

"Eat the Rare!"

Did I remove my cleaver from the back of my pants? I honestly don't remember. I know I fought, but it was chaos, batons slapping, fires spreading, people running. I was so drunk that before I knew it, we were back at Cori's apartment in Common-5. The stars blinked through an open tenement window, and Cori sat beside me with a bowl of rice. I sat shirtless on a bedroll, body still covered in sweat, my ribs aching from where batons had hit me. Dried blood almost a Perfect copper in my mouth.

"I'm no chef," Cori said, pushing the bowl over to me, "so no complaints."

I barely ate, my body completely disinterested in it. And Cori didn't lie. It was simultaneously bland and oversalted. She'd added a handful of sauteed vegetables but nothing that worked well together. It was a meal of sustenance, not flavor.

When I was finished, Cori eased me back onto my bedroll. "You took quite the beating before we pulled you out. Who convinced you to lead the charge? I didn't even notice you'd gone until it was too late."

"I don't remember. Did we burn it down?"

"Partly, but there'll be time for that tomorrow. We should get some rest. Daylight ain't far."

Then much to my shock, she pulled off her sweaty, sleeveless shirt, revealing a bare chest and a handful of tattoos along her ribs, one of which was a carnephon's head side-by-side a badgeboar's.

A startled choke burst from my lips.

She rolled her eyes and lay down beside me. "They're nipples, killer. You have 'em too."

I coughed, embarrassed. "Yeah, totally. We, uh, can—"

Cori snorted a laugh to cut off my frantic thoughts. "Calm down, killer, we're not. It's hot, and if you aren't going to suffer the night sleeping in a shirt, why should I?" She scooted in, forming her back into the curve of my body. Warmth radiated along the length and breadth of me. Even through the pain, I stirred to life, which felt exceedingly counter to the point of taking shirts off because we were hot. I stifled a choke as I unwillingly rose and pressed against Cori's lower back, but Cori didn't say anything. She reached behind herself, found my arm, and threw it over her stomach, pulling me tight.

"Goodnight, killer," she whispered.

"Goodnight," I said, cuddling into her, head still pounding.

No nightmares disturbed me for the first time in months.

31

MISSING

CORI AND I sat at a small table in her threadbare apartment in Common-5. I'd made breakfast—just porridge, because Cori kept little around—and we were getting ready to go see my moms when Yenne pounded on the door, breathless.

"Laven didn't return to his flat last night," she said, pushing in.

"Good for him," Cori said, tossing her a habanero. "Any idea who he spent the night with?"

"You misunderstand," Yenne insisted. "He informed me of his intentions to pursue a lead on Paprick's missing spice and didn't return."

I knew the Academy's dangers. "Let's go find him."

"Those bruises implicate you in the riots," Yenne countered as she produced makeup. "We need to cover them."

I'd never even considered that. "Were the riots that bad?"

Yenne stopped preparing the concoction. "Half the factories in the Arid Fields are in ruins. The king promises girders for all suspected rioters. Carvers flock the streets. Even you can do that maths."

Cori prodded at her porridge. "Things got further out of hand than Vanil intended."

"They were planned?"

"More like expected." She sighed. "If things are that bad, I'll need to keep to the Commons. My fake ID is passable, but not that great. Plus, Vanil'll need help keeping the instigators safe."

When Yenne was done, I went looking for my cleaver. "Must've dropped it in the tumult," Cori said, handing me a bread knife. "Best I can do."

I kissed her goodbye, reveling that I could do that, and hurried toward the Clouds. In the light of day, it was a different city. Common-5 was the farthest point from the Academy, east to west, tucked against the wall beside Common-6. Carvers rarely ventured past the pepper fields between Common-5 and the river, but two battalions marched through the street in front of the Commons, weapons ready and Endurance clear in their glares. As we crossed the river and made east through Tall Grass, the message grew louder and clearer: common were being snatched off the street and beaten without reason, forcing Yenne and I to stick to the shadows.

Our passage was slow, but Yenne was an expert in stealth, so we reached the white tower unnoticed. "Where do we start?"

Yenne produced a map from nowhere. The fact that she never wore a bag infuriated me. Where did she keep all this stuff? "Laven's been mapping secret areas of the tower."

That was news to me. "How long has he been doing that?"

"Each night since you two discovered those common."

"Even without his key?"

"He's industrious," Yenne said, a note of approval in her voice. "I believe he returned to the substacks as he reclaimed his key from his father yesterday, and most of the upper floors are mapped now."

"He told you all this? I didn't realize the two of you were so close."

Yenne rolled her eyes as if these questions were an unnecessary inconvenience. "Our friendship predates yours by two years. He still perceives yours as precarious, despite your obvious trust. His intention was surely to present you with satisfactory evidence before interrupting your busy schedule."

We arrived at the locked door to the substacks. "Can you pick this?"

"Easily." Yenne removed a set of lockpicks from a fold in her skirt. Just how much did she store in those folds? "An adoption present from Dyl. They wanted to ensure I had access to nearly any place in the city. Information always lies behind locks. Quite a surprise at first."

Slowly, we descended into the substacks, snaking through warrens of shelves holding books, pantries full of Alchemic Gastronomy equipment, and meat lockers that hadn't been used in years. After checking the locker we'd found the original nightmare in, we descended another level, and I knew something was wrong immediately. The dusty musk I'd grown accustomed to on the previous floor transitioned to the faintest scent of iron. Could be metal equipment. Could be blood. By unspoken agreement, we stalked quietly inward, and I wished I'd thought to get a new cleaversaw.

Yenne produced a thin blade from within the folds of her skirt, which widened my eyes. It was long. Really long. Practically a sword. "Where did that—"

She shushed me and we crept through the older stacks heavy with books. Pulling one off the shelf showed a cookbook published fifty years before my moms were born, from some place called Ryespur. If I weren't so worried for Laven, I might've flipped through it to get a sense for the cuisine.

Yenne had stalked ahead. She stopped suddenly, bringing my attention to a light up ahead, and I drew my weapon.

As long as my forearm, the breadknife provided more range but lacked a cleaver's heft. A cleaver could chop like an ax, or in desperation, even throw with some accuracy. A breadknife is a rounded, serrating blade, used specifically to keep structures intact by massaging fibers out of the way. Against a human, my best chance would be to drag it across a shallow artery, like the carotid in the neck or popliteal behind the knee—things I remembered from the factory and Military Matters. Both required me to be behind the person I was attacking. Luckily, I could be stealthy for my size when I wanted to be, lithe and thin as a whip. And just as silent until the moment something cracked.

As we approached another meat locker, I ached for Endurance. If whoever had done this was Enduring, I was probably dead already. Famines, if Yenne hadn't been beside me with courage enough to boil a stew, I might've rushed away and called for Vanil, but I didn't think he'd care about some random Rare. I needed to start carrying a greater recipe with me somehow.

But I wouldn't leave my friend because I was unprepared. Reckless, I spied through the crack, not nearly as headstrong as my last encounter.

They wore masks. Neither mask depicted an emphon I'd seen properly at that point, but they had the distinct reptilian likeness, and based on what I knew of the Twelve, I had some idea. One, completely scaled, had a long canine snout in a toothy grin, a goat's eyes, and a ram's horns: a wolphon. The other was fishlike, but no salmon or tuna. Not a lobster either, which rounded out my knowledge of seafood at the time. The dolphon mask bore a long, scaled snout, spherical fish eyes, and a hole in the crown of its bulbous, blubbery forehead.

Behind them, Ilantra and Laven hung from hooks. Blood dripped from Ilantra's nose and cheeks like tears. From her removed skull.

I charged into the room despite Yenne's attempt to grab my belt. Before the wolphon cultist—because by this point, I had decided this was a sick cult composed of disgusting people—could react, I drew my breadknife across their throat. My cut was too shallow but startling and skillful. They backpedaled and screamed, slipping to the bloody floor.

Dolphon wasn't so surprised. I swung around to stab them, but they caught my wrist, preternaturally quick. Their grip became boulders against my bones, and they snatched my arm behind my back to disarm me perfectly, a maneuver Vyson taught in Military Matters.

It could've led straight into snapping my neck, but my attacker's grip went slack as Yenne dove, stabbing multiple times in quick succession. None hit home, but they gave me time to free myself.

I kicked at Dolphon's flank, allowing Yenne to strike at openings I created. But like they already knew what was coming, Dolphon caught and deflected both our attacks with ease. Almost lazily.

I readied myself to upset the balance and tackle their knees, but I didn't get a chance. Wolphon tackled me from behind, and my ankle flared with pain as I collided with the ground. Before I'd even rolled onto my back, Wolphon stood over me, lightning crackling between upraised hands. Desperately, I kicked them as hard as I could in the genitals.

I don't know which they had, but they reached for them the way everyone does. Lightning still raced through those hands, and as soon as they touched their body, it arced. They twitched and fell to my side like a plank.

Hastily, I rolled to my breadknife and sawed along the wound I'd left in Wolphon's neck until arterial blood sprayed across my face.

Yenne fought off Dolphon with admirable fury, but was losing ground steadily. Blood trickled from her lips and her left eye swelled purple. Dolphon's speed and ability to predict our attacks were too incredible.

I dove at their right knee. Even as they spun, I slashed my knife across the back of it, but the military leathers they wore were thick and my blade only frayed them. Their fist spun into the side of my head, cracking against my temple and sending the candlelight swimming out of focus. My nose slammed into the tiled floor, blood pouring out instantly.

I blinked rapidly, attempting to regain myself.

Tried to stand.

As I failed, Yenne pushed Dolphon hard enough that they stumbled back over my crouched body, flipping off balance and falling hard.

Dolphon's mask split down the center, and even with my swimming vision, I recognized the asshole that had taught me how to fight: Lt. Vyson.

No wonder he'd seemed to know what was coming.

As we made eye contact, the soldier planted a boot in the center of my face. I splayed over onto my back, and my limbs gave out on me.

32

AFTERMATH

GROANING, I ROLLED to my side, vaguely conscious. As if through the murky waters of Ranch River, I watched Yenne land several attacks on Vyson before he caught her by the wrist, turned her blade around, and stabbed her in the shoulder. She fell back with a yell, and despite my anger, I couldn't rise to my feet to stop him as he ran through the door.

By the time I made it to my feet, Yenne had ripped strips from the bottom of her skirts to press them against the wound in her left shoulder. Her knife still stuck from it and her eyes fluttered as blood escaped down her blouse. She didn't have much left to lose, and I couldn't abandon her to go after Vyson.

On instinct, my hand reached to pull the blade out, but my butcher's training overwrote all that. If I removed it, nothing would stop the blood flow. I maintained pressure, noting how much blood sluiced down her arm.

We didn't have much time. "Do you have more of the dehydrated milk?"

Grunting, she reached into her skirt folds and withdrew two pills.

I swallowed one and offered the second to her, but she shook her head. "I can't heal with the knife in."

"One, two—" I ripped it out before three, supposing her body would tense if she expected it. The blade came free with a splash against my face. Yenne's scream could've split the sky. But she bit it off and swallowed the pill.

With her in half-decent shape and the pill affecting me, I darted over to Ilantra. "She's got no pulse!" I shrieked as I checked Ilantra's throat. Why had I taken the pill? I'd seen them. I should've saved it for them.

Yenne hurried up behind me, still panting. "Her skull's been removed, Paprick. She's gone."

Tears washing over my eyelids, I moved to Laven. I didn't even want to press my hand to his neck. Couldn't take the idea that it'd be just as cold and still.

Yenne grabbed his wrist. "It's weak, but he's alive. We need to hurry before someone else shows up."

She guessed only two or three common still lived, but I couldn't leave Laven. His breath was shallow as sleep. Despite the hole in his hands, he appeared almost peaceful.

"Wake up, wake up," I urged as I slapped his face, but no luck. I couldn't call the carvers, not if a lieutenant was involved in all of this. How was I to know it wasn't the whole military? But I couldn't leave him either, not with the reinforcements potentially on their way. So I took him off the hook and piled him over my shoulder with a groan. Damn Rare likely never missed a meal in his life. My back quaked under the weight.

I tried to pull a common woman off her hook, but I nearly dropped Laven. "We don't have time for them," Yenne said. "We can't save anyone else."

I tried to protest, but we heard a noise from outside the room and fled. In a daze, we reached the dumbwaiter and rushed to the Academy House's kitchen, where we had emergency supplies. Yenne and I tried to feed him some Emphon Milk, but he wouldn't swallow. I didn't want to risk bringing him to a Rare hospital, and couldn't come up with a better idea, so I hurried to Cutler's while Yenne stayed hidden in the pantry to stitch his hands shut.

"A wagon?" Cutler repeated. "What madness are you making, boy? No, don't tell me. Just get it back to me, and make sure my bison stays watered."

After learning to drive on the fly, I pulled up to the back door of the restaurant, and we hid Laven in the wagon. Yenne was the better driver, so she smuggled him to Common-3. The gate guards never check wagons leaving Rare districts as strictly as those going in. I sat with him in the back, hoping he would survive. Someone had to survive this.

The stairs were the worst. There's no easy way to get a body up them other than to hoof it. I sweated and groaned, but finally, I made it to my moms' apartment.

"Pappy?" Mom gasped when she saw the blood. "Who is this? What happened? Come in, come in!"

Mother took one look at the three of us and raced out the door. "I'll get Cay-Anna."

"Pappy, boil wraps," Mom commanded. "You—sorry dear, I don't know your name—there's tequila hidden under our bed."

We were there for another day, and the door revolved. Cori came first, throwing her arms around me and kissing me right in front of my moms. Which, of course, resulted in a lot of embarrassing conversations in which my moms were far too smug.

My childhood "doctor," Cay-Anna, tended to us and ensured that Laven would wake eventually. "He's been drugged," she confirmed. "He's dehydrated, but broth and time will clear it from his system."

Vanil also came, his typical calm demeanor forgotten, angry that Ilantra had been murdered before his plans for her could be achieved, upset that we'd smuggled a Rare into Common-3, concerned the military was involved.

Fury doesn't even begin to describe how I felt. Ilantra wasn't just a potential tool for the Herd. She was my mentor. She'd taught me flavors, recipes, a whole new way of imagining a kitchen. And Laven had become my best friend. It couldn't be a coincidence that the two of them were down there together. This was my fault, and there was nothing I could do to help Laven. To make up for what it'd cost Ilantra.

Ilantra's murder made the Rare news sheets the following evening, a few hours after a librarian found the bodies. The morning sheets had focused on a substantial win for the Rare military: they'd found a carnephon herd out east, and were bringing six adult bulls back to Ranch. But even with the control the Rare have over the media, there was no silencing the murder of a Tribunal member and the kidnapping of another's son.

So what did they do? They blamed it on the common rioters!

Hoppus Florento was quoted promising ransom and hellfire in equal measure to whoever had Laven. The High Consumer and the Commander preached equal disappointment that their friend, the great Missiloan-starred Chef, had been murdered, though the Commander's version had more to do with disappointment that she wouldn't see the return of the bulls he'd captured than their supposed friendship. As if they didn't bemoan her at the Tribunal. As if the Commander's own military personnel hadn't been involved. Even the king released a statement, claiming that any common found guilty of involvement would drop from girders over and over until the corpse was no longer distinguishable from the stained streets below the courthouse.

Days passed, nightmares plagued, and even cooking couldn't calm me down. When I sliced bread, I crushed it into crumbs. I burned peppers over the stove just to watch them burn. I'd never wasted food in my life, but I was so starving mad. Mad at the cultists. Mad at the Rare. Mad because there was to be a funeral and mourning feast later in the week for Ilantra, but Vanil forbade me from going. Like he deserved to forbid me anything. He'd asked me to trust him with the cultists!

"Your image is still fragile," he explained. "If you are seen wallowing in the death of a Rare, and a Tribunal at that, it will weaken the movement."

"I don't care. She was a decent person!" I countered. "She helped me when no one else would."

"She was a liar who believed herself your savior. Why give her credit for giving you what you already deserved?"

At that, I stormed into the hallway. Everyone was so starving concerned about how this would affect the Herd and their politicking plans. Did no one have the decency to mourn the murder of good people? No one even mentioned the other common in there. It felt like I was the only one who cared. Who wanted revenge. Ilantra didn't deserve to die dulled on some drug, hung like meat.

I punched a wall. Roared. Glared at the family that poked their head out to examine the hole I'd put in their apartment.

"Testosterone satisfied?" Yenne stood beside the door to my moms' apartment. She wore one of Mom's dresses—a remarkably plain ankle-length sleeveless gray thing, its neckline shallow but wide and revealing much of her bandaged shoulder. It was an eerie sight compared to the Rare clothes she so often wore. As if it didn't belong on her. "When you're finished renovating that flat, let me know. I want to know who's behind all this."

"Why?" I asked. "This is probably, what, the longest you've been in a Common since you elevated? What do you care who kills common?"

"One, starve. I do care." She took a step back toward the door, stopping only long enough to say, "But two, they have secrets."

"You need a better outlet for your anger, killer." Cori stood down the hallway, carrying fresh bandages for Laven's hands. "Making holes ain't going to help anyone."

"It helps me," I said, my anger tempering at the sight of her.

"Does it?" She frowned and took my hand, holding my bleeding knuckles up for inspection.

"It feels like it's my fault," I admitted instead. "It happened, again, in the same place. I should've been there to stop it."

Cori kissed my knuckles. "You couldn't have. Not without knowing the future."

"Do you think there's a greater recipe out there to do that?"

She shrugged. "I've heard rumors, but who's to say? There're rumors for everything under the sun. It doesn't matter. What matters is that he's alright because your first inclination was to go looking for him. Who knows what could've happened if you'd chosen to come see your moms with me as planned. Focus on that. Your actions mattered."

"He's awake!" Yenne shouted from inside.

We rushed into my moms' bedroom where Laven sat up, holding a shaking dinner knife at the doctor with his bandaged hand, fear frozen on his face. Mother and the doctor had their hands up, and Yenne held up a hand to calm Laven. There wasn't much Laven could've done in his state, but he was confused and scared. Until he spotted me.

His hand trembled and he dropped the knife.

"What happened?" he asked. "Why aren't I at hospital?"

"You're in my moms' apartment," I said softly. "Yenne and I found you in the substacks. Do you remember being attacked?"

Laven inspected his hands. "Not attacked," he whispered. "Not exactly."

"What happened?" Yenne asked, approaching.

"I found a memo from the military on my dad's desk. It said a shipment of classified culinary materials of value had been delivered to the Academy to analyze, so I was searching the substacks when I overheard voices. I crept closer and saw those masked people dragging Ilantra inside." He lowered his gaze. "I panicked and bumped into a jar. It shattered, and the next thing I knew, they had me. They forced me to eat something. It's fuzzy after that. Ilantra argued with them as they hung us from the hooks, said they had no right to do this. But the one in the dolphon mask laughed and said, 'We have His Majesty's blessing,' or something like that."

"They referenced His Majesty, specifically?" Yenne asked.

Laven nodded.

"I'm sorry," I said, taking his attention. "You never should've been there. You were only there for me."

"Paprick." He struggled for words temporarily. "After that, I—I felt this pressure against my mind. It was like a voice, whispering that I should want them to kill me because…"

"Because?" Yenne prodded after a suspended moment.

"Because the voice said it would free me from you."

"From me?" I said, confused.

"He said that you were coming to kill us all. That he'd seen the future, and it was painted in the blood of your victims. Paprick, the voice said you'd kill me one day."

My eyes met Cori's, struggled to figure out what to say, and blinked back at Laven. "I… I wouldn't. I don't want to hurt you."

Laven shook his head. "I believe you. It's just, the voice was so sure. So terrifying."

"Did you recognize the voice?" Cori asked from the door.

Laven peered to look at Cori, a question obvious on his expression, but he answered anyway. "I don't know. It was familiar and had a Rare accent, but I can't place it." He cleared his throat and affected his voice as he quoted, "'They will call him Butcher, and he will earn his name. He'll destroy the Commons, and by his hand, you'll become lame.'"

"It sounds like a sick nursery rhyme," Cori said.

We didn't know it was a prophecy.

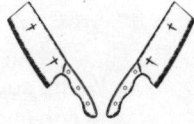

Course 4: Grilled Steak Fries

Equally capable of filling the role of appetizer or main, Grilled Steak Fries are best served with light dollops of guacamole, sour cream, and your choice of red, green, or mango salsa. They should typically precede a grain bowl main dish or be served alongside a black bean salad. Consider sharing as an appetizer. Pair with a beer flavored with a squeezed citrus rind.

Ingredients (serves 1–2):

Marinade:

- ◊ ⅓ cup oil
- ◊ 3 limes, juice of
- ◊ ½ cup fresh cilantro, chopped
- ◊ 4 cloves garlic, minced
- ◊ 1 tsp chili powder
- ◊ 1 tsp onion powder
- ◊ 1 tsp ground cumin
- ◊ ½ tsp paprika
- ◊ Salt and pepper to taste

80–120g bull emphon skirt steak
Fries:

- ◊ 2 russet potatoes
- ◊ 2½ tbsp salt, divided
- ◊ 1 liter water
- ◊ 1 tbsp oil
- ◊ ½ tbsp paprika
- ◊ ½ tbsp garlic powder

Wood of your choice (applewood works best)
Optional toppings:

- ◊ ¼ cup guacamole
- ◊ ½ cup pico de gallo
- ◊ ½ cup shredded cheese

◊ ¼ cup sour cream
◊ ¼ cup choice of salsa

Salt to taste

Steps:

1. Whisk the marinade ingredients together in a bowl until oil and lime emulsify.
2. Immerse steak in bowl for at least 1 hour (or up to 24 if chilled).
3. Prepare the fries:
   - Skin (optionally, don't skin) and cut potatoes into 2cm thick fries.
   - Add 2 tablespoons salt to 1 liter of water and soak the fries for at least 5 minutes (an hour works well).
   - Dry fries and place into a large bowl with oil, salt, paprika, and garlic powder. Toss until coated.
   - If baking fries, coat baking sheet in oil, place fries in a single layer, and cook for 30 minutes at 220°C, flipping halfway through. If deep frying, drop in frier for 2-3 minutes until golden.
4. Preheat grill.
5. Grill marinated steak to desired rarity and let rest for 4-5 minutes.
6. While the steak is resting, pat fries dry carefully and layer into a bowl or plate.
7. Chop steak into cubes or slices and layer over fries.
8. Garnish with optional toppings of your choice. Serve.

Expected Endurance Effect(s):

Endurance, 2-3 hours
Hyperobservance, 2-3 hours

33

A TOUGH EGG TO CRACK

SCREW VANIL. SCREW finding leverage for myself by searching for the spice. I was on the hunt for cultists. I wanted revenge. But we had to deal with Laven first. He was understandably curious how we'd managed to stop the attackers and why we'd chosen to bring him to my moms' apartment.

As much as we trusted him, we couldn't tell him about the Herd, so I told half the truth. "We had reason to believe that the carvers—er, Enduring Defense Branch officers—might be involved in the attack. Safer to bring you here than to a hospital. Plus, there'd been some unrelated riots during the festival and things were chaotic. Better to go to people we could trust."

We couldn't tell him about Vyson specifically. He was our only lead, and telling Laven who'd nearly killed him was as good as telling his father, which was as good as telling the whole Tribunal—especially if the attackers really had possessed "His Majesty's blessing."

Regardless, we returned Laven to his father after Laven promised he wouldn't reveal us as his saviors. He implied that it would be great for us financially if we did, but much as I hated working two jobs, it was too risky. No, only one job now. The realization was a stab in the gut.

We planned to investigate Vyson, but I needed to return Cutler's wagon. Yenne drove it to the shop the next morning, where Cori (in Rare disguise) and I met her. Vanil hadn't even wanted Cori to go, given how closely carvers were monitoring IDs, but Cori was scary when she was insistent. Even Vanil backed off. Gone were the days of me moving around the city alone. I needed the protection.

I was glad I had them when I walked in. Something was wrong. For one, there was an unfamiliar person behind the counter shining a teapot. For another, the store smelled of lemon and lacked a shelf I'd painstakingly installed. The individual with the teapot wore a male-cut suit and tie—both the moldering green color of Rare mourning—and had a thin beard, but their topknot, painted fingernails, and long dangling earrings blurred gender. When I entered, they lifted the teapot and pulled their arm back as if to throw it at me.

"Who are you?" I asked accusingly.

"How did you get in here?" they fired back.

"I could ask you the same."

Cori and Yenne stood carefully behind me.

"*I* own this place. So I'll ask you again, how?"

I produced my key with distrust. "Try again. I know who owns this shop. *I* work here."

The key seemed to relax them, and they lowered the teapot back to the counter. "You must be Paprick. I'm called Soryl. He or they."

I calmed slightly, and we each introduced ourselves.

"You're back from the Front?" I asked after introductions.

Soryl took a steadying breath. "We're given accommodations back home for exigent circumstances."

Cori reached forward to grip my hand.

"Exigent how?" I said, fearing the answer. The mourning green, the smell of lemon, it being so soon after losing Ilantra. Spry as he was, Jives Cutler had been on the older side… My world was coming down around me.

"No one told you? Pa was attacked."

"Attacked?" I asked, my hand shaking in Cori's. Her grip tightened around mine.

"Right there," Soryl informed, pointing toward the missing shelf.

"Who?"

"They wore masks."

"He's not...?" I couldn't say the word.

"He survived," Soryl said proudly. "Felled three, or so he claims. No bodies were recovered."

"What exactly happened?" Yenne asked.

"He'll want to tell you himself," Soryl assured, leading us to the back room where Cutler had taught me to make Sleepless Salad. "Says it's your fault. Jives, we're coming in."

Yeah, Soryl was the kind of person that called his dad by his first name. I know.

Cutler was in a wheelchair that looked too large for him, small and frail as he was. And that was worse than usual. He looked as if at least a decade had caught up with him since last I'd seen him, hanging bags from his eyes and wrinkles from his forehead like coat hooks. A bandage wrapped the crown of his head, a thin line of dried blood peeking through to show the cultists had tried to cut him open.

"About time you showed up," he snapped before I could say a word. "Didn't expect you to bring a harem though."

"Excuse me?" Yenne said sharply.

"Leave an old man his bad jokes," Cutler grumbled, waving a hand. "It's all I've got left. That and my doting child."

"What happened?" I asked.

"A bunch of arseholes tried to pry knowledge out of my noggin because they think you're going to burn the world down," he said. "You wouldn't happen to know anything about that, would ya?"

Soryl glared my way. "You weren't that specific before."

"I save my words for those who need them."

249

I swallowed. How was I supposed to respond to that? Thankfully, Yenne answered for me. "They attacked our friend and named Paprick a harbinger of murder. They said the same to you?"

"Said it? Locusts, no! They bloody screamed into my brain like a bunch of scalding Panchons."

I exchanged a look with Cori.

"Laven, Ilantra, and Cutler, all after the riots?" she suggested. "That can't be a coincidence."

"Retaliation against the Rare who look out for you," Yenne concluded.

"Can we get back to the fact that someone tried to kill him?" I asked, partly because guilt was gnawing deeper into my gut.

"Ah, so you do care." Cutler pouted. "Good. Next time, don't start riots. How would you have felt if I hadn't proved so incredibly capable of defending myself?"

"How *did* you defend yourself?" Yenne asked.

"My family has been on this plateau since before they changed its name," Cutler said, as his eyes tracked over to Cori. "We know a lot about what's been forgotten."

"Jives," Soryl warned, "don't."

Cutler shot his kid a withering look, but otherwise ignored the comment. "Now, what are you doing about all this? I assume you and your Herd are already on top of it?"

All three of us froze. "Who?" I stammered.

"Look at me!" Cutler ordered. "Do I really look like I was born yesterday? I might be wrinkly and pink, but that comes at both ends of life."

"How long have you known?" Yenne asked. Despite the accusation, she looked placid as ice. Cori, for her part, looked ready to bolt from the place and burn it down on the way out. If I hadn't been holding her hand, she might've.

"Since papwit used his day off to go to Black Spice."

"How do you know about that?" I growled.

"I was there."

"Rare can't enter Black Spice," Cori accused.

Cutler rolled up his sleeve to reveal the same tattoo that I had on my forearm: the spice pouch. "You're lucky I already took a liking to you," Cutler said as he showed it off. "If I'd heard what you did to my brother before I hired you, you would've never set foot in this shop."

"Brother?" Yenne said.

I recalled my first time in Cutler's, how I thought Cutler looked so like Old Man Banan. "But you're Rare," I said, still confused.

"I've told you," Cutler said sharply. "Common, Rare, those words mean nothing. Rancher is the only acceptable term for people from here."

"Okay, but your brother—" I started.

"Has a different father," he said, cutting me off, "and is no less my kin because of it."

I nodded with a head pounding from unexpected information. I'd gone into that store to return the wagon. Only to find out my boss had been attacked. That Cutler and Banan were half-brothers.

"We're trying to put together the pieces," I said finally. "Understand their cult."

"Cult?" Yenne repeated. "Is that your hypothesis?"

"Why else the masks?" I asked. "Why cut people's brains out? That's culty stuff." It sounded a lot less plausible when I said it out loud. I tried to brush past it. "At the very least, we know the king gave permission to attack Laven. Both Laven and Cutler had voices digging around in their heads, just like I did when the king interrogated me. That's no coincidence."

I turned back to Cutler. "Now, jokes aside, can you tell us anything of actual use?"

"Fine, fine," he complained. "Soryl, get those two items I told you to put aside."

Soryl threw Cutler a stubborn look but obeyed, returning a moment later with one item I recognized and another I didn't. The first was a carnephon mask, remarkably similar to the one I'd seen on the cultist I'd killed that first night.

"This came off one I killed," Cutler said, taking it from Soryl and handing it to me. "On the inside, there's a signature or engraving. I can't make beets or carrots of it, but maybe one of you can."

"Where did you get that?" Cori asked, staring at the other item. Her tone was somewhere between accusation and awe, like she couldn't quite believe what she was seeing.

As far as I could tell, it was a pineapple-sized rock, speckling slightly under the light. It should've weighed more than it did based on appearance, but Soryl carried it as if it weighed no more than a coconut.

"You recognize this?" The corner of Cutler's mouth twisted as he appraised Cori. "What did you say your name was?"

"They're supposed to be long gone," Cori redirected. "How did you get one?"

"It's been in our family for a long time," Soryl answered pointedly.

Cutler cut them a glare. "None you mind."

"What is it?" Yenne prodded, a little jealousy in her voice. Not often Cori knew something Yenne didn't.

"An egg," Cori announced.

"What kind of creature lays eggs like that?" I asked. It was a bit too small to be the egg of a carnephon and far too big to be anything else.

Cutler flicked my ear. "Ow!"

"No creature *lays* eggs like this," he answered. "You can only get these one way."

Cori's voice dripped disgust. "You've got to cut it out of the ovary of a carnephon. Before it's matured."

I blanched. "Famines."

"Oh, I've read of these," Yenne offered with a satisfied smile. "In the early days of the kingdom, the Panchons culled dozens of young bulls to get them. The room in the palace in which they were stored

is still called the Nursery. They don't rot like normal eggs, intrigu-
ingly."

"What's so special about them?" I asked, reaching over to take it
from Soryl, who looked more than a little displeased to hand it over.
"Why do something that raving?"

"A greater recipe," Cori said, "called Omniscient Omelet."

"What a stupid misnomer," Cutler complained. "As if such a power
existed. *Observant* Omelet, and it lets you perceive the past."

"The past?" I repeated.

Cutler sighed. "Soryl, go get my things. Apparently, these children
are too dumb to do anything. I guess I'll have to make it myself."

"No," I said, moving over to his demo kitchen. "I'll do it. Just tell
me what to do."

I didn't like the idea of making anything from an egg old enough
to have been in their family for a very long time and taken in such
a gruesome and inhumane manner, but the ability to look into the
past wasn't something I wasn't willing to squander. I wanted to know
exactly what happened to Cutler.

These people had killed and attacked people I considered friends.
I wanted them dead. And while I knew Vyson was involved, I needed
more information before I could do anything about it. Hurting him
wasn't going to get me anywhere unless he named others. I didn't want
to rely on that. I'd been interrogated before. It's not hard to lie.

I needed more, and that meant cracking an egg older than anyone
alive.

34

LESSONS

I CHARGED OUT of Cutler's like a carnephon, tucking the cleaver I'd used to break the egg into my pants.

"Paprick." Cori hurried after me. "Wait."

I pulled out of her grip and stalked forward. What I'd observed with the omelet had changed my perspective. Vyson had been there, had put his knife to Cutler's head and pressed it deep enough to reveal something vicious and terrible in the old man.

I wasn't waiting for answers. I would be demanding them.

Yenne followed Cori out and dashed in front of me to block my path.

"What did you see?" she asked. It was one serving per egg, and I could still see the jealousy in her eyes.

I tripped over my momentum. What I'd seen had been unexpected. Cutler wasn't just an old man with a knowledge of cutlery and greater recipes. He was something else. Something that was old in a completely different way. Even the memory of it was unsettling, and it wasn't something I was willing to dwell on just yet, let alone share with Yenne or Cori. It would be years before I dared ask Cutler about it.

The archivist's eyes shoot to the Butcher's. "Of course. That old goat touched the Source, didn't he? Oh, don't deny it. We both know what he's done. And he has tattoos. Famines, how did I not recognize it sooner?"

Hastily, the archivist scribbles a note and bids the guard, arm still broken, to deliver it to the Commander. "Make sure this goes directly into his hands. His eyes only."

With a nod, the guard exits, and a waft of smoke enters the room, hinting at the battle outside.

When the archivist looks back to the Butcher, he's staring out the door, left ajar. Much too intently for the archivist's liking. Quickly, the archivist closes it, and the pen returns to the ready position. But the archivist doesn't continue just yet. "You knew, even then, what the Source could do and you said nothing."

"I didn't understand what I saw."

"Tell me."

"It isn't relevant," the Butcher counters immediately.

"Shouldn't I be the judge of that?"

"No," he insists. "This the story of murders, blasphemy, regicide, and cannibalism."

"You're forgetting about seven counts of espionage, Butcher."

"Am I?"

I pushed past Yenne gently. Mad, but not unraveling. "If you want to come, come. But don't think about stopping me."

Vyson lived on the Academy's thirteenth floor. The whole way up the central stair, Yenne and Cori, who both followed, pestered me with questions.

"What's the plan?"

"Shouldn't this wait?"

"Why don't we go back and talk with Vanil?"

I ignored them. The plan was simple. I was going to break Vyson's toes, and then his fingers, and then start pulling out teeth and fingernails until he told me what I wanted. If that failed, I'd start cutting.

I obviously wasn't going to tell Cori and Yenne that. They couldn't understand. Observant Omelet doesn't just look at the past. When you use it, you hear, smell, *feel* from different perspectives. A chaos of conflicting senses. I understood why the stories called it Omniscient. It wasn't that you could know everything. It was that you experienced every sensation from anyone who'd lived the memory you focused on. I had been unprepared for it. I don't even think Cutler himself had ever done it. He couldn't have known what I'd experience.

But I'd *felt* Vyson's knife go into Cutler. The sharp sting against his cranium woke a part of me that glamorous cooking classes had tried hard to bury. Before I ever joined the Culinary Academy, I spent sixteen years living on meager meals, under the certainty of a lifelong indenture, and with the promise that I would never amount to anything because I was common. I might've spent months feeling pretty damn free, but elevation could only hide the darkness of systemic oppression for so long. When Vyson stood over a kind man who'd welcomed him and his fellow soldiers into his shop, despite masks, and spoke of sending me a message in blood as he cut Cutler, it reminded me who they all were underneath their masks. I'd seen Rare mistreat common my whole life. I'd become so numb to it, so passively accepting of it, it took seeing a Rare attacking another Rare to see how deep the poison went. No more acceptance. No more passivity. I'd joined riots on Flyover.

Now it was time to lead them.

I raced up the central staircase of the Academy, knocking sniveling Rare aside, becoming the common they feared as I kept a hand on my cleaver. I made them *see* me in my rage. Fear the assaults I'd learned to expect from overseers and carvers. My fury didn't quiet when I made it to the Teachers' Wing on the thirteenth floor.

As I slammed the hallway door open, Chef Sagen exited his office with a protest on his lips, but whatever he saw in my eyes was enough for him to suggest the students waiting outside his office come back later. Quietly, he closed his door.

I came to Vyson's door, with Cori and Yenne still following nervously behind. My shoulders were bunched up, tension flooding my muscles. The color of my face. I bet they thought I was going to kick the door down.

I wanted to. I knocked politely instead.

I had this whole plan. Vyson would open the door a crack and then I'd kick it in, sending him on his ass while I burst through to pin him to the ground. Yenne and Cori would hurry in behind, closing the door to the hallway by the time I had my hand over Vyson's mouth to muffle any screams.

But he didn't answer the door.

Huffing, I knocked again. Rattled off a little cadence too. The same one he used to give rhythm to the blows students of Military Matters exchanged. But no answer.

"Maybe we should go," Cori encouraged.

Yenne opened her mouth to say something but stopped, angling her ear toward the door.

"I heard it too," I confirmed. "Groaning."

I spared the barest moment to check the hallway on either side to ensure no one was close before I kicked the door. Wood strained under my Endurance-enhanced strength, but it wasn't until Cori slammed a shoulder against the door with me that hinges snapped. Cori cursed and cast her gaze back in either direction. "Someone will have heard that."

Yenne and I hurried in.

We both stopped short.

Furniture lay tossed over or pushed aside. The far wall wore a deep, spiderwebbed crack, and Vyson lay spread and drawn in an X across the floor of the apartment, his ankles and wrists pulled by taut ropes anchored into the ceiling so that he hovered a few centimeters off the ground. His naked body was pale against the blood welled below him, which leaked slowly from what looked like a thousand cuts along his arms, legs, and torso—all the places where shallow cuts would allow the victim to feel each one, to slowly burn in the torture of a conscious death. It reminded me of Bessa, cut and bleeding above the floor of the King's Factory.

In Vyson's chest was carved the word "failure," and sea salt had been rubbed into the wounds. Piss and shit pooled in the blood beneath him, creating a coppery ammonia-clogged stench that made me retch, even after my time in the factory surrounded by Bessa's offal.

The torture was gruesome, inhumane, and very, very fresh.

Vyson still quaked with pain when we entered, though he was gagged. His head snapped up to meet my gaze, and I sensed all the anger that had been directed at me in Military Matters, but no longer for me. For being caught like this.

For all my talk of torture and answers, I moved to help him.

Cutler hadn't deserved his attack. But no one deserved what Vyson had gotten in return. Back then, I still believed that.

Still, rage and compassion fought within me. I wanted to help him almost as much as I wanted answers. I settled on a middle ground. "I'll help if you answer my questions."

Vyson's eyes flicked to Yenne, who stood, arms crossed, glaring down at the scene, and then to Cori, who was lifting the remains of the door back into the portal. It wouldn't pass inspection, but a glance might disguise its destruction.

Vyson nodded sharply, and I pulled the gag from his mouth.

"Why are you bound?" I asked.

"Punishment," he said, as if that wasn't obvious.

"Who did this to you?" Yenne asked before I could ask my next question.

Vyson seemed to consider Yenne for a long time, as if debating whether to answer. When she pushed the heel of her shoe into the

F in failure, however, his voice became urgent. "The Seekers! And His Majesty."

Confirmation that the king was involved only stoked the flames of my anger. The man already sold us into indenture the moment we were born. Now he kills us too? For what?

"What do they want?" I shouted. "What does this have to do with me?"

"Everything." A bloody smile made a too-large crescent on his face. "To find it before you. And to punish you for your rebellion."

"To find what?" Cori asked.

Vyson didn't answer right away, staring at Cori with confusion.

"To find what?" I repeated, drawing the cleaver.

Vyson eyed it with equal invitation and apprehension. "Paprick the Butcher. So it is true. My sacrifice…"

"What did you call me?" I asked, confused.

He smiled wider and coughed blood. "I die with or without your help."

"I can help end it then."

"Paprick," Cori whispered in warning. "We could use him."

"He'll never survive these wounds. Not with what time we have," Yenne countered, as if taking a perch on my opposite shoulder.

"What is it!" I slammed the cleaver into the floor beside Vyson's ear. I'd meant to miss. I really had. But my hands were shaking. He screamed as blood sprayed from the artery at the base of the tragus.

"The recipe for control!" Vyson screamed, writhing against his bonds. "The Source! All the things that must not be undone."

His words sent a chill down my spine.

"We need to go," Yenne urged, breaking my shock. "Before someone comes to investigate."

"Give us something, Vyson. Anything. They did this to you."

His eyes darted away, for the briefest moment, and he spat in my face. I didn't think anything of it, but Yenne smirked.

"The drawer," she said, pointing, over my shoulder to the drawer of the upturned desk. "He's looked to it twice now."

"You think there's something there?" I asked.

Without answering, Yenne stepped over Vyson, picked the lock quickly, and removed a sheaf of papers.

"You'll kill them," the soldier said, his eyes full of tears, though his smile remained. "Your mums, your friends, every last common roach."

The chill in my bones grew deep. He was raving beyond repair. His own people had strung him up like a bull, and he still defended them, would still kill for them, surely. There was no point in saving his life because it wasn't a sound life—or at least, that's what I told myself.

In that moment, all I saw was the angry eyes of the man who'd killed Chef, hurt Laven, attacked an old man.

I wouldn't hear him speak another word. Not when it felt like a prophecy locking off any other futures I could have.

"It's a mercy, then." I lied to myself loud enough for Cori to hear so that she wouldn't think less of me, but the words were cold, with lucid vengeance. No one in that room thought I was saving a poor, unhealthy man as I chopped the cleaver down between Vyson's eyebrows. The defenseless soldier died instantly, his eyes not even closing.

It hadn't been mercy, at least not for Vyson. If anything, it was for me.

The last remnants of Vyson's bowels evacuated into the bloody pool, and I looked away from my cleaver. Cori, still using her back to hold up the door, whistled. "Killer, indeed. We gotta go, quick."

I tried to yank my cleaver back and found it too deeply embedded. Leaving it, I nodded a silent message to Cori, who dropped the door. The three of us dashed down the tower, back toward my apartment.

"The papers?" I asked Yenne after three floors of silence.

"Written in some kind of cipher."

I didn't know what that was, but I nodded and tried to ignore the carvers that ran upstairs at full sprint. No doubt Vyson's body had been found and the search was on for his murderer. It was the third body that I'd left in my wake and the first that I can't claim was self-defense. But Vyson was a murderer, a cultist, and would've died with or without my intervention. As he'd said.

"Let's get back to the Greenhouse," Yenne suggested. "You've gotten your revenge."

I bit off an objection and shifted my attention to Cori, looking for a supporter. "Maybe Vanil will know something about these Seekers and the greater recipe they seek," she suggested.

If he had, he would've done something to stop them sooner, I thought.

But I didn't say that aloud. I just wanted to leave that murderer's shit-stained body behind.

35

SOLITARY

WE BROUGHT THE papers to Vanil, who set Crooked Rish to decoding their contents. Cipher was a new concept for me, and one I didn't enjoy learning. Weeks to decode? I couldn't wait weeks to know what was in those papers. What if they were attack plans?

And then, in his infinite starving wisdom, Vanil decided that I needed to stop running around the city killing people—his words, not mine—before it put the revolution in jeopardy. "Buy your school supplies and prepare for another term at the Culinary Academy." Because, and again, his words, if I was going to discover the Chili Control recipe, I needed to study. *Study*. And I would be confined to the Clouds, preferably the Academy, and even more preferably my apartment, until the investigation into Vyson's death died down. "No searching for the Seekers either. We can't risk you."

He forbade both Cori and Yenne from seeing me because they "lacked sensibility in restraining *my* moods," and would need to add to my moms' guard rotation. He had the audacity to claim he'd have guards bring me back to the Academy if I tried to enter a common district. Seriously? My birthday was a few days away. I was supposed to sit in my apartment and not see anyone, not Cori, not even my moms?

Yup. Starving awesome that was. Nightmares of Vyson's face each night. Followed by nightmares of Seekers attacking my moms, Cori, Laven again. Crying because I'd starving murdered someone in cold blood. Wondering, by day, why the Seekers hadn't come to kill me if I was their prophetic harbinger of death.

Not that I was left alone. The day after Vyson's body was discovered, four carvers broke down the door to my apartment and beat the living shit out of me looking for a confession and evidence. I didn't give them either, though they gave me enough burns and bruises to make me regret my silence for days.

But why were the Seekers only after the people I cared for? If the king wanted me dead, it seemed like he could've easily done it. So why was Vyson punished? Why did he die?

What was I missing?

All these questions and more haunted my isolation. I couldn't even distract myself with work, forbidden to see Cutler and with the Academy House closed until Ilantra's replacement could be chosen. Honestly, if Laven hadn't shown up, I might've broken into the substacks just to find something to do.

Or someone to hit.

"You expect me to believe that you didn't go see your mothers?" the archivist asks. "That you merely pondered and toiled your days away in unguarded solitary confinement?"

The Butcher shrugs. "Not entirely. The one time I tried to see my moms, guards at the entrance to Common-3 caught me and brought me to Vanil. He sent me right back."

The archivist produces a letter. "This is an affidavit placing you in Common-3 for the majority of that time period. It swears you spent the entirety of your 'isolation' cooking. Bull emphon heavy in the scents exiting the flat. Moreover, it claims a certain Macen Common-1 visited you thrice during that time."

"Well, then it's obviously false. Macen and Musta died in the collapse of Common-1. Besides, the king sent raids into all the Commons in retaliation for the riots. He killed hundreds. If I'd been there, I'd have been arrested or killed."

"I have a hypothesis, Butcher. If you have been truthful, if in fact you did not touch the Source as you claim, perhaps Macen did. You might have been the Herd's symbol, and you certainly did wrangle that bull, *Bessa*, but Macen invented Emphon Rub. Macen discovered the concept of Enhancement."

"Enhancement? We haven't gotten there yet, and you already want to discredit me for it? Starve."

"You're lying, continuously."

"You were there! Did *you* see Macen? Do you have any actual proof he lived beyond rumors and coerced affidavits?"

"You're deflecting. Why lie? Why not talk about spending time with your mothers during that time? Let's pretend for a moment Macen was dead, why not talk about your mums?"

The Butcher takes a deep, steadying breath. "If I was lying, which I'm not, maybe it's easier this way. Maybe not talking about them is better. *Maybe* there are some things that I just can't bring myself to talk about with *you*."

"Lying invalidates the Rite, and I know you know that, so why call upon the Rite at all? Why are we in this room together, Butcher? Revenge? Distraction? Pettiness?"

"Maybe I came to tell you about the Source and knew this is the only way you'd believe me."

"More lies. You wouldn't tell me. Not after what I did."

"Probably, but you have no idea how desperate I've become." The Butcher glances at the darkening window. "Either the smoke's thickening or night approaches. Do you want to be here through the night? Do you want to be here when the Empheron arrives?"

The archivist stands. "I have need of the facilities. If you insist on lying for the remainder, take this time to rehearse. You're slipping."

As the archivist exits, the Butcher waggles the empty cup to the remaining guard. "More water, mate? I'm parched."

"I'm not leaving you alone," she says.

"Ah, well, worth a try."

And so he waits, and waits, and waits, until finally the archivist returns, and he worries that time really is against him now.

36

BIRTHDAY
PRESENTS

MY SEVENTEENTH BIRTHDAY fell three days before my second term. I'd already received my course list and supplies delivered from Cutler's, but I was still confined.

As pissed as I was, unable to investigate, I was eager to start classes for a distraction from my nightmares and guilt if nothing else. I had another with Chef Sagen, called Cooking with Emphon; Alchemic Gastronomy II with Chef Chikor; a free period for independent study; and two new courses, one called Advanced Combat and one being offered for the very first time: Recipes Revisited. The title alone had piqued my interest in the latter, but, even better, it was being taught by Dean Dyl, the author of the redacted paper Laven found. Laven, Yenne, and I immediately signed up.

I was doing the required prereading for that class when a knock on my door sent hope through me. Had Cori gotten out of Vanil's blockade? Or my moms? I'd never celebrated a birthday without them. Famines, I would've settled for silent study hour with Yenne.

"Happy birthday, mate!" Laven said as I opened the door. A large icebox rested in his arms, somehow supporting three large takeout boxes. I helped him inside, but before I could ask about the boxes, he pulled a wrapped parcel from his messenger bag and shoved it into my hands.

"You shouldn't have," I said instinctively, taking it eagerly.

I ripped it open and found a beautifully illustrated cookbook that stilled my heart. *A Dash of Cilantro* by Chef Ilantra Andala. I turned the pages slowly, passively noting the lesser recipes and drawings of the meals Chef had included. Almost all graced our menu at one point.

"It was the first cookbook I read," Laven said. "Part of the reason I decided to pursue cooking."

I set it on the table and took my friend into a hug. "It's wonderful."

"Something to remember her by," he said more quietly.

I nodded, feeling a tear at the back of my eye.

"I missed you at her mourning feast," he continued, taking a seat at the table. "Winta asked after you, too."

"With the riots, Yenne and I thought it was a bad idea to attend."

Laven nodded. "A lot of Rare say you caused those."

"Unsurprising, but no one's said anything to me."

Laven scowled and reached for the takeout boxes, which he opened to reveal my favorite spiced potato tacos from the pub, tortilla chips with salsa, and a burger. Our typical pub lunch.

"You aren't the only one," he said, pushing the tacos to me. "I told my dad that I was rescued by some friends and that was it. He sent word to the EDB to have an officer come by to get my statement, but they didn't even bother to do so. It's like they don't even care I was attacked."

He'd clearly kept the identity of his rescuers a secret as promised, but I didn't want to involve him in the Seeker stuff more than he already was. He might be a brilliant alchemist and a good cook, but even the wok on his back wouldn't save him from another attack.

"But I didn't come here to dwell on that," he said. "Eat, eat. There's cake, too. Homemade, of course."

"Cake?" Laven couldn't possibly understand my surprise. I don't think I'd ever known a common who'd eaten cake.

267

"Cream cheese frosting," he said, like it was normal to put cheese on cake. I suddenly wondered if that *was* normal.

"Thank you. This… this is too much. It means a lot."

"Too much? But then what will I do with this?" Laven withdrew a stack of papers from his bag and showed me the title. It was Dyl's paper about my spice.

"You got it?" I said, snatching it from his hand.

"The whole paper, unredacted. Pretty lish, if I do so say myself. I read through it and knew I had to get it to you. My dad's been pretty unwilling to let me out of the house—I had to sneak here! Me, sneaking. Scalding ridiculous, ain't it?" He took a bite of his burger. "It's a bit dense. Which makes sense given it was co-authored by Chikor *and* Sagen."

I was momentarily startled, but it *did* make some sense. Chikor was the city's most profound alchemist, and Sagen was probably the most talented Chef left after Ilantra's murder.

"What's it say?" I asked, my eyes glazing over almost immediately.

"It's half maths, half flavor theory, all centered around your spice. They call it skyroot powder, and get this, mate. It has endurium in it. That's what the maths is about."

Taco nearly slid out of my gaping mouth. "I thought endurium is only present in emphon?" In my surprise, I wasn't thinking about endurmite.

"That's what's so secret about this," Laven continued. "Ten grams of this powder has almost as much endurium in it as a glass of emphon milk."

"That's like 200 grams worth of carnephon."

"Exactly!" Laven agreed. "The paper goes into all the implications of a plant-based endurium source. Apparently the trees it comes from are huge too. Root systems that are thousands of cubic meters large. According to the paper, it takes a thousand grams of root to get a gram of the spice powder, but still, that's a ton of endurium. No wonder it's so secret."

I chewed in stunned silence, savoring the bitterness of the nopales hidden behind the potatoes. For decades, Rare had known that eating endurium was what gave us Endurance. (I'd only learned it after being elevated.) But during that time, everyone had thought you could only get it from emphon or maybe inedible endurmite. Skyroot powder opened up a whole new world of possibilities.

How much had I used to make Emphon Rub? A pinch? If skyroot powder weighed anything like salt, that was maybe three, four grams. No wonder I'd been so powerful. It had been like dipping the meat in milk.

"Does it say where it came from?" I asked.

Laven frowned. "No, and no matter where I looked, I couldn't find anything unredacted. Not even when I indexed skyroot powder specifically."

"How did you get this unredacted, anyway?" I asked.

"I was too afraid to go back to the substacks looking for the spice, so I used my dad's master key to access the teachers' library on floor nineteen. Figured the paper might be up there."

I reached across the small table to grab him by the neck. "You're a genius."

Laven blushed under the compliment and made a show of pulling out the cake, which was intricately piped in a way I could never compete with. "If we're going to go all the way to become Chefs, one of us is going to have to be."

I gave him a friendly shove, and we cut into the cake.

"Why's it red?" I asked.

"You've never had red velvet?" he said, incredulous.

"I've never had *cake*, Laven."

He stood and rushed over to my tiny kitchen. "Have you got flour?"

"What? What're you doing?"

"Mate, we've got a lot to do. That is *not* going to be the only cake you have today. Not on my watch. No best mate of mine is

269

walking around never having had at least three different types of sponge."

We hung out for the entire afternoon and evening, eating *cakes*—I didn't know what lava was, but it sure made for a great chocolatey texture—and drinking, until he worried his dad would send the entire military looking for him. By then, I had a new plan. Sagen, Chikor, and Dyl all studied skyroot powder sometime within the last six months—or at least that's what the publication date indicated. That meant they'd had some. Might still have some.

I wanted to stop the Seekers. I wanted to protect Ranch. I wanted to be a Chef.

I needed that powder.

37

TEACHER'S PET

SAGEN WAS MY best bet among the three teachers. He liked me—the full marks I'd earned on my TOF final made me confident in that. Dyl had stuck up for me at the Tribunal, but I didn't think they were likely to discuss state secrets with me on day one, and since Chikor had as much willingness to speak to students as I did to eat another bowl of shellfish, I figured him for a last-ditch effort. The last-ditch after I tried to get Yenne to talk to Dyl for me. But I didn't know how I'd broach it with Sagen either.

I kept to my class-day routine, embracing the familiarity of bergamot oil in my Earl Grey tea and savoring something new from the cafeteria—on that first day, a Semoli pastry called a cornetto. Catching lunch with Laven once or twice a week. Practicing with my cleaversaw after classes. Before, I would go from that practice to the Academy House. I wasn't sure how I'd fill my evenings anymore. Maybe I'd try to find Winta to see how she was doing. Maybe see my moms, if I could sneak away. Dates with Cori? I didn't know. But I was trying not to think too much about it either. The Academy House without Ilantra... I didn't want to dwell.

Yenne appeared beside me as I climbed the central stair toward

Recipes Revisited. "You look surprisingly well, given how furious you were last I saw you."

"It's good to see you, too," I said. "And that's because Laven is a genius."

"He's found something," she said, no hint of a question in her eager deduction. "What is it?"

"After class," I whispered. The Academy had changed in the days since Vyson's death. Thirty- and forty-year-olds posing as students leaned against walls and traveled up the stairs around us. They might not be carrying their customary carving fork prods, but it only took a common like me one glance to recognize a carver in the wild. I couldn't tell if they were investigating or watching me, but they definitely didn't let my words go unnoticed. The Academy was starting to feel like the centerpoint of all Seeker activity. The king might be behind them, but the cultists were operating here.

On the next floor, we met up with Laven. He and I had all the same classes; we even had the same room for independent study, and we had both looked forward to spending those courses together. He needed my help in Sagen's class, and I needed his in Chikor's. What I didn't need and hadn't expected was his new worst enemy, a security guard named Aniss.

Aniss was as tall as me and twice as wide, with a dark hat lowered over his eyes, a darker suit, a war spear strung across his back, and a crossbow perpetually glued to his hand. His head was a swivel, and his presence was a wall. Despite the size of the staircase, I felt claustrophobic a meter from him.

"This is my new shadow," Laven said by way of introduction. "He's to follow me everywhere. Scalding wonderful, ain't it?"

"Even into classes?" I asked.

"Even into the toilet," Laven confirmed. "My dad doesn't want me disappearing again."

I offered a pained grimace on his behalf, knowing that was due to my birthday, but mostly I was cursing the varied gods of different religions. I was counting on Laven to assist me in my quest for skyroot powder. Having Aniss around took him off the table.

The Recipes Revisited classroom was packed tighter than a burrito. And not just with students. Two uniformed carvers stood in opposite corners, watching everyone. Despite my previous misgivings, Aniss proved useful. After seeing the crowded room, he glared open a table for us in the back, about as far away from a carver as we could be, too.

A moment later, the Dean took the podium at the front of the classroom. They wore a stylish magenta suit that androgenized their form. The webbing of chained piercings I'd seen at the Tribunal was now covered by a new hairstyle: long, asymmetric bangs dyed a matching magenta. After glancing disapprovingly at the carvers in the corner, they clapped for the room's attention.

"Welcome to Recipes Revisited," Dyl said warmly. As they spoke, a teaching aid subtitled their words on the slate board behind them—a nod toward accessibility I've never forgotten, as someone that much prefers reading to listening. "In this class, we will explore the difference between a lesser and greater recipe. We shall philosophize about what leads to the distinction, and we will appreciate the alchemy of endurium as we do so. This class is listed as an elective, but I assure you it will be the most rigorous you have. Moreover, the final will be unlikely to treat you gently, as it will be your task to communicate why a greater recipe grants power."

"But no one knows that," someone in the front row commented.

"Quite right," Dyl confirmed. "No one *knows*. Not with certainty. But mark my words, you will have an opinion. Or rather, you will at least pretend to if you have any hope of passing."

A few chuckles marked the Dean's words, mine included.

"Now, today, we will begin by challenging the very nature of your understanding of a greater recipe. Tell me, anyone, what must a greater recipe include?"

Laven raised his hand.

"Ah, yes, Florento," the Dean called.

"Emphon?" he said, his tone sure he was being bated but not how. "Meat, milk, broth, or egg?"

Dyl surveyed the class, head cocked as if asking for contradiction. A moment later, they voiced it themselves. "No, I think not."

Dissent whispered the room as people quietly objected, but my voice wasn't among them. I was silent, couldn't believe my opportunity was already presenting itself, and in the most unexpected manner. I raised my hand, drawing a suspicious look from Yenne, whose voice hadn't joined the rest but whose expression certainly supported the general uncertainty around the classroom.

Dyl tilted their head further. "You have another answer?"

"A source of endurium," I said confidently.

Before Dyl could respond, a Rare who'd often enjoyed beating me in Military Matters groaned loudly. "Scalding suns, I wish my servants were here. The roaches think you'll liberate them like some rumored hero, but you can't even tell that's the same bloody thing Florento said."

I kept a straight face. "It's not."

"Bullshit."

"Bessa is correct," Dyl settled. "It is not the same thing."

I pushed my luck. If I wanted their help, I needed their respect, and the only person I knew they respected was Yenne, who'd earned it with a clever, unique argument. Over the course of my isolation, I'd had a lot of time to think, to flip through Ilantra's cookbook, and to remember my attempts to make a greater recipe. I didn't know exactly, yet, but I had an idea. "Nor is it the only necessary ingredient to a greater," I suggested loudly. "There's another."

Dyl and Yenne both narrowed eyes at me. It was almost unsettling how similar their distrustful gazes felt.

"Alright," Dyl said, sitting on a table near the podium. "I'll bite. What else is necessary?"

"Intent," I said, and one of the carvers perked up. Maybe I shouldn't have said anything, but it was too late.

"Go on," Dyl instructed.

"In order to create a greater recipe, you have to have a specific intent for its creation. It's not enough to add a source of endurium and make something."

"In order to create, you must intend to create?" the same chided student asked, clearly looking to regain the support of his peers or his teacher. "That's got to be a logical fallacy."

The students turned to Dyl, who said nothing. In fact, I wasn't sure they'd heard the objection, because when they spoke next, it was a completely different critique of my statement. "Greater recipes have been recreated by unknowing contemporaries, which negates your theory of intent. Refute."

Unsure what they were asking of me, I looked to Laven and Yenne for help.

Yenne whispered, "The Dean wants you to offer evidence against their counterclaim."

They wanted me to prove them wrong, but how? I'd created Emphon Rub practically by accident, but I'd also somehow intended to create it. Each other greater recipe I'd made had been made on purpose. When Cutler and Mom had taught me, I'd known that we were making a greater, and I'd intended that outcome. None of those situations included unknowing contemporaries.

Unwilling to risk any goodwill I'd earned, I shook my head. "I cannot, Dean. Yet, anyway."

They nodded warmly. "I look forward to the day. Now, class, let us return to Bessa's initial suggestion: a source of endurium. He and I both assert that this is not the same as Florento's initial claim of emphon."

The TA pushed the slate aside to reveal another with a set of pre-scrawled directions, which Dyl then read aloud. "Answer the following question: If emphon is not the single necessary ingredient to create a greater recipe, what is, and how might we use it to alter our perspective of cooking? Cite at least three sources from the texts to support your claim."

Groans followed. If there had been any doubt the Dean had been conflating their statement about this being a hard elective, this put it to rest.

"Bessa has already given you the first answer," they continued. "I recommend you give thorough and strategic thought to the second. I will be grading your statements. Bessa, you are excused from the assignment. Come with me. Yenne, as well."

One of the carvers moved to follow, but Dyl stared them down until they slunk back into the corner. I was impressed, honestly. I didn't realize Dyl had that in them—the glare would've rivaled Ilantra's.

A pang of grief followed the thought. In silence, probably for different reasons, Yenne and I followed Dyl to the eighteenth floor, which was guarded by a locked door. "How did you know that emphon wasn't the only source, Bessa?"

I had prepared a lie for this question: it was the logical next step if Laven was wrong. But I worried then about giving it. I had been too confident, too knowing. They wouldn't believe I'd be that confident with a logical next step. I was *too* sure. Too pleased with myself.

So I thought, oh well. If I wanted to talk about skyroot powder, then I might as well. "I know of another source of edible endurium."

Yenne gasped, unable to contain her surprise. I hadn't had a chance to tell her about skyroot powder yet.

"I see my protégé still has much to uncover," Dyl commented. "Valuable to know."

"You've been reporting on me to the Dean?" I asked, spice on my tongue.

Yenne looked away, and I wondered if Vanil knew she informed Dyl, too.

We arrived at a door labeled DEAN. The room within was one part library, one part alchemist's laboratory, and one part living quarters. Bookshelves lined the right wall, and before every third one, a table with anywhere from a single book to a dozen rested. Along the left side of the room, there was a full kitchen with chimneys and hoods, a laboratory full of alchemic equipment, and a grand desk. In the far corner, an open partition revealed a bed and wardrobe.

"What exactly do you study?" I asked cautiously.

"In a word, 'everything,'" they offered. "More specifically, I seek to understand how endurium works through the lenses of alchemy, anthropology, and philosophy. But more importantly, I would like to return to your statement. What other source of endurium?"

I couldn't give that information away too willingly. Not only would it be suspicious, it would appear naïve to someone who clearly valued intelligence and knowledge above all else. And I hadn't forgotten the message I'd found in my apartment that first day either. I couldn't be sure who'd sent it, and I could think of only one follow-up question to revealing I knew a source: Have you used it?

"I think we both know it would be unwise for me to share that so readily," I said. The statement felt weird in my mouth. Political and so unlike me. Rare.

Dyl nodded concession. "I would be remiss if I had not inquired."

"Is that why you brought me up here?" I asked.

"Not completely. I wanted to pass my condolences for the loss of Chef Ilantra. Yenne communicated your grief's intensity."

Despite the guilt Ilantra's name stoked, I side-eyed Yenne. "I appreciate it. Thank you."

They asked how my finances stood without the Academy House shifts and about how I was adapting to life as a Rare. They admitted to knowing much of the answers already thanks to Yenne, but they were never rude, and despite their bookish nature, I felt empathy in their inquiry. But that didn't stop me from casing the room in sideways glances.

When the bell rang to end the period, they stood from their desk. "I look forward to hearing more of your theory. In the meantime, should you need anything, inform Yenne. I don't want you working yourself to exhaustion to pay for course materials. I want you sharp."

"Yes, Dean," I said, a little surprised. Had I just found another ally?

"Good day, Paprick," they said, dismissing me. "Yenne, let's begin at table four."

I took my leave alone, memorizing the route we'd taken to get there on my way back. I was nearly late to Sagen's class, taking my time to commit the passages to memory, and I didn't get a chance to speak with him about skyroot, but I no longer considered him the best lead. Dyl's wing, and more specifically, their lab, felt like exactly the kind of place where I'd find some, which meant that I needed a way in there.

Laven's dad hand-delivered his key to Dyl personally to ensure his son wouldn't go wandering into danger again, which killed my initial plan. So over the new few days, I went to my other classes, half paying attention as I considered next steps. Evidence suggested the king was behind the Seekers, but Vyson said that the Seekers were trying to find the recipe for control before I did. The king already had Chili Control. Why would he be looking for it? The obvious answer was that the recipe for control was something else, but I wasn't looking for any other greater recipes. Until I figured out how to get into Dyl's, I needed to learn more about the Seekers.

That brought me back to the mask Cutler had given me. It was signed.

I needed to figure out by whom.

38

PANNA COTTA
FAVORS

"I NEED ANOTHER favor," I whispered two weeks later, when *finally* carvers were becoming less frequent attendees of my classes.

Laven leaned closer, his hands still quick at work stirring the agar-agar into water while Chef Chikor droned on about proper stirring technique. Laven applied the technique to one half of the lesser recipe, while I applied it to the other: a solution of powdered milk, sugar, and water. Aniss glared from corner, where he cleaned his crossbow, but at least he wasn't a carver. And if he was, he was out of earshot anyway.

"You can copy my work," Laven offered quickly, "but try to actually understand it this time. I don't want to spend the entire week before finals going over the same stuff."

I feigned shock at such a scathing insult as the powders swirled within the beaker, slowly dissolving into the milky substance I'd seen, quietly impressed.

"That's not it," I replied a moment later, "but I'll take you up on that about a week before finals."

"Of course you will. So what is it then?" He cocked an eyebrow, handing me the agar solution, which I swiftly dumped into the milk and sugar solution. A moment later, I transferred the combined solutions to a saucepan for heating.

"If the carvers won't investigate what happened to you, I want to."

Laven chopped rhubarb. "How?"

"I got one of their masks, and it's signed."

"Quiet over there!" Chikor barked.

I lowered my voice and removed the simmering pan from the heat to cool, moving to the other side of our station so my back was to Chikor. There, I placed Laven's rhubarb in a deep dish for sugar sprinkling.

"When were you going to tell me that?" he asked.

"I didn't want to talk about it in front of Aniss."

Laven nodded, drizzling white wine over the rhubarb, and I crimped foil over the dish.

"Whose signature?" he asked as I popped the dish into the oven and checked on the agar-milk. It had cooled enough for the ramekins, so I hurried to pour that in before answering.

"That's the favor," I informed. "I don't know how to track a mask-maker down. I didn't even know there were mask-makers."

Laven worried his bearded chin and moved over to the pressurized nitrogen cartridge. At the same time, Chikor moved in to observe us, silencing our conversation. "You must be precise with the bath," he taught. "Two seconds in either direction will lead to a runny panna cotta or a shattered ramekin. Neither excusable!"

"How long, Chef?" I asked dutifully.

He harrumphed. "Do the maths. And be quick about it or risk losing your canister pressure."

Laven jumped to the calculations, quickly exercising control over unwieldy variables: the differing freezing points of coconut milk and bison milk, the dissolved sugar's volume, the agar-agar, which we'd never used before.

For my part, I guessed on gut. "It can't be more than two minutes."

"Two seconds in either direction is a lot more specific than, 'can't be more than two minutes,' mate. Do it properly. It's important."

"Is it? No self-respecting chef is going to take ten minutes to do math during dessert prep."

"No, they'd do it when creating the menu," Laven argued, his pen sliding across the math so dutifully my vision doubled, producing his father in his place.

I accepted defeat and waited for the answer. One minute, 59 seconds. Laven was displeased I was within the margin of error, but he didn't get long to complain. The rhubarb finished the moment he double-checked the math. The ideal serve was bone-cold panna cotta over warm rhubarb, both covered with the strawberry-hibiscus syrup we'd already prepared.

I lowered the ramekins into the pressure canister quick as a whip and resealed the cap, careful to preserve pressure. We spent a pair of frantic minutes preparing the dishware for plating, lining the rhubarb nicely, and placing our syrup boat within reach—but not so close it chilled—for a quick pour.

"So what do you think?" I asked as we used tweezers to adjust the garnish on the plate. "Any ideas for mask-makers?"

"I doubt they walked into a Plateau store and asked someone to make them creepy cult masks," Laven mused, "but it wouldn't hurt to quickly check the signature against Dad's tax records."

"I'll get you a rubbing."

"In the meantime," he offered, "there may be another avenue that you can pursue."

Our timer dinged, and I quickly removed the panna cotta from the pressure canister. Deftly, I inverted them over the rhubarb beds. For a moment, they stuck in the ramekins and Laven made nervous eye contact with me, but I gave a confident smile—we had done this together. No way it failed. I have it a gentle wiggle, and we both grinned as they plopped out, jiggling gently. Laven placed the flowered strawberries in perfect position, and I reached blindly for the boat to pour the syrup, still entranced by the movement of the favors.

My hand smacked against the side of the boat, causing it to wobble. Before it could topple and ruin the work we'd done, Laven snatched it off the table. "Whoa, mate, don't you dare ruin my plating."

Head shaking with admonishment, he poured it himself.

"One day you're going to knock something over, and I'll have the last laugh."

He gave me a smile. "Right."

Chikor inspected our work: first pressing the bowl of the spoon over the bevel of the panna cotta to check for imperfections and then knocking it against the dessert's side to test its jiggle. Satisfied, presumably, he took a small bite, cutting his spoon through the rhubarb.

"Acceptable panna cotta favors," he said, but I smirked as he dipped his spoon for a second time—something he didn't do for any of our classmates.

When he walked away, Laven nudged me and lowered his voice. "The masks depict different emphon, yeah? What if that's religious? There are emphonists among the common. Maybe ask around in common circles and see if anyone knows anything?"

Why hadn't I thought of that?

"Yeah, good idea."

He smiled. "Now let's taste these things ourselves."

39

LEGENDS

I COULDN'T EXACTLY walk around holding up a mask and asking if anyone had seen it before. For one, it was as good as asking to get attacked. For another, I could barely walk around common districts at all anymore. Between the murals, the greetings, the singing that came my way, I felt like shrinking into my skin. I was the center of attention in every possible way. I was astounded Rare weren't talking about it more or using it to goad me everywhere I went in the Academy. As we ducked through the door into the building housing Black Spice, I mentioned it offhand to Yenne.

"The Herd's suppressing your involvement. We have news-sheet editors working alongside us. As far as Rare are concerned, the most interesting thing about you is who your father is, which restricts mention to the gossip columns."

"Still, you'd think they'd hear it more from their house staff or the carvers, like we heard in class."

"Each time a story is spoken it changes," she commented. "More so if the speaker is biased about its contents. Those who want your story to be great and heroic make it so with set dressing that becomes increasingly fantastic; those who paint you the villain tweak a word here and there to cast shadow. Both lead to such outlandish claims that Rare who hear them discount their original validity. The only way to set history straight now is to pen it yourself. Though I could write your story."

"You could?" I raised a skeptical eyebrow.

"Easily," she answered, "but I'd fill it with lies."

I stopped descending the tunnel to the market momentarily. "Why?"

"The truth is rarely what we want others to hear."

I gawped after her as she hurried into Black Spice, and we went our own ways. Yenne to go debrief Vanil and the others in the Greenhouse, me to Crooked Rish's stall.

"Ah, Pappy!" he exclaimed as I approached. "It is not every day that I stand before a legend."

It'd been a long time since I'd had a candied lemon, and I took it eagerly. "Not you, too. You aren't even standing."

He laughed, wheeling himself into the tent and closing the flap behind us. "I'm not sure you are allowed to say such things."

I frowned. "I—"

He waved me off. "I jest. What brings you to me today? A certain style of penmanship, perhaps?"

I regarded him skeptically. "How could you possibly know that?"

"Oh, my friend, Crooked Rish has ears where others see only walls."

I rolled my eyes. "Can you keep this a secret? And not from my moms or from the Rare or from anyone else I already know you can keep quiet around. From the Herd."

"It pains Crooked Rish that you would even ask, but I appreciate the necessity. Yes, you can rest assured your words will remain locked in my brain's vault. It is not a cheap lock, though, Pappy."

"What does it cost?" I asked nervously.

"It depends on the secret," he replied, "but rarely would I deal in something so fickle as money backed by a state I wish to overthrow, eh?"

"I'll pay it, whatever it is." I pulled the mask from my bag and put it before him. "What do you know about this?"

He examined it, noting the signature inside with a click of his tongue. "Emphonists wore such masks for their services once."

So Laven was right.

"But not for a long time." He motioned for me to take an adjacent seat. "You seek the Seekers."

"What do you know of them?"

"Not much more than you," he admitted. "Not until I crack the cipher. But I have wondered why they would take the faces of emphon. Not likely to be emphonists, eh, so why hide behind the masks worn by them so long ago?"

"Misdirection?" I suggest.

Nodding, he motioned to the signature. "Look at the words here. What do you see?"

"I don't know. It looks like a bunch of swoops and crosses followed by the number 124."

Rish's smirk made angles across his cheeks. "Not a number, but a date."

"Year 124?"

"Indeed," Rish confirmed. "You cannot read the name, but I can. Olivo. From olive, and from a time when it was popular to name a common by a fruit and not a spice."

"So it's a dead end," I complained.

"Ah," Crooked Rish tsked, "what would you make me to be, eh? Never a dead end in Crooked Rish's tent."

Before he could say more, Yenne burst into the tent. "There you are."

"Ah, young Yenne, my brain," Rish said affectionately. "Join us. I am about to enlighten the legend-in-making."

"Please stop calling me that."

"What is that doing here?" Yenne demanded, pointing at the mask. "Vanil ordered—"

"I don't care!" I interrupted. "It's been weeks."

"Children, children," Rish cooed. "Bygones can be gone from my tent. For now, Crooked Rish's services have been requested, and rendered they will be."

Bygones weren't going anywhere, but Yenne didn't interrupt as Rish continued.

"Imagine for a moment that you are a member of a secret group. Difficult, I know. But imagine that your deeds require you to strike fear into those who would witness them and simultaneously protect your secrets. What are two ways you would do so?"

"A mask," I said, obviously.

"A legend," Yenne answered, simultaneously.

I turned to her, confused.

But Rish kept his promise of enlightenment. "A legend," he confirmed as he lifted the mask. "And a mask. Tell me, Paprick not-a-legend, do you know of Queen Pistachia the First?"

"I'm guessing not truthfully," I said bitterly.

"She was a genius and a fury. Under her rule, Ranch defeated the Duckbill Kingdom—weird name, I know—and expanded west, closing the Empire of the Badgeboar into its coastal mountains."

"That was Fen the Victor," I said.

"Only according to *his* history books," Yenne grumbled. As she did, she moved to lean against Rish's desk at the side of the room.

"Her victory cost sixty years of careful tactical attack," Crooked Rish continued. "And the day it was secured, her son poisoned her with the gorge, sneaking extra emphon into her victory feast. He claimed the throne and the victory for himself."

"What does this have to do with masks and legends?" I asked.

"During her reign," Rish answered, "she found a cabal of emphonists so desperate for power that they earned the derogatory term 'faunatics' by killing anyone they believed to be a Consumer. They wore masks made by the common sculptor Olivo, an emphonist himself, and they wore their masks to strike fear.

"But Pistachia used their fanaticism against them. Never were they seen without their masks, even amongst themselves. So Pistachia kidnapped Olivo and forced him to make masks for her and her most trusted. With their masks, they infiltrated a gathering of the cabal, marking themselves with small pins on their lapels so they could identify one another. Swiftly, they killed everyone in attendance without a pin."

"What happened to the masks?" I asked eagerly.

"They were reportedly destroyed," Yenne answered. "I can't believe I didn't think of it sooner!" As she exclaimed, she tossed up her hands and knocked one of the ledger books on Rish's desk onto the floor. Sighing loudly, she picked it up and placed it back.

The outburst, the clumsiness—it was very unlike her, but Rish continued, and I gave him my attention.

"As far as Crooked Rish knows, and Crooked Rish knows much, they have remained in the palace ever since as a trophy of Panchon success. Legend says the prince wore that of the drakephon when he poisoned his mother."

"Then the Seekers really are working for the king," I said. Even as I said it and I felt the truth of it, I couldn't reconcile the inconsistency about finding the greater recipe. Why look for a greater they already had?

"Crooked Rish guesses they wore these masks to pass scrutiny upon emphonists and common, should anyone of clout have caught them." Crooked Rish smiled and bowed his head. "And now services have been rendered, eh?"

"What will it cost me?" I asked, remembering.

"Crooked Rish hears whisper of a new spice with tremendous power: skyroot powder. Convenient for me that the two I think most likely to find it sit before me. I want some."

"I don't know what you're talking about," Yenne said, staring straight at Rish.

"Ah, but Yenne the Brain, the cleverer response would have been to say it is not your debt for me to collect, no?" He smiled. "Crooked Rish thinks you do know, and that you forget your cleverness in defense of that secret."

Yenne looked away. It wasn't often she was outsmarted.

"I don't have any," I said, speaking for myself.

Rish tsked twice. "And you, my little legend, should think before you speak. The better response would have been to say you have no idea where to find some."

I tried a different method. "And what if we don't give it to you?"

He shrugged. "I am but a humble trader. When someone trades in bad faith, I stop. Crooked Rish does not deal with knives in the dark or poisoned food. I simply ignore."

Somehow, that felt more dangerous than a knife in the back.

"I'll do my best," I said.

"That is all I ask."

"Thanks, Rish." I stood. "Come on, Yenne, it's time to go talk to Vanil. I need Cori's help."

Vanil wasn't immediately available, so, sat on a park bench in the Greenhouse, Yenne and I spent the next hour attempting our most recent Recipes Revisited assignment: an analysis of the Grilled Steak Fries recipe. We were to infer why this meal granted Endurance and hyper-observance though similar meals that used the time-old combination of meat and potatoes didn't, using the specific ingredients and steps. Despite being the most advanced students in the class, we couldn't form an argument we actually believed. *I* had suspicions toward an answer, but it wasn't an answer to the question the assignment posed, and Yenne disagreed.

I think we were both relieved when Vanil appeared, staff over his back, Rare clothes on his body, eyes Enduring.

"Paprick," he said. "I wasn't expecting you. I'd begun to think you'd grown angry with me and the cause."

"I need you to stop keeping Cori from me." I made no effort to hide any anger in my tone. "I need her help."

"Help with what?"

"We need to steal skyroot powder," Yenne answered simply.

Vanil faced the Greenhouse for a moment, considering. "You've been reckless as of late. Leading the riot. Killing a teacher. Now you ask for help to steal a new source of endurium—yes, Yenne informed me. Dare I ask from where?"

I looked away from Yenne as I spoke. "Dean Dyl's office."

"Pardon?" Yenne asked.

"Are you sure it's there?" Vanil asked, turning back.

"I can't think of a better place. I know they worked alongside two other teachers to write a paper about its qualities. They couldn't have done so without it."

"Cori is guarding your mothers. Why is she better served with you than with them?"

"It's a three-person job," I lied. "Put your next-best person on my moms' guard."

Yenne narrowed her eyes skeptically.

"If I agree to this, I expect that spice delivered to us. I want to research it."

"Okay," I agreed.

"Okay," he said, tossing me a honeycomb. "I'll send for Cori. On one other condition."

40

THE TRAPPED
DRAWER

"HURRY," I WHISPERED for the second time. "A carver could show up any second."

"Would you like to attempt it?" Yenne offered with zero patience as she worked her lockpicks against the door's lock. "I told you, I checked the patrol schedules. None should be up here."

"Should," I emphasized.

Cori waited farther down the hall. It'd been three days since Vanil released Cori from my moms—who provided Cori with so much blackmail about my childhood antics, I never heard the end of it—and since then, we'd waited for Dyl to leave for a Tribunal meeting. Laven let us know one had been called, but we lost time waiting for the courier who managed the roadrunner office in the Clouds to deliver it to me. So here we were, rushing against an unknown clock.

Cori glanced over at me, face illuminated by the moonlight coming through the window. I smiled, and she winked back. I'd missed her presence in the weeks she'd been with my moms, but until that wink, I hadn't realized how much. Insomnia and nightmares had wound me tight and irritable, which was partly why I lied to Vanil, but having her a few meters down the hall filled me with a relaxed warmth.

The door beside me clicked.

As planned, Yenne and I burst into Dyl's laboratory office, and Cori waited at the door. We figured it was best she stood guard—she could pretend to be lost, and the carvers who frequented the Academy were less likely to know her than Yenne or me. But as we left her out there, tension settled into my shoulders as deeply as during my isolation from her, and I worried what Dyl might do to an unfamiliar student outside their door. At least carvers wouldn't hurt someone with a Rare ID. I turned the lock and grabbed a chair to brace against it for good measure. Cori could and would take care of herself.

Yenne lit a bullseye lantern and made for the laboratory area, her footsteps feathers compared to my own.

"How do you move so quietly?" I whispered.

"By keeping my mouth shut, for one."

I restrained a complaint and turned my attention to the illuminated shelves of the laboratory area. Yenne and I agreed the skyroot powder was as likely to be there as anywhere else. We searched quickly, no way of knowing how soon Dyl would return, combing through cabinets containing standard pantry items like grains and butter as well as rarer stores: a jar of powdered agar imported from Semoli, dried and hulled soybeans labeled for lecithin extraction, and a fresh solution of seaweed and sodium carbonate.

"Famines," I cursed as I came upon the jar of solution.

"What is it?" Yenne asked.

I pointed to the solution. "Dyl's making algin."

"I'm a historian," Yenne responded, deadpan.

"It's an alchemic gastronomy thing," I said, unwilling to explain the spherification techniques I'd memorized for our final. "Point is, it takes about two hours to extract from the seaweed. How long ago did they leave?"

Yenne checked her pocket watch, and even though I was looking for it, I still couldn't find where in her skirt folds she produced it from. "We need to hurry."

I reached for the next drawer and nearly popped my shoulder from its socket failing to pull it open. "This one's locked," I said.

Yenne approached with picks, and I checked the rest of the drawers in the laboratory. None were locked. If skyroot powder was here, it was in that drawer.

"Don't forget the secondary objective," Yenne said as she fiddled with the lock.

Vanil's second condition was that we take full advantage of being within the highly restricted living quarters of a Tribunal. "Powder will get us your greater recipe, but the intelligence within that office might win us the war."

Taking the other bullseye lantern, I surveyed the shelves and came across two tomes that I stuffed into my bag: *The Lost Family Herdon* and *Forgotten Flavors and Techniques of Olearth*. I was hoping to find something like *Secret Greater Recipes of the Panchon Kings*, but no such luck.

I had just found another locked drawer in Dyl's desk when Cori's knuckles rapped against the door frantically.

"Oh, thank the Consumer," she yelled loudly outside in a Rare accent, unnecessarily heavy footsteps stomping away from the door. "I've been lost up here for an hour!"

"How's that lock coming?" I whispered.

"The lock isn't the problem," Yenne hissed. "It's the tripwire connected to a gas vial inside that vexes me."

"It's trapped?"

"Stay quiet and let me focus! If Dyl finds me in here, I'll be unadopted in a heartbeat."

If hers had a gas vial, I guessed the second locked drawer did, too. I figured we weren't getting out of the room undetected anyway, so I grabbed the algin Dyl had been preparing and hoped it would do what I needed.

Summoning my strength, I pulled on the locked desk drawer as hard as I could. The wood groaned against my fingers but started to give. Gritting my teeth, I flexed my digits harder, desperate to get more out of this than two tomes that might not even prove useful.

The desk shattered open loud enough to be audible outside the room. As a plume of gray smoke exploded outward, I poured the algin, which was now a gel, into the drawer and held my breath—neither of which I would've thought to do if Yenne hadn't mentioned the gas vial inside her drawer.

Good thing I did.

The algin sponged up half the gray smoke, trapping it within the gel. The other half burned caustic against my nostrils and eyes, and I feared what it could do to someone's lungs—or skin—even as I threw my hands into the open drawer. The gas attacked my flesh like a nest of bees, reminding me of the burns I'd suffered to make my Emphon Rub in old Black Spice.

Inside the drawer, I found a scroll made of thick, leathery vellum unlike any I'd ever touched. Despite the pain, I felt the algin gel coating the vellum, so I wrenched it out quickly, and flapped it into the air to disperse the gas and gel. A corner burned to ash in the air, older and thinner than my hands, and I threw myself away from the lingering fumes.

As I hurried back to Yenne, the lock turned in the door. "Who's in there?" Dyl called.

"Full marks for me," Yenne whispered as she used some apparatus to produce a slicing sound from within the barely opened drawer. It slid open without an explosion, and we tossed the contents—three different colored pouches—into my bag alongside the scroll and the two tomes.

Dyl threw their meager frame against the door, but the chair held in place.

"Is there another way out of here?" I asked.

"Not that I know of," Yenne said, shaking her head.

I failed to see an alternative to hurting Dyl and escaping.

Then I recalled where I was. An alchemic kitchen.

I couldn't pick a lock, but I could cook. And anyone who cooks as much as I did thinks often about the most prevalent pest of the kitchen. Not rats but smoke.

No one cooked in an enclosed space. So why were there no windows in this place? Covered by bookshelves, maybe?

I tried to move one out of the way, but the thing must've weighed two hundred and fifty kilos.

I tore my attention from the shelves to the oven along the wall. The fume hood above was about the size of my shoulders. Hastily, I pushed Yenne toward it and bid her climb through.

"What if it narrows?" she protested, but I didn't think it would. This was a big room with precious tons of books. The Dean wouldn't want smoke accumulating.

Yenne tied the bag's straps around her ankle, and I had to dodge a kick to the face as she wriggled upward to the smoke shelf, muttering complaints to herself as she struggled. My hope of fitting was slim, but I remembered the pantry items. As she climbed the flue—confirming it didn't narrow—I hurriedly stripped off my shirt and rubbed a stick of butter over my sweating shoulders and arms.

The chair fell as Dyl finally knocked it free, and I hurriedly squeezed into the chimney's throat, pulling myself over the smoke shelf as my greased shoulders ached against the tightness.

The door banged open as Dyl entered and cursed.

Impossibly nimble, Yenne climbed from the crown of the flue to the roof. I tried to mimic her grace, but my fingers were larger, and I scraped them against the edges of the bricks I clung to. My buttery hands kept slipping. I could hear Dyl muttering curses, presumably finding the remains of the desk and the empty drawer. The strain and soot made me desperate to clear my lungs, but if I coughed or panted, I'd be heard. I tried to cover my mouth with one hand, but the moment I did, my other lost its grip, and I slid, my boot scraping against the flue. I had to do a shallow split, my boots pressed against either side to keep from sliding back down.

"Hello?" Dyl called out. "If you're hiding, I'll find you. The EDB will be here momentarily. Come out now and the punishment may be reduced."

My legs shook with the strain, but I used the moment to wipe my greasy palms against my pant legs.

Footsteps approached the chimney. I was out of time. But I looked up to find Yenne reaching down. If I could just get up the last two meters to reach her. I strained and pulled. By the time I escaped onto the roof, my cuticles bled and stung, my whole body covered in soot.

Atop the tower's roof, I couldn't help but take in the city. The vantage was staggering. I'd only ever seen the city in the daylight from Fen's Plateau. In the late evening, candles illuminated nearly every window in the Commons, but half the Rare homes lay dark. I knew we had more people from what I saw on the Plateau, but the illusion was shattered. We dwarfed them. Substantially.

I followed the river winding around the Clouds and running south to the ruin of Common-1. Even in its wreckage, lights danced, unhoused common finding shelter where they could. Rare had access to these vantages and didn't even have the power to root out squatters. How could we ever let ourselves be subjugated?

Hissing, Yenne led us off the roof. She had to pick another door to get us into the central staircase, which she checked was clear, allowing me to dodge into some hallways to avoid notice—I wasn't exactly explainable, buttered up, shirtless, and covered in soot. Eventually we regrouped with Cori behind a pub on 11.

"What exactly happened in there?" she asked, running a hand across my buttered chest. "And can it happen any time I want?"

Rolling my eyes, I removed the tomes, pouches, and scroll from the bag for investigation.

Two of the pouches were mysteries. One was packed with flat mulchy bark with a chalky consistency that smelled like a powerful combination of malted caramel, vanilla, and citrus, with a hint of lavender. The other, a claylike salt that tasted sharp and earthy. I imagined it would be great for broth or soup. The final pouch contained at least half a kilo of skyroot powder.

But the scroll was the true treasure.

Vanil had hoped for secrets we could use in the war, but none of us expected to find the greatest of all.

I unfurled it far enough to see the title and the first ingredient, both inked in blood on what we later determined to be human flesh.

This was not the place to read that scroll, not while I was still covered in soot, attracting attention. Because the scroll contained a greater recipe. *The* recipe. Chili Control.

We didn't celebrate. Because two things soured the taste of success.

Dyl, someone I'd thought harmless—if not an ally to the Herd— had it locked in their desk. Why? How? Questions we weren't ready to ask aloud, let alone answer.

And far worse, the first ingredient of Chili Control was far more gruesome than carnephon.

Human blood. And a lot of it.

ENTREMET IV

UNDERSTANDING

"DESCRIBE IT TO me," the archivist commands.

"You've seen it," the Butcher replies with a hint of defiance.

"For years I've wondered if your eyes saw more than mine."

After a long moment, the Butcher scratches his chin and sighs. "Remember the assignment I mentioned? Analyze Grilled Steak Fries and argue why it worked the way it did? It wasn't until I read that scroll that I really understood the assignment."

The archivist's heartbeat rises. This felt close. A path to the Source at last?

"But that's the thing," he says, pausing a moment. "I didn't actually read the whole thing right then. I saw the first ingredient and decided it wasn't worth using. I didn't read it until later, and what happened before I read it was crucial to understanding."

The pen cracks in the archivist's hand, grip tightening into a fist of frustration. "Tell me, Butcher."

"That's not how the Rite works. Skipping ahead would invalidate the process. Kings are excused from all crimes under Rare law, and if I'm to prove I'm the Chef King, I need to go in order."

"Don't lecture me on the laws I uphold."

"I wouldn't dare to."

"Then let us be quick to it, Butcher."

"Don't worry. It all happened so fast after that." His eyes, no longer Enduring, fall to his hands. "Gods, was it really only two days?"

41

INFLECTION POINT

CHAOS REIGNED OVER the Greenhouse, and it had nothing to do with us. More people than I'd ever seen there dashed through the garden. Black Spice was empty, the guard only letting us in because we were expected.

We found Vanil in a small garden, his head bowed over a desk covered in papers. He spoke with a handful of advisors that I'd seen but rarely spoken to. Beside him stood a bloodied and bruised woman, not much older than me, who I'd never seen. Exhaustion hung in her eyes and the stink of the road clung to her dusty clothes. Among the small crowd, there was another surprising face, one that belonged to the merchant I'd first gotten skyroot from, Ruda.

As we approached, I reached for almonds, but quickly realized this wasn't a time for greetings.

"We shouldn't rush to conclusions!" Vanil said, clearly trying to ease tensions.

"They brought six carnephon to the Front," a white-haired woman who couldn't have been more than thirty countered. "Nearly everyone's dead. We're done!"

"What happened?" Yenne asked, stepping into their circle.

Vanil opened his mouth as if to explain, but the white-haired woman cut him off. Even as she spoke, she looked as if it pained her to do so. "Vanil, I appreciate the vision you've shared with them, but you've put too much stake in these children. Enough is enough. We don't have time."

"Excuse me?" Cori asked, affronted.

Vanil cut a sideways glance at Cori and his lips tightened as if suddenly uncomfortable. After a second, he calmed his voice and addressed Cori directly. "Cori, take Yenne and Paprick to find Crooked Rish. We'll talk later."

"Respectfully, sir," Yenne interjected. "There's something you should know."

"By the Twelve," the woman cursed. "That was an order!"

"I found the recipe for Chili Control," I blurted.

Everyone froze, including three different messengers who'd come to hand Vanil a message or take one from his desk.

"It appears she spoke truth." It was Ruda who broke the growing silence.

"Show me," Vanil said, and despite how much I didn't want to hand it over, how much I didn't want *anyone* to read further than I had, I slapped it into his outstretched palm.

His eyes widened immediately as he reached what I assumed was the part about the blood, but he didn't seem as disgusted as I'd been. He kept reading, and nodded confidently when he finished.

"This is it," he confirmed to the small council. As if a great weight of many days had been taken from him, Vanil fell back into his chair. "We lost the battle at the Front, but with this? We've won the war."

"How did you come to possess this?" the woman asked.

Vanil nodded his permission, so Cori relayed our story. I tried to hide my grimace as she informed everyone about the skyroot powder and its importance to Emphon Rub, but my face must have given me away.

"They already know it's in the recipe," Ruda said smugly. "I told them that night. Oh, and I will be expecting repayment for what was stolen."

"You already took my kn—"

"There will be time later," Vanil placated. "For now, we have an advantage. They decimated the entire Front and think they've won."

"They what?" Cori interjected.

"But they'll bring the carnephon back to Pen Stables. With this, we can steal them and all the others besides. This is the inflection point. This is the beginning of the end."

I startled as I realized what he was saying. "You can't intend to use it. It's wrong."

"Wrong?" Vanil examined me as if I were some unknown bug. "What's *wrong* is that the Rare slaughtered our army and torched Far Common."

"Torched?" Cori's lip made the slightest tremble.

Vanil frowned. "I'm sorry. Your parents are safe, Cori. I should've led with that. The carnephon the General bragged about capturing? He didn't bring them here as our intelligence suggested; he brought them to the Front and attacked in the night. Within a few hours, they'd marched all the way to our headquarters in Far Common. It was razed. This is Kay from Far Common-11. She managed to get away on a bisonback and bring word from your parents."

"Marched them?" I clarified. "Do you mean...?"

Vanil nodded. "I believe the king must have been among them. Chili Control was in use."

I wanted to give the rebel army's sacrifice room to breathe, but I couldn't stand by and let it be used as justification for using human blood.

"It's cannibalism," I continued. "I don't care how the Herd benefits. It's wrong, and the amount needed is disgusting. It specifies that each serving requires a different murdered person."

"A few lives are no cost compared to that of all common," Vanil answered. "Or are your own murders somehow different?"

I looked away, appalled at the validity of his retort. I *had* used that argument to justify myself, even after I'd admitted my hypocrisy. But I was no more willing to accept that someone be killed so that the Herd could capture carnephon. Not even to hurt the king's plans. "If you use that greater, you do so without me."

"We don't have time for this!" the white-haired woman shouted. "Send the children away, Vanil, and let us get to planning. Someone could've already given up this place."

Vanil looked from the white-haired woman to me, to the scroll, and back to me. Before he could speak further, a voice called from our backs. "Pappy, a word."

Crooked Rish waited at the end of the trees, motioning for me to follow.

"All three of you, go with him," Vanil ordered. "You need to hear what he has to say."

I didn't move.

"Go!"

Cori grabbed my wrist and pulled me over, using the movement to cover her mouth as she whispered in my ear. "We'll make it right."

I flared my nostrils and stared Vanil in the eye. "It's wrong," I said, but turned to follow Cori and Rish.

42

CROOKED KINGDOM

"BEFORE WE GET to Rish," the archivist interjects. "I'd like to share where I really went while I used the facilities."

Suspicion creases the Butcher's brow.

"Earlier, you asked about the Empheron. A few weeks ago, several Tribunal members, myself included, journeyed into the Southern Desert to observe it from a distance. During our journey, I found a young girl, no more than twelve, her throat drier than a sponge. For just a bit of water, she told me her name, Musta, and all about her father. She was a nice—"

"Was?"

The archivist smiles. "Sorry, is. Anyway, it just so happens that her father's name was Macen. Quite the coincidence if you ask me."

With some effort, the Butcher retakes his seat. "There are only so many spices for common to name themselves after. It was bound to happen."

"Right, well, I could have her brought here, if you want?"

The Butcher waves a hand, nonchalant. "It's a coincidence. Besides, it's what Rish said next that clarified the whole Chili Control situation. You still want to know about the Source, don't you?"

"If you insist."

Rish led us out of earshot before pressing candied lemons into our palms. "You have recovered payment for services rendered, no?"

"This is the important thing we needed to hear?" I complained as I reached into the bag.

"Don't give it to him," Yenne said, staying my hand.

"Why not?"

Rish narrowed his gaze upon Yenne. "What is it you know, Yenne the Brain?"

After a long moment, she removed two pieces of paper from the seemingly endless abyss of her skirt folds. One appeared to have been ripped from a book... or ledger. I recalled her knocking that ledger off his desk after her dramatic outburst. She must have used it to cover her ripping a page out. The other was a crumbled piece of excessively white paper that I recognized immediately.

"Where'd you get that?" I asked.

"Your trash," she said.

Crooked Rish smiled as laughed. "Brain, indeed."

"What's going on?" Cori asked.

"The handwriting matches," Yenne said, ignoring Cori and showing me the papers.

I frowned over the note and looked to Rish. "But why?"

"Y'all need to explain what's going on before I stop asking questions," Cori threatened.

I handed the two papers to Cori. "I got a message the day I moved into my apartment, threatening me if I told anyone the recipe for Emphon Rub. Apparently, Rish wrote it."

Rish smiled, a crooked thing that was less guilty than sincere. "I am revealed."

"Why?"

He shrugged. "It is neither as nefarious nor as self-important as you are likely to think. I didn't send that so I could take what I remembered of that night—the spices you smeared upon that meat—and recreate the greater for sale. But if Crooked Rish is honest—a very strange thing, eh?—you will not believe me."

"Try me," I said.

"I feared for the son of Sesa, and I did not want him to have a loose tongue in a place that would so readily cut it free and dine on it."

He was right, I didn't believe him.

And Cori didn't either. "Then why do you want the powder?" she asked, returning to the point. "If you know Paprick's greater, it's pretty suspicious to ask for it if you ain't trying to recreate it."

"Is it so incredible to believe I merely want to interrupt Ruda's monopoly?"

"Probably," I decided. "But I don't care. Vanil is going to murder people to use Chili Control."

I handed Rish a small portion of the skyroot powder and turned to head back to Vanil's gathering.

"I would not be so quick to return," Rish said, halting me.

"Why not?"

"Because there are more cooks in this kitchen than anyone knows."

"Anyone but you?" Yenne grumbled.

"Indeed," Rish answered soberly. "I have it on very good authority that the king was not in fact with those who attacked the Front."

"Whose authority?" Cori asked.

"For once, my own," he said.

I ached to return to the gathering, but curiosity got the better of me. After all, of everyone, I'd known Rish the longest. Rish who my moms trusted and loved. Rish who'd once promised to buy me skyroot powder before we even knew its value because I wanted to taste it.

"Then he sent someone else with the greater recipe," Yenne suggested. "Why does Vanil think that we three need to hear this from you?"

I can't know if she wanted the answer because she was naturally curious or for a snippy need to one-up Rish, who seemed to constantly outsmart her, but I sometimes wonder what would've happened if she'd not asked. I know I didn't think to ask it.

Rish reached into a bag hanging on his chair and produced a stack of papers. "I broke the code on Vyson's notes earlier this day." He handed them to Cori, who quickly began leafing through them. "The lieutenant kept notes on you, Pappy. Your grades. Your skill with the cleaversaw. Your comings and goings, the people with whom you spent time. Your mothers, your friend Laven, even Jives Cutler. They attacked Laven, Ilantra, and Jives, purposefully."

"We knew that," Yenne said. "For revenge."

"In fact, no," Rish said. "Well, not in entirety. You see, these notes detail darker tidings. First, that they knew Cori's song, your place amongst the rioters, and your comings and goings within these walls. Things he could not have known without having a mole within the Herd."

That froze everyone.

Rish rolled closer.

"Secondly, they mention a prophecy seen with Foresight Fried Gryphon, a greater recipe to glimpse a person's future. The king saw your future after the Tribunal. You destroy the Commons and kill your friends. Pappy, they have spared you so that they can use you to destroy the will of the common. To turn their symbol against them. But they also saw that you would touch the Source—whatever that is—and it would be their undoing."

"I wouldn't," I insist. "I'd never do that. And I haven't touched the Source. I told the king that!"

"What is that?" Cori asked. "This Source?"

"It is the subject of myth," Yenne answered. "To some, a god. Anyone who touches it learns all greater recipes, or so the myths indicate."

"Well, I sure as hell don't know all greater recipes!" I yelled, my anger getting the better of me. "So clearly this Foresight recipe is bullshit. Maybe it's misunderstood, like Observant Omelet."

"There's more," Rish said, removing two more pieces of parchment. "I finished decoding this as news broke about the Front."

He handed me the first, which was dated a couple weeks before the Flyover Festival.

"'Almon's notes mention Enhancing a greater recipe,'" I read aloud. "'Dyl thinks they figured out what that means. I'll need time, but we're closer to the recipe for control than ever. But first I need to see what he knows. Set up the demonstration with Ilantra and prepare some collateral as distraction. Friends, family, I don't care who. Find me some targets. Maybe something that destabilizes the Herd as well. Talk to my servant about options.'"

The second was immediately familiar. The parchment I'd seen the king write after interrogating me. "'The roach's memories were the final piece. I know how to make the greater recipe. Start with that bitch, Ilantra, and lure in the Florento boy. Both have proven disloyal, but we can't have his father thinking he was taken intentionally. Kill the old man, after. His family has always irked us. We'll save his mums for now.'" I faltered momentarily but continued. "'No telling what trouble killing them will have. We can't have him touching the Source before he destroys the Commons.'"

I looked at the people around me, as I took all that in.

Cori spoke first. "So the king thinks Paprick knows something about Enhancing a greater recipe? Am I getting that right? What's that mean?"

"That was my reading as well," Rish confirmed.

"And the king has a servant," I repeated. I turned back to Yenne. "You were telling Dyl about me. Dyl had the Chili Control recipe."

"Paprick," she said, very gently. "I only told them about how you were acclimating to school. That's all they ever asked about! I swear. I can't believe they had that greater." She paused. "I'm disgusted."

Rish looked characteristically skeptical. Cori spoke up in Yenne's defense. "Yenne's had plenty of opportunities to betray us. She just helped up break into Dyl's office. Let it go, killer. A witch hunt's only going to play into the king's hands right now."

"Thank you, Cori." Yenne sighed, seemingly with more exasperation than contempt. "I don't blame you, but Paprick, this is weeks old. The mole could already be gone. We need to focus on the now. Do you have any idea what Enhancing is?"

I bit my lip. "I—I've been wondering about what happens when you add more endurium to a greater."

"You gorge?" Cori said, as if that was obvious.

"If that's the case, why did Emphon Rub work at all?" I asked. "It has more endurium than anything I can think of, with both carnephon rib and skyroot powder." I held up a hand to stop further argument. "Gorge, as far as I know, only happens when you eat more than one greater recipe."

That gave everyone pause.

"How long have you been sitting on this?"

"Ilantra showed us a bunch of different ways to make similar dishes with tomatoes. How different cultures have different techniques. She even asked us what defines our cuisine so that we'd think about how techniques define lesser recipes. And then Laven told me how Dyl was studying endurium quantities: skyroot powder vs meat vs milk, etc."

Crooked Rish shook his head. "Pappy, help a broken man mend these different pieces. How are those two things related?"

I raised my hands, searching for the words. "We," I gestured to Ranch, "have always made greater recipes one way. In fact, the only thing we even know about making them is that they need a source of endurium. We always focused on that element. That's our *technique*. But then I made one that used two sources and I didn't gorge. What if I add a second to an existing greater?"

Crooked Rish tossed and caught the pouch in his hand. "You needed a second to test your theory."

"The king confirmed he was working with Dyl," Cori added. "And they had a second."

"Maybe even multiple," Yenne said, motioning to the bag with two more pouches within.

"We need to test your theory," Cori said. "Now."

"I can't let Vanil use that scroll," I said.

"Killer, think," Cori said. "Dyl's working with the king. They're going to tell him what's missing. We're out of time."

"What ingredients do you need to test your theory?" Rish asked.

"Truthfully?" I shrugged. "I don't know. More than anything, I need time to think, to figure out how this all comes together."

"Then I will do the impossible and buy you time you do not have," Rish said, holding up a candied lemon. "Easy, peasy, lemon squeezy."

First, we groaned. Then we planned.

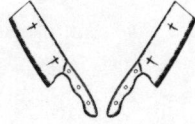

Course 5: Chili Control

A meal best left untouched.

Expected Endurance Effect(s):

Endurance, 2–3 hours
Telepathic control over living creatures with endurium bones,
   2–3 hours

Noted Side Effect(s):

Loss of rationality, 2–3 hours

43

THE FUTURE
OF A NATION

WE RETURNED TO Vanil as his councilors were leaving. He saw my expression and sighed. "I understand your morals, but we have no other options."

"That's not necessarily true," I said, stepping forward and handing him the letter. "I have a theory I need to test, about Enhancement."

"What does that mean?" He read it over quickly, but it didn't have the same weight for him that it had for us. "Paprick, I can ensure victory with the Chili. You want me to give that up because the king read something in his thieving ancestor's notes?"

"I have to try. I'm common; I don't waste. And that goes double for lives. Even if you murder Rare to use that greater, you prove we're no better than they are. That we'll do the easy thing to win."

"Nil," Rish said delicately. "I believe in him. *Cori* believes in him."

"Belief only carries us so far. At a certain point, we must trust history. History tells us that he who uses Chili Control wins, time after time."

"Then you betray us," I said.

And as Vanil sighed, I punched him in the jaw as planned. He went down faster than a brick, completely unsuspecting. Cori grabbed the scroll, and we ran.

Vanil attempted to scramble after us, but Rish blocked his path, encouraging us to run faster. It was hell dodging through the guards that came after us, but no one was ready for an attack from within. Before long, we were in the Clouds, the scroll still in my hands. I needed a kitchen, but Vanil knew all the ones I'd like use: mine, my moms', Cori's, Cutler's.

I was desperate and afraid. Feeling as if the future of a nation was resting on *my* shoulders. Me, a factory boy from Common-3. A kid who just liked to cook. I'd just betrayed the Herd, risking my moms' safety if Vanil wanted revenge. Even Yenne looked uncharacteristically unsure of things. But Cori took my hand, calming my heaving lungs, and I had a key to one other kitchen, a place I suspected would affect me deeply—and not in a way that was going to be helpful.

The Academy House.

No one had been inside since Chef's death. Not even Winta. Some unspoken agreement among the staff that it wasn't our place to enter, but it felt right. I'd invented a greater recipe in the flames of Black Spice and honed my craft at the Academy. If I was going to Enhance a greater, then I'd do so where I'd been enhanced: Chef's kitchen.

I said it before: I always prefer to read rather than listen to new information, and now was the time to learn. So I went to Chef's station and unrolled the scroll.

In the Greenhouse, I'd rambled out a theory about using multiple endurium sources as a means of Enhancing a greater, but I still didn't fully know what led to a greater. Why I couldn't just swallow some carnephon and grow large. Why I'd had to create my rub, specifically. Why the ingredients I used. Why then. Why there.

I'd given Dyl the beginnings of a theory, some kind of intent, but I needed more, and when I saw the human blood in the recipe, that theory grew stronger. Because that recipe was appalling. And not just morally, but flavorly, if that's a word.

Reading it confirmed my suspicion.

SEVEN RECIPES FOR REVOLUTION

No one could want to eat this.
No one could stomach it.
Not with that much blood.
So why require it?

ENTREMET V

INGREDIENTS

"ARE YOU SUGGESTING the scroll was a lie?" the archivist asks.

The Butcher runs his hands through his damp hair, which has grown greasy with the agitation of recalling that evening. "No, it was perfectly accurate. You know that."

"Then what are you getting at? What did reading it reveal about the assignment for Recipes Revisited and for creating greater recipes?"

"Have you ever tasted human blood?" the Butcher responds.

"I've sucked a paper cut or two."

"Not even a teaspoon then. Human blood is rich as mines with iron and salt. A teaspoon will kick you in the teeth. A few tablespoons? You'll gag on it. Cups? Most people couldn't get it down without vomiting. So why did I read the scroll?" He rises and presses his head between the bars, coating them with the sweat and grime of his hair. "I wanted to know what else was in it. What starving ingredients made human blood palatable."

"And the assignment?"

"Tit for tat. What else do you know about the Empheron?"

"You show me yours," the archivist goads.

The Butcher nods. "Fine. When I read that scroll, I knew, without the slightest hesitation, that greater recipes need only two ingredients. Everything else, all the onions and spices in the world, they're meaningless. Just tools really."

"Elaborate," the archivist demands after a moment's pause.

"Do you remember what I said to Ilantra at the Tribunal? 'Food is identity.' I didn't realize how right I was."

"What do you want from me, Butcher? To say, 'You, Paprick Herdon, are the smartest, absolute best Chef alive; please, oh, please explain to my poor, insufficient mind what you're getting at?' Is that what you want? I'm over your riddles!"

"I never got to write my Recipes Revisited final," he answers. "To argue what makes a greater different from a lesser, but if I had, I would've argued this: A lesser recipe is a culmination of its ingredients' individual flavors and a greater recipe is the culmination of the dish's identity. It is the culmination of the *identity* its creator and its community give it. Endurium doesn't give greaters power, we do."

The archivist's fist balls around the pen. "Is that supposed to be philosophy?"

The Butcher licks his lips, clearly pleased with the archivist's frustration. "I've told you a dozen times over that the greaters I tasted all tasted like something else, except for one: Emphon Rub. Why? Because I expected it to taste the way it did."

"Well, yes. You made that one."

"Exactly." He pauses a moment. "You still don't get it. Well, once we get to me eating the chili, you will. Now, show me yours."

Unsatisfied with the answer, the archivist considers protest, but the guard returns with a note from the Commander, and its content brings a smile to the archivist's weary face.

"The Empheron isn't natural. It was once human, though certainly is not now. We believe we know who it was and why it seems obsessed with composing its army with all twelve emphon. Why it seems to have waited for you to reappear before it leads its army here to kill every last one of us. Which it will, unless you help us find the Source."

"How is it killed? When whoever looked at it with FFG, did they see how it's killed?"

"I'm disinclined to share, Butcher."

"Of course, you are. Fine. The deaths are about to stack up, and with them my charges. You ready? It only gets worse for you after this."

"You say that as if the same isn't true for you."

44

LEATHERBOUND

I COMMITTED CHILI Control to memory before handing it over to Yenne, who was desperate to read it. When she was finished, I took it back—which was easier said than done—and contemplated what I was going to say to Cutler in the morning. There was nothing more for Yenne to contribute that night, so she headed back to the home she shared with Dyl.

"We shouldn't leave that out," Cori noted while I was still lost in thought.

I nodded. "Right, I know where we can hide it." I should've destroyed it, but destroying a greater recipe is something that, to this day, feels akin to blasphemy. Cooking is my religion, and you don't burn your belief down. Not even in the darkest moments.

It's often all we have.

When I returned, Cori unsheathed her flatsaw and inspected a knife sharpener with a suspicious expression that shifted to me as I entered. "I'm not sure I should use this on my flatsaw."

"Not if you want a durable edge," I said, taking the sharpener. "They're meant for thinner blades."

"Did you mean what you said back there?" she asked suddenly.

"What part?"

"That if Vanil used the chili, you'd leave the Herd."

I shrugged. "I believe in the Herd's mission, but the methods… What's the point of being a symbol if I don't believe in the symbolism?"

"Alright, killer. Gettin' all poetic." Cori sheathed the flatsaw and reached into her bag. From within, she produced a wrapped parcel. "I got this for you for your birthday, but I never got the chance. I don't want to miss it now. Your moms helped me with the size, so it should fit."

I freed a bundle of folded leather from the parcel and gasped as it opened into a leather apron with shoulder straps rather than the traditional neck loop—something that was never comfortable on someone as tall as me. It had two deep front pockets that actually rested where my arms fell and an off-center pocket on the chest. As I lifted the apron to try it on, a butcher's cleaver fell out of it—apparently wrapped inside it—and struck the counter with a clamor.

Cori squeaked an adorably un-Cori sound and fumbled to grab it, looking embarrassed as she did. "I should've realized that would happen." She set the knife in my hand, and I turned it over to see an engraving that read *Chop chop, killer*. Its weight was perfect.

"There's a secret sheath on the inside for it," she informed, guiding my hand to it.

Maintaining eye contact with her, I put on the apron and found the secret pocket. The cleaver slid in perfectly, fitting across the front of my torso at the V-line of my oblique, so I barely had to bend my elbow to retrieve it.

The perfection of the gift, of the fit… It was obviously one of a kind and tailored to me. Not something Cori could've found in a store, not even Cutler's, or the type of thing a leatherworker could've put together in the amount of time between our date and my birthday. I knew immediately that this was something Cori had requested far, far earlier and at no minor expense.

"When?" I asked, tears straining at the back of my eyes. It was so much better than the one I could never afford from Cutler's.

She looked at the sink where I did dishes, where she'd visited me that night. "The next morning." An embarrassed flush colored her cheeks.

"Well, I'll be, you can blush."

"Keep making fun, and you won't get your other gift."

"Other gift?" I asked, stepping closer.

"Butcher," the archivist complains. "Must w—"

"Can I have it now?" I asked, touching her cheek.

"If you're ready, yeah."

"Ready if you are."

This time, her lips were flavored with salt and steel. Not irony or metallic, but the essence of steel. The Perfect approximation of it; sharp and lethal as a flatsaw, firm and playful as a duel. Each flick of her tongue brought me deeper into her, forged me in the warmth of her care, and promised an escape. After pulling my shirt free, Cori lifted herself onto the island and swept it clear of dishes and knives. I followed, eager but careful.

Even then, my moms were in the back of my head. A thousand little hints and warnings disguised as jibes.

Cori rolled me with her hips, flipping me onto my back atop the island as she removed her shirt. It wasn't the first time I'd seen her skin—all those little scars on her biceps from training with her father, the tattoos, the birthmark left of the navel—but there was a freedom to the invitation that sent my spine arching toward her. My lips met Cori's skin with a sound that could've been from my mouth, hers, or both, and no space distanced our flesh.

Stars danced through the windows and across my skin, until we couldn't any longer, until the night's heat and our passion wrung the last water from our bodies. Until we lay on our backs atop the island, panting and bare, soul and body. Until every aspect of me knew that I loved this person, that I would die for her at the cost of anyone else.

That if ever anyone robbed me of Cori, that person would find themselves inserted into a hell so deep and so Perfect stories would be written about it. An entire book.

That I would cut out their tongue and eat it as the blood leaked their body slow.

The Butcher rises back to his feet, that smile manic and starved, and approaches the bars. For the first time, the archivist fears the man within the cell, worries the bars can't possibly restrain his urge for revenge.

Slowly and carefully, the Butcher tucks his hair into his smile, licking the split ends as if they were the ends of a basting brush. When he wipes the hair away from his eyes, they glow a gruesome yellow.

"Your hair," the archivist realizes. "It's in your hair!"

Not for the first time in this life, the archivist stands and hurries away from Paprick the Butcher, knocking frantically against the door.

Guards rush in as the archivist rushes out into the hallway. The Butcher laughs, throwing his hands wide as the soldiers throw open the cell door. A loud *pop* stings the archivist's ears as several of the guards are thrown back through the door.

"But mostly," he shouts, "as we lay there, I was happy! Happy knowing I had a person, and that I was theirs. That I had a love some people could never achieve."

The wet slap of bodies colliding stiffens the archivist's spine. The Butcher, for it has to be he, grunts as more slaps follow. The cadence of beating rising as the guards subdue the Butcher by any and all means.

But still, the Butcher's gleeful shout carries into the hallway. "Because it was reciprocated!"

And it is the archivist, then, that feels beaten. If he knows enough to salt this wound...

What else does he know?

45

THE TYPE
OF KNIFE

AN HOUR LATER, the Butcher leans his freshly shaved head back against the wall of his cell, breathing deeply. The archivist watches him from the still-open door. Not a moment before, the archivist had taken a similar moment in the hallway, calming with forehead to cold masonry. His words still lingering.

It was unprofessional and unbecoming of the archivist's station, being affected so.

But most wounds ignore professionalism.

"We'll be finished soon," the archivist whispers to a guard stationed beyond the door. "Alert the Commander."

The guard nods and moves silently up the hall, leaving the archivist to stare through the door at the Butcher, a familiar if distant activity. When the Butcher's boredom manifests as fingers tapping against stone, the archivist does the professional thing, entering the room as if nothing had happened and sitting back at the desk without a word.

And the vengeful thing, making him tell the rest of the story.

The pantries were much as I'd left them before Ilantra's death, the difference being that all the produce was rotten. I needed to try Enhancing a greater recipe, but without the right ingredients, I couldn't, and I wasn't really sure what those ingredients were yet, like I'd told Rish. So to calm the nervous energy twitching through my hands, I cooked with what remained.

Wearing only the apron, I spread flour over a counter—Cori still lay on the island, not sleeping but watching me with a smile—and stoked the oven. Sending smoke from a chimney of an abandoned restaurant was easily one of the greatest oversights of my young life, but I was drunk on sex's afterglow. Never occurred to me.

As I began to grease the loaf pan with some butter I deemed safe enough, Cori spoke up. "There's something you should know."

I cocked an eyebrow and moved to the scale, measuring flour, baking powder, and salt. Distracted, I marveled at how the simplest ingredients can take you so far, but Cori broke my moment.

"Crooked Rish wasn't the only one who saw you make your rub. Old Man Banan was there, too."

"Okay," I said, whisking, unsure where this was going.

"He's been working with Vanil to recreate it, and I think they figured it out."

I waited for a salting of anger or a bitter disappointment to flavor my reaction, but neither came. Instead, I felt a distinct frustration that I didn't have any of Mom's sourdough starter as I measured water and oil into the bowl with my dry ingredients. Started to knead.

"With Ruda back and no Chili Control," I surmised, "you think they might use it to attack the king?"

"I reckon," Cori said with a distinct note of disappointment. "What do we do? Who can we trust?"

Rish would find us if he could, but I wasn't holding out hope. At that point, I didn't trust him to breathe when he said he would; the man had too many secrets. Yenne would be back in the morning, and Laven was stuck with his bodyguard, though I was going to send him a roadrunner in the morning anyway. That left only three people outside of Cori that I felt I could seek guidance from.

Cutler would help me; I was sure of that. He'd known so much about what I was hiding and trusted me anyway. The Omelet had showed me enough of his mind to understand where his loyalties lay. Not with the king, Herd, Rare, or religion, but with the land. With the food. And I was coming to share that loyalty.

I had once told Ilantra that food defined us. As I worked dough into elasticity, I recalled the menu the king had ordered and all its pomp. It tasted great, sure, but there was no heart in it. It was all precision and technique. No storytelling. Tartare? Bisque? Mousse? Winta had taught me that those came from Olearth's most "elevated" of cooking traditions, but that even then, there was a never-ending debate about who got to define "elevated" or whether it was even valuable. Tortillas, tacos, peppers, they're some of the oldest ingredients in human history, steeped in tradition and community. Foods that could make you cry. That was what Cutler valued with his cooking demonstrations. What I cared about when I cooked. Our religion.

I knew I could trust him for that reason alone.

The other two were my moms, of course. I could trust them with anything. But I wasn't sure what they could offer beyond telling me to trust my gut, and more, I was worried about them. With all this focus on me from the Seekers and the literal threat made against them by the king, I didn't dare see them. Cori'd been protecting them, but now they were alone. What if they were attacked because of it? I didn't think Vanil would hurt them—not when that would risk angering other common—but the king's message to Vyson mentioned them explicitly.

"You're going to squeeze the life out of that bread," Cori said, interrupting my thoughts.

"It's still dough," I said reflexively, then chuckled.

"What're you thinking about?"

"My moms. The Herd won't stop protecting them because I stole the scroll, will they?"

"I don't think so," Cori assured. "Asabi might be critical of us, but she and Sesa have been supporting us since you joined. Vanil ain't so short-sighted."

It was time to check the dough's consistency, and a strange conflict pulled inside me. Mom had always done it by touch, just sliding a finger across it and knowing. Chef Sagen had taught us to run the flat of a dry knife against it to see if any of it pulled away. Was I someone that did so by touch or by technique? Could I be both, cooking with technique in order to tell stories? Cutler had made fun of the Culinary Academy the first time I'd visited him, and he didn't know any fancy techniques. I'd invented a greater without them.

Ilantra had though, and she'd told stories. Of a kind. Her techniques were the reason I had ideas about Enhancement. Her cookbook helped me understand.

Sighing, I used the knife technique, still unsure what that said about me. The dough didn't pull away, so I used the same knife to score an X into the top and placed it on a bread stone in Patisserie to rise, wondering what Ilantra would do if she were still alive.

"Be a knife," she'd said.

"I don't think I've ever seen someone so troubled by bread," Cori said, coming over to place a hand on my neck.

"I don't know what to do," I admitted quietly. "Nothing I can do will stop violence. Not without violence."

I wasn't waiting for a response. I don't even think I wanted one. So I went to the pantry and removed the only other unspoiled ingredients, peanuts and honey, and placed them alongside the salt beside a mortar and pestle, wondering how exactly this process went. I understood the principles, but unlike bread, I'd never actually made it myself.

Cori kissed my cheek before dressing quickly. "How can I help?"

We both knew she wasn't just talking about cooking, but I didn't know how she could help me with the king's plans. I felt responsible for that.

"Grab that baking tray," I said, pointing, as I began to deshell the peanuts. "Then come help me break these."

"You want me to help with your nuts?" Cori teased. "Again?"

We both laughed like the teenagers we were—even if we rarely felt so young those days. Several minutes later, we popped the sheet in the oven, and set them to roasting. I could've moved the dough closer to prove by the oven, but I didn't think I needed to. Though winter approached, heat lingered over Ranch, perpetually cooking us alive.

"Do you know why I fight?" Cori asked from behind me.

"I'm guessing it's not because your parents are generals?"

"Did I say they were generals?" she asked.

I thought back. "No, I guess I just supposed because you said they led the army at the Front."

For a moment, the only sound was the idle cracking of discarded peanut shells as Cori fiddled with them. Then Cori's tone grew distant, like it was coming from outside the city and time itself.

"About ten years ago, my family moved from Far Common to a village near the Front. For a bunch of reasons, but primarily because carnephon started ranging out that way. The Herd had spent a lot of good years making sure the Rare didn't capture any, and we didn't want them finding that herd. If anyone could track them and get them out of the area without anyone finding out, it was Papa.

"It was nice at first. We were out in the middle of nowhere, really. This small village where we had to hunt our own venison and trade with the local common for rice and beans. When Papa wasn't on a mission, we'd do the hunting. Me following behind him as he did the real work. Him always telling jokes while he worked.

"But then every so often a bull was spotted. I was young; I couldn't go with him, and I'd mostly complain about Mama's boring lessons on history, healing, you name it. After I saw my first bull up close, though, I was never bored. I was worried every moment he was gone. When he'd leave, I'd ask him questions like 'what if they step on you?' or 'what if your bison bucks you?' and he'd tease me.

"His words weren't cruel," she clarified. "It was good-natured. Fatherly. Stuff like 'do you worry that the sky will fall, too?' or 'and what if I should get the runs from bad mushrooms while I'm herding?' but I would spend the whole time he was gone thinking about all the different things that could happen, especially the ones he teased me about. Sometimes, he was gone for days at a time."

A shell cracked under Cori's thumb, and I moved closer, allowing her to nuzzle into my side.

"When I was old enough, I went with him and saw I worried for nothing. He knew what he was doing. Showed me a lot of it. But I never really shook the worry, not when I wasn't with him. And eventually, I couldn't go with him as much. The Front got closer, and Papa had to balance organizing with hunting. Mama's healing kept her busy, and she needed me helping her."

Carefully, Cori arranged all the shells into a little square.

"But I started worrying Papa would run into carvers, and I stopped being much use to Mama either. Got so fed up, she sent me out with Papa permanently. Only one day when we came back to the village, it was gone." Cori took the last of the peanut shells and swiped them off the counter into a compost bin. "Wiped off the map by lightning and fire from a battle with the carvers."

"Your mom?" I asked gently.

"We found her and some others a few days later, holed up in a cave, half-starved and worse for wear. She was racked with fever and covered in cuts. Half the group had some sickness or another. I did the best I could, and Mama pulled through, but we lost good people. People I cared about.

"I kept thinking I should've been there. I'd been so worried about Papa because he was alone that I didn't even think about the common who weren't. Like numbers meant safety in a starving warzone."

"But being there wouldn't have stopped the fight," I said, understanding why I was hearing this now.

She kissed my cheek. "And they say you're just a dishwasher." But her expression darkened again. The story incomplete.

"Papa never teased me after that," Cori continued. "If anything, he became the troubled, worrisome type. But angry. Spiteful. He refused to let me come with him on his missions because he wanted me to be with Mama. He never said it, but there was a pretty clear 'in case something happens' at the end of his excuses. Mama saw how it hurt me to sit around waiting. She told him to let me come so I could fill the shoes he was going to leave me. But he just couldn't. 'The land needs you, Cori,' he'd say." Her impression was so spiteful and mocking that I wondered if there was something else in that spite. "Eventually, I took that to heart and left in the middle of the night to make my way here."

With a final flourish, she lifted the compost bin under an arm and brought it out to the outside. I could've followed, but space seemed more important.

"Do you regret leaving?" I asked when she returned.

Cori gave my question a fair amount of thought, which I can't deny hurt a little. I wanted her to immediately say there were no regrets, because if there were regrets, it meant I wasn't enough to outweigh them. But there was a lot I still didn't know about Cori, and that pause had a lot more weight behind it than I would know for a few more days.

"I don't," she decided, and my shoulders relaxed. "I know Mama and Papa were pissed. Are pissed. They told Vanil to send me back, but for all his flaws, he saw the good in having me here and he let me stay. I wouldn't change coming. But I'd sure as hell change how I left."

"You miss them."

"I do, but I miss the simplicity more. Being here, it's revealed a lot about who I am and what I care about." She gave me a wink, but I knew that part of it was for her own sake.

"Maybe I can make you something that will remind you of home," I offered. "What did you eat out there?"

"Rice and vegetables, like I made for you. Nothing better."

My face must have given me away because Cori broke out laughing. "I'm teasing. Papa used to make me milk tea, fresh from the bison while we were out hunting."

I nodded. "I can do that. Not tonight, but soon."

With that, I removed the roasted peanuts from the oven and placed the dough in. Cori used a tea towel to remove the skins from the peanuts, and I began pasting them with mortar and pestle. The night's darkest hours continued on like a warm blanket around us. I don't think either of us was at peace, but we were content.

When I pulled the bread from the oven and the smell hit me, a wave of understanding shot through me: why she'd finished the story, rather than stopping after the battle destroyed the village.

"You couldn't let your Papa stop you from growing," I suggested. "From learning how to better help the people you cared about."

She stopped polishing her flatsaw. "In a way. It was more like I couldn't let him protect me any longer. Not if I wanted to help others. I didn't realize it until I was making my way here, but if you spend too long thinking about protecting people, you can forget people rarely need to be protected from evil. They need to be liberated from it."

"What do you mean?"

She looked off toward where I'd hidden the scroll. "Evil doesn't come for you nearly so often as it paralyzes the world around you. I mean, look at Chili Control. When was the last time anyone used it to actually hurt anyone?" She frowned. "The attack at the Front notwithstanding."

"I don't know," I admitted.

"Not in a hundred years. Common just lived in fear of it. Stayed rooted in place until Ranch became Ranch. Mama used to say that healing is good work. I always agreed, but I don't think I understood until now. It ain't good work like you make good food. It's work that is good. She taught me to heal so that when she needed healing, I could provide care, and so that I could teach others. And then they could teach. So on until everyone could do good by helping each other and teaching." Cori offered me a surprisingly shy smile, pulling her hair out of her eyes. "I'm rambling."

As I held her gaze, I reflected on the night I'd invented Emphon Rub. I'd done it because I wanted to help the city. But what had I done to help it since? Though I couldn't see it, I could feel the weight of the scroll nearby.

The smell of freshly baked bread filled my nostrils, reminding me of Shank Stew with my moms, of the fire that I could literally summon from within me to affect change.

I couldn't control what would come next. And I wasn't going to be healing any wounds. But good? I could do good with what skills I did have somehow. I had to believe that.

A breadknife, rounded and designed to separate without damaging, rested in my grip. I'd used one to stop a Seeker once, doing damage, nonetheless.

The scroll, the smell of bread, the knife in my hand.

Cori's eyes.

They all coalesced into an idea.

"I'm not so sure that was rambling," I said finally, releasing Cori's gaze. "What you just said gave me an idea for how to try Enhancement."

Before she could speak, I cut into the bread. The smell filled me with a sense of sureness, and Cori sighed with the fragrance of it as she dipped a finger in the peanut butter.

"Wise to your attempts at seduction," she joked, smearing the peanut butter across my cheek.

46

THE PLACE ⊕ OF BITTERNESS

WE FINISHED OUR peanut butter sandwiches as dawn's first pink rays broke over the back of Fen's Plateau. Cori left to share my new plan with Crooked Rish, and I waited for her to get a good distance before departing myself, headed to Cutler's.

On the way, I passed a newsstand, where I learned of the parade. We knew something like this was coming after the victory at the Front, but the news sheets made it official. The victorious carnephon would march from the South Gate to Pen Stable later that day to celebrate. Surely, Vanil would attack somewhere along the route. With access to Emphon Rub, he could pick any spot he wanted for an ambush.

It wasn't a bad thing, attacking the parade, not exactly. But if things got out of hand and they couldn't free the carnephon, the animals might suffer in a firefight, and I didn't think it particularly helpful. It wouldn't kill the king or be the final rallying point behind which the common could liberate themselves. They feared the king and Chili Control. Carnephon only entered the city's walls because of those two.

The Plateau was desolate at this early hour, but I couldn't shake the feeling I was being watched. After sending a roadrunner to Laven, I rushed into Cutler's and locked the door behind me. Neither Cutler looked particularly surprised to see me, but Soryl's frown countered Jives's cockeyed grin.

"Did you hit your head and remember finally that you have a job?" he inquired.

"I've been indisposed," I said.

"Fancy way of saying you killed a lieutenant," he cracked back. "You tell him I sent my best?"

I didn't bother wondering how he knew that. "Something like that."

"What is it you want?" Soryl asked tightly.

"More than I deserve," I said.

"Probably," Cutler responded. "But I'll be the judge of that. Out with it."

I fumbled for a moment, unsure where to start. "You ever had potato tacos with nopal?" I asked.

Two hours later, I returned to the Academy House with the supplies I needed, including carnephon. Cutler had laughed at my plan in several places and insulted my intelligence, but in the end, he gave me the knuckles I needed for the supplies and some advice that would prove useful. "Enhancing a greater recipe isn't much different from creating one."

"Cutler knew of Enhancement?" the archivist interrupts.

"Of course he starving did," the Butcher answers. "The old goat knew every godsdamned thing I ever asked him. Not that he always wanted to share it."

I'd never eaten an Enhanced greater, let alone tried to Enhance one, but Cutler confirmed Enhancement took the effects granted by a greater recipe and either made them last longer or added something to them.

I wanted to Enhance my Rub. It was the one I knew most intimately and the one I understood best, but I couldn't exactly grow twenty meters tall in the middle of the Academy unnoticed. I started with an old favorite. Which is why I needed nopal.

"Rish is willing to help," Cori said as I returned to the Academy House kitchens, "but he wouldn't say how."

"No surprise there," I groused. "Anything else?"

"You hear about the parade? Rish says Vanil plans to slay the carnephon and incite a final insurrection."

"I suspected as much. What do you think?"

Cori frowned. "It's too early. The people are educating, and the Herd has transitional plans, but we don't know what defenses the king has in place. And it feels like a trap. A parade through a city half in the throes of riot? The king ain't that dumb."

"We don't have a lot of time then. Cutler gave me what I needed." I tossed the package onto the counter. "If this works, I can offer Vanil a different path."

"I trust you. What do you need from me?"

As Cori fetched the cookware, I forced myself to remember how Sleepless Salad smelled like the Perfect lime and tasted like lightning. My rub, earthy, gritty, and spicy as common justice, came about when I'd wanted all those things. I can't tell you how. Call it instinct. Call it the Source. Call it divine starving intervention for all I care. But I believed that meant Sleepless Salad's inventor, whoever they were, *intended* to communicate the very idea of alertness through its flavor.

Cutler said Enhancing was like creating, which required intent. That meant, in order to Enhance this meal, I had to intend to take that communication further. I had needed to literally create the Perfect version of alertness.

"Stop trying to mislead me with impossible logic. Speak plainly!"

He tosses an uncaring hand to the side. "I'm doing my best, here.

It isn't orderly like Laven's math. It's pliable, stretchy like dough."

"Cute," the archivist complains. "But you're being purposefully opaque."

"If so, it's because that's how it was. I can't help you understand what came naturally."

I made the same salad I had before, but I added julienned nopals to it, deepening its bitterness and expanding its tartness, and I subbed skyroot powder for paprika in the marinade. As I prepared the meat, I immersed my thinking in the different directions of alertness. There was being awake and there was being asleep. The normal version of the greater recipe already dealt with that. But my daily Earl Greys showed there was more to being awake. There was a level of awareness where you were faster in mind, eye, and energy. (Laven recently identified an alchemic called caffeine that causes this.) Anyway, it's like eagerness bordering on overstimulated. A quickness of wit.

I cooked the meat in butter instead of oil, still thinking about the running, popping quickness of butter on the brink of boiling, and the meat didn't smell like the Perfect lime. It hit the air with the bitter, tangy Perfect nopal. The smell almost had a snap to it, like the texture of the cactus I added. Which I'd discovered through those pub tacos with Laven.

When it was done, it tasted like a thundercrack.

As I finished the last bite, the sleeplessness kicked in, but there was more. I was *fast*. I could chop like a blur. Run from one side of the kitchen to the other in the time it took Cori to blink.

"That seemed to work," Cori laughed as I swept past her, lifting her hair in my wake.

I stopped and nodded. Tried to smile, but knowing what came next made it hard.

"You don't have to watch this," I informed, and Cori left the room.

Reluctantly, I forced myself to vomit. I needed to confirm emptying myself would immediately end the effects granted by a greater recipe, otherwise I wouldn't be able to eat Enhanced Emphon Rub full of endurium already. Not without gorging, anyway.

The good news was I lost the salad's effects instantly.

The bad news was the door to the kitchen burst open behind me as I did so.

And the Seekers came through it.

47

COLD

THOUGH THEY'D PUT a black bag over my head, I had a pretty good sense of where we were. We'd been descending steadily, and we'd just entered a frigid room noxious with the stench of blood. It seemed it was my turn to face the Seekers in a meat locker. I just hoped Cori had escaped.

With a grunt, a Seeker lifted my bound hands over my head. I braced for the pain of a meat hook driving through my palms, but to my relief, they hooked me with the leather bindings. A chain grated against its pulley as the hook lifted, pulling my arms until my feet left the floor.

The stretch stung my ribs where the Seekers had punched me with their steel knuckles. There had been six of them: carnephon, badgeboar, dolphon, wolphon, and two new masks. One had the short, curved horns and long bovine face of a bison but the eyes, whiskers, and ears of a mouse: a yakrat. The other was red, narrow, and beaked like a vulture, but with two enormous eyes on stalks that rose out of the top. Those gray eyes were like orbs that were barely contained in their housing, with three slit-thin black pupils inside, one on top of the other. Everyone's favorite flying nightmare, the gryphon.

Candlelight flickered into my light-shy eyes as the bag wrenched off my head. Ignoring the badgeboar-masked Seeker in front of me, I quickly surveyed the cold, tiled room. A chill that had nothing to do with the cold rippled down my spine as I turned my head. I'd assumed I was in another meat locker, but this wasn't like the one where I'd found Laven. It was more like a morgue.

Hundreds of human corpses piled all around me in varying states of decay. The cold had preserved some, but there was no mistaking how awful others had become, flesh purpling and bloated.

A second Seeker, dolphon-masked, with blood dripping from gash in their left arm, wrestled Cori into the room. A bag covered her head, and she was soaked in gore, but I couldn't find a scratch on her. With a wrench, the Seeker tossed Cori onto the ground, her head smacking against the tile so hard it made me wince. Dolphon motioned to their arm without speaking, and Badgeboar nodded.

The two departed the locker, shutting it tight behind them.

"Cori?" I groaned, trying to walk toward her but failing to get my toes to the ground.

Slowly, she pulled herself up to a sitting position, which looked difficult with her hands and legs bound. When she finally made it, she whipped her neck and flipped the bag off her head to reveal a bruise forming on her cheek and a busted lip. "Howdy, killer," she groaned back.

"Are you okay?"

"You should see the other guy," she said. "Guys."

"Are those two the only ones left?"

"Think so." She shuffled herself to the nearest body, a desiccated woman, and began to scrape the bonds behind her back against the woman's teeth.

Stretching, I finally got my toes to the ground and rotated myself to survey the bodies. Despite the varying levels of bloat and blackening, I recognized several immediately. The ones I'd seen the first time the Seekers had been in the substacks. Two common I'd known from the King's Factory. A rebel who'd thrown a firebomb in the riots.

Then, in the corner, one I knew all too well.

One of the most decayed, her skin puffed to the point of bursting in places. Skull open, brain removed. I stared at the features I knew best. Her eyes. The whites were flaccid sacks of goo, sunken into the back of the socket. No trace of the life, Endurance, and anger present when I'd last seen her in the Factory on her final day.

"Meg," I whispered.

We were such fools. Why would a king let his workforce exile itself? Why send people to a desert where they could easily join the Herd? No wonder we never heard back from anyone that chose exile.

Meg didn't wander into the desert. She was brought to the king.

So many of the common around me were roughly eighteen. Just past the point that indenture locked, and their debts assured. How many thought they'd free themselves from their indenture only to end up in here?

We should've seen it.

Cori walked up beside me, hands freed.

"I'm going to kill the king," I said, my eyes still on Meg's corpse.

"I'll help," she offered, undoing my bonds.

48

THE PARADE

I WON'T BORE you with the specifics of our escape. We didn't have to kill anyone, so it won't affect your body count, and we both know the Seekers only captured me to keep me off the table while the king goaded the Herd.

Laven came looking for us at the Academy House with Aniss, as I'd asked. When he found a lot of blood and neither me nor Cori, he knew there was only place we could be. How he convinced Aniss to escort him down into the substacks, I can't be sure, but when the door to the locker opened and I rushed forward, using a femur bone as a make-shift club, I nearly took Aniss's left knee out. I had no idea where the Seekers went or why they left us, though I had my suspicions.

They were partially confirmed when we got back in the Academy House. All of my ingredients—including the skyroot powder and the two other sources of endurium—were gone. Presumably on their way to the palace, which left my plan to Enhance my Rub impossible.

We decided we'd figure something out on the way to the parade. Not that we really did. By the time we exited the Academy, the sun had dipped below the city walls, casting deep shadows and bathing the western sky an ominous red.

"Where will Vanil attack?" I asked Cori.

She didn't hesitate. "Tall Grass. Open space, symbolic, and dead center between Pen Stable and the South Gate."

"If this is a trap, Vanil could ruin everything the rebellion's built toward," I said.

"Then less talking, more running, killer. We've gotta tell him your plan."

Before we could take off, Aniss grabbed Laven by the wrist.

"Sir, I can't allow this," he said. "As it stands, your father is going to kill me if he finds out I brought you back down there. If there's going to be an attack, we need to return home."

"No, mate," Laven said. "No way. You've been with me for months, sat with Paprick. You're going to let the people who did this to him get away free? The people who did this to me?"

"My job isn't to get revenge, and it certainly isn't to stop an attack on common rebels. It's to protect you. We're going."

He wrenched Laven by the arm hard enough to make my best friend cry out in pain, and before I knew it, I swung a fist at the mountain of a man before me.

Aniss was so shocked, no one moved for a moment. Then he shouldered me away and turned to grab Laven, but Laven hadn't stood idle. The moment Aniss turned, Laven elbowed him in the groin. After kicking him behind the knee and knocking him howling to the ground, Laven slapped his giant wok across the man's chin.

"Pain in my arse!" Laven shouted as he backed away.

"Damn," Cori and I said simultaneously.

Then we ran.

We arrived in Tall Grass as the parade entered it. Gone was the usual chaos of the market. Instead, the food wagons and campfires formed orderly rows and columns, busy with activity. Along the center row, three times as wide as the others, Rare cheered from parallel barricades and formed a path for the carnephon, which arrived in a line.

Angus, the male carnephon I'd partially butchered when I started my indenture, led the line, the largest among them. From a howdah on his neck, two carvers steered him with loose, braided ropes. Two more ropes stretched from the end of his tail to the horns of the following female, Heffa, dragging her along in file, and two from her to the next and so on. Angus cantered a perfect, steady cadence, never straining against his guides. Free bulls didn't move like that, so no doubt he and the rest were under Chili Control's effects.

"What do you see?" I asked as we neared the crowd.

"All of the carvers on the lead bull are Enduring," Cori noted. "There are a few hidden in the crowd too." She pointed subtly. "I don't see any Herd or anyone else I recognize."

"Oh, that is definitely not lish!" Laven shouted as he shoved us both hard.

The three of us landed in a tumble as a wagon smashed through the barricade mere centimeters away from where we'd just stood and rolled into the parade's path. A deafening explosion sent Angus rearing onto his hind legs. Smoke rose from it and three other flaming wagons that blocked the parade route. Nearly everyone began to run.

Another explosion boomed from behind the carnephon.

Laven grabbed my outstretched hand, and the three of us disappeared into the panicked crowd.

"What's the plan?" Laven asked.

Suddenly, a foot the size of a wagon cratered the ground before us, shaking the earth. Half a dozen Herd, led by Vanil himself, thundered into Tall Grass from behind the tenements around the square. They were each twenty meters tall and clad in enormous scale mail armor, fashioned from what I assumed had to be carnephon hides. A range of bone weapons—from war spears to swords to axes—completed their war kit. And though they were outnumbered by the bulls and the carvers on their backs, I didn't think it would be a one-sided fight—not with those weapons at their disposal.

"That's your greater!" Laven marveled.

"I know," I complained, still searching for a way out of this.

As carvers severed the ropes linking the bulls together, the Second Battle of Tall Grass began in earnest. Angus charged Vanil while us ants scrambled for safety. Campfires and wagons were destroyed in moments. A bone javelin speared into the rear left haunch of the smallest bull, sending it flailing and crashing to the ground ahead of us. We turned sharply, stalling as two bulls simultaneously charged a Herd woman from either side and slammed her down in our path.

"There!" Laven pointed to a Rare office building near the entrance to Tall Grass.

By the time we reached it, human and emphon blood alike spilled across the market, and I couldn't tell if my breath heaved from the sprint through a battle of rampaging giants or from plain fear. The doors were locked, so we caught our breath behind marble columns at the building's entrance.

"Alright," Cori said. "The first step in wrangling bulls is to get on their backs. We had greaters for it at the Front, but unless Laven's got Jump Jerky or Stormsquall Steak in that backpack of his, we're gonna need to find a way onto a roof."

"And then what?" Laven said, incredulously.

"Then we wait for the right moment, jump on, and get to the head. If we pull on the horns until their eyes face the sky, they'll quiet down enough for the Herd to subdue them peacefully."

As if in defiance of her words, Vanil lifted a flaming wagon and threw it at the howdah on Angus's back. The carvers leapt away, spilling to the ground as they sent shocks of blue lightning, fireballs, and spears back at Vanil. As the howdah became kindling, Angus screamed and bucked until he went chillingly still, flames burning his feathers as he glared Vanil down.

"Would that even work with them under Chili Control?" Laven asked.

Vanil grabbed an ax dropped by one of the other huge Herd members and cried a rally to his fellows. "STAND TALL!" The sound boomed across the square like a thunderstorm as he charged a smaller bull, ax lifted above his head.

"We have to try," Cori said.

In a display of strength that gave us all pause, Vanil cut the hind leg off the surprised bull, cleaving straight through endurium bones. It screamed and pitched onto its side as he lifted and smote down into its ribs, cleaving the scales open in a splash of gore.

"Do we?" Laven asked, motioning. "Looks like they've got it well in hand."

"They're slaughtering them," I said.

"It ain't right," Cori said, echoing my own disgust.

As Vanil lifted the ax for a second strike, carvers swarmed him from behind, slicing at his giant calcaneal tendon with flatsaws and cleaversaws. As blood spurted and his calf muscle rippled free of the tendon, snapping upward like a bowstring, he fell on a knee screaming.

But he wasn't stopped.

He swung the ax back around like a scythe over wheat, not so much cutting three carvers in half as turning them to paste.

All around the carnage, common and Rare cowered, just like us. No common rose to overthrow anyone. No one felt empowered. We were ants afraid of the flood.

"This is what the king wants," I said. "It's only helping him."

Laven scrunched his face. "How? All this chaos is doing is making him look weak."

"No," Cori said. "It makes the Herd look reckless and blasphemous. Half the Herd's common are emphonists. We need to put a stop to this."

"How?" I countered. "We can't get to a roof, and we're useless down here. They can't even see us. Oh, shit!"

We'd been sheltering behind large columns atop the stairs of what the Rare insisted was a courthouse, directly opposite where Angus was recovering. But just then, Angus charged at Vanil. Hit or miss, the courthouse about to become Angus's next victim. All three of us scrambled down the stairs into the cover of an alley.

"VANIL!" warned a Herd as she wrestled a bull.

Limping on his bad ankle, Vanil dove aside at the last possible moment. Rubble exploded around us as Angus crashed through the brick building.

By the time we ducked behind the next building, Angus was back in the fight, and I was reeling in living nightmare. Common-1 falling. The smell of blood. The meat locker. Meg.

"It's too much," I whispered. "I can't. I can't."

I'd been fighting the fear, the terror, the pain since the day Common-1 fell. As those buildings fell around me, it finally boiled over. I fell back into a wall, shaking and clutching my knees.

Blood rained over the wall.

The walls shook.

People screamed.

And then a face appeared before me. Hands on my hands, eyes on mine. "Hey, killer, it's alright now."

I don't know what, if anything, I said.

"You're okay," she insisted. "We're all going to be okay."

Laven put a hand on my shoulder.

"Talk to me, killer," Cori said. "What sounds good right now?"

"Sounds good?"

"To eat. You haven't eaten since this morning. I know you're hungry."

I was hungry, hungry to punch something, to scream, to let my frustration out. I felt so starving scared. So starving useless.

Cori cradled my head and turned it slightly away from the battlefield, to where a young bull lay dead beside flames. "How about some carnephon? How about you show them what you've learned?"

My eyes drifted to hers.

"I was wrong before. When I said we could only help if Laven had a greater in his backpack. We learned how to butcher for a reason, right? Come on. What we need is all right here."

Laven squeezed my shoulder. "I always did want to see how you do it."

"I don't have skyroot powder," I said.

Before she could answer, Laven reached into his bag. "I got you, mate."

I gaped up at him.

"What?" He shrugged. "You don't think I've just been twiddling my thumbs while my babysitter kept me company? Mate, I'm wealthy, *and* I know people."

"But why?" I asked, taking the pouch.

"A friend of mine let me know he'd come into some." His lips quirked. "Figured if an oaf like you could come up with a greater recipe using it, I might be able to alchemic my way into one."

"A friend of yours?" Cori asked critically.

"Just a guy who knows how to get things. Nothing nefarious."

"Why didn't you mention this earlier?" Cori asked.

"When would I have? You two tore out of the substacks like rabid jackrabbits. Next thing I knew, I was slapping Aniss with my wok and running farther than I have my entire life."

I still wasn't sure. "It might not be enough to stop all this. It won't kill the king."

Cori shook her head. "Stop that. One step at a time. Look." She pointed to a carver's corpse, the sword laying beside it. "I've already found me a flatsaw."

Angus and Vanil crashed into another building, so much like when I'd fought Bessa.

It was all happening again. Becoming elevated, rallying the common during the Flyover Riots, Chef's death—none of those meant anything if we landed back in the same place. I'd risen to stop Bessa when no one else would. I'd stopped *her*, but I hadn't stopped the cycle of death.

And once again, the common suffered.

No more.

"Let's go."

49

BUTCHER, SOLDIER, CHEF

AS WE SCRAMBLED across the burning battleground, we scavenged supplies from food wagons. Smoked paprika. Ground pepper. Salt. Tortillas and tomatillos rescued from an overturned broiler.

Laven tossed me a spear as he pulled the armor off a dead carver. Cori grabbed the flatsaw. When we reached the downed bull, Cori started cutting.

Half of the Herd fighters were down by then. Three of the eight bulls, too. Scattered throughout Tall Grass, Herd armed with other greaters—like Shank Stew or Emphon Tartar—fought carvers on the ground, and common with pitchforks clashed with Rare civilians wielding the weapons they carried for exactly this sort of possibility. Vanil and Angus still shook the sky with their battle as I expertly extracted scales to expose this young bull's flesh with Cori's help.

Laven watched in awe, spouting some nonsense about how it wasn't as he'd imagined. I guess he thought it would be more dignified.

When we had the cuts, I smeared my rub together and borrowed Laven's wok. It wasn't equal to a grill, but smoke from the battle had clung to its iron, and I knew that would provide an unparalleled seasoning. I tossed in nine pieces—one piece per serving more than the normal version required—and basted them in lime juice, quick on each side. Then I grabbed the spear we'd found and used it as a spit, slowly rotating the pieces over a burning wagon, glad that I didn't have to melt my hands again.

Those minutes were hell.

We hid from charging bulls running overhead. Grieved as two familiar Herd took goring blows in the stomach and chest respectively. I second, third, fourth guessed myself.

By the time the meat was medium rare, Vanil, limping worse, and one other Herd remained against five bulls. Quickly, I heated tortillas over the spine of Cori's sword and Laven finished a green salsa.

As we all cooked together, I thought of my Uncle Macen and the Perfect taco. Full of spice and fresh herbs. The cool salsa over the hot meat, both full of heat and life. I thought of my pub tacos, the nopal that brought bitterness and crunch. Bitterness like what I felt for the Rare. Crunch for what I'd do to their bones. About how my greater recipe could save the common people. *My* people, who ate tacos from commonsaries and waxed poetic about the best way to press a tortilla, who spurned the king's mousses and tartars, who loved cheap, greasy, godsdamned tacos more than anything after a long day of sanctioned slavery. About the fullness such a large portion, a portion my people rarely got, would generate. How I'd be solidified by it—solidified like when I'd eaten that stupid scalding Rare tartare. Rare thought they knew strength? Steel bones and iron knuckles. Eat 'em.

Common knew strength. Emphon, endurium for bones, *they* knew strength.

My rub would know strength.

As it all cooked, I watched the common cowering around the field, those too afraid to even run. They'd lost the fight. I almost had, too.

But Cori'd pulled me up. Laven'd shown me there were good people here.

No more Megs.

No more cowering.

Hoping I'd added enough endurium to the total, I slid my Emphon Rub cubes into war-grilled tortillas, loaded them with toppings, and covered them in Laven's salsa.

I handed Laven his taco. "You sure you want to do this?"

"No," he admitted. "But I won't watch the city burn." His eyes lit up as he took his first bite. "Scalding sun, mate, this isn't half bad."

I bit into my own, senses flaring to ecstasy as I approached the limit of flavor—a spice away from overwhelming, an acid away from scouring, emphonic beyond belief. Cori gasped as she bit down, eyes dilating with Endurance.

We each rose to the height of a tenement, and I knew that my Enhancement had taken effect, that the only way to be so big and still draw more was to be like the tenements and emphon themselves: supported by bones of endurium. Teal knuckles, hard as endurmite.

We quickly scavenged some armor and weapons from the ground. I had an ax, Cori took a sword, and Laven surprised me by lifting the bull leg Vanil had severed. "IT'S AS SOLID A CLUB AS ANY."

His words alerted the remaining Herd to our growth. Both had backs pressed against a tenement, weapons raised, as the five remaining bulls closed a circle around them. Unnatural behavior. In the wild, they would never corner prey like that. But whoever controlled them fought like a human. Knew to use numbers' advantage.

Problem for them, the numbers were even now.

Cori, Laven, and I charged across Tall Grass. Dozens of supporting carvers leaped in our way, throwing lightning and fire. I batted two bolts away with my bone ax, confirming it was made of shock-resistant emphon spine from tip to grip. Laven swept his makeshift club low, throwing the soldiers out of our path. From somewhere behind me, two carvers landed on my shoulder and thrust spears into the muscle. By instinct, I swatted with my wagon-sized, endurium-reinforced hand, crushing them into my body in an instant. Then we were on the bulls, but as we got close, a strange buzzing like that of cicadas chittered in the back of my mind. My joints slowed, and my two friends seemed to slow, too.

Vanil and his ally used our arrival to make a break for safety, rolling under the kicking claws of the bulls on either side before turning and attacking. Cori jabbed a sword to the left of the bull she'd chosen, forcing it to dodge right as her other fist collided with the side of its head like a hammer. Laven took a more direct approach, jumping meters off the ground and two-handing his club down across the forehead of his bull with the full weight of his size and hardened bones.

That left me with Angus. And gods, if I didn't see recognition and revenge in his eyes as he caught my scent. He remembered my butchery.

Not wanting to bunch up and get in my allies' ways, I shuffled back into the main area of the square, beating my chest. "COME AND GET ME."

Angus, or whoever controlled him, charged. At the last moment, remembering my fight with Bessa, I spun left. This time, though, I had an ax and more than two months' training with a cleaversaw. It wasn't exactly the same, but I knew every ligament, tendon, and muscle in a bull's body, and together, they gave me the edge. Spinning away, I arched my ax into the back of his leg at the gastrocnemius muscle. Scales ripped free, drawing blood, exposing the meat of his haunch. Another strike to the same spot would render the leg useless.

I stalked toward Angus's hind leg. Shuffling, he kept his head in my direction, and each time I attempted to circle, he bucked and quickly pulled himself sideways. Four times I dove and thrust, but each missed and earned me a horn strike to the gut or side. My scale mail and endurium bones held against them, but it would only take one lucky blow to get me in the flesh.

Cori crashed into him from the side, knocking him over as she landed on top.

Angus scrambled, rolling Cori to the side, and the bull Cori'd been fighting clawed the ground as it prepared to charge. Cori hadn't moved since hitting Angus. A gash splayed open on her back, and blood welled from beneath her left eye.

If I let Cori take the attack, I could bring the ax down on his neck as he hit her. Cori's life for an end to the mania and destruction. Who knew how many lives her sacrifice could earn?

It wasn't a question.

Summoning all my strength to my legs, I dove in front of her, turning my body to put as much of my armor in the bull's path as I could.

I was fully perpendicular to the ground when it struck me, and my back took the full brunt of its steel pan of a head. If not for the strength offered by the Enhancement, I would've shattered my lower ribs. Spinning like a weathervane in a desert storm, I slammed into a building and fell to the ground.

Following me, the bull raised on his haunches to crush me underfoot. Screaming, Cori tucked her knees to her chest, rocked back, pressed her hands overhead, and pushed off the ground in an inverted jump. Her knees uncoiled and her steel heels cracked the falling bull in the side of the head so hard the blow snapped his neck. As Cori crashed back onto the ground, the bull listed and fell far enough to my left that I rolled over and avoided becoming a pancake.

Behind her, Vanil mimicked my fight with Bessa, squeezing the windpipe of his bull—though he'd angled his body so that he wouldn't be crushed by her weight like I had been. The Herd woman lay dead, the horn of her bull sticking straight from her chest, but her bull twitched on the ground beside her, dying as it exsanguinated from a deep slash across its side. And last was Laven, who uppercut his club into the chin of his bull and shattered its jaw as I groaned on the ground beneath Angus's glare.

Four bulls lay dead.

Before I could celebrate, the buzzing in my head crescendoed into a riotous, noxious tumult of sound, and I dropped my ax to grip my skull. Locusts seemed to be swarming through my brain, devouring every thought before any could become action.

351

Stop fighting, the king's voice ordered. *Lay down. Surrender. You are mine. It's time to end this.*

The buzzing crushed my will to fight the commands. Everything that made me *me* withered away like a pepper charring into ash over the roaring flame of the king's control.

Tell them to stand down.

"STAND… DOWN," I said, the words coming out my mouth against my will.

"PAPRICK?" Vanil questioned.

Punch him in the gut.

My arm flew into Vanil's stomach with such force, he crumpled and vomited. As the chunks spewed, his body shrunk.

Now, stomp.

I lifted my foot to crush Vanil beneath it like a bug, but Cori tackled me before I could.

"KILLER, WHAT THE HELL?"

Her, next.

No, no, no, I raved, but I tackled Cori to the ground and pulled her into a chokehold. She struggled, trying to wrench free, but strong as she was, she wasn't doing anything that might accidentally hurt me. I had the upper hand. Even as Laven tried to pull me off her, I tightened my hold, squeezing her, smiling the king's smile until she fell unconscious.

Before I could subdue Laven as the king willed, he ran. I could feel the king in my head, considering whether he should pursue, but he eventually chose to stick with his plan.

Quickly, but not hurriedly, he forced me back to the parade route, where I found the braided ropes that connected the carnephon. As Cori lay unconscious, the king made me bind her. It wouldn't do anything if she shrunk, but carvers gathered round.

That night, he said, *all those months ago when you "Stood Tall," I'd finished making the recipe to get that pathetic animal under control. I had my hand on its mind, ready to turn your precious rebels to paste, when I* felt another presence. Smarter—barely—and human. Imagine my surprise, cockroach, when I touched your mind and realized I could've taken control of you, too.

I decided to leave you be. I wanted to see what a cockroach would do with power. A mistake, maybe, but one I quickly rectified by looking ahead.

I've waited. How I've waited, butcher.

Because I knew you couldn't resist. I saw you grow into this form again. I saw what you'd do, what I'm about to make you do.

It's time your roaches see who they really follow so blindly.

50

RUIN

ONE FOOT IN front of the other, he forced me to destroy the remaining Herd and common fighters in Tall Grass.

As I trampled alongside his carvers, he made me say things I won't repeat. Threatening the common. Demanding subservience. He made it clear he'd taken me, their "savior," and proved no common was outside of his control. By smashing wagons and stomping at the common that dared fight, he made me his greatest weapon. Through my mouth, he dared them to use my greater and see what it meant to Stand Tall before their rightful ruler.

Then, when they'd all fled or cowered, he started walking me toward Common-3. A stranger in my own body, I could only watch as he bent me to all fours before the tenements like an animal. He made me snort. Made me stamp my arms and wag my imaginary tail.

Then, when people finally tried to run from inside, he made me roar. In a sickening and intentional mirror of the day Bessa destroyed Common-1, I bucked and kicked and rampaged through Common-3, swinging my endurium knuckles. All as people screamed. All as people died.

My friends, who I'd gone dancing with. Cay-Anna, Meg's dad, my neighbors, all people who'd helped raise me, who I'd shared meals with.

My moms.

It was rubble in seconds.

I thought my nightmares had come to life as Angus fought Vanil. I thought I hit my low as I cowered and needed Cori to pull me out.

"HEAR ME, ROACHES," I said over the flames and ashes. "YOU ARE NOTHING. YOU LIVE BECAUSE THE KING ALLOWS IT. STAND TALL AND RIOT ALL YOU WANT. EACH TIME YOU DO, WE WILL DESTROY ANOTHER COMMON. WE DON'T NEED YOU. WE NEVER HAVE. WE NEVER WILL. YOU ARE EXPENDABLE. YOU WILL KNEEL."

In the aftermath, I knelt, my feet and knees burning in the flames, until slowly, painfully, I shrunk, and my mind was freed from him.

If not from what I'd just done.

After a long stretch of minutes, the Butcher wipes the tears from his cheeks. "For years, I hoped my moms would show up, smiling, and tell me how they'd fled Common-3 when the violence started at Tall Grass. That they'd been stuck outside the city or some other excuse for why they'd only just returned. That the things I remembered were only another nightmare."

"They loved you," the archivist assures, unwilling to offer him condolences or apology. No point in trying again after how poorly the first apology went.

"Don't you say that." He hangs his freshly shaved head. "Don't you say that. They would hate what I've become."

"Why?" The archivist stands, taking the book to keep scribbling. "What makes you sure?"

"Why?" The Butcher's eyes rise, violent as ever as he laughs. "*Why?* Because despite their best efforts, I turned out to be my father's son!

They spent their lives trying to make me good like them, and in the end, I wasn't theirs at all. I was his."

"You have no father," the archivist says, pointing to the pages.

But the Butcher doesn't rise to the bait. "Even though I'd destroyed their home, the survivors rushed to me, gathered me in blankets away from the smoke and the flames. 'We don't blame you,' one said. 'We'd never blame you.'"

"But you blamed yourself," the archivist prods, knowing.

"I always will."

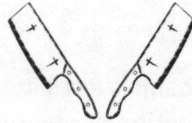

Course 6: Emphon Rub (Enhanced)

Also known as the Emphon Taco, the Enhanced Emphon Rub is best paired with a light or sour beer and a light salad, refried beans, and/or rice. For those with a lower spice tolerance, sour cream is recommended.

Ingredients (serves 1)**:**

Tomatillo Salsa:

- ◊ 2 tomatillos
- ◊ ¼ cup white onion, finely chopped
- ◊ 1 clove garlic, minced
- ◊ ¼ cup cilantro, chopped
- ◊ 2 jalapeño peppers, whole (removing stem and seed may reduce potency of flavor and cause greater recipe to fail)
- ◊ Salt to taste

3 30–50g bull emphon rib chunks, cubed

½ cup oil, for dredging

Rub:

- ◊ 2 tsp smoked paprika
- ◊ 1 tsp chili powder (ancho preferred, but any will do)
- ◊ ¼ tsp oregano
- ◊ ½ tsp garlic powder
- ◊ ¼ tsp onion powder
- ◊ ½ tsp salt
- ◊ 1 tsp skyroot powder
- ◊ 2 tsp lime juice
- ◊ 1 tsp oil
- ◊ Cayenne pepper to taste
- ◊ Black pepper to taste, typically no more than a pinch

1–3 applewood skewers

2 small tortillas, white corn

Optional toppings:

- ◊ Cilantro
- ◊ 20g pineapple, sliced or cubed (not recommended alongside guavacado)
- ◊ 1 dollop sour cream
- ◊ Grilled veggie mix (green and red bell pepper, red or yellow onion)

¼ avocado or guavacado (if sweetness is preferred)

Steps:

1. Prepare the salsa:
   - Preheat broiler on low.
   - Remove tomatillo husks and rinse well.
   - Halve tomatillos with a tomato knife, slicing sideways rather than down the button, and place halves down on an oiled or lined baking sheet.
   - Broil for 5–7 minutes until lightly browned and lighter in color.
   - Allow to cool before transferring to a bowl for blending.
     - If using mortar and pestle, mince jalapeño, retaining all seeds and stems.
   - Combine all ingredients.
2. Ignite flames, whether in a grill or open.
3. Tenderize emphon, forking or tenderizing the meat for rub to sink in deeply, and dredge in oil until slick. Set aside.
4. Whisk dry rub ingredients in a medium-sized bowl.
5. Transfer oiled emphon into the dry rub bowl and work rub into meat for approximately 30 seconds. There will be leftover rub.
6. Firmly drive one skewer through the meat and prop over flame, rotating regularly. Cook 4–6 minutes.
7. Heat tortillas over fire lightly so that they warm but don't solidify.

8. Place one tortilla halfway across the other so that they appear like overlapping circles and place meat in the overlapping areas.
9. Top with all desired ingredients, including a spoonful of salsa and avocado slices.

Expected Endurance Effect(s):

Endurance, 15–30 minutes
Heightened Senses, 15–30 minutes
Quickened Reflexes, 15–30 minutes
Emphonic Growth, 15–30 minutes

Enhanced Endurance Effect(s):

Endurium Bones, 15–30 minutes
Burst knuckles made of endurium, 15–30 minutes

51

HOLLOW

ANY COMMON CAPABLE dug for survivors. Bare hands. No Endurance. Burns and bruises. It didn't matter, we tried to find hope. I tried to hope my moms were alive, knowing at least five thousand had just died.

What was left of the Herd joined us in anonymous clothing sometime later, led by the white-haired woman, no Vanil. Some Rare even helped, though they kept their distance. Among them were Soryl and another handful dressed in mourning green who set bones and bound wounds. Medics. I couldn't help but wonder if the king sent them to ensure his workforce wasn't completely obliterated.

Carvers arrived almost immediately after I shrunk, but none helped, only watched me like Factory overseers. No concern for anyone but me.

The sound of the search lives in my memory. Crackling fires, shifting weights slow and then sudden. A thousand different shouts, some crying, some desperate, all names. Hoping, knowing that as it went on, reuniting was unlikely.

We dug deep into the night, until our hands bled and our hearts numbed. The occasional survivor kept us going. Voices would ring out, "We got one!" and everyone would rush to see if it was the one they searched for.

Not my moms though. Never them.

At dawn, the last of us dispersed by some silent agreement. There was no one left to find. Exhausted, numb, broken, I collapsed to my knees. It was then that a carver stepped forward and handed me an envelope.

"You are cordially invited to the king's victory banquet," the soldier said. Then he kicked me in the gut. As I spluttered onto the pavement, familiar hands eased me from the ground.

"Come on, mate," Laven said, throwing my arm over his shoulder. "Let's get you patched up."

Common parted as the Rare carried me away from Common-3. The person who'd rushed to me when I first shrank had said the common wouldn't blame me, but in the eyes of those we passed, I saw only disappointment. So much worse than hate.

No whispers of "Stand Tall," no words of encouragement. As we crossed the battle-torn remains of the city, only silence accompanied us. I could tell my friend wanted to say something to me, but no words came until we arrived at Common-4.

"There's no lift here, I'm afraid. You'll have to climb."

My burned feet were numb by then, their soles unrecognizable. We made it up the stairs in between fits of pain so powerful my whole body quaked. Then he gave me Emphon Milk from the icebox and lay me in a bed.

I barely had the strength to wonder whose apartment this was, with milk in the icebox, before the milk lowered me into a dreamless sleep.

I awoke to find Laven leaning over me. "Easy, mate," he said as he helped me sit up.

The room came into focus around him. A desk pressed against the opposite wall fought a losing war with the volume of papers stacked atop it, but no desk chair rested within reach. On the nightstand, a familiar sheaf of papers written in cipher caught my eye, and I suddenly knew why the air was sweet and sour with sugar and lemon.

"Ah, Pappy, it's about time." Crooked Rish rolled his chair over and joined Laven.

I wanted to know why Laven had brought me to Crooked Rish's home—and more importantly, how he knew where it was in the first place—but the color of the sky through the oily window gave me pause.

"How long was I out?"

"About a day," Laven answered. "Dawn just broke."

"Did they find them?" I said, turning to Rish.

Rish rubbed at his eyes. "No."

I felt too hollow to cry, my tears spent over the rubble of Common-3. "It's my fault."

"It's not," Laven said. "The king controlled you. It took some explaining, but everyone knows."

"That won't bring them back. This never would've happened if I'd minded my own business and stayed common."

Rish tsked. "That isn't the man I have become proud of. Take your own advice, Pappy. Stand tall."

"Stand tall?" I yelled. "What good has that done?"

I turned to Laven. "What are you doing here? With him?"

"It is not important, Pappy," Rish said. "What is important is the victory banquet."

"Why would I care about that?"

"The king has Cori," Laven answered. "We're sure he's going to have her on display."

"We?" I shook my head. "Who's we?"

"Now is not the time," Rish cautioned, looking at Laven.

"He deserves the truth. What good does it do now? Our plan failed."

"*Our?*"

Laven sighed. "I told you I couldn't make Rare friends. When I was ten, I made friends with the only person I could, a servant in my house called Ander. After a year, he confessed to spying on my dad for Crooked Rish. He'd only become my friend to spy, but now he really did see me as his best friend. I pushed him away, but I got so lonely that, eventually, I went back and told him I'd help him do whatever he was supposed to do for Rish.

"Two years later, after I'd fallen in love with the cause, the carvers caught Ander, and even though they tortured him, Ander never told them I helped. He died quiet, and I promised to repay Ander's sacrifice by helping Rish topple the king."

Laven looked away and said, "You asked if my dad put me up to being your friend."

"But it was Rish," I finished.

He nodded sharply, still unable to meet my eye. "Now, I know how Ander felt when he told me the truth."

"Was it real?" I asked. "Our friendship?"

"By the end of that first day in AG. When you gave me your ice cream even though I could see how much you wanted it? Scalding suns, mate, I couldn't help but be your friend. All those pub lunches. Then you went and bloody saved me from the Seekers. Brought me to your mums' flat. I swore I'd die for you like Ander died for me. You deserve that."

"I don't want anyone else to die for me." I started to sob. "I lost my moms, Laven."

"I hope I never have to. But I will if it comes to it. We all will."

"No," I said. "No."

"Is this what becomes of the son of Sesa?" Rish asked. "To snivel and cry. What of revenge?"

"He turned my recipe into his weapon!"

"Then the legend will make another," Rish replied.

"I destroyed Common-3! It's over. The people are broken."

"I'm not," Laven said. He put a hand on Rish's shoulder. "And he's only crooked."

Despite myself, I laughed through a sob.

"Trust us, Pappy," Rish said. "The people, they still hold the faith. You can, too."

No one can survive without faith, whether it's in the Consumer, the Twelve, the Source, a country, an idea, or just one person they love. My moms were dead. Uncle Macen was dead. Chef Ilantra, cold as she was, was dead. Cori was captured and possibly dead. And Cutler, well, Cutler wasn't exactly alive now, was he?

"Excuse me?" the archivist interrupts, but the Butcher continues, unfazed.

I needed to believe, however naïvely, there was something worthy of my faith. Ranch itself, the common within it, freedom, food? All too conceptual for me. But my best friend? A man who'd been like an uncle to me? I could put faith in them, even if they'd lied. Because they loved me, and I loved them.

It took me a long time to stop crying. When I looked back up, Laven was holding breakfast tacos, fluffy yellow chicken eggs slathered in salsa. The smell of lemons had left the apartment, replaced by fried potatoes and eggs. Had I really been crying that long? How hadn't I noticed the smell?

"So what," I said eventually, "are you two? Part of the Herd?"

Rish shrugged. "I am the spymaster everyone needs and no one trusts. Herd? Not Herd? It does not matter. People need us. I grieve, my son, deeply, for your moms. I understand that you want to lie here and make it go away. But you can't. You need to take up the king's invitation."

He handed it to me, and I saw that it wasn't just to attend some stupid banquet but to cater it.

"He's arrogant enough to believe he's won," Rish continued. "When the carnephon destroyed Common-1, loyalists claimed the king had been elsewhere and couldn't save them. That we owed him our trust after all the Panchons have done to protect us. Now, he's convinced himself that he won't be loved and so he must be feared. He used you to sow fear, and it worked. Most are too afraid to speak two simple words, let alone lift a weapon. But even his loyalists have lost faith. They may be afraid, but all common are Herd.

"You have the chance to cook for him. Exploit his arrogance, Pappy. Get revenge for Sesa and Asabi, for all of us."

"How?" I asked. "He'll be ready for me to poison him."

"The people are afraid, but if you speak to them, they will listen. You can convince them that they can take the city, Pappy. And if we can take the city while you cut the head off the snake, the Rare will flee."

"You make it sound so easy," I said. "Rally the people, take the city, and kill the king. This isn't a list of steps in a recipe, Rish. What if he makes me destroy another Common?"

"He can only do that if you eat your greater," Laven said.

"I can't beat him without a greater," I said.

"You're a Chef, mate. Capital C. Make a new one."

52

RALLYING CRY

I'M PROUD TO say it was my idea to use the Greenhouse.

That afternoon, as the sun sparkled through its curved roof, thousands of common stood within the garden, all staring at me. We'd used the crates and barrels of Black Spice's stalls to build a stage, and though I'd helped with its construction, it never occurred to me I'd be the one standing on it, alone. But Rish insisted. So there I was, stuffed with the First Flavor to give me a bit of clarity and focus, about to convince common to risk everything one more time.

Truth be told, I would've preferred I go straight to the palace. Though I'd put my faith in Rish and Laven, I'd spent the hours leading to that stage thinking of Cori. Of how much better she'd be at rallying the common. At how much strength she'd shown, how much support she'd given me throughout. Of how starving ridiculous it was that men like the king were always using women as proof of their victory. If he so much as touched her, the things I would do to him.

I think I've mentioned it. I'd cut out his starving tongue. As I stood on that stage, I intended to, and I intended for everyone watching me to leave there dead set on doing the same.

With a deep breath, I addressed the quiet masses.

"I'm not much of a speaker," I admitted. "The last time I was on a stage, I let other members of the Herd, like Cori, do the talking. I prefer cooking, honestly."

Crooked Rish nodded to me from the crowd. "You can do this, Pappy," he mouthed.

"But, yesterday, the king decided to make me a mouthpiece. He *used* me, made me tell his lies. He wanted you to be afraid."

Boos and jeers rang off the glass roof, singing the crowd's anger.

"So, now, I'm going to tell you the truth!"

When they cheered...

I think that was the moment when *I* started to believe.

"The truth is, I'm starving! I'm angry! I've seen enough of what Rare do to us."

I told them about Meg, that last shift in the factory. How she'd left to find freedom. How I'd found her. Those eyes, tears streaming from my own.

I told them about my uncle, my cousin. About how his tacos had served as the inspiration for my tacos.

I told them about Cori, how she believed in all of them, how I knew in my heart that she was fighting against the king right then, for them.

And then, as much as it hurt, I told them about my moms.

"They met in Tall Grass, you know?" I said, choking up. "Mom was selling bread, and well, Mother used to say that day, she was buying." I laughed to a silent crowd. "They loved food. Mom with her zaatar crackers and her sourdough. Mother with the stews and spices my grandma passed down. They loved me. They loved our family. They loved common. But more than anything, they loved each other. Hugging constantly. Holding each other through the hunger, through my tantrums, through so many common deaths. They were rocks. Just like so many of you. And he took them from us. The king and his starving Rare."

I wasn't expecting cheers, and no one did. This was a moment of mourning.

"They take and they take. Our labor. Our voice. Our food. And when that isn't enough? Common-1. Far Common. Common-3! All gone.

"We're nothing to them, nothing. And I've had enough of being nothing. I'm too hungry to be nothing. Too angry to starve!"

They roared.

"What should I do about it? What are *we* going to do about it?"

From the back of the crowd, someone called out the last line of Cori's song.

As the common chanted, I descended from the stage, and the revolution began in earnest.

The archivist yawns. "You finished buttering yourself up, or are you going to feed me further drivel? Perhaps how they carried you to the palace? How they called you hero, legend, savior, princeps, and whatever bullshit Vanil convinced them? Or perhaps, instead, we can advance to the banquet and finish this story."

"You sound bitter," the Butcher observes.

"Apologies, oh great Chef King, please do tell me how you freed us all. Pretty please, with a cherry on top?"

"Well, if you insist."

53

THE PALACE KITCHEN

LATE THAT SAME afternoon, enormous marble doors swung open on silent hinges before Laven and me. Two Seekers in masks—carnephon and gryphon—flanked the door. As we entered, two more greeted us, a wolphon and a badgeboar. Wolphon patted me down, looking for weapons, and I held my breath. Laven had done well to scoop up my apron when he'd fled Tall Grass and kept it safe for me. I wasn't foolish enough to try to smuggle a cleaver into the palace in the hidden sheath, but I was banking on the sheath itself going unnoticed. After their hands groped up and down my legs, Wolphon nodded to Badgeboar, who'd just done the same to Laven. Satisfied, they pointed us in with the practiced grace I'd seen only in the maître d' at the Academy House.

The chamber was enormous. Far, far more intricate than anything so rudimentary as a dining room. Six oven stations stretched along the right wall, each supported by large islands brilliantly illuminated by copper pots hanging above marble countertops. Between the third and fourth station, a knife block akin to a weapons rack offered a hundred different hilts. A spice rack stretched the entire wall between the ovens. I counted no less than four pantries on the left side of the room, doors open to reveal their splendor, and what looked like a vault door to a walk-in freezer in the corner.

Beyond all that, on the opposite side of the room, an enormous banquet table bore a white tablecloth. The glass wall behind it showcased the palace cacti gardens and a gorgeous vista of Fen's Plateau beyond. The room was better categorized as an eat-in kitchen with a view than a dining room. But when I entered, I didn't notice any of it. Through all the glitz and glamor, my eyes snapped to Cori. She was bound to a chair at the left hand of the center-seated king. Blood seeped from a re-opened scab on her cheek to the gag wrapping her jawline and dripped over a plate thick with its collection.

I said I wanted to cut out the tongues of the people I held responsible for my moms' deaths. When I saw the blood collecting on that dish, I didn't just want the king's tongue for what he'd done to her. I wanted to take every digit from his hands and his toes. I wanted his kidneys, his liver, his sweetbreads. I wanted to find the dullest knife in that starving godsdamned kitchen and slowly carve my way to his heart so that I could take all of it and shove it down the throats of every Seeker in the room, one piece at a time.

So all-consuming was my anger that when I saw the figure at the king's right hand, it wasn't the gut-punch it should've been. My anger almost cooled me. Because the truth was, I'd had all day to wonder where she'd been, and there was only one logical conclusion. Yenne, the traitor, wore a carnephon mask, her green and pink hair hanging around it like a carnephon's feathers, the pins holding up an imitation of one's tail. I should've realized it the moment she left. Rish had said there was a mole, and she'd gone straight to Dyl. But we'd been distracted.

There were others I recognized, too. The High Consumer wore no mask, apparently preferring her ceremonial headdress. Maybe she refused to sully herself with the visage of an unholy emphon. To her left loomed a wolphon-masked soldier with square shoulders I guessed belonged to Commander Wenson. I was pretty sure Dean Dyl sat next to Yenne in a dolphon mask, their maroon hair giving them away. And of course, there was the king himself, his drakephon mask twice as large and more ornate than any other Seeker's, with fangs that dripped blood in a gruesome mirror of Cori's gag.

I itched to shatter it. But the room was filled with armed Seekers. Dozens of them, each representing a Twelve, though no other wore the drakephon. Famines and locusts, I was thankful I'd eaten the First Flavor before the speech. A bit of Endurance coursing through me gave me so much more courage than the last several times I'd encountered the Seekers. Thankfully, Rish had another set of contacts, too, so with my Endurance hidden, I had a trick up my sleeve against them all.

Before I could think of anything else, the king snapped his fingers.

"Butcher, welcome. I'm glad you accepted my invitation. And, ah, I see you brought the Florento boy. Good. I tried to invite him, but he wasn't home. I found someone else though."

Two Seekers dragged Hoppus Florento, shivering, from the freezer. Laven called out to his father as the pair thrust the captive toward the empty seat beside Cori, but the Treasurer shook his head, meeting Laven's eyes. He was similarly bound but far, far bloodier, his right eye swollen shut and the entire right side of his face gored from a cut in his forehead. The fact that his place setting had a bowl rather than a plate made my stomach churn.

"Well, come in!" the king waved. "Everyone else is here."

"You'd really let me cook for you? Risk poison?"

He smiled. "Please, try."

Beside him, Cori shook her head subtly. She knew something I didn't.

"Now, I don't know about you, but I'm famished. Should we get started?"

Several Seekers moved at once toward the pantries and the cold storage, pulling out dozens of containers, an enormous slab of bull rib, and another package of what looked like chuck. The king stood, turning to look out at the garden.

"What am I cooking?" I asked as the ingredients were brought over to the island closest to the window.

"Well, I was thinking we might have a few different meals. A true feast." He turned to those seated at the table. "Guests, I should warn you that the roach is what we in the industry call 'relaxed.' Don't expect any patisserie or bouquet garni. He prefers simple fare suited for his common ilk. Still, we can likely palate his *tacos* without gagging. Probably."

He removed his mask to give me a shit-eating smile.

"As for the rest of the menu, well, your girl here is looking a little peaked. She'll need some milk. And for the final dish…" In a flourish, the king drew his knife across Hoppus Florento's throat, spilling it for collection into the large bowl. "My family's famous chili."

54

FIRES HOT,
KNIVES SHARP

LAVEN'S RAGE ECHOED across the tiles, and mine reared so hard
that I drew blood from my lip, biting back my malice.

"Ah, ah," the king warned, wagging his blade as he stood behind
Cori. "The greater recipe only calls for one, but I've found two can
really deepen the flavor."

I kept my tongue and hands in check, blood boiling beside Laven.
He'd fallen to his knees, stock still as he stared at the tiled floor and
the little medallions of the king's emblem set into the center of them.
"Why?" he asked the ground. "Why did you kill him?"

"His son was seen fighting alongside rebels. Surely you realize this
is your fault."

Commander Wensoan added, "He was a greedy, embezzling pig,
blind to the traitor in his own house. He deserved it."

"Now, now, Thymen. There will be time for that later. Butcher, if
you don't mind. I'm quite famished."

There was still so much I didn't know. Why did he want me to cook
these meals? Sure, he didn't know my taco recipe, but he knew Chili
Control. Seeing no answers or sense, I decided to bide my time. I had
to figure out a way of saving Cori and stopping the madness. So I

374

washed my hands at the sink and examined my ingredients. When Laven didn't immediately follow, I worried that any chance of keeping him at my side was slipping. What use was he to the king now that Hoppus was dead? If anything, the king should've seen him as a liability. I had to keep him useful.

"Laven," I said. "Come wash your hands. I'll need your help if I'm cooking for all these people. You know I can't plate for shit. Remember the panna cotta? Wouldn't want me to get a laugh now."

He stared at me with wide eyes, but I made the subtlest of expressions, hoping he'd recognize what I'd said. Thank the gods, Laven Florento was probably the smartest person in that room, Yenne and Dyl included. Laven's eyes flashed with recognition, and he joined me at the sink.

On any other day, the archivist would counter the insult, but the Butcher nears the end, and the sound of violence grows louder beyond the walls. Rite or not, their time together is coming to an end.

We didn't speak. There were too many Seekers standing practically on top of us for me to feel secure in that. But I had to get a message to him if we were going to plan something. Laven had cooked alongside me for weeks in Sagen and Chikor's classes. We knew each other's preferences and styles. So if I deviated from my norm, if I did something *intentional*, I trusted he'd catch on. But I'd have to make sure no one else did.

"If I'm making my tacos," I said to the king, "I'll need skyroot powder."

The king tapped the table. "Be a dear, dear."

Yenne stood with effortless poise and sauntered to a locked cabinet. Producing a key from within her dress folds, she unlocked it and reached inside. Her dyed hair bounced behind the mask as she walked over to me, the million folds of her dress swishing with each step.

"So he's your mystery partner?" I asked as she approached.

Without so much as a word, she dropped the familiar pouch of skyroot powder on the counter and turned to walk away.

"Were you ever common?" I called after her. "No greeting foods, barely any accent, no care for us. Was the elevation thing just a means of getting in with the Herd? Or are you so blind you don't even see he's using you? What did he call you in his letter, his servant?"

She ran back up to me, hands swinging beside her skirt with the speed of her movement. As I balked at her sudden outburst, she took me by the front of my apron and threw me onto the preheating oven. "Criticize my loyalties as you desire, but your ignorance is documented fact! Or have you forgotten your inability to support a single one of your arguments in Dyl's class?"

Before I could retort, she hurried back to her seat, threw her arms over her chest, and glowered at the window.

My arguments in Dyl's class? It struck me as the weirdest sort of insult, until I straightened out my apron and found a pouch tucked between it and my shirt, right where she grabbed me. My eyes flicked to the open cabinet for the briefest moment, just long enough to see that Yenne had picked up two of the pouches that had been within, not one.

I didn't dare touch the pouch, but as I returned to the kitchen island—in plain view of the king—I mentally noted the sticklike shape of the items pressed against my chest. It had to be the vanilla-malt-citrus bark.

Was Yenne on my side after all? Was she being controlled against her will? Was that why she was called servant?

I didn't know what to think, told myself that I had to stay focused on keeping Cori and Laven alive. Throwing a glare at the back of Yenne's head to avoid suspicion, I moved over to the enormous knife block and made a show of examining the variety. There were thirteen rows, one for each of the knives Ilantra had taught us in Knifecraft. I'd hoped they'd be disorganized, that I might slip a cleaver into the sheath hidden within my apron unnoticed, but if two were removed from a row and only one appeared on the counter, my deceit would be plain. That didn't stop me from grabbing a half-dozen knives though. I handed a few to Laven, directing him to begin on the vegetable prep, and grabbed the enormous slab of ribs.

"How many servings?" I asked as I angled my blade to carve.

"Four tacos, one milk, and two chilis," the king responded.

"Two chilis?" I choked. "I'll need more blood."

The king smiled ruefully, drawing out the moment such that fear fueled my limbs and my muscles twitched with anticipation. "Of course! My apologies. Would someone be so kind as to tap one of the exile kegs from the basement?"

A Seeker disappeared, and my gut roiled. Kegs. There were kegs of exile blood. I don't know how I had the capacity to feel more loss at that point. So many had died.

"Oh, and butcher?" He paused picking the knife beneath his fingernails. "Blood burns easily. Be very precise with your technique. If not, you'll have to start again with fresh ingredients. I'm sure your girl's blood will do."

He was right about blood burning easily. Mine was on fire. "Do you get off on feeling superior or is it so baked into your privilege that it comes naturally?"

The room silenced completely as everyone stared at me. Then back to the king, who remained silent for a long moment, as if considering my question. "I can think of only one other person who's spoken to me that way," he said. "She was an arrogant bitch. Liked to prattle on at the Tribunal and in the classroom about how we were all on a team together. By the Consumer, you cannot know the joy I felt when I learned she was helping your Herd. But not so much as when I cut open her head and tasted her brain."

"Am I supposed to be scared?" I pressed, slowly moving the cleaver I'd placed beside Laven into my apron.

"You're supposed to be cooking!" the king answered. "But if you aren't feeling particularly motivated, perhaps this will help."

He slammed his knife down into Cori's thigh. Her eyes bulged and her scream cut through the gag. It stung as if I'd taken the knife myself. All the more because I'd been expecting it, knowing that distracting him was a cost Cori would pay for me. But I promised myself it was worth it to get the knife into my apron, that it was what she would've wanted.

Her head lolled and her pained cries died into stifled sobs.

"Get to work, common, or the next one is in her eye."

Teeth clenched, I finished organizing my ingredients and planning how to simultaneously execute tacos that took all of six minutes and a chili that took over sixty, along with the rest of what I was planning. When I was ready, I held a knife out in front of me and rang my fingernails across its spine in an approximation of a bell.

Laven, tear streaks still pale against his dark skin, gave me his attention. He'd never worked in Ilantra's kitchen, but he'd wanted to. We'd pored over her cookbook dozens of times since my birthday. I'd told him how we did things there.

"Fires hot," I whispered.

He nodded, a small smile barely bracing his cheek. "Knives sharp."

"Plates clean." We both took a deep breath, and I finished the mantra. "Let's make this day his last."

"Heard, Chef."

All I could return to him was a curt nod. With that, we began. I quickly lost myself in sending messages to Laven through angled cuts and awkward procedures where I could. Which wasn't often. It was the first time I was making Chili Control, the first time I was making two greater recipes at once. I felt pushed to the very edge of my cooking ability. The chili was a complicated procedure without having to balance my tacos and my worry for how the hell I was going to get out of this situation on top of it. I had to concentrate on the Taco Enhancement and its relationship to the flavors. I had to taste as I went, which was starving awful with all the blood in Chili Control.

"Mate," Laven warned at one point.

I looked down to find that I'd forgotten to fold my fingers beside my chopping blade. If I had cut the bell pepper beneath it, I would've taken a finger off with it. Adrenaline knocked at the back of my eyes like I'd swallowed shellfish again.

Desperately, intensely fatigued, I chopped and I cubed. I sliced and I diced. With each bit of knifecraft, I struggled to pass a message to Laven that I couldn't even be sure he was getting.

In time though, the meals took shape. The smells danced through the space, seductive and salivating. Acid and spice mixing in the taco marinade, sizzling aromatic beauty as onions, garlic, and chuck came together for the chili. Seekers gathered around us, some presumably to inhale the aromas and watch, but one brought fresh blood. Hoppus Florento's and someone else whose sacrifice will never be named.

Simmering inside, I found the emphon milk the king had left for Cori. I knew it wasn't a gesture of goodwill. It would heal Cori, yeah, but it was also a danger to her. It was the comment about poison that gave it away, that and the proportions. He was going to have her sample all three meals I'd prepared. If they were poisoned, she'd show it. But that wasn't my only concern. Even if she barely tasted a drop of chili or a bite of my tacos, it would be a lot of endurium to swallow. Cori would heal at the risk of gorging.

That's what worried me most about the pouch Yenne slipped me, but it was also my only chance. Skyroot powder was packed with endurium. If I mixed it with the high concentration of endurium in the milk, the chance Cori gorged went way up. I didn't dare make a greater recipe from it. But the spice bark Yenne had given me? It'd been in the same drawer as the skyroot powder when we'd stolen from Dyl. It *had* to have endurium in it. How much? Did Yenne know? Was it a trap?

So many questions rushed through me, filling me to the brim with the unknown. But I'd promised Cori I'd make her some milk tea, and it was feeling like it truly was now or never.

As Laven plated for me—because I was so bad at it, right?—I took a monumental risk.

The Butcher's sigh startles the archivist. The weight of it carries a reverence, a maturity that's so often lost in his recount. One might even call it guilt.

"It wasn't the first time I'd done something raving," he admits, "but it could've easily been my last, Cori's last, Laven's last. I told myself it was worth it. None of us were all that likely to survive the day anyway. Sure, the king was high on victory at Tall Grass, too arrogant to notice that his use of me hadn't caused the level of fear he needed. But he'd have to make an example out of us eventually."

He shakes his head, disgusted with himself. "Really, though, I was starving angry, seeing red, absolutely raving. I lost my moms. I didn't want to live. I didn't want to leave Cori in a world where she became the king's plaything. I thought it was better if we all died. If she gorged, well, at least we tried.

"If I'm guilty of anything, it's that I bet Cori's life on my revenge."

"I hope you die crushed by that shame," the archivist says pithily. "It was that risk that proved it to me. You were what the king claimed you would be. A bloodthirsty butcher who put himself above all else."

The Butcher laughs. "Starve. I don't need your forgiveness, or anyone else's. Let us be done with this."

As Laven plated, I remembered the story Cori'd told me in the Academy House. Her song. How deeply she loved the common people and wanted them free. I didn't want to risk her life. I loved her. But I had to believe that she would want me to take the risk.

So I attempted to make a greater recipe of bark and milk.

55

PLATING

KNOWING I HAD little time while Laven plated, I focused all my skill on Enhancing the most basic and pure greater recipe on the planet: carnephon milk. One ingredient. One step. An incredibly potent outcome: healing.

I'd talked to Cutler about Enhancing before I'd Enhanced Sleepless Salad—even then, it felt like it'd been weeks. "Enhancing a meal isn't all that different from creating one, but it is harder," he'd shared. "So don't get all arrogant and smart with yourself. You're still a daft idiot. Be careful! Use your tongue and your brain."

It's not as simple as taking more endurium and adding it to the recipe either. You have to will the greater recipe to add a physical outcome. When I Enhanced Sleepless Salad, I added physical speed. To my tacos, I added endurium-strengthened bones. But the addition also had to make sense. Physical energy was the natural progression of mental energy. Bones strong as an emphon's added to emphon-sized growth. Milk was not only extremely high in endurium, but its outcome was pretty spot on. What was *more* than healing your wounds?

I *hoped* I knew the answer I needed. I hoped it counted.

But there was one more thing I couldn't control.

Come on, Laven, I thought. *Please tell me you understood the message.*

As I'd cut, I'd intentionally used all the same knives and techniques that we used in Chikor's class to make the panna cotta. I'd even put the green salsa in a syrup boat so that he could pour it out easier when he plated. Just like when we'd made the favors.

He had to have gotten my message. I'd said I needed his help plating.

As Laven picked up the salsa boat to finish the tacos, his hand slipped, dropping the ceramic boat to the floor. It shattered.

Using the distraction, I quickly measured the smallest pinch of shaved bark into the milk and imagined the taste of the tea I had become so familiar with at the Culinary Academy. It wasn't so difficult. Earl Grey lives in the interplay of sharp citrus, malty assam, and delicate lavender. The bark Yenne had given me wasn't that far off—not that she could've known that was how I'd use it— and its vanilla taste only enriched the flavor. But though I imagined the taste, I forced the smell of Perfect milk into my senses, trusting the Enhancement I was crafting to smell one way and taste another like so many of the greater recipes I'd eaten. I *needed* it to do that. I intended for it.

And so it did.

"You changed its smell with intent alone?" The archivist's eyes narrow skeptically. "Explain."

"I've gone over this."

"We can't all be savants that touch the Source, Butcher."

"You and your starving Source. A greater recipe needs a source of endurium and intent. That's what I said in Recipes Revisited. And I've also said that no greater recipe other than my own tasted the way I expected. None of them *smelled* the way I expected—because taste is mostly smell. So why? Why should the recipes *I* made taste as expected but not those that other people tasted?"

"Because things taste and smell different to other people," the archivist answers, catching on. "And greater recipes taste and smell the way the creator intends."

"Full marks for you," the Butcher cheers sarcastically. "Now, no more interruptions. I hate this part and I'd rather be done with it."

As I bent down to help Laven with the mess, I wafted the milk, disguising my motion as a gesticulated tirade. I smelled only creamy, normal milk. Nothing at all beyond the expectation. But at the same time, I knew it wasn't just milk. I knew it was greater. That not only would it heal Cori, but it would Enhance her with something a step beyond healing, something greater.

I nodded sharply to Laven. "Well done," I mouthed.

We cleaned it up, remade the salsa, and finished plating.

I felt closer than ever to success.

But I still needed to kill the king. I didn't know what he had planned for this meal, so I did the best I could. I hid something up my sleeve.

56

A MEAL TO ⊕ REMEMBER

THE TABLE WAS set for twenty, but most were unfilled. I was commanded to sit opposite the king with Laven to my right, across from Cori. As we sat, three final seats were quickly filled by masked Seekers, helped into their seats by other Seekers, which I found odd. One beside me, and two beside Laven.

The moment all diners were seated, the meals were carried forward on silver platters with polished cloches. A serving each of milk, chili, and tacos was placed in front of Cori as expected. The other chili went to the High Consumer, and the tacos were distributed to Dyl, Yenne, and Wensoan. From another room, a Seeker brought a gold cloche, which revealed a golden bowl of orange bisque beneath, and set it before the king.

My whole body seized in reaction to the smell. A Perfect lobster smell, ripe as the sea. My stomach pulsed with familiarity, and I thought I would puke with proximity.

"Ah, that's right," the king regarded, smiling at my discomfort, "you're allergic." He wafted the steam to his nose before blowing some toward my face. "It was the crux of this whole plan, did you know? I was worried for weeks that you might manage to wrench the meal

384

away from me and swallow enough to wrest control away. But when I learned from Ilantra that you couldn't consume it?" He squeezed his fingers and kissed them before opening them to the air. "Perfection! Finally, that bitch knew something useful."

"What is it?"

"The recipe for control," he answered. "Brain Bisque. One part common brain, one part bisque, a dash of that glorious powder of yours, and some salt Dyl discovered."

"But you already have the chili."

At my confusion, he laughed. "You still haven't figured it out? Consumer, you're duller than my childhood knives. What's better than controlling carnephon, butcher? Take a guess."

"Killing you?"

"Controlling people," he answered. "But it's still too hot, alas. We'll have to wait a moment." He reached for Cori's gag, pulling it down slightly. "Eat."

Cori's hands were bound, so the king lifted the milk to her lips himself. It was the most crucial moment of my plan. If he sensed anything off about it, we were lost. He even sniffed it. I actually thanked him for making Brain Bisque in that moment, because the lobster disguised my nervous gag as a symptom of my allergy. But he sensed nothing irregular, and brought it to Cori's lips.

Her eyes darted to mine and I nodded, my eyes taking on the smallest warning I could, hoping she wouldn't react. That moment stretched across years for me. The lips I had become familiar with, the milk dribbling from the corners due to the king's awkward angle, the dilation of Cori's eyes as the taste washed over her tongue, unexpected. But hopefully familiar enough to remind her of the promise I'd made and what it meant.

Cori choked on it. The surprise of the flavor caught her so off-guard, even with my warning, that she couldn't hold it back.

We were ruined.

Except the king in all his arrogance had already told himself he'd won. "Scalding sun, the roach's never even tasted milk," he chuckled, making eye contact with the Commander.

"A relief she has no right to enjoy," Thymen answered. Always the sycophant.

Cori drank the rest down at the king's insistence, and immediately, the scabbing wound on her cheekbone began to close. The strength familiar to her posture returned, and those singular arms of hers began to press against her bindings behind the chair ever so subtly.

My plan was never to save Cori myself. It was to give Cori the power to save herself. And the first step was underway with her healing. I could only hope she'd understood the Enhanced power I'd provided and could take advantage of it.

"Wonderful," the king said. "Now let's check the rest."

In that moment, I told myself it would work. Gorging killed because it damaged the body, flooding it with too much endurium. But emphon milk healed the body. Could it heal the damage?

I suddenly regretted the risk I'd taken. How could I bet someone else's life for them? I almost reached out to stop Cori before she sampled anything, but then the king saved me.

"Just enough to make sure it isn't poisoned," he said. "I won't have you dying of gorge before I know whether poison killed you."

To my relief, Cori barely took a nibble of taco and a spoonful of chili. Still, the chili was hard on her. Consuming human blood, no matter the anonymity, was torture, and vengeance morphed her expression into a defiant mask.

The king announced his pleasure and signaled a server.

I expected the Seeker to remove the taco plate and the chili bowl, but instead, they carried it around the table, setting the bowl before me and taking the taco to one of the three Seekers who had joined Laven and me on this side of the table.

Panic raced through me. If he was putting it in front of me, I would have to eat it. But I was already Enduring. Twice in my life I'd worn those godsdamned contacts, and again it was coming back to haunt me. I needed to get them out.

"I refuse," I said, staring at the king.

"Oh? I think you'll find sufficient motivation momentarily." He laughed, but I didn't understand. Cori was almost safe.

The king snapped his fingers and each of the Seekers removed their masks. The ones on the opposite side of the able did so quickly, with practiced movements, but the three on my side of the table fumbled with theirs, taking longer.

My heart stopped.

To my left, the recipient of the tacos, was Vanil.

To Laven's right: my mothers.

I had truly thought them dead. To this day, I imagine them appearing from the wilds, lost when Common-3 collapsed and returned years later, because it's still easier than what came next. Gags were removed from Vanil, Sesa, and Asabi, and immediately my mothers began promising their love and encouragement to me, but the king cut them off. "Enough!"

A Seeker pressed a spear into the nape of my neck.

The king waved across the table. "If you have tacos, you will eat quickly and immediately proceed around the table to the doors on either side, exiting to the gardens for your transformation. Those without will remain.

"Butcher, you will use Chili Control to take control of your leader and force him to the remaining Commons, all of which he will destroy. Yenne and Dyl will aid in this endeavor. Meanwhile, Thymen will use his advantageous size to hang your mothers and the Florento boy from the girders atop the palace. Should you choose not to take control of the rebel rat, they will drop, and High Consumer Orega will immediately assert control to continue with the destruction. Is this clear?"

"Why are you killing all of these people?" Mother asked. "What have they done to deserve this?"

"Do you know what a monarch's greatest privilege is?" the king asked.

"I can name a few," I responded.

"Information. Every book, story, and memory in this nation is available to us. My ancestors used Observant Omelets to learn so much about the past. But they should've been working with the Empire of the Badgeboar. They have a greater recipe that grants foresight. That's the ability to see into the future, common. And what I've seen is a creature that intends to kill us all, swallowing this entire city in its maw. I won't stand for it.

"The truth is," the king continued. "Common didn't do anything to warrant death. They lived, they loved, they worked to support the nation. But the other reality is that they ate, they shat, and they supported *him*. He who they hoped would destroy me. The fabled princeps come to liberate them from the evil king. On its own, none of those things would warrant mass erasure, but there's another war coming. One that requires an army stronger than any before. And I won't have cockroaches leeching resources I'll need to fight against the Empheron. So they die."

If we were going to get to the next stage of my plan, I couldn't let him prattle on for hours. Cori's Enhanced power could wane any moment.

Wiping my face, as if hiding tears, I dragged the contacts out of my eyes and closed them. Without looking, I dug my spoon into the bowl in front of me.

The king smiled. "Bon appétit."

After that first bite, I knew a great deal about the person who had invented Chili Control. The flavors should have been salty, metallic, and bitter. That much blood would've easily done it. And it was all those, but it was so much more. It wasn't just disgusting, it was the Perfect disgusting. I understood immediately why Cori had gagged. It wasn't just the knowledge of the cannibalism, but the physical repulsion of swallowing made intentionally abhorrent. If I intended for my tacos to taste like the Perfect representation of common heart and the will to succeed, this was the Perfect representation of evil and hope of failure.

The High Consumer didn't so much as flinch at the taste. The king regaled in it, his canines glistening. "You develop a taste for it."

In their reactions, I learned a great deal about them too.

Vanil had told me that the Panchons stole the greater recipe. As if transported into memory by an Observant Omelet, I imagined the woman who had made it. Amid the War of Eleven Recipes, she must've known that this world was full of greed and desperation. She must've known that at some point, someone would think to use the resource they slaughtered, carnephon, as fodder for the slaughter. To kill two birds with one stone. And so, she'd beaten them to it. Imagining the most disgusting ingredients, the most abhorrent flavor, to complement the power she'd considered most immoral, she'd forced herself to make Chili Control. Not to use, but to deter. Hoping no one could stomach it. That they'd puke before they ever got the power.

Imagine that woman's horror when she realized the depths of Almon Panchon's gluttony for violence and disgust. That he could eat it, that he could use it so often and to such devastating effect that he could build a kingdom on the bones of its victims—human and bull alike.

That was when the solution came to me.

How to stop the king.

Just like with other greater recipes, one bite was enough to get a small amount of the meal's benefit. So that's all I ate. The Endurance warmed my tired muscles and calmed my concerns for what would come next. As I finished, my mind expanded and touched three intelligent and scared carnephon, kilometers away in Pen Stables. They flinched against me like beasts from a flame.

"Tacos up!" The king waved his hands excitedly.

At spearpoint, Vanil rushed into the garden, growing with every step. The others followed.

As they left, Cori caught my eye and flexed her shoulders enough to show me she'd slipped her bindings but remained still. I casually inclined my head to the empty glass of milk, a silent question as to whether she'd figured out the other effect.

She shook her head.

I couldn't blame her. It wouldn't be obvious until it was. But how to clue her in on it?

"Butcher," the king said as he slowly began to enjoy his own meal. "I do hope you're remembering your role here. Your leader looks awfully independent."

Sneering, I turned my attention to Vanil. His mind was a buzzing insect I couldn't see, yet familiar to my ears. While I couldn't read his thoughts, I could speak with him, and reluctantly, I set him toward Common-2.

"WE'LL START WITH COMMON-2," he said, as if deciding for himself.

Dyl and Yenne followed, flanking him, as promised. All three had been given armor similar to those the Herd had worn at Tall Grass. Perhaps the very same.

The buzzing connecting me to Vanil stretched away like a rope spooling further and further, still there if I tugged on it, but gradually disappearing into the horizon. If I closed my eyes, I could send my perception down its length, thrusting eyes and ears into him to see and hear as he did.

Meanwhile, Seekers led Laven and my moms at spearpoint to join the giant Commander.

"I love you!" I shouted to my retreating moms. "I'll fix—"

But I was cut off by a slap from the king.

I didn't dare try to take over the Commander, but I used the recipe to see through his eyes as, one by one, Wensoan lifted them to the girders atop the palace and tied them to the dangling ropes.

Maybe I held him in place for a moment longer than he wanted, watching them sway from by the wrists and bake under the beating sun.

I could still save them.

When he was finished, he headed off toward the Commons, following Vanil. I checked on him, seeing Dyl frowning beside him. I wondered about the Dean's commitment to the cause. I didn't know them well, but they'd never struck me as particularly ruthless. They'd fought for my life and gone out of their way to stake interest in my ideas in class. Yenne had given me the bark, and she had suggested Dyl was being coerced back in the Greenhouse. That felt exploitable.

"ARE YOU IN THIS FOR THE CAUSE OR THE KNOWLEDGE?" Vanil asked, his thunderous voice amplifying my silent thoughts as if they were his own, which gave me a chill.

Dyl's gaze fell over Vanil's shoulder to Yenne, but they said nothing.

"PAPRICK PROVED HIS THEORY."

Dyl's eyes widened over Vanil, drawing back. "TRULY?"

Wensoan was nearly caught up with them, so I left Vanil with some further points to address and pulled back to my own sense. The king still picked at his bisque, eating slowly and diligently as his eyes grew in Enduring intensity with each swallow.

"So what now?" I asked, spinning a fork around my fingers as if defeated and bored. "You mind control me to make sure I keep mind controlling Vanil. Why eat your Brain Bisque?"

"Control you? No, I love the taste. To me, this tastes like victory."

I stopped spinning my fork, pointing it at the High Consumer. "Right. So what now?" I tapped the fork idly, still pointed at the High Consumer.

"Now, we wait for the roaches to be exterminated."

"I hate waiting." I made eye contact with Cori for the briefest moment and crossed my arms, fork still in hand. "Ow!"

Seekers sprang into action, pointing spears at my throat. Feigning shock, I pulled the fork I had been twirling out of my arm where I'd crossed it. I dropped the utensil as if I'd forgotten it wasn't in my hand when I stabbed myself in the arm.

No one noticed the spice pouch leaking skyroot powder into the rest of my chili alongside my blood.

"Prick yourself, Paprick?" The king giggled. "Should I get you some milk?"

"Don't trouble yourself." I massaged the small wound. "Flesh wounds only bother some of us."

And then I waited for Vanil to do as I bid.

57

TABLE MANNERS

AS THE KING finished his meal, his eyes became rings of luminous intensity, bright as the inside of the oven. "Whoa," he gasped, clutching the table. "What a rush."

A second later, most of the Seekers turned to him in perfect synchronization and saluted as one. "The problem with carnephon," he prattled, "is that you can only control so many at once. Humans? Much easier. Hundreds at my disposal if I need them." The king rose to look out the window and pointed at Tall Grass, across the river. Hundreds of people were standing in the market. He, of course, had no idea why they were there. Probably assumed they were shopping, even though the city was in shambles and common never shop when there's work to be done. "Watch."

All at once, hundreds raised their left hand.

As he marveled at his power, I lowered my new chili to the floor, resting the bowl gently. The High Consumer started to say something, but Cori acted in the same breath, grabbing the steak knife set before her and spinning it toward the neck of the priestess.

When the king turned back, I yanked the cleaver from the inside of my apron and vaulted the table toward him. Startled, the king raised his arms in front of his face. Seekers scrambled to spear me or grab me, but their number became a detriment. Too many weapons crashed into the space at once, knocking others aside. I sailed over the table and my cleaver fell toward the chopping block of his face.

Blood sprayed across my lips, but his ulna bone stopped my blade in his forearm. I landed atop the king, his head smacking against the tile. Before I could take advantage, a sound from behind caught my attention. My eyes flashed up, even as I yanked the cleaver from the king's arm, and I froze. Cori stood over me, a spear through her arm and a second through the right shoulder as she shielded me from an attack I surely would've taken. The High Consumer twitched on the floor beside her chair, clutching at her draining throat.

Another Seeker charged forward at Cori, weaponless and already speared twice. She spun at the last moment and deflected the blow with her arm, taking a deep cut across the thigh instead.

The king elbowed my chin, knocking me off him, and scrambled toward his servants. I chucked my cleaver at his back desperately and actually managed to clip him in the calf. But I didn't have time to celebrate. As he tripped into the waiting arms of a Seeker, several spears came for me, and I rolled sideways under the table.

Cori broke off the spear in her shoulder and used the shaft to club an attacker in the knee. With a growl, she pushed the bladed end through and out, grabbing the spearhead like a dagger, and dropped to the floor, planting it in the Seeker's chest as she fell.

I grabbed Cori's arm and yanked her under the table as another spear fell where her head had been. We both sprawled on the ground, catching our breath as the other Seekers hurried to surround the table.

"That hurt more than I thought it might," Cori drawled.

She repeated the process she'd used on her shoulder, breaking the shaft of the spear and pulling the bladed end through. The shoulder had already begun to seal itself, healing at a million times the normal rate.

"When you said flesh wounds wouldn't bother me, I thought you meant my skin would be impenetrable."

"I did the best I could," I admitted. "Continuous healing is pretty good if you ask me."

She kissed my hand and smiled. "Well enough, though that tasted nothing like my papa's tea. You have a plan to get us out from under this table, killer?"

I reached for my discarded bowl of chili.

"I believe you've outlived your usefulness," the king huffed from out of sight. "Time to join my army, Butcher."

I felt a pressure against my brain, and I instinctively flinched away, falling back into Vanil's mind, its buzz thoroughly distracted by a fight with Wensoan. I felt the king scramble, trying to grab for control of me, but I wasn't there, not fully. He quickly gave up, and tentatively, I returned to my senses.

The doors to the dining room opened, and from beneath the table, I glimpsed a series of booted feet joining the rooted boots of the Seekers around the table. Reinforcements.

"No point wasting my time," the king decided. "This is why kings have armies. Perhaps instead I'll visit your mums."

The boots all slapped the ground in salute before backing away. Cori cried out as a sword bit into her ankle. All around, mindless Seekers flattened to the floor around the table and started crawling toward the two of us.

I had my cleaver. Cori had a broken spear.

There were easily fifty Seekers.

Not the best odds. So I decided it was now or never. I shoved my fingers down my throat, forced myself to puke, and spat bloody chunks on the floor. My throat burned, but I managed to evacuate the original chili from my stomach and swallow the pain back. The last thing I wanted to do was eat anything—well, the second to last. The last thing I wanted to do was die, and eating was the alternative.

Seekers crawled within striking distance of Cori, and she slashed as quickly as she was attacked. I didn't know how long her regeneration would last, if she'd only be able to heal a finite number of times.

Carefully, I stirred the blood and skyroot powder into the rest of the chili, careful to use the technique Chikor had taught us for equal distribution during the panna cotta class. I didn't know if it counted, exactly. I wasn't cooking anything new, but I hadn't cooked Cori's milk. I'd only stirred using *technique*. In my mind, that was enough. Ilantra said techniques change meals, and I needed to change this one.

As I stirred, I thought about what I intended to do. About the depths of Almon Panchon's gluttony for violence and disgust. The bones he'd built his kingdom upon.

Because I cherish every moment with Cori, who reveres all emphon, I remembered one of the very first questions she asked me as we stared down at the offal and waste cut from Bessa. "Where does all that go?" and its follow-up, "Bones, too?"

I thought about skyroot powder's earthiness, how the roots of a tree as tall as the clouds must dig down into the bones of the earth for nourishment. About why we used that phrase, bones of the earth. About what must be below us all.

I thought about the carnephon that died in Tall Grass.

I thought about Bessa.

I thought about revenge.

I crafted all of that into a flavor and willed my intent to create it as I stirred skyroot powder and blood into a chili designed to treat emphon like weapons until they died.

And I asked for more.

58

ARMIES

MY ANGER FLOODED into the flavor, and it took on something vicious. Astringent, pungent, gritty. Like dirt and decay. Death and decimation. The razing of Commons, the persecution of a people. The taste was of a knife whittled from the bones of those the kingdom had betrayed, common and emphon alike.

And I swear, that chili glowed with Endurance as I Enhanced it.

The flavor burned all the way down, hot as a flame and caustic as poison. As I stomached it, the Endurance raced outward from my core, a searing that ripped my stomach lining with a weight I recognized from the time I'd eaten the First Flavor in Ilantra's kitchen.

Too much endurium for one day.

I gorged.

How long before the poison took me, I didn't know. Didn't care as long as it was enough to see this king killed.

As Seekers continued to attack Cori, I reached out with my mind. Instead of the living bulls in Pen Stables and Vanil, I sensed the endurium skeletons of carnephon in Tall Grass, not yet moved, and those of Bessa, a dozen other carnephon, and something truly ancient buried beneath Fen's Plateau.

Even then, when I felt that corpse, I gasped and turned to behold what I had thought to be a natural formation. The grave.

But I didn't have time to reckon with it. With my cleaver, I decapitated a Seeker that had reached me and said, "Time to go."

Cori and I fought our way from beneath the table, reliant on so much Endurance to strengthen our attacks. Together, we made it outside to the cacti garden, only possible because Cori could regenerate. The Seekers pursued us, and within moments, we were surrounded. Even through the throng of a hundred Seekers, I saw the king's army growing, thousands upon thousands of carvers flooding across the garden from Pen Stables to the north in uncanny synchronicity.

I took a moment to look up at the Palace roof, to see my moms and Laven hanging from girders. At least they hadn't dropped.

And then I used my newest greater to raise *my* army.

It took a moment, reanimating the corpses of the carnephon in Ranch. I had to remind the ligaments and muscles how they worked in a way that only a butcher who knew them well could.

"You'll have to protect me," I said to Cori. "While my attention's away."

"I've got you, killer. Don't you worry."

The first bull I controlled was the smallest, barely more than a calf but sharp and thin like the best filleting knife. She had been the first to die in Tall Grass, and I rewarded her early sacrifice with a name that befit her: Shanka. At my command, Shanka's skeleton, dripping rot and flesh, reformed, ran to the palace, and crashed the gates with horns low, bursting through the king's army like a filleting knife between scales.

Through the hollows of her eye sockets, picked clean by vultures, I watched as she cut through them, deeper and deeper. Two rows in. Four, creating Rare corpses for me. Even as they swarmed her. As they ripped the decaying flesh from her bones. As they threw themselves against her like a thousand hammers, over and over until her ligaments detached and she was brought low.

I lost control of her corpse, but Shanka had done her duty. She'd skewered down to the center like my cleaversaw and opened a path for my next soldier.

Chuck, stout and thick as a santoku knife, was also from Tall Grass. At my command, he crunched through the spines of those left in Shanka's wake. With his weight, he pulverized and broke, more of a tenderizer than a knife.

As he fell to the horde, I raised the first bull I'd ever butchered, Heffa—I hadn't realized she'd fallen at Tall Grass—and swept her into the army from the side. She was my carving knife, as I'd once been to her, sticking herself into the meat of the army and tearing it apart with equal parts malice and grace. When she fell, it hurt deeply, but she'd earned a rest.

I raised three more from Tall Grass, and I used them like a cook's most versatile knives: nakiri, utility, and chef. I named them Reba, Flanker, and Brisk, and they fell upon the remaining bodies with dicing speed. Annihilated the remains of the army like it was nothing but an onion. When the three emphon were brought low, there couldn't have been more than a dozen scattered carvers still standing.

All-in-all, my bulls must have crushed three thousand into pulp around the palace. I'm not sure, frankly, how that factors into your twenty score counts of murder. I guess we'll assume it covers most?

As I let my consciousness back into my eyes, I saw the corpses piled around Cori and me. My moms and Laven still hung, which was good. Now I just needed to get to the king before he could drop them. Which meant I needed a ride up to the roof.

I closed my eyes and called for the most familiar bones in the city. Bessa.

She was to be my cleaver.

Hurry up, girl, I said, from across the city. *I need you over here.*

If she could've roared, she would've. Ready.

"Hey, killer," Cori said behind me. "You gotta see this."

Floating behind her was a transparent teal outline of a person.

399

Short, but with a mighty posture. Big ears. Though the rest of the body was somewhat opaque, eyes that I would have recognized anywhere bored dismissively into me with Enduring yellow.

"Cutler?" I questioned, extending my hand through the transparent specter.

"Stop that!" the ghostly figure snapped. "It tickles."

It was Cutler's voice alright. But what? How?

"Soryl just got back from Tall Grass. All is set there," Cutler explained, "but it seems like you could use some help."

"How are you here?"

"We don't have time for all that, Papwit. Climb your bull and follow me."

As Bessa arrived, the spectral form floated toward the second floor, directly above the kitchen. At my command, Bessa dipped her fully decayed skull low enough for Cori and me to each wrap our arms around a horn. Eyes dripping ichor into my hair, she lifted us to the window, which I broke with my cleaver.

The hallway within was eerily quiet, save for my breathing and the slap of our feet against the floor. Cutler's ghost led—

"Ghost?" the archivist interrupts. "Is this what you meant by not alive?"

"Hush, pencil neck, I like this part."

The archivist startles to see a transparent outline of Jives Cutler floating in the room.

"Good, you got my message," the Butcher says, noting the ghostly figure.

The archivist scrambles to get the guards, but the Butcher raises a hand. Endurance blazes in his eyes as he says, "YOU AREN'T GOING ANYWHERE. KEEP WRITING."

∽

400

Cutler led us inside a familiar room. The doctor's desk remained right where it had been when she'd tended to me. The bed still bore my straps.

"In there," Cutler instructed, pointing to a cabinet, and I recalled my first taste of emphon milk, its bitter, sweet, citrusy quality. Chef Sagen would have been ashamed I didn't describe it as piquant.

I rushed the closet and ripped through it, tossing aside vials of useless elixirs and tonics that I didn't know or understand. "What am I looking for?"

"Ipecacuanha root syrup," Cutler answered.

"Ipe—how do you spell that?"

Cutler groaned and pointed to the top right. "Drink that when you're out of options."

"What's it do?"

"It makes you puke," Cori said. "Momma used it all the time up north."

"I knew I liked this one! Anyway, I can't maintain this form any longer. The king's reached the roof. Don't die, alright? I can't find anything at the store without you."

"You're going to have to teach me this greater," I said as I tried and failed to hug the air.

"Ha, as if this were something you could get from food."

And then he disappeared.

59

WHO WE
CARE FOR

AT MY COMMAND, Bessa lowered us back to the garden.

"Why are we going down, killer?" Cori called from the opposite side of Bessa's mouth. "The king's on the roof. We're wasting time."

"The Herd is finalizing the revolution in Tall Grass." Pain streaked through my stomach as gorge stilted my words. "They need your help."

"You're trying to get rid of me? Now? After all this?"

"I'm sorry, but I don't know how long your healing will last. I can't lose you again."

"Again?"

"He had you for a full day."

"Exactly. I want revenge, killer."

I hopped off Bessa and pointed to Tall Grass, hiding my face so the gorge's pain wasn't visible. "Those people need you more than they need me. If things go bad…" I hesitated. "It was your song. You took the time to get to know them, to organize the strikes and the riots. You were responsible for freeing Bessa, not me. But the king won't go down without a fight. If someone isn't coming back from it, it should be me, not you."

"I won't let you be a martyr. Paprick, please."

I halted at my name on her lips, but then pain stung through my stomach and chest. "I'm sorry," I said. "I can't lose anyone else I love."

Cori bit her lip in an adorable, embarrassed smirk, despite all that was happening. "So you love me, huh?"

It must've been the biggest blush in history.

"I love you, too." She took me into a deep kiss. "And killer? Butcher him."

As she jogged away, I patted Bessa's horn. "Alright, girl. Let's go."

She lifted me to her full height, and famines, she was a titan among carnephon. A queen among bulls. From her vantage, I saw the city in flames, the people marching in Tall Grass, the Rare fleeing the Clouds. But I saw the king standing beside Laven's girder, his hammer ready to break the wood holding it up.

Mother's eyes were vengeful. Mom's were worse off, staring straight through me. Her mouth quivered with prayers I'd never seen her so reliant on. In my gut, I knew she thought her fate was sealed. That she'd fall from that rooftop.

Laven just looked happy to see me.

As the king saw me, he raised the hammer. So starving sure of myself, I thought he was bluffing. Just like I risked Cori before, I risked Laven again, knowing I was running out time before gorge took me. At my command, Bessa reared onto her skeletal haunches and brought her claws down through the roof around them, nearly crushing the king.

But the king hadn't jumped away like the coward I thought him to be. He hadn't bluffed. He slammed the tenderizer down on the wood, shattering it.

Laven fell.

Frantically, I forced Bessa to dive away from the roof, to catch him in her hard, skeletal claws.

Crunch.

She'd caught him, but to what end? Heart thundering, I hoped he was alive. *Take him to Cori*, I commanded Bessa. *If anyone can save him, it's her.*

Then I turned back to the king and watched as he lifted the hammer above Mother's girder. She screamed and wrenched with her bound hands, fighting to the end. I may not be her blood, but I was and am ever her son. All my courage, I owe to her. My passion to make the world better, what I am now.

But then, then I was a child watching it all end.

Frantically, I calculated paths that would get Bessa to her before it was too late. But I already knew. I'd make a mistake. Bessa was already on her way to Tall Grass.

The king's eyes locked on me.

Mother lifted her chin and nodded. "Eat the—"

The rest of her words were stolen by the fall.

60

PAPRICK THE BUTCHER

AS MOM'S WAIL echoed across the silence, I clutched my bloody cleaver with a feral snarl. Enhanced chili roiled in my belly, its conflagration stoking my anger beyond quenching. Grime on my face from Bessa's mess. Eyes haunted by what I'd just seen and what I intended to see done.

If ever I became the Butcher, it was then.

Pointing my cleaver to the king, I made a promise. "I will carve out your tongue and feed it to the vultures. There will be no feasts in your name. No mourning for your soul. Any who dares dip their bread for you will answer to me. With your blood, the Panchons will meet their end."

"Cute speech," the king said.

A lead weight struck my gut, the gorge deepening. I was out of time.

"I'll kill her, too," the king promised, gripping his giant tenderizer hammer. "Your blood mum."

The truth that haunts me to this day is that I didn't care. Mom was lost without Mother. There was no coming back from what she'd seen, what she would see if she lived through what I wanted to come next.

The violence I would sow would make me a monster to her, and if she lived, she'd feel as if her wife and her son had died on that rooftop. Death would be a mercy.

I wanted to tell her I was sorry, wanted to say something to comfort her, but pain lanced down my torso, starting in my gut and to the very center of my pelvis. I didn't know what it meant, hadn't gotten this far into gorge's side effects in the Academy House, but I couldn't delay any longer, couldn't spare my conscience for her.

If I died before I stopped the king, the common were dead, every last one. Two days before, I'd weighed Cori's life against killing the king and chose Cori. How many died between then and now?

"Pappy," Mom whispered, catching me off-guard. "He killed her."

"I know, Mom," I said. "I know."

"I was never hungry with her arms around me."

"She could make anyone feel full," I told Mom.

"Make sure no one goes hungry, Pappy?"

I fixed my eyes on hers, but there was a catch in my throat. Somehow, I knew these could be the last words I spoke to my mom. I could've said "I love you." I could've said I was sorry. But Mother had raised me, so I forced out the words Mom needed. "I promise."

Tears spilled from Mom's eyes, clouding her vision of what would come next.

A devastating pang roiled through me, nearly dropping my cleaver from my hand, and the edges of my vision pulsed black. Still, I met Mom's eyes, and she spoke to me a single word.

I launched forward, intending to bring the cleaver down into the king's jugular. But he sidestepped and brought the hammer down again. But not on me. On mom's girder.

Then she was gone.

Fallen.

The king turned back to me, ready for a fight.

But I hadn't *stopped* and watched my Mom die. No, I never stopped avenging either of them. The moment he'd looked down to find his target, despite the pain forcing me to clutch my ribs, I'd pivoted out of my lunge for his throat. While he concentrated on hitting the girder, I reared back my blade.

So a second later, when the king turned, when his Enduring eyes fell on me with glee and expectation, all illusions of his leaving that rooftop fled them. Fear dulled the yellow of his Endurance. His mouth hung open.

My cleaver split through forehead, nose, and lips, falling out of my grip as it chopped into his brain's permanent block. Just like it had Vyson's.

Scrambling, I leaned over the edge and looked down the four stories where my moms lay below.

Mom had fallen atop Mother. One of her arms was around Mother's waist. The other was behind her head. If I lied to myself, I could pretend they were holding each other in their sleep. But I couldn't, not after I'd brought this on them. Not as their blood pooled together, growing wider and wider around their bodies on the hot, dry earth of the palace cacti garden.

So I took solace that even in death, they embraced.

A final pang brought me to my knees, and I fought the urge to let myself die to be with them, to escape the guilt of the deaths I'd brought—Rare Seekers and innocent common alike. To let someone else take up the responsibility of cleaning up my mess. It would've been easy, dying. Letting a legend be told about the Butcher that destroyed Ranch and then its king, or whatever martyr Vanil wanted to create.

It would've been so much easier than the years that brought me here, to this cell.

But I reminded myself that I was still just a dishwasher with things to prove in the kitchen. Reminded myself of Cori and Laven. Reminded myself that the only way to control my story was to dictate it myself.

I drank Cutler's root syrup. My eyes bulged and vomit geysered up my raw throat, stripping the endurium out of me. My bones rattled with pain. My breathing labored into a sob.

The Butcher locks eyes with the archivist. "I saw flashes then. As if from a bird's eye, I observed the desert south of the city, seemed to cross it for kilometers on vulture's wings. Then a cave, its mouth sparkling with endurmite all across its rim, a drakephon asleep outside its mouth. I was inside it next. Standing before a massive stone, shaped like an acorn. Taller than Bessa. Tealer than any endurmite. Pulsing with power. No, that's not right. It *was* power. The Source of it all. I saw it there, and I stretched out my hand, but before I could touch it, I was back on the roof."

It was a long time before I could see or breathe normally. And I've never felt weaker, as if my bones lay at the bottom of the palace walls while my skin stretched to its roof.

My throbbing eyes fell back to my mothers. And finally, finally, I summoned what strength remained in my lungs and cried.

In part because I'd lost them, but also for what I'd become.

He who would sacrifice his mothers.

Butcher.

ENTREMET VI

NAMES

WITH A FLICK of his hand, the Butcher releases the command.

Quickly, the archivist surveys the room for Cutler's ghost, finding nothing, and pens a message for the guard waiting beyond the door. The Butcher doesn't deign to stop her, which only worries the archivist more.

As the archivist returns to the desk, the Butcher takes a satisfied gulp of water, emptying his cup. With flames of rebellion shedding red light through the window, the last drops clinging to the Butcher's lips look almost as red as skyroot powder or blood.

Silence stretches beneath them, allowing each the moment they require. For the Butcher, it's mourning with eyes closed. Even after ten long years, the memory is a vice grip on his throat. For the archivist, it's victory. She finally has what she wants. The location of the Source.

But there's always more knowledge to chase, so it's the archivist that breaks the silence. "What did she say?"

The Butcher does not look up. "Who?"

"Asabi, before she died."

"Nothing important," the Butcher pretends. "Only a name."

"That of your father?"

"Who else?"

The archivist brings the pen to painted lips, considering for a moment, sure that death is just around the corner. She already knows that name, so why not ask for something more? "Was it worth it?"

When a pale excuse for a laugh runs its course, the Butcher's tone shifts. "Why don't you answer a question for a change?" Still, he does not look up.

"It's only fair."

"Were you ever on the king's side, you and Dyl?"

"It's hard to say," the archivist admits. "It was I who first learned of the Source—while I was writing that paper on religion. The one that got me adopted by Dyl. I shared it with them, and they shared it with the king. In a way, you can say that it was the two of us that inspired the Seekers. If I had to answer, I would say we were on our own side, pulling strings where we could."

"But you did love him."

She can't help it, she shudders, physically disturbed by the thought. "Is that what you thought? No, not at all. His tactics were consistent. Just as with you, he held my partner in chains to ensure I served."

"The king wasn't the mysterious partner?" The Butcher's surprise is apparent.

"Of course not. The king was a brute."

"But you couldn't even make it through the sex scene."

The archivist glares. "Some wounds only seem related, Butcher."

He shrugs. "Butchers open wounds. So who was it?"

"Have you ever wondered, Butcher, who cooked the Brain Bisque for him that afternoon?"

"I have."

"Well, there you have it."

For a long moment, the Butcher considers her. Does he dare push further? Seek the answer?

"Where were you and Dyl when it happened, anyway?" he asks.

"Vanil told me later that you two left amicably when he shared my theory. But he lost you both when he fought Wensoan."

"Atop Fen's Plateau, watching through a telescopic lens."

The Butcher's anger seems to glow through his eyelids. "How long were you there?"

"Long enough to know where in your encounter you've lied, but I believe your question truly seeks to know when we left, which is as soon as it was clear the king was dead."

The Butcher smirks. "Lied? I don't know what you mean."

The archivist doesn't indulge his bait. The story he told was clever, but not enough to exonerate him under the Rite. Surely the Butcher knows that, here for a different purpose. What that is, the archivist isn't yet sure, but frankly, she doesn't care. After all these years, she finally knows where the Source is.

"If you left right after, then there's still a surprise or two left for you."

"Is that so?" The archivist checks a pocket watch from within the folds of her skirts. Dyl wouldn't have gotten the message yet. No need to hurry. She readies the pen. "Feel free."

"Before I do, why did you give me the greybark pouch? It's the only thing I never really understood."

"Ah, that."

The archivist lays down the pen and speaks, choosing not to record the words. It is not the archivist, then, that answers, but the historian that hid behind that mask for years. Yenne Corzon, first and last of her name. The Butcher merely nods, never looking up, but listening as his once ally speaks.

"You asked why I should be called Chef King by my supporters," he reminds. "I told you that there are two types of kings: those born into it and those that seize it. In the vacuum of the king's death, I was neither. I *am* neither. I was never the lost princeps Vanil promised, I never had any desire to seize a throne, and I never wanted to lead less than as I mourned my moms. But there were others who did. And it was they who brought me down from the roof."

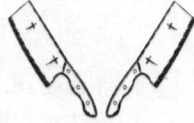

Course 7: Shank Stew (Enhanced)

Also known as Sesa's Sourdough Stew, the Enhanced version of Shank Stew is a complete meal by itself. The bread bowl provides ample starch, and the stew itself, all the variety of flavor you could need. Enjoy with a beverage of your choice and feel satiated by its completion.

Ingredients (serves 4)**:**

1 large white onion, diced
2 medium carrots, diced
1 green bell pepper, chopped
6 tbsp oil, divided
4 cloves garlic, minced
1 tsp chopped thyme
4 cup vegetable broth
4 oz tomato paste
½ cup white wine
½ tsp black pepper
3 tsp skyroot powder
½ tsp oregano
800g bull emphon shank, sliced into 1cm wide pieces
1 lime, juice of
1 russet potato, peeled and cubed
¼ cup room temperature water
Bread Bowls:
◊   1½ cup sourdough starter
◊   ¾ cup warm water
◊   ½ tbsp sea salt
◊   up to 4 cup bread flour

◊   1 tbsp olive oil
◊   4 tbsp butter, melted

1 tsp chipotle powder
1 tsp cayenne
salt and red pepper to taste

Steps:

1. In a large pot, sauté onion, carrot, and bell pepper in 2 tbsp oil on medium-high heat for 6 minutes.
2. Add garlic and thyme and cook for an additional minute.
3. Mix broth, tomato paste, wine, and seasonings in a bowl or measuring cup and pour into pot.
4. Bring the mixture to a simmer and cover.
5. In a cast iron skillet, heat remaining oil on medium-high heat and add shank. Immediately squeeze lime over the meat and let cook 2 minutes on each side.
6. Remove skillet from heat and transfer shank from skillet to pot. Add chopped potato.
7. (Optional) Let skillet cool for 1 minute before adding water to the skillet to deglaze the remaining oil and grease. Transfer liquid to the pot.
8. Simmer on low with lid closed for up to 6 hours.
9. Meanwhile, mix starter, water, salt, and 2 cups of flour in a mixing bowl and beat until smooth.
10. Using a sieve, add remaining flour ¼ cup at a time and beat until dough holds together.
11. Knead until no longer sticky, about 10–12 minutes, on a floured surface.
12. Oil a glass bowl and roll dough to coat.
13. Cover bowl and let rise in a warm space until doubled in size.
14. Peel dough from bowl and smack dough hard onto the floured surface so that it flattens slightly. Divide into four equally sized pieces.
15. Roll pieces to a round shape and place on parchment paper to rise till doubled.

16. Preheat oven and baking stone to 230°C.
17. Brush dough balls with butter and score tops with a knife to make an X.
18. Bake on baking stones for 30–35 minutes until bottoms are golden brown and slapping the bottom of the bowl creates a hollow sound.
19. Let bread bowls sit for 5 minutes or until cool to the touch.
20. Cut open top and gently press bread tightly into the sides of the bowl where possible, until firm.
21. Ladle stew into the bowls until three-quarters full.
22. Top with chipotle powder, cayenne, salt, and red pepper flakes.

Expected Endurance Effect(s):

Endurance, 18–20 hours
Spontaneous creation of fire, 1–2 hours

Enhanced Endurance Effect(s):

Ability to project fireballs at a range of up to 1 km
and detonate in a shape of your choosing,
1–2 hours

61

ROYALTY

THE MESSENGER WAS kind enough to cough loudly.

I still kneeled at the edge of the building, looking down at them. My tears had begun to dry in the dying light. Even if I had wanted to, I didn't think I could stand. I was just as likely to fall over.

"Paprick," the visitor prompted when the cough was unsuccessful. "The Herd needs you to come down now. There's much to discuss."

"I can't stand," I admitted, so she came and lifted me to my feet, bearing some of my weight on her strong frame.

"We'll have your mothers brought inside."

I thanked her and allowed her to ease me to a door. It opened onto a staircase landing barely two meters across, but it was out of the sun, and the coolness gave me confidence enough to wrap my hand tight against the stair rail. I needed her help, but by the time we reached the chamber minutes later, my mind had regained some coherence, if not my strength.

In the time I'd mourned on the roof, the world had gone on. The walls of the palace grew packed with Herd in new uniforms. Including my escort, all wore armored suits eerily similar to those of the carvers, but rather than the king's medallion, their uniforms bore an emblem

417

depicting a bull's head side-by-side with a badgeboar's. Familiar, but I couldn't place from where.

I caught snippets of conversation about a mounting defense, people missing, and tallies of deaths and destruction. My escort brought me to the Tribunal chamber. The throne, as ever, sat empty on the far side while Vanil, the white-haired Herd leader, and Crooked Rish sat beside it.

Rish's agent eased me into a chair below the table and backed away a respectful distance before addressing the group. "Permission to bring in the bodies? I saw vultures."

"Please." Rish's voice was hoarse, as if he'd been screaming or crying. Probably both.

"I'm not in the mood for an interrogation," I said, barely able to look at them.

"You'll be glad to know this isn't one," the woman informed.

"Then what is it?" I asked.

"Orders."

"No," I declared. "My moms are dead. I'm done."

Vanil forced a pained smile. "Now that the king has been deposed, we all, you included, must take our rightful place as the governing body beside its sovereign."

"I don't care."

"And why not?" the woman with white hair asked.

Before I decided it was worth answering, I needed to know who she was. Thinking of her as the white-haired woman was getting on my nerves. "Who are you?"

"Semary," Rish answered for her. "Semary Andala."

I spotted the faintest hint of yellow in the brown of her eyes. "Andala. Of course."

"I believe you knew my late sister, Ilantra," she answered coldly. I couldn't be sure if the coldness was for me or her sister or both of us, but the family resemblance only grew deeper with her scowl.

"I won't be your puppet sovereign," I said in answer to the original question. "And I won't be taking any more orders."

"Pappy." Rish's voice cut through my fatigue, filling my throat with a new rage. "You mis—"

"*Don't*," I interrupted, furious he was calling me that. "I don't mistake anything."

"You mis*understand*," he clarified.

"What do you people want?" I groaned. "I just lost them!"

"And many more will continue to lose their loved ones," Vanil answered. "It is time for the people to have their leader, time for the Herdon princeps to return from the shadows."

I scoffed, motioning to the blood along my arms and legs. "Do I look like the person who should lead this country?"

"No, killer," answered a familiar voice from the entrance. "You look like shit."

I smiled.

As Cori strode forward, I pulled myself to my feet and threw my arms around her. She was dressed in fine leathers, blood cleaned from her face, hair stripped of grime and gore. Her flatsaw and sheath sat returned to her waist, and beautiful earrings that somehow matched the sword dangled to her shoulder. Practically regal.

"I'm glad you're okay," she said, helping me back into my seat.

"Likewise," I said, squeezing her hand. "Did Bessa bring Laven? How is he?"

Only then did I see that Vanil and Semary were on their feet, heads bowed. Rish had likewise lowered his gaze as well. Cori waved a hand and those standing reclaimed their seats.

I blinked rapidly as Cori strode around the table and sat. On the throne.

"Not well, killer," she answered. "I did what I could, and I've given him to the best people I can spare, but I don't know."

"What's going on?" I asked.

Cori lifted a corner of her mouth. "Surprise."

"Surprise?" I repeated incredulously.

Cori unbuckled her flatsaw and handed the sheath to me. Pressed into the leather was the same emblem I'd seen on the arms of the Herd soldiers. The one I remembered was tattooed on her ribs.

"I told you my name was Cori Common-5," she said, reclaiming the sheath from my hand. "My name's actually Chicori Herdon."

The archivist's pen juts across the page. "What?"

"Surprise," the Butcher says again.

"That can't be."

"It is. Y'all thought I took the name to keep up with Vanil's legends and never bothered to check when Cori used it too."

"It changes nothing."

"Oh, but it changes everything for your Rite. What's the law? Something about how royals can't be held accountable for crimes."

"I'll have to check into the validity of your Cori's parentage," the archivist says. "And it only matters if you married. Did you?"

The Butcher glares. "You know exactly what happened at our wedding."

"As I recall, it was interrupted."

"We married," he says forcefully.

"Two hundred years ago," Cori continued, "my ancestors were forced to flee this city when one was slain by her neighbor, a boy named Almon."

"The woman who created Chili Control."

Cori nodded. No wonder everyone in the Herd had always listened when Cori spoke, how it seemed like she was the highest-ranking person in the room. I thought it was because her parents were important—and well, they were.

She looked away. "I'm sorry to have lied to you."

"Why did you?" I asked, the sting of this betrayal moving my lips.

"Rish identified the presence of a mole in our organization over a year ago," Semary informed dryly. "But we were unable to determine their identity. When *circumstances* necessitated that the princeps join us in Ranch, we couldn't risk her identity getting out. Princeps Chicori became Cori Common-5."

"Which do you prefer?" I found myself asking. "Chicori or Cori?"

"Princeps," Semary insisted, but Cori waved a hand. "From you, always Cori."

"So that wasn't a lie then, everything between us?"

"Just a mistake," Semary muttered.

Cori cut Semary a silencing look, and I got the sense that Cori's position gave her some power over this group, but not absolute power. That level likely lived with her parents.

"If you already had your royal family, why all the rumors? Why the focus on me?"

"In that," Rish said, leaning forward in his wheelchair, "I am to blame."

Vanil jumped in. "Since before either of you were born, the Herd has worked toward a day when it would come out into the open. More than a year ago, we decided we'd do so the day the master butchers would be concentrated cutting the chuck from the bull you so affectionately named Bessa. We'd suspected that chuck was the meat used for Chili Control due to the secrecy surrounding it, and decided that it could be an ample blow. From there, we would lead a full-scale rebellion against the Panchons, and the 'lost' royal family, so well hidden for so many generations, would join us when all was concluded to serve as stewards until we established the new government.

"As Semary so eloquently said, circumstances led to Princeps Chicori arriving in the capital early. We could not let the king's spy know that we had the heir, and your arrival as some hero of unexpected origin granted us the opportunity to shroud the princeps further. We needed the king to believe that you were the focus of the Herd's efforts. Cori's *interest* in you proved problematic, but eventually, Rish convinced me of the benefits to having a hero of legend beside the future sovereign."

"So you used me as both bait and stick," I said, glaring at them both.

"You did as you insisted," Crooked Rish reminded. "Often without the Herd's consent."

"Why risk Cori protecting me? Especially when the Seekers started coming after me."

Vanil lowered his gaze. "You may recall I *tried* to keep her with your mothers."

Their mention stung my grief, and I looked down. "And they died anyway."

"What?" Cori jumped to her feet. While Vanil and Semary protested about time for mourning later, Cori wrapped her arms around me, hugging me over the chair from behind. Just like Mother had Mom. The embrace was warm, her lips on my cheek a comfort I didn't deserve. She held me there for a long time before Semary cleared her throat.

"I'm so sorry," Cori whispered as she released me. "I really liked them. Loved them even." She turned to Vanil. "How did they get captured in the first place? You were specifically ordered to protect them at all costs."

Vanil lowered his gaze. "I pulled all available assets for the attack on the parade. I'm to blame."

"It's fine," I lied. "I've already avenged them." In the meantime, I still had questions about Cori's role and the Herd's new missions, but my fatigue was catching up. "You said that I was here to receive my orders. I won't take them from the two of you," I said pointing to Vanil and Semary. I didn't even look at Rish as I said, "And especially not from him. But I will from Cori. Whatever you need."

Cori smiled at me, and only then did I realize how much this secret must have hurt to keep. That expression was so earnest, so vulnerable. She might have lied about her name and her role, but she hadn't lied about anything else. I was sure of it.

"We need to know what you did and how you did it," she replied. "Resistance's cropping up from the Rare already, and at least two others want this chair. Fennel did all of this, built this army to fight something called the Empheron. We don't know what that is or why he was so concerned, and it worries us. His methods were insane, but we don't know if his concern was, too."

"Will you fight for the Herd?" Vanil asked.

"I will fight for the Herdons," I said.

In the hours that followed, I told them about each of the greater recipes and Enhancements I'd made in the last few days, and about what I'd sensed inside Fen's Plateau. I didn't tell them about my vision of the cave.

They pressed me for information about how I'd made the greater recipes, how I'd known they would succeed. It was barely logical and orderly as I've recounted it here. Back then it was a lot of nonsense instinct. I didn't have words for intents, outcomes, and flavors. I had feelings, the same kind of feelings I'd had when I first made Emphon Rub, only more specific. I couldn't give them anything practical, and I didn't much want to. Cori, sure. But Semary, Vanil, and especially Rish? I didn't trust any of them at all.

When I was finished, I was given leave to rest. I stood, but I was quickly held in place.

"Before you go," Cori prompted. "I, Princeps Chicori Herdon, do name you, Paprick Bessa, a—"

"Common-3," I interrupted. "Paprick Common-3."

Cori's eyes filled with a bright and earnest light. "I name you, Paprick Common-3, a Chef of Ranch, with all the licenses and permissions that come with it. I will need you, especially when my parents arrive, but you are welcome to open a house as befits your title." A glint entered her eyes. "I can think of one with a wonderful little kitchen island in need of an owner."

I bowed my head to her and cleared my throat. "I'm still a dishwasher, a stage. I haven't earned it."

She nodded. "Then consider the Academy House your classroom. The Culinary Academy's curriculum will need to be examined and its

Chefs vetted for loyalty. In the meantime, you can learn on the job. How's that sound?"

"I'm not sure I'm ready for that either," I admitted.

I think that's when Cori really understood how low my moms' deaths took me. "Alright," she said. "Get some rest. I'll find you soon and we'll get you something to eat."

62

RESOLUTIONS

PEACE WAS SHORT-LIVED, and the world didn't wait while I mourned. The Herd occupied the city, its soldiers using Emphon Tacos and a dozen other greaters to overwhelm the carvers that fought back, but with the entire population of common at the Herd's back, it wasn't difficult to maintain control. The Herd had planned well, and common seamlessly took the place of the Rare, who fled in droves, many of the more powerful families rallying rogue carvers as personal guards.

Most went east to Palm Oasis, where Commander Wensoan, who'd escaped from Vanil, rallied a resistance around a supposed five-year-old princeps, Zesta Panchon, a secret bastard of the king. We didn't buy her legitimacy for a second, but it didn't matter. Those that flocked there did so because they preferred the old world.

More open-minded Rare stayed and offered their support to the Herdons—Cutler and Sagen among them. Not that anyone was ever going to convince Jives Cutler to move out of his shop. Soryl stayed, too, but he was less supportive than we would've liked. That's another story.

We said goodbye to my moms. Only a handful of people, Cori and

Rish among the number. I really, *really* didn't want to cook, could barely stand the sight of the kitchen, but my moms deserved a mourning feast, and I wouldn't let anyone else do it either. I decided to make them something special, something they could enjoy in the afterlife that they never had in this one.

I recalled Mom's bread and how well it flavored the first greater I'd made, Shank Stew, passed down by Mother. I thought of the warmth of a hearth and the fire the stew generated with its power. Using my still confusing skills, I Enhanced that, making what I believed was the Perfect version of what Mom sought with her sourdough and that stew. As I cooked, I thought about stories that Mother had told me, passed down from her grandmother's grandmother, about some of the celebrations on Olearth. How they had enormous explosions of fire in the sky in the shapes of flowers and palm trees. I thought about the fire granted by Shank Stew. Imagined that extending to the sky in brilliant shapes.

As we finished our mourning feast, we sent our fires into the sky and sent my moms off like no one ever had. Silent little flowers. The kind that could've grown in the pot we used to hold rusty tongs. Had she survived, I knew Mom would've wanted to grow some.

The day after that we held a mourning feast for all lost, and Cori asked that I share the Enhancement with all of Ranch, and though the Herd complained about revealing recipes, I knew it was what my mothers would have wanted. With the bodies of all those carnephon, we had enough to feed the entire city, and they'd shared the original version once too. It was fitting.

Sagen oversaw the largest-scale multi-House service in Ranch's history. Each of the remaining fifteen Chefs—most had fled—executed the Enhancement, and for a night, the city was bright with celebrations honoring the dead.

I didn't cook.

The attacks began the morning after. We knew they were being coordinated by Thymen and Rare agents within the city, but the Herd had so many other problems to deal with. There were all the unhoused common. While we could fit some into the Clouds and other emptying Rare districts, the common had always outnumbered the Rare. A refugee camp was built in Tall Grass, but that became its own problem.

Starting the day I'd killed the king, the Herd had burned bodies at an impressive clip, but the destruction of the Commons and the presence of so much rot spread disease quickly. A pox raced through the refugee camp. Common-2 and 4 caught it. Then the Rare districts. All as Thymen's insurgents kept attacking and adding to the bodies.

We wouldn't have survived it without Laven.

Bessa caught him, but she'd shattered his left arm and leg, and in healing him we learned the limits of emphon milk. It could heal most flesh wounds, but there was a window of opportunity for bone damage, and we missed it. Bessa, and by extension I, had saved his life, and for that, he was grateful to the point of annoying reminder, but he lost fine control over his left hand and walking was difficult.

His mind was as powerful as ever. We spent several days in the new hospital together—gorging had decimated much of my intestines— and I shared the ideas that I was beginning to understand. He and Cori were the only ones I spoke to on them. The only two I trusted.

Laven created his first greater recipe about a month after the king's death. Panna Cotta Favors with powdered emphon milk. Using my theory of intent, he wrapped a bitter resilience into the rhubarb's sharp flavor. The resulting greater burned the pox out of everyone who ate it. We didn't have much milk to spare, but it was enough to turn the tide.

Six months after the king's death, Cori's parents returned to Ranch. The Herdon Stewards, king and queen. Common-6, brand new, standing taller and stronger than any before, welcomed their arrival. The unhoused common were granted new homes, and the first act of Cori's parents was to dismiss the idea of common and Rare, decreeing all as ranchers—as it had been in their ancestors' time.

But then, the war—

〜

"I think we can skip the intervening years," the archivist interrupts. "We know what came next well enough."

"Okay, then. If I count correctly," the Butcher announces, facing the back of his cell with his arms crossed behind him, "thus concludes twenty score counts murder, one count regicide, one count blasphemy, and one count cannibalism."

The archivist draws a pocket watch from the folds of her skirt. "Am I correct in assuming, then, that your final defense, beneath the Rite, is that of sovereign exemption? Your marriage to Cori invalidates all crimes?"

"Like I said, 'Chef King.'"

"Then let us skip ahead to your marriage. I don't recall it completing."

"That's a completely different story," the Butcher argues. "For it to make sense, we'll have to go over the time I spent outside Ranch, the Butcher's Apprentice, the drakephon, the Sourcerers… Gods, we'll have to go over what led me to the Source. Telling that would take another day."

"You touched it?"

Before the Butcher can speak further, the door opens, and Commander Thymen Wensoan enters, sweating and gray in his old age.

"About time," the Butcher says.

ENTREMET VII

EPILOGUE

"WHERE IS IT?" the Commander demands.

"Where is what?" the Butcher mocks.

"You know what! You said it was in Fen's Plateau."

The Butcher approaches the cell door and carefully removes, one after the other, a pair of contacts from his eyes. "Oh, it *was.*" Eyes like wildfire, burning with Endurance.

"How?" the Commander gasps. "Your hair! We took your hair!"

His gaze flicks to the archivist, but before the scholar can speak, the Butcher tosses a small compact through the bars, and all watch as it clatters across the floor.

The archivist's eyes bulge, recognizing the container that holds the lockpicks stowed always in her skirt folds. Her mind grows suddenly fuzzy as if there's something she's been forced to forget. Was that possible?

"I promised that I would see the Panchons and all that sat at that king's table die for what they did to my mothers," he reminds them, drawing attention back to his blazing eyes. With his kick, the cell door slams open, metal ringing against metal as it bangs on its hinges.

The Commander, for all his skill in war and bravado, freezes. The archivist rises. But neither is fast enough.

As if he's eaten Sleepless Salad, the Butcher moves like a blur, leaping the archivist's interposed table, and landing on Thymen with a tight grip around his throat.

"You think *I* would be captured? That I would let myself fall? That I'd sit for even a minute in this place without more Endurance than your pathetic body could even contemplate?"

As the archivist considers fleeing, the Butcher shatters the Commander's windpipe. Killing him instantly.

In a flash, the Butcher wrenches the archivist's wrist, eliciting a scream quickly silenced by his sweaty palm against her lips.

"I was going kill you, too," he muses. "Planned to until you spoke up."

The archivist mumbles something beneath his hand, but the Butcher doesn't listen. His head cocks to the sound of beating wings outside the building.

"Perfectly on time," he says.

Feet slap toward the door. The archivist expects to see more soldiers, but instead, two emaciated figures rush inside: Jives Cutler and Musta Common-1. Both wear the prisoners' garbs they were given when they were captured weeks earlier, when they became bait for the Butcher.

With the Butcher's story fresh, the archivist is unsurprised Cutler managed to break the pair free. Guards follow the two prisoners inside, weapons ready.

"There's nowhere to go," one says, her eyes glowing with Endurance and ready for a fight.

But then the entire building shakes as a tremendous weight collides with it. The Butcher releases his hold on the archivist in response, smiling broadly. The ceiling rains dust. Smoke forces the archivist to cough.

As she does, the Butcher reaches into the folds of her skirt and removes her knife. "It took me a long time to figure out how you managed this trick," he says, stalking over the Commander's corpse. "Behave if you intend to live long enough to leave this place."

The archivist blanches. She's about to be taken captive, then.

The guards surge forward, but Cutler's eyes glow suddenly. Not the yellow of Endurance, but teal as endurmite. A blast of air *whomps* through the room, sending the guards flying back.

On the floor, the Butcher cuts out Commander Wensoan's tongue with a practiced motion.

An enormous wrenching shudders the archivist's bones. Light pours in as a colossal skeleton rips the roof free. Its bones glisten gold in the flaming dusk, having been gilded and preserved in a manner most unfamiliar to the archivist's eyes. The holes of the undead emphon's skull stare beneath staglike antlers of polished endurium, bright and blue against a sky burned black with smoke. Until they're blocked by leathery wings pocked with holes.

Drakephon.

"Cousin," Musta says, mouth agape, "do we get to ride her?"

"If you'd like, swe'me," the Butcher says with a smile.

Once again the guards attempt to charge forward, only to be blown back by Cutler.

The fleshless drake lowers a fraction of its massive jaw into the room as the guards pour in, only to stop in their tracks. The Butcher points the knife at the archivist. "Climb on."

No point in resisting, she steps onto the open jaw, hooking one arm around a tooth for support, and the second around the Rite book, no longer willing to let the tome out of her sight.

The Butcher turns back to the gathered guards and sweeps the blade out to point at each before settling it on the Commander's corpse. In his other hand, he raises the tongue above his mouth.

"Remember this," he says, his eyes glowing with so much Endurance they illuminate the motes of dust in the sunlit room. "In Ranch, we eat the Rare."

He swallows the tongue.

END OF BOOK ONE

ACKNOWLEDGMENTS

To my family. Brooke for everything. Mom, Dad, Debbie, Alicia, and Brit for a million different things. Marcie, Tom, Erin, Talyn, and Ryan for all their encouragement. Patty, Steve, the dogs, and even the bird, I guess. And, for Jake and Juno. I hate hurting the animals in these books, but I do it hoping no pets will ever have to suffer like you both did.

To the community of people around me. Brendan, and because I cannot stress it enough, *Brendan*. Sunyi Dean for being the first stranger to believe in me. All of *the Growlery*, but especially Essa Hansen and Wayne Santos for being some of my first readers; Shaylin Gandhi for making the romance palatable; Clay, Richard, and JT for putting your name on this thing before it was even edited; and Scott for never keeping Publishing in the dark. *Iller's Killers* and the hundreds of messages I wake to each morning. *Cactusland*, which has welcomed me like no group ever has. Storm, Mack, Matt, and Connor for reading a *lot* of awful books. I appreciate every note on every book. Bew, Pro, Rob, and Shi for listening to me go on and on about Paprick.

To my champions in publishing. My agent, Harry Illingworth, for loving this book so much he offered before finishing it. That alone kept me hopeful. Helen Edwards and everyone at DHH who bring it to as many readers as possible. My editors, Davi, Cat, and Tori for making this story the best version it can be. Kerby, Jane, and Luan for making this book look absurdly good. Nate and Dan for dotting my Is and crossing my Ts. Daphne for founding the most author-friendly publisher there is. Caitlin and Jamie for convincing people to read it. Whoever it was with the divine power of choosing me for Special Editions, and the reviewers and booksellers who make it all worth it.

To my influences. Peter, who I hope never reads this, for filling me with so much hate that I conceived the Butcher. Essa Hansen, again, for *Nophek Gloss*, which inspired me to challenge tropes. Jay Kristoff for *Empire of the Vampire* and for actually reading this book. Piotr Musial for the *Frostpunk Soundtrack*, without which this book would have no melody. YA Dystopian, you might be dead, but I'll never forget the lessons you taught me about revolt. *Dungeon Meshi*, *Food Wars*, *Attack on Titan*, and *Monster Hunter World* for burning an aesthetic into my mind. Bovard Auditorium, the UCLA School of Law, the MIT Welcome Center, and the Goldman School of Public Policy for accepting me as is. Il Cielo, Beverly Hills, for being the first place I can remember crying over food. Nana Rose's lasagna recipe and all its secrets, for inspiring me to cook. Nana Smith's "cooking" for inspiring me to cook well. LA Street Tacos, for existing. All the cookbook authors and recipe bloggers for opening another door, and another, and another.

And finally, again to Mom. Nana's recipe might've inspired me to cook, but you were the one who invited me into the kitchen. Thank you for that and for so many things along the way. Sorry for what I did to the moms in this book!

ABOUT THE AUTHOR

After escaping his hometown in Central Florida, Ryan began studying to become a chemical engineer. He was sure he would one day be an asteroid miner. Since then, he's worked in tabletop game design, Broadway musical production, and even taught English to middle schoolers. These days, Ryan lives in Oakland with his partner and their dog, which may be a demon. He now works to defend democracy at UC Berkeley, which still doesn't involve chemical engineering. You can find Ryan on the good socials, assuming there are any at the time of this printing.

THE ART OF PROPHECY

By Wesley Chu

"An ambitious and touching exploration of disillusionment in faith, tradition, and family—a glorious reinvention of fantasy and wuxia tropes."—Naomi Novik, *New York Times* bestselling author of *A Deadly Education*

Prophecies don't make heroes: they only choose them. When Chosen One Jian falls short of his prophesied quest, he must find his own path to greatness.

The prophecy is clear: Wen Jian is the Chosen One, born to defeat the immortal Eternal Khan and save the kingdom. The only problem is that the prophecy is wrong.

Jian has been raised in splendor, trained by the best warriors, and celebrated before a single battle has been won. After all, he's the chosen one, selected by prophecy to defeat the immortal god-king and free the kingdom for good. But when the prophecy is proven to be incorrect, Jian still has to find a way to succeed—and maybe even become a hero in his own right.

To save the kingdom, an unlikely band of heroes rise: Taishi, an old grandmaster who swore her days of battle were over; Sali, a warrior re-evaluating her allegiances; and Qisami, an assassin with questionable values. Together, the four embark on a journey more wondrous than any prophecy could forsee.

❿ Daphne Press

TO CAGE A GOD

By Elizabeth May

Join the rebellion to burn down a cruel tyrant in this heartracing fantasy duology, perfect for fans of *Shadow and Bone* and *The Wolf and the Woodsman*.

To cage a god is divine. To be divine is to rule. To rule is to destroy.

Using ancient secrets, Galina and Sera's mother grafted gods into their bones. Bound to brutal deities and granted forbidden power no commoner has held in a thousand years, the sisters have been raised as living weapons. Now, the time has come for them to overthrow an empire—no matter the cost.

With their mother gone and their country on the brink of war, it falls to the sisters to take the helm of the rebellion and end the cruel reign of a royal family possessed by destructive gods. Because when the ruling alurea invade, they conquer with fire and blood. And when they clash, common folk burn.

Forced into a desperate plan, Sera reunites with her estranged lover who now leads the rebellion, while Galina infiltrates the palace. In this world of deception and danger, her only refuge is an isolated princess whose whip-smart tongue and sharp gaze threaten to uncover Galina's secret. Torn between desire and duty, Galina must make a choice: work together to expose the lies of the empire—or bring it all down.

▶ Daphne Press